David Brewerton, a past winner of the London Business School's Financial Journalist of the Year Award, has spent his life in the media. From his first job as a reporter on a City newswire he has worked his way up to senior editorial positions on four national newspapers.

He has extensive first hand experience of investigative journalism and has also mastered the black art of public relations as a director of London's leading financial PR consultancy.

It is this experience he brings to his writing, to create the intriguing situations and unusual characters who populate the media and business worlds.

DAVID BREWERTON

IMPECCABLE SOURCES

A photographic image ... is a message without a code
Roland Barthes

Matador
9 De Montfort Mews
Leicester LE1 7FW, UK
Tel: (+44) 116 255 9311 / 9312
Email: books@troubador.co.uk
Web: www.troubador.co.uk/matador

ISBN 978 1906221 300

Typeset in 11pt Stempel Garamond by Troubador Publishing Ltd, Leicester, UK

Matador is an imprint of Troubador Publishing Ltd

For those who encouraged me

ACKNOWLEDGEMENTS

My heartfelt thanks go to my friends who took the trouble to read early drafts and who offered such valuable comments, especially Chris Ross, Kathy Berriman and, of course, Patricia.

I would like to thank the staff at the British Embassy in Rome for guiding me through the labyrinth of Italian procedure, and Caterina Albano for anwering my many questions.

A big thank you as well to Phil Meech who took my photograph for the website and to everyone at Matador for making the path to publication so painless.

Finally, thanks to Marcus, Miles, Sid and Max for keeping my feet on the ground.

CHAPTER ONE

THIS much is certain:

John Warham and his wife Ruth were taking a holiday in the Cinque Terre, a collation of five ancient villages that tumble along a spectacularly beautiful stretch of the Ligurian coastline. On the afternoon of May 22 they checked into their pre-booked hotel, a pleasant but unremarkable establishment in the picture-postcard fishing village of Manarola. It was their wedding anniversary, a fact that may, or may not, prove relevant.

The following morning, at around 06.40, Warham walked out of the hotel and failed to return.

The next day, Ruth reported her husband missing. After some persuasion, the Italian *Carabinieri* launched a search that proved fruitless. Just over a week later, a battered body was pulled from the sea. It was identified as being that of John Warham.

Stop.

However, from transcripts of police interviews with Ruth Warham, other records from the official investigation, a limited amount of CCTV footage and information arising from enquiries made by private detectives, we can deduce much more.

When they arrived in Manarola, Warham and his wife took a drink at his favourite bar and enjoyed ice-creams beside the harbour. They returned to the hotel to celebrate their thirty years together with supper on their balcony, overlooking a garden. The hotel manager, one Giovanni Riolo, recalled they ordered a bottle of *Prosecco* and ate grilled sea bass, caught by a local fisherman that morning. By a bizarre coincidence, it was the same fisherman who, several days later, found Warham's body.

According to Ruth, they enjoyed an intimate, romantic evening together, an event that was, by some accounts, quite unusual for the couple. They went to bed around ten o'clock.

The following morning, Warham woke early. Ruth was already awake, but feigning sleep, a deceit she later regretted. As he opened his eyes and brought the room into focus he would have seen the revolving brown blades of a slow, silent ceiling fan. It barely moved the air. He may have stared at it for a while, marveling at its inelegance, on which he had commented when they arrived.

He would have noticed the open windows and the closed shutters, through which some sunshine seeped into the room. A long, thin oblong of gold marked the spot where the sun struck the ancient chestnut wood of an antique wardrobe, the door of which stood ajar. Its mirror later reflected back to Ruth's half-closed eyes a mottled image of her husband's surreptitious preparations to depart.

Ruth remembers Warham raising an arm to look at the Rolex clamped on his wrist. He lifted his head from the pillow, apparently in response to a scraping sound, possibly a boat being dragged down the street to the harbour. There were other noises: a cock crowing, an outboard motor, the inevitable reciprocal barking of dogs.

Had Warham spoken to his wife, she would have admitted her subterfuge. But he seemed intent on not waking her, so she tried to keep her breathing regular, suppressing the beginnings of a smile.

She was aware of him looking at her closely, no doubt watching the occasional flicker of her eyelids, perhaps willing her not to wake. Her clothes lay where they had been dropped.

Ruth later said, in answer to a question from the *Carabinieri,* that at this point she must have dozed back to sleep, for the next thing she remembered was Warham standing naked in front of the gold-tinted bathroom mirror, pulling in his abdomen and pushing back his shoulders. He was in fine condition for a man of any age, let alone fifty-eight. She watched him through half-closed eyes, still pretending to sleep. Her artifice may have cost Warham his life.

A meticulous man, Warham would usually have showered and shaved before going out, but that morning he did no more than slide a toothbrush over his teeth and allow a trickle of water to flow through his fingers, which he then rubbed over his tanned face.

From a tangle of clothes he selected a crumpled pair of cream linen shorts and a blue shirt. He dressed quickly, carelessly according to his wife, sitting on the side of the bath to put on a pair of deck shoes, and walked silently back to the bedroom.

Piled on a small glass-topped table was the stuff from his pockets. Taking elaborate care not to make a noise, he selected a handful of coins, a few banknotes and his mobile phone. He slung his camera around his neck.

Everything else – passport, credit cards, keys – he left behind. He stared at his wife for a few moments while arranging the items in various pockets. Then Ruth said he suddenly turned and crept, soundless save for the soft squeak of rubber soles on ceramic tiles, from the room, gently closing the door behind him.

From the CCTV system Riolo had installed around the hotel only a few weeks before, we know that Warham went down the stairs and into the cloakroom off the foyer. It was probably there he took some pills, because the medication was present in his stomach at the time of the *post mortem*.

He returned to the foyer, unlocked the front door, and walked into the street. The alarm system recorded the door being opened at 06.39.

He turned downhill, in the direction of the still-closed shops tucked into small openings in the ancient buildings, towards the sea. Beyond the harbour wall, where gentle waves lapped against the rocks, a small *gommone* buzzed into view. At 06.43 Warham checked his mobile for messages. There was just one.

By then, the little inflatable had tied up against the stone wall of the harbour.

He walked briskly, past boats moored high and dry outside houses. Outside the bar, a man waved. Warham immediately turned, heading back up the hill. He stopped to tickle the head of a little black cat, glancing behind him as he did so. The CCTV showed nobody else on the street.

Warham switched on his camera and pointed it towards the sea. In the viewfinder he would have seen the street, already half lit by the sun. He may have zoomed the lens and adjusted the focus, noting the contrasts of light and shade. By this time, one man had climbed from the *gommone* onto the harbour wall. Warham took a photograph.

He then must have drawn back the zoom, taking in the café at the foot of the hill. When they examined the camera, found several weeks after Warham's death, the bar owner, Ezio Tesorieri, was frozen in the act of wiping the outside tables. The picture was timed at 06.49, just ten minutes after Warham left the *San Rocco* hotel.

A postman told the magistrate that he saw Warham turn and head back down the hill. Just beyond the hotel he stopped, apparently examining the ancient way-mark painted in red and white on the wall. He looked all around him and disappeared into a gap between two houses.

Behind the village, the sun was driving a morning mist from the hills; it was going to be another hot day. All along the coast, the little white ferries were being wiped down, their tanks filled. In the villages, fresh bread was being baked. Peaches, peppers, tomatoes, lettuces and *zucchini* were being carefully arranged on displays in front of small food shops on steep streets. The first customers were drinking coffee standing at the counter of the café.

Back at the *San Rocco,* tables were being laid for breakfast. When he went to open up, Riolo was surprised to find the front door already unlocked. It was barely seven o'clock. Ruth said she was asleep in her room at that time.

CHAPTER TWO

THERE are better ways to start the week than with a bollocking from your news editor. Especially when you are rooted, you got up at five in the morning in a second-rate Dublin hotel to catch a flight back to London and you've spent the best part of two hours, and seventy-five quid, in a battered Toyota mini-cab trying to get to work on time.

It's even worse when it's pouring with rain, your shoes are soaking wet, your hair looks like a bush pig's arse and the bollocking is delivered in a text message. "Where the f★★★ are you".

None of your business, Curley, OK?

Cassandra Brown rubbed away the condensation and stared out of the car window at the rain-sodden East London landscape. Was this why she had come to Europe? She sighed and caught the eye of Alex in his rear view mirror. "Would you like the *Metro?*" Alex offered, picking up a copy from a pile on the passenger seat and passing it back to her.

"Why have you got a whole pile of freesheets, Alex?"

"So I can give every client one of their own, Miss Brown. It's value added."

"Wouldn't a better car add more value, Alex?"

"Then I'd have to increase my tariff, Miss Brown." He winked in the mirror. She turned back to the paper, flicking from headline to headline searching for nothing in particular. Her phone rang again. She ignored it. After his shitty text, Curley Baird could bloody well wait.

But even so, she felt guilty. Finally she dialled her voicemail. "Cass, it's Curley. I need you in here as soon as you land. The editor's going ape-shit for a big story on John Warham. The WBC share price has collapsed. Call me soonest, OK?"

Brown closed her eyes and prayed for instant redemption.

"Have you ever drunk too many black velvets, Alex?"

"Can you drink too many, Miss Brown?"

"I can, Alex. And I did."

"I'm sorry to hear that Miss Brown."

There was more to Alex than a toned body, clapped-out wheels and the scent of Paco Rabanne. One day, she might find out how much more. But, first she had work to do. Somewhere in *Metro* she had seen the name Warham. She scanned the pages until her eyes found a small story at the foot of an inside page. "Holidaymaker missing" above a single paragraph: British tourist, Henry J Warham, reported missing while on holiday in Italy. So, Henry was John, and John had gone missing.

This was a story she did not want to lose to another reporter. It could put her name on the front page. Prove that financial reporters could cut it with the hairy-arsed hacks who had done-their-time-in-the-provinces-and-were-bloody-proud-of-it. Show she could run rings around the Oxbridge brigade who monopolised the features pages. But she was tired, hung-over and possibly getting a cold. Why did the best opportunities come on the worst days?

Brown had worked nearly two years on the *Post* Business Desk, reporting financial and economic news. She had made her mark within the department, but it was tough for financial hacks to make the breakthrough to the front end of the paper. The Business desk was a ghetto – the stars were made in home news, foreign news and politics, not in the arcane world of stocks and bonds. She had met the *Post* Editor, George Cameron, only twice and he seemed scarcely aware of her existence; tough since the reason she came to London from Melbourne in the first place, screwing up her marriage in the process, was to make her name as a hot-shot reporter.

Alex bounced the Toyota through pot-holed side streets, negotiating his way around a variety of speed humps and width restrictions, every jolt hurting her head from the inside.

"Does this thing have any springs, Alex?"

Alex squinted into his mirror. "They've been damaged by the state of the roads, Miss Brown."

Touché. "I could really use a coffee, Alex, if you see somewhere."

Alex looked up again and nodded.

She must get herself together. After a coffee and a shower, she would feel better. If there was time for a sleep, she would feel perfect, but there wasn't. Better would have to suffice.

Right now, before speaking to Baird, she needed to find out something about Warham's disappearance. She'd met him several times, most recently in a VIP box at an Eric Clapton concert hosted by his company, WBC, for journalists, City people and others. Somebody from the Prime Minister's private office was also there. Warham's connections were impeccable.

Brown balanced her Filofax on her knee and keyed the private number of a senior WBC director into her mobile. The call went through to his voicemail. She left a message. She did not expect Charles Elwood to return her call.

As she rang off, a one-dimensional rendition of Bach's Toccata and Fugue in D Minor rattled around the Toyota's interior, cheap competition for Mozart wafting softly from the car's eight speakers. It took her a moment to realize the interruption was from her mobile. Alex turned down his precious sound system.

"Hello."

"Hi Cassandra, it's Curley, where are you?"

"On the M11, or somewhere."

"Christ, Cass, didn't you get my message? Why haven't you called? I need you here."

"You agreed last week I could come in after lunch today Curley. Give me a break. I'm on my way in, OK? As agreed, OK?"

"Oh, yeah, I remember now." Baird paused momentarily — it was as close as you'd get to an apology. "But look, I've got the editor pacing up and down demanding to know what's going on at WBC. The bloody PR man's gone AWOL and the share price has fallen off a cliff."

"Calm down Curley, for God sakes. I'm already on the case. Now, why don't you get yourself a cup of coffee, relax, and trust me. Eh?"

A loud sniff echoed down the phone. "Ring me as soon as you know anything. Are you on your way in now?"

"After lunch, Curley, alright. But you can put my name against WBC. I'll call you as soon as I know anything. Oh, and Curley, try not to shout at me again today. I'm feeling a little fragile after too much hospitality."

She rang off before Baird had a chance to reply.

Alex looked into his mirror and caught her eye. "New ring tone, Miss Brown?"

She felt the beginnings of a blush. She loved the way he said "Miss Brown". And being addressed through a mirror always gave her a buzz. It was the same at the hairdressers. There was no need to reply.

Brown searched again through her address book, and then dialled the number of a contact in the City. Two minutes later, she had the latest gossip. As she rang off, the tinny Toccata started again. "Cassandra. Charles Elwood, WBC. How are you? I thought you'd soon be baying round our doorstep."

Sarcastic bastard. "You're always so complimentary Charles. Anyway, I was wondering if you'd noticed the WBC share price is taking a hammering this morning. All sorts of stories flying around. I guess you must have heard them?"

"Oh yes, Cassandra, my brokers are quite assiduous when it comes to relaying market ..." he paused, "... tittle-tattle. Some of these, these rumours, yes, speculation, are quite ridiculous, you know, quite unfounded." Three "quites" in two sentences. Not as laid back as he wanted to sound.

"So what's the story, Charles? Will WBC be making a statement?"

"About what, Cassandra?"

Enough bullshit. "I hear John Warham's been reported missing in Italy. True or false?"

"As ever Cassandra, your sources are quite impeccable. Now, let's see. You pose me a dilemma. I'm always happy to help a friend, as you know, but there are a number of, what shall we say, issues, yes, complicated issues, arising here."

The Toyota pulled into the kerb, perilously close to a tower of dripping vegetable boxes. Alex cut the engine and got out, locking the doors as he left. He walked to the main road and disappeared round the corner. Was he abandoning her?

"What sort of issues, Charles?"

"I knew you'd ask, Cassandra." She could sense the smirk on Elwood's face. The man had an ego the size of St Paul's Cathedral. He continued. "Now. I have a suggestion. Would you happen to be free for lunch today? I would feel more comfortable talking over some white linen than over a mobile telephone. Strictly *entre-nous*, of course. All quotes to be checked, nothing to be used without my express say-so. And no fingerprints."

"I could be free, Charles, as it happens."

"Oh, and one more condition."

"Yes?"

"You withdraw your photographer from our front steps. There's really no point in him hanging around in the rain. He makes the place look so, so untidy." There was no mistaking the sneer. "I can assure you he won't miss anything: our chairman is not expected in today. No, not today."

"It's a deal, Charles. When and where?"

"La Lune Blanche. One o'clock."

"OK." She rang off. The Lune Blanche, eh? Very up-market. Alex returned carrying a paper cup, unlocked the car and handed her a cappuccino. He really was too good to be true. The car squelched over rotting cabbages and turned into Kentish Town Road – they would be back at Brown's home in a few minutes. There was enough time to put Baird out of his misery.

"It looks like Warham's gone walkabout, Curley. I'll know more this afternoon. I'm lunching with Charles Elwood in less than an hour."

"Who's Charles Elwood?"

"Where've you been Curley? He's Warham's number two at WBC. By the way, can you get the picture desk to call off the snapper from WBC. Warham's not going to put in an appearance today."

The car stopped outside the stuccoed Georgian house in Primrose Hill where Brown had rented a flat since arriving in London. Alex was instantly out of the car, her overnight bag in one hand and an umbrella in the other.

"Curley, I've got to go now. I'll be in after lunch."

She drunk the last of the coffee and asked Alex if he could

wait. Walking up the steps to the front door under Alex's umbrella, she thought of asking him if he would be more comfortable waiting upstairs rather than in the car, but immediately thought better of it. Alex retreated to the Toyota. The car's hazard lights blinked fiercely enough to frighten off any traffic warden who might have been waiting to dispense a soggy ticket.

Cream silk shirt, black trouser suit, shoes with a small heel, hair tied back. Sexy but business-like. Minimal make-up. She looked herself up and down in the bedroom mirror: a bit dark under the eyes. She changed her shoes to a pair with a higher heel. Elwood was, after all, a good six feet tall. A simple silver crucifix around her neck.

Her head was clearing: adrenalin and caffeine were winning the battle against alcohol. Reflected behind her she saw the debris from her weekend away. With a sigh, she went to the window. The rain had sharpened the scent of the trees in the square and brought the colour of the worn York stone pavement back to yellow. The children's swing in the playground dripped water. Alex had turned the car round and was waiting beneath the large umbrella which she was amused to see was inscribed with the name of one of London's top auction houses.

Fifteen minutes later, after first driving past WBC's offices to make sure the *Post*'s photographer was no longer hanging about outside, she was sitting at a table in La Lune Blanche, and wondering why Elwood had chosen the advertising industry's favourite restaurant, where their lunchtime assignation would be observed by half Charlotte Street, for what he insisted was to be a private lunch. Hadn't he said, "no fingerprints"? Who would need fingerprints when there would be at least a dozen eyewitnesses?

Brown sipped a mineral water and tried to ignore the basket of bread. She had eaten far too much in Dublin. Elwood strode into the restaurant, ten minutes late, nodding and smiling his way to the table at the rear.

"Don't get up," he commanded as Brown made to greet him, "sorry I'm a little late, but as you can imagine, it's been a busy morning. How delightful to see you, Cassandra." His manners were as immaculate as his suits. Seated incongruously beneath the photographs of celebrity diners, Elwood was nevertheless totally at ease. A glass of white wine arrived without apparently having been ordered. Elwood put his menu aside unopened as the waiter stood back a step or two, notepad poised. Brown ordered; Elwood merely nodded to the waiter. A soupspoon was already laid at Elwood's place – he was clearly a man of habit.

"Now, Cassandra, what would you like to know?"

"Shall we start with what has happened to your chairman?"

"I wish I knew, Cassandra. It is a quite extraordinary situation. Mrs Warham, Ruth, is naturally very distressed, and completely at a loss to know where John could have gone. Or why. WBC is doing all within its power to help her, of course, but it's not really a WBC issue, you know. No, not a WBC issue at the moment."

"What do you mean, Charles, not really a WBC issue?"

He grinned briefly and then appeared to think better of it. "Well, Cassandra. John was, and still is for that matter, on vacation."

The first course arrived. Could Cassandra be tempted to a glass of wine? No, not with the aftermath of a Dublin night still curdling her bloodstream.

"I don't follow you Charles. Why doesn't it concern you just because John was, is, on holiday?"

"I didn't say it didn't concern me. I said it was not a WBC issue, not the same thing at all, not at all."

He was a pedantic sod. Brown put down her fork and looked him full in the face. "So you did Charles. But, forgive me for being slow, why is it not a WBC issue?"

Elwood's spoon stopped halfway between the plate and his mouth. "Slow is never a word I would apply to you Cassandra. Quite the reverse. It is, I would be the first to admit, a subtle distinction, but an important one. You see, if John fails to return to the office at the end of his vacation, then it will become a WBC issue. Meanwhile, however inexplicable his behaviour, it is actually none of our business. Do you see the difference?"

Brown nodded, her mouth too full to speak. Pompous ass. Elwood continued. "But it's not only the board which takes that view. I rather think Ruth wanted to keep it within the family for as long as she could too."

Brown swallowed hard. "What do you mean?"

"Well, without, without, necessarily drawing any conclusions, I find it a little odd, shall we say, yes, a little strange, I would put it no stronger than that, that Ruth did not feel it necessary to let us know of the situation when it arose."

Was it the Guinness and Champagne still in her system that made all Elwood's statements into riddles? Couldn't the man simply say what he meant?

"She didn't tell you? So how did you find out?"

Lamb arrived, pink, garlicky, perfect. Pepper was ground. A glass of red wine joined Elwood's half-finished white. Brown looked covetously at the glass and took a sip of fizzy water.

"A client, I am sorry to say, telephoned me on Sunday, yes, yesterday, from Italy to ask if rumours of John's disappearance were true. John had worked with the client on a big campaign last year. Yes. It's where he first met Bia Gonzales as a matter of fact." He sipped the red and pushed the white away.

"Where he met who?"

Elwood's face lit up. "Bia Gonzales. The model in John's fur coat campaign. Oh Cassandra, I'm sure you must remember the picture of him with Ms Gonzales at the London Fashion Week party, published in the *Post*'s very own gossip column if I remember rightly?"

Brown shook her head as Elwood pressed on. "Not a popular campaign with some of our staff, as you might imagine, Cassandra. And it unfortunately brought WBC to the attention of the animal rights people."

The waiter arrived to pour Brown more water. Her head was almost back to normal.

Elwood continued. "Now, as I was saying, Cassandra, I was quite taken aback by the question. Yes, so taken aback that I didn't know how to respond."

"That's not usual for you, is it Charles."

He ignored the remark. "I said there must be some, some misunderstanding because John was simply on holiday. But I was concerned, obviously, so I called their London home to learn that not only was the story true, but that he disappeared on Wednesday morning. Nearly a week ago, Cassandra. You can imagine how embarrassed I felt. I had to ring the client back immediately."

Brown captured a few flageolets on her fork. "But as you yourself said, Charles, it's not really a WBC issue at the moment."

Elwood put down his glass, leaned back, and allowed a condescending smile to brush momentarily across his lips. "Quite, Cassandra." He leaned forward again, changed his facial composure to 'serious' and lowered his voice to a whisper. "But it is slightly odd, don't you think?"

"So what are you going to say to the stock market?"

"We'll simply report the facts, Cassandra. People can then form their own conclusions."

"And what conclusion should they draw, Charles?"

"Really Cassandra, you cannot ask me to speculate."

The waiter arrived to clear the plates, and Brown ordered an espresso. Elwood looked around to make sure he was not overheard and then once again leaned across the table to speak in a whisper. His scent smelled very expensive.

"As you will doubtless discover, Cassandra, John is under a modicum of pressure from some of our shareholders."

"Over?"

"Over him holding the positions of both chairman and chief executive. Some believe it gives him far too much power in the boardroom. They feel it would be better, yes better, if he held only one of those positions."

Brown knocked back her coffee in one swig. "How much is a modicum, Charles?"

Elwood laughed tidily behind his knuckles. "I think it's time we each went back to work, Cassandra."

"So what's the story?" Baird demanded. Outside La Lune Blanche, Brown tried to manage an umbrella in one hand and her mobile in the other. She watched Elwood stride off up the street, after air-kissing her on both cheeks. She was no nearer finding out what had happened to Warham than she was before lunch. But one thing was clear. Elwood regarded Warham's "bizarre adventure", as he called it, as an opportunity to further his own career. She had just had lunch with a man in whom ambition was growing like fungus.

"It's all pretty odd, Curley. Apparently, he was on holiday with Ruth. That's his wife. She woke last Wednesday morning and he'd gone. Hang on a minute Curley, here's a cab."

The cab splashed its way down New Cavendish Street. Brown

drew a smiley in the condensation on the window. The taxi driver scowled into his mirror and she rubbed it out. "The weird thing is, she didn't do anything for twenty-four hours. The police weren't told until Thursday. And there's a mash-up about who actually called in the police. Their son Tom flew out, and it seems it was he who got things moving. Well, it was either him or the British Embassy. Oh, and did you know the story broke in Italy over the weekend? The Embassy tipped off a local hack on Friday afternoon, but the joke is nobody seemed to twig who they were talking about. It's in *Metro* this morning, but his name is given as Henry Warham rather than John, so nobody picked up on who it was."

"No joke, Cass. Not only *Metro*, we ran it in the first edition and then dropped it. Cameron's already had a tantrum about it. Foreign got their arses kicked 'cos they ran it as a News in Brief in just one edition. By the way, the *Standard* says he was on an upmarket walking holiday. Is that right?"

"Sounds like a contradiction in terms to me, Curley. Look, I'm on my way back. See you in fifteen."

Baird was finishing the afternoon news-list as Brown arrived at the office. She went straight to the news-desk, dropping her bag on her own desk as she passed. Her message light was flashing. "Hi Curley. What do you want me to do?"

Baird showed her the news-list on the screen.

"What the hell's this?" she said, pointing to the second of the two stories she was due to write.

"What it says."

"Listen Curley, how am I supposed to know there's a distraught family waiting by the phone?"

"Then use your imagination," Baird snapped back.

"I'd better get on," said Brown, retreating to her own desk before Baird thought up any more stories to put against her name.

On her voicemail, she heard the soft Irish accent of Conor Hogan, saying how much he had enjoyed entertaining her in Dublin. She emailed a reply: "Hi Conor. Sorry I was out when you phoned. Frantic right now. Will call you later from home. Cx."

Brown called up the news-list on her screen. She really did not want to write a piece about a distraught family she didn't know. She would try again to persuade Baird to drop it. He was walking back and forth beside his desk, stretching his telephone cord as far as it would go, talking to the picture desk. "Nothing? Tell him to hang on and get any family he can. News wants a human interest angle. Get him to knock on the door and ask for some family pics. And for Christ's sake tell him to be polite. OK, OK, I know it's a reporter's job but there's nobody I can send. Oh, and can you get out the library pics. You have, right. See if you can find any of him and his missus." He banged the phone down, dropped into his chair and took a large gulp of brown liquid from a plastic cup.

"Curley, have you put a photographer outside the house?"

"What do you think?"

"Call him off, Curley. If Elwood hears about this he'll think I organised it. You know he asked for the snapper to be called off outside the offices."

"Which I did. So I sent him to the house. Cassandra, can you leave the pictures to me and get on with your stories."

"OK, but don't blame me if the source dries up. Curley. Look I can't do the distraught family angle."

Baird swivelled his chair. Why?"

"First of all it's too corny and surely we have to be a bit understanding about their feelings. By the way, you might sooner have a shot of Warham at the Fashion Week party. His wife wasn't there and he was there with some model."

"Can we talk about it later. I've got to get to afternoon conference."

When he returned, Baird pointed to the City Editor's office. Henry Marshall, the man paid to run the business section, had not yet arrived and nobody knew, nor much cared for that matter, where he was.

"OK to use Henry's office?" Baird asked Marshall's secretary.

"Sure. Tea?" With Marshall out all day, she had little to do and was obviously quite happy to play hostess to Baird, who some suspected might one day be her boss. Tea in Marshall's office was china cups and a pot on a tray, rather than the instant variety in polystyrene. Baird settled himself in Marshall's chair. Brown sat on his desk.

"So Cass, what do we have?" said Baird.

"As you know, Curley, WBC officially refuses to add a word to the statement, not even confirming where he was on holiday and when he disappeared. But that's all on the wires anyway."

The tea tray arrived and Baird helped himself to a chocolate digestive from the plate. "So why did Elwood want to take you to lunch?"

It was an obvious question without an obvious answer. Brown poured the tea. "I think, Curley, to make sure I knew Warham is under pressure from a couple of the big shareholders to loosen his grip on the boardroom. They want to put in somebody else to run the business."

"Elwood, perhaps?"

"You're not such a dubbo after all, Curley. He's already installed himself as acting chief executive until Warham turns up."

Baird grunted. "Anything else?"

"Well, although he's not been seen since last Wednesday, no-one at WBC knew a thing about it until yesterday evening, and only then after Elwood found out from someone in Italy."

"I like it."

"Oh, and there's another thing. Elwood couldn't wait to remind me that Warham's been hanging out with this model." She looked at her notebook, "Bia Gonzales."

Baird picked up a second biscuit. "Great stuff, Cass. You'd better get writing." One bite took half the biscuit into his mouth.

"This one's got legs, Curley. By the way, what do home news want?"

Baird grinned from ear to ear. He wiped his mouth with a crumpled tissue pulled from his pocket. "You've got the splash, Cass, but it better be bloody good. Mystery surrounded the whereabouts last night of a prominent London businessman and friend of the Prime Minister ... you know the angles. Five hundred words by five fifteen?"

"You bastard, Curley, why didn't you tell me before."

If she had been a footballer, Brown would have run around in a circle, leaped on Baird's back and punched the air. Yes, the splash. The lead to the paper. Her name on the front page. The kid who had started in the library of the *Melbourne Age* during her college vacations had made it to the front page of the *Post* in London. All she had to do was deliver what London's most demanding editor wanted. Her hangover had gone completely.

Brown swung her legs off Marshall's desk, aware of Baird's gaze and relieved she was wearing trousers rather than a skirt.

By six thirty, all the pieces were written and sent through to the news-desk. She had persuaded Baird that a story about relatives comforting Ruth Warham was better than his proposed "distraught family". She had no idea whether or not it was true.

Brown stood behind Baird looking over his shoulder as he made a few minor changes and zapped her stories through to the Back Bench, where the sub-editors who control the nightly production of the paper would add their own twist.

"Nice package, Cass. Just what Cameron was looking for."

Brown got herself a coffee from the machine and sauntered back to the news-desk. "I'll just hang on until the page is made up and then I'd like to call it a day, Curley. I'm bushed after the weekend and I should get home and catch up on my chores. I'll be at home if anyone needs me."

Baird shouted across to the sub editors. "Any problems with Cass's stuff?"

Nobody replied. She went back to her desk and called up pages of property ads on the Internet, looking for flats in either Primrose Hill or Belsize Park, the area of North London she now regarded as home.

The chief Business Desk sub-editor called her across to his oversized screen. "Thought you'd like to see this before you go."

There was her story at the top of the *Post* front page, carrying the biggest by-line she had earned since arriving in London.

"Shall I bike you the first edition?" he asked.

"That would be great, if it's not too much trouble." She turned to Baird, "OK to go, Curley?"

He nodded, his mouth being occupied with crunching something from a crinkly plastic packet.

Brown walked down the stairs from the business section and then along the whole length of the noisy newsroom. This was where Brown felt she belonged, at the hub of the news operation. She wanted one of those small grey desks for her own, to sit amongst some of the most respected journalists on Fleet Street. The business section was just a stepping-stone.

As she passed the back-bench she could see her story on the

big screen in front of the News Editor. He nodded in her direction and spoke to the Editor, who was watching the electronic front page take shape. Cameron glanced up briefly and immediately returned to concentrate on the screen. She had hoped for a smile at least. On their way she passed, coming in, Henry Marshall, City Editor. It was his first appearance in the office that day. He nodded and mumbled a few words which could have been "good night".

Brown took the tube to Chalk Farm and as she walked the last few hundred yards home, the rain stopped. The air was fresh. Even the graffiti-daubed bridge over the main line into Kings Cross had lost its smell of piss. The pavements were clean and the tables outside Primrose Hill's many cafés were busy. It was still light. She stopped to look at the flats and houses for sale in an estate agent's window.

There was one she liked the look of. Huge living room, ultra modern kitchen, one bedroom, bathroom, private roof terrace, for sale at £335,000. How on earth could she raise a mortgage sufficient to bridge the gap between what remained of her share of the proceeds of their Melbourne flat and the asking price? But the rent on her current flat was killing her. She telephoned the agent, got the message service, left her name and number and headed home to the square, where there were always several 'For Sale' boards, but at prices well beyond her reach.

Brown did not want supper. Her work clothes felt tight and uncomfortable, and she changed into a tee shirt and an old pair of blue jeans, sufficiently well worn to be comfortable even if she had put on a pound or two. She set about putting her home back in order, pondering on the strange lunch with Elwood. Why was he so keen to make sure she knew about the pressure Warham was under to loosen his stranglehold on WBC?

As chairman and chief executive, with a handpicked group of non-executive directors behind him, Warham was in virtually complete control of the board. But with the downturn in the economy, WBC was struggling to maintain its growth record and the shares had fallen. Investors had lost money.

Elwood had also been too keen to remind Brown that Warham had been busy with interests other than WBC. What was it he had said? "Some of our friends in the City seem worried that John has been spending more time on the helping out the government than on WBC. Of course, I have been telling them they are quite mistaken, quite wrong."

I bet you have, thought Brown as she closed the door of the washing machine.

She needed to get out, so pulled on socks and a pair of trainers. The wide pavements were again dry. She was struck once again by the beautiful curve of Regents Park Road, the heart of Primrose Hill. She thought about taking a coffee at one of the places still open, but she wanted to spend some quiet time walking in what was left of the evening light in order to focus. Too much had happened in too short a time.

She had promised to phone Hogan, but what was she going to say? Could she chatter on and avoid the question of whether she wanted a relationship? But as she climbed to the top of Primrose Hill Park and looked out over a darkening London, at the lights on the London Eye, the BT Tower, the flashing light and glowing roof of Canary Wharf, and the last planes of the day heading westwards along the flight path to Heathrow, Brown nearly convinced herself that a little fling with Hogan might be fun. On the other hand, it might not.

Watching the television news less than half an hour later, Brown was struck, not for the first time, at what a poor job the telly did of reporting business stories. Their piece consisted of little more than a reading of the official statement issued that afternoon by WBC, along with some background footage and commentary on Warham's involvement with the government. There were shots of him arriving for the Fashion Week party with an exceptionally pretty girl on his arm.

Although tired, Brown wanted to see the other papers, to find out what the competition was running. So she called Central Executive Cars, and asked them to pick up copies of all the next day's papers available from the stall outside King's Cross station. Half an hour later, she was surprised to find it was Alex who was ringing her bell.

He handed over the papers. "Long day, Miss Brown."

"For both of us I think Alex."

"Good night, Miss Brown."

Brown delayed her reading until she had watched Alex climb back into the Toyota and disappear down the road. She idly wondered when, where, and with whom, Alex would go to bed that night. With a sigh, she poured a small shot of vodka direct from the freezer, added tonic, selected *The Times* and began to read.

SECTION	News 1
CATCH	Missingman
HEADING 1	Prime Minister informed as key backer reported missing
HEADING 2	Top businessman vanishes on Italian holiday trip
AUTHOR	Cassandra Brown
STATUS	Live

Mystery last night surrounded the whereabouts of a leading British businessman who vanished whilst on a family holiday on the Italian Riviera.

John Warham, one of the circle of "Blairite" businessmen who worked closely with the Government on both the ill-fated Millennium Dome and London's winning 2012 Olympic bid, has not been seen for nearly a week.

According to officials, the millionaire advertising chief walked out of his hotel last Wednesday without telling his wife where he was going. Despite an intensive search by Italian police, there have been no sightings of him.

A coastguard helicopter called in by the police failed to find any traces.

News of his mystery disappearance wiped tens of millions off the stock market value of his company, WBC, the advertising giant. The company announced that Mr Warham "has been reported missing while on a family holiday in Italy". Beyond the brief statement, however, the company is being tight-lipped about the affair. "We have nothing to add to our statement," said a spokesman.

However, industry insiders point out that the advertising business is going through difficult times and that WBC has lost some key accounts recently.

The British Embassy in Rome has asked anyone who may have seen Mr Warham either to get in touch with them or the local police.

Interpol has been alerted and a watch is being kept at ports and airports.

Warham, known as "Mr Genius" following his high profile role in the "It doesn't take a Genius" general election campaign, is married with one son. His wife is thought to have returned to the couple's £2.5million London home.

Staff at WBC's plush Charlotte Street offices were informed of the mystery yesterday morning as the Stock Exchange forced the company to make an official statement.

The 58-year-old advertising guru is due to return to his desk next Monday. "At this stage the directors have no reason to suppose that he will not return on the due date," the company said.

A spokesman admitted the company had "no idea" where their chairman might be, but promised to keep investors informed of any developments. Asked if there was any reason why the company's founder might have wanted to disappear, the spokesman said he would not be drawn into "wild speculation".

He pointed out, however, that the company says it is on target to meet stock market profit forecasts.

Downing Street said they were "concerned" about Mr Warham's disappearance and had instructed the British Embassy in Rome to give the local police "every assistance" in their search.

SECTION	News
TITLE	Rellies
HEADING 1	Relatives comfort missing ad chief's wife
HEADING 2	
AUTHOR	Cassandra Brown
STATUS	Live

Relatives were last night comforting the wife of missing businessman John Warham at the couple's exclusive North London home.

Callers at the house, in the desirable "Little Venice" area, were referred to the millionaire's company, the advertising giant Warham Blazeley Cotts.

His wife Ruth was said by friends to be "at a loss to understand" her husband's sudden disappearance. A two-day search of the Italian Riviera, where Warham went missing, revealed nothing.

Meanwhile, details began to emerge of his mysterious absence, when he walked out of his hotel and failed to return. He did not tell his wife where he was going.

The British consulate in Rome raised the alarm after Warham's son Tom contacted the Prime Minister's office. The Italian state police, the Carabinieri, brought in a helicopter to help the search of the rugged cliffs which form the coastline.

A spokesman for the company appealed to the media to respect the family's need for privacy "at this difficult time".

The Warham's were on a £1000 a head walking holiday along the beautiful Italian coast known as the "Cinque Terre". They had reached the midpoint in their trek, the artists' colony of Manarola, when he vanished.

CHAPTER THREE

IN THE distance, she can hear her mother. "Cassie, Cassie", the pitch of her voice rising at the end of each call. But Brown is sitting at the organ of Melbourne's St Patrick's Cathedral in a wedding dress. At her neck hangs a small silver crucifix, a seventeenth birthday present from her sweetheart. She looks over her shoulder and can see Steve sitting in the front pew. He glances behind him but doesn't look up. The congregation waits below. "Cassie. Now. Start now," shouts her mother. In front of her is the sheet music of Bach's Toccata in D minor. But one entire keyboard is missing, the stops are gone and she cannot operate the pedal board because her feet are tangled in the dress. Suddenly the music starts.

She wakes to the ringing of her mobile. The bedclothes lie scrumbled in a heap. She stretches across to the bedside table and sees who is calling.

Hogan. She simply wasn't in the mood for pressure, and let the phone ring unanswered.

The floor was littered with newspapers. She caught sight of the front page of the *Post* and grinned.

Baird bit into a bacon sandwich dripping with tomato ketchup, swallowed hard and wiped his mouth with the back of his hand. "So where's the WBC story going today, Cass?"

"Well, I thought I'd follow up on the shareholders wanting Warham out."

Baird balanced the sandwich on the top of an upturned plastic cup, rubbed his hands down his trousers and leaned back in his chair. "That's fine for our pages Cass, but what about a news story?

Cameron wants to keep it running in the front of the paper."

Brown perched on the corner of his desk. "I don't know, Curley. I haven't got anything particular. Not unless Warham turns up somewhere. Nothing on the wires I suppose?"

Baird retrieved his sandwich and looked at it, as if seeking inspiration, before bringing it to his mouth. He raised his eyebrows and closed his teeth around the soggy bread. He pulled the sandwich away, wiped his mouth with the back of his hand, and shook his head.

Brown stood up. "Then I don't have anything. I'll get to work on the city story."

Baird flung what was left of the sandwich into the rubbish bin. Abruptly, he stood up and pointed to Marshall's office. Brown followed behind. She sensed she was not going to enjoy the next few minutes. Baird walked straight past Marshall's secretary and sat himself behind Marshall's desk. The office carried a whiff of stale cigars, despite the air-conditioning. There was an old butt festering in a large onyx ashtray. The day's newspapers were arranged neatly on his desk, the *Post* right on the top of the pile. If Marshall came in, he couldn't fail to see her story.

Baird took off his spectacles and rubbed them furiously with his tie. "Do you want to hang on to this story, Cassandra?" He did not wait for a reply. "Because if you do I suggest you get your arse into gear and find an angle for the news pages. Cameron was planning to put a news reporter onto it but I persuaded him you could hack it. Now, you'd better find something before afternoon conference. OK?"

Baird was right. If she was to get anywhere, she needed to show she could find stories good enough to make the front page, not just once, but day after day. She was in danger of throwing away the best career chance she had ever had. Journalists are only as good as their last story. And today's papers will be wrapping up tomorrow's rubbish. She did her best to grin. "Sorry Curley. I'll come up with something. And, thanks, by the way."

"I didn't do it for you."

Somehow she knew that to be true.

A routine call-round of City contacts confirmed Warham was not flavour of the month: far from it. It was also clear somebody was out there stirring up trouble for him. Was it a coincidence that Elwood's own term "inexplicable behaviour" came up repeatedly?

The more she spoke to the City stuff-shirts, the more she sympathised with Warham. The establishment was all too ready to write him off. They spoke as if he were some troublesome teenager, not an astute businessman who over the years had put a great deal of money in their pockets. And he was still officially on holiday, for God's sake. But at least it confirmed her story.

The first City edition of the *Evening Standard* flopped down on her desk. She muttered "thanks" without bothering to look up. A picture of "John Warham, missing tycoon, arm in arm with fashion model Bia Gonzales" at the London Fashion Week party dominated the front page. The story, datelined Milan, said "friends of Bia Gonzales" claimed she was "distressed" at the mysterious disappearance of John Warham. Clearly the reporter hadn't managed to talk to her.

Because she was holed up with Warham? Not impossible. Where? Milan, maybe. But why would he not at the very least not let his family know he was not dead? Don't thirty years of marriage count for anything?

Inside the *Standard* were two more shots, including one of Gonzales wearing nothing but a fur coat. The image had graced the hoardings and Metro stations of Continental Europe the previous autumn. Behind her, the Ligurian coast basked in sunshine.

Brown had nearly finished writing the City story when Baird pulled up a chair and sat on it backwards, arms resting on the seatback, head directly in Brown's line of sight. His manner was conversational, rather than confrontational. "So, Cass, how're we doing? What've you managed to find? By the way, the editor's dropped a packet on WBC shares."

Brown looked again at the notes scribbled in the taxi after her lunch at La Lune Blanche, and wished for the millionth time she had learned shorthand. But she had trained as a corporate lawyer, not a journalist. Despite promising Baird she would come up with "something", she didn't have anything new. Would he settle for a story about the delays in bringing in the Italian police and the fact that the family had not told WBC about Warham's disappearance?

She avoided Baird's eye. "Well, Curley, the investors story stands up and will give us a good strong piece for business. I've nearly finished it, as a matter of fact. Now, for news, we could offer a piece on how weird it was nobody told the police for twenty four hours and then the family said nothing to WBC until Elwood heard rumours on Sunday night."

"You told me that yesterday, Cass. What have you picked up today?"

"We didn't use it yesterday Curley, and neither did anyone else. I've got this to myself."

Baird swung the chair from side to side. "But what's happening today Cass? Something must be going on. It's your job to find out what. Have you talked to the family yet, Scotland Yard, Interpol? Have you called up the Italian police? What's Elwood got to say for himself?"

Brown stared down at her notebook. She didn't want to see Baird's face, because she had no answers. Finally, she managed to look up.

He wasn't angry; his face and voice expressed concern and encouragement rather than command. "Come on Cass, for fuck's sake, what's the matter with you today?"

He stood up abruptly and began a walk around the office, going from journalist to journalist, cajoling them to greater efforts.

Bach announced a call from the estate agent. Luckily Baird was out of earshot. The flat in Gloucester Avenue was still available, although inevitably, "there were quite a few interested." She needed to see it immediately if she was going to be in the running. Shit timing. Brown glanced nervously at the vacant news-desk. With luck she could get to Primrose Hill and back in less than an hour, and she could use her mobile on the way. It wouldn't really interfere with her day's work. She agreed to meet the agent in twenty minutes, grabbed her bag and fled.

The estate agent was waiting outside the front door as the cab, not black but hideously red and decorated with a huge jumping kangaroo advertising Qantas Airways, drew into the kerb. Before she even got out, she knew she did not want to live there. She asked the cabbie to wait. The house was of grey brick, a set of cracked steps leading up to a front porch, already dismal but made worse by a dirty plastic plant trough in which a red geranium struggled to survive.

The agent was putting the key into the lock when she told him she was not interested because of the state of the outside. He replied she would have to think of spending perhaps another £150k to get something with more class. His firm could, of course, help her to find a mortgage. They shook hands with his promise to get details to her of what was on offer. Disappointed, Brown climbed back into the Qantas cab. The 'roo wore a knowing smile. For the price being asked for this flat she could buy something huge and modern overlooking Sydney Harbour.

Beside her a red light glowed to indicate the driver had switched on the intercom. "So what did you think, sweetheart? Didn't you like it?"

"No, not much."

"You want to look a bit further out, love. Have a decco at Crouch End."

Brown smiled, but the cabbie wasn't even looking in his mirror.

Somewhere around the Bank of England, the traffic came to a dead stop. A water main had burst. Brown looked at her watch. She had already been out of the office for forty minutes. The intercom light came on again. "Want me to try another way, love?"

"Could you?"

The taxi backed up slightly, did a tight U-turn and ducked into a tiny street Brown had never noticed before. The driver weaved through a succession of narrow streets and two minutes later they were right across the road from the *Post*'s green glass offices.

Baird was still not at his desk when she returned, barely three quarters of an hour after leaving. But she had spent £30 on a taxi fare and, worse than that, risked her job, to see a dump. If Baird knew she had been out, he did not mention it when he came past her desk, spilling coffee from a plastic cup as he overshot and went into reverse gear. "Got time for lunch?"

Was it a loaded question? Had he seen her empty desk? Been looking for her? She looked at her watch. "Sure, a quick bite would be nice."

Lunch with Baird was an altogether different proposition from lunch with Elwood. No fancy restaurants: it was either the staff canteen or the Three Dragons. He chose the latter. Baird was not a tall man, but walked surprisingly fast, taking steps too large for the length of his legs, so that with each one he had to swing his whole body to make the desired length. Walking beside him was not only challenging but also potentially dangerous. If that were not enough, Brown was suffering the additional handicap of high heels. "Slow down Curley, for Christ's sake," she panted, "I'd like to get there in one piece."

Baird slowed, but his attempt to saunter was a dismal failure. They were both relieved to arrive at the grubby blue swing doors of the pub. The barmaid picked up a pint pot and began drawing Baird's bitter even before they crossed the distance between the door and the bar. Over ham, eggs and chips Baird got to the point. The Warham story was a chance to show the editor just how good his team were. He promised to take Brown off all other stories so she could concentrate exclusively on Warham's disappearance, but only on condition she gave it all she could. Over his second pint, Baird confided that he did not see the City Editor, Henry Marshall, staying in his job for very much longer and that, should he get Marshall's job, he would be looking at her as a possible deputy.

Brown was as keen as Baird that they should make a good show with the WBC story. But not because she wished to be his deputy. Being a deputy was not in her career plan, except as a short-term measure if necessary. She kept her thoughts to herself.

As Baird outlined his plans for the future, Brown's mind drifted back to the flat she was hoping to find. How far should she raise her sights on price? Perhaps another £100K? But £150K was too much. She tried to focus on what Baird was saying about how he would run the department, but the vision of plain wooden floors, white walls and a view of trees kept returning to the dark brown interior of the Three Dragons.

On the way back to the office, Baird returned to the Warham story. The editor would demand she come up with an original angle every day if "they" – the Business Desk – were going to hang on to the story and not be forced to surrender it to a news reporter. It was going to be bloody hard work, and her private life would have to be put on hold. She got the message. Subtlety was not part of Baird's armoury.

"Hope you've got your passport with you, Cass." Baird's Inverness accent, dulled by years in London, had been rejuvenated by his two pints of bitter.

Brown looked up from her screen and cocked her head on one side. She said nothing.

"You're off to Rome tonight."

"Why?"

"To look for John Warham."

"Jesus, Curley, the story's here, not Rome. Why can't foreign cover?"

"Because in the immortal words of George Cameron, Cass, our man in Rome couldn't recognise a news story even if it had a fucking papal bonnet on it."

"But why me, Curley? There are so many angles to chase up here."

"One, the editor is convinced there's some funny business in Italy. Two, you speak Italian. And three, George has told me to send you ASAP. Didn't you listen to anything I said to you at lunchtime?"

"OK. But not tonight, Curley. I've not got my passport with me, let alone a change of clothes. And I've got a story to write — remember? Anyway Curley, Rome is nowhere near where Warham disappeared."

"George wants you in Rome. Oh, and by the way he doesn't think you've got enough for a separate news story on the delays and so forth." Baird pursed his lips. "Unless you can come up with something better, he doesn't want anything on the news pages tonight. Have you?"

Brown shook her head. Baird raised his eyes and the palms of his chubby hands to the ceiling.

Shit, this was not a great start to her career as one of the *Post's* top reporters. Time to give in on the Rome assignment. "OK. But not tonight, please. My flat looks like it's had the burglars in."

He sighed. "First flight tomorrow then."

What the hell was she supposed to do in Rome? Come up with a bloody good story if she wanted to hold on to her job, let alone get promoted. Who would know anything about Warham? Well, she could start with the British Embassy. She got the number from the Foreign Office and made an appointment to see the vice-consul the following day. So far, so good. Telephones work as well in Rome as London, so she could try to get to speak to Gonzales.

Failing that, Gonzales was bound to have an agent who might talk. Would the *Carabinieri* say anything? Possibly. In truth, it could all be done just as well from her desk, but what the Hell?

She was wrapping up the "Warham under pressure from shareholders" story, checking the closing share price, when a city money manager to whom she had spoken earlier called her back. He said Elwood had agreed to meet some big shareholders "when Warham returned from holiday." At least she had a decent business story, even if she'd not found anything for the news pages.

She slipped past the news-desk without saying goodnight and went home feeling thoroughly dejected. Nemesis was clearly on her case, but divine retribution — for what? Brown was running out of chances to make her name, and could not afford many more days like this. Writing the lead story for the business pages was no longer good enough, neither for her nor for Baird.

SECTION	Business
TITLE	WBCDemands
HEADING 1	WBC crisis: Fund managers demand urgent meeting
HEADING 2	
AUTHOR	Cassandra Brown
STATUS	Live

CITY INVESTORS are demanding to meet with the missing chairman of Warham Blazeley Cotts as soon as he returns to the advertising firm he founded.

Institutions are unhappy with the board structure at WBC, where John Warham holds the jobs of both chairman and chief executive. They point out that under corporate governance guidelines, the arrangement is not regarded as "best practice".

Warham, 58, was last week reported missing in Italy while on a family holiday. A police search and local publicity failed to produce any clues to his whereabouts.

When news of his disappearance surfaced in the City on Monday, WBC shares virtually halved in a few hours. Investors are unhappy that a morning of speculation was allowed to elapse before the company made an announcement to the Stock Exchange.

They want the Stock Exchange to investigate dealings on Monday morning, as news of his disappearance had already been reported in Italy and in some British newspapers. A spokesman for the Exchange said yesterday that they always investigate suspicious share price movements ahead of price sensitive announcements. She refused to be drawn, however, on whether WBC was being targeted for investigation.

One fund manager commented last night, "There was absolute chaos in the market yesterday (Monday) morning, and then when the announcement came it said nothing. What we want to know is, 'is he coming back or not, and if he is, when will he split the roles.' Warham needs to be reminded that the shareholders own the company now, not him."

Charles Elwood, the WBC finance director who has stepped into Mr Warham's Chief Executive role until the position is clarified, said that Warham's disappearance was "inexplicable", but maintained that since he was not in any case due back to the office until next Monday, June 5, he felt the company had acted properly. "We put out an announcement when the share price became unstable. We acted as quickly as we could in these unusual circumstances".

It is understood that WBC directors were kept in the dark about Warham's sudden absence and learned about the crisis only late on Sunday afternoon, when an Italian client called Mr Elwood at home to ask for an explanation of rumours already circulating in business circles in Milan and Rome.

Bruce Fentiman, a leading industry analyst at investment bank SBA, said that the shares of WBC might now be undervalued, but that before they recovered the company needed to restore City confidence.

"Two things need to happen", he claimed. "Firstly John (Warham) has to account for himself, and secondly the board has to settle the management structure issue once and for all. Investors would like to see John give up his role as CEO and concentrate on the chairmanship. We feel WBC lacks a certain amount of strategic direction, and this could be because John is trying to do too much."

Mr Elwood said that he had been in touch with the leading shareholders and recognised their concerns. He added he would be happy to meet with them in the near future, but any such moves would not take place before Mr Warham returned.

"At the moment, our concern is to support Ruth (Warham) through this difficult time. We are as concerned as anybody and look forward to hearing that John is fit and well and back with his family," he added.

CHAPTER FOUR

AT EXACTLY 6am, Brown's doorbell rang. The Toyota was outside, engine clacking, blue smoke curling from the exhaust.

On the doormat she picked up an invitingly plump brown foolscap envelope. The estate agents had moved quickly.

Alex held the car door open. Several copies of *Metro*, so fresh she could smell the ink, were piled on the back seat. The sun was already warm, and she was heading for Rome.

Alex engaged the gears and released the hand brake. "Stansted, Miss Brown?"

"If you think we can make it that far."

"No problem, Miss Brown. Please help yourself to a newspaper."

She looked into Alex's eyes in his mirror and no longer cared she had to spend an hour driving all the way to Stansted when the Paddington to Heathrow Express took only fifteen minutes. "Thanks. I do appreciate the added value."

East London was almost deserted and what traffic there was seemed to be going in the opposite direction.

Alex glanced in the mirror, catching her eye again. Brown looked quickly away, concentrating at the headlines on *Metro*. "Beautiful morning, Miss Brown."

When did he sleep? This was no worn out driver at the tail end of a night shift, but a fresh, sweet-smelling man new from the shower. After no more than a glance at the paper, she laid back her head and allowed her thoughts to wander, and the next she knew the car was stationary outside Departures, with Alex standing by the car door, her bag in his hand. She hoped she hadn't snored.

Over a glass of orange juice and an espresso, Brown decided, having read the competition, she was just OK with her efforts of the previous day. The *Post*'s coverage was as good as anybody's and better than most. The *Financial Times* had the disgruntled investors angle, but it looked like a last minute rewrite of her own piece.

Somewhere over France, Brown remembered the estate agent's package. When she opened up the envelope, it contained not details of flats for sale, but a series of photographs of a girl she immediately recognised as Bia Gonzales. They were a mixture of glamour shots and stills from the advertising campaign for furs. Gonzales was indeed a most beautiful girl. Brown was relieved the seat next to her was unoccupied, but was nevertheless anxious to get the pictures back into the envelope as quickly as possible. There was no indication as to the identity of the sender, either in the envelope or on the outside. None. Her address was on a white label, printed from a word processor.

Not until she was in her room in the Ambasciatori Hotel on Rome's Via Veneto did Brown open the envelope again, spreading the pictures out over her bed. They were very sexy, and even the more *risqué* examples were beautifully composed, well lit and, for their type, tasteful. In one, Gonzales is standing, naked, at the foot of a sweeping carpeted staircase, one hand on the rail, one exquisitely pedicured foot on the stairs and the other on the marble tiled floor of the hall. Huge modern paintings adorn the walls. The setting reminded Brown of somewhere, but she could not place it. In another, Gonzales, in front of an ornate mirror, is wearing one white lace stocking while she leans forward, a foot on the red velvet seat of a gilt chair, to pull on the other. In the mirror can be seen a rumpled four-poster bed. In other pictures, she is on the bed itself, sometimes reflected in the big mirror. Brown looked again closely at every picture, disturbed by the pleasure they gave her. The toenail polish in the bedroom shots was bright red, while in the hall it was a delicate pink. Such attention to detail.

The stills from the advertising campaign consisted of six glossy 6 x 8 professional prints. In every one, the girl has her fur coat, but is otherwise naked apart from a pair of delicious red high heels. Brown had almost bought a similar pair herself, but with a trip home to Melbourne planned for the New Year, had decided she couldn't afford them. The coat is draped over Gonzales' shoulders, she carries it, it is spread over a rock as she leans back against it, she has it bundled up under her arm, she wears it open, she wears it closed. In the background, tumbling cliffs and blue seas. Finally, there were two 6 x 4 snaps, the kind you get when you take a film to a photo shop for processing. One showed Warham talking to the girl on location, her nakedness mitigated only by the coat clutched to her chest. The other shows her on the beach, wearing half a bikini, alongside Warham in shorts.

After puzzling over them for some time, Brown gathered the pictures into a pile and replaced them in the envelope.

Feeling grubby from her journey she undressed, watching herself in the mirror. What made girls strip for the camera? Money, fame, vanity perhaps. She turned sideways on, pulling in her stomach, straightening her back. She needed to lose a few pounds, and improve her posture. Pilates would be good. She turned away, looking back over one shoulder, her long hair brushing the other. Even a professional photographer with amazing airbrush skills would never make her a rival to Gonzales, but if she took herself in hand she could be a little more presentable. She quickly showered and dressed; she felt better. Time to call Curley.

"Hi Cass, how's Rome?"

"Great, Curley. I'm about to lunch on the via Veneto and then head off to the Embassy. What's happening your end?"

"Via Veneto eh. Very chic. Don't spend too much. Now, Elwood's been trying to get hold of you. I told him you wouldn't be in today."

"He's got my mobile number. Did he mention an envelope?"

"What envelope?"

"Never mind. What are you looking for today?"

"What've you got?"

"Right now, not much." She thought she heard a sharp intake of breath on the other end of the phone. "But the Italian papers are full of the mysterious disappearance. The police claim they've done a thorough search. They believe he is still in the country, as his name hasn't appeared on any airline passenger lists. They seem to forget you can drive 100 miles along the coast and be in France. I can give you something on that?"

"OK. Look, the editor wants you to stay close to the City story. By the way, he was OK in the end with this morning's piece. So depending on what you get from the Embassy, I'll put you down for four hundred on the City angle. But remember, he'll be looking for something for news as well."

Brown looked out of the window at the broad pavements of the via Veneto below, lined with smart hotels and restaurants. Fiats, Alfa Romeos and Mercedes jostled for space as they approached the bend in the road. She took a deep breath. "Christ, Curley, make your bloody mind up. You send me to Rome and then want a story on the City. I could do this better at my desk, you know. You don't make it easy do you?"

"You've got your mobile and your contacts book. It makes no fucking difference where you are. I'll speak to you later on, when you've calmed down a bit." He hung up.

The street was busy with pedestrians, ladies who lunched and businessmen who discussed deals across smart restaurant tables. Baird might have irritated her, but since she was in Rome, she decided to make the most of it. She slipped the little mobile into her bag and took a last look at herself in the mirror. She did look better dressed than naked.

As she stepped out onto the warm street, the smell of Rome was almost intoxicating; a mixture of food and exhaust and for a shoe maven like her, the place was heaven.

Her appointment with the vice consul was set for two o'clock, which gave her time to read the Italian press over lunch. There was Gonzales again, yet more pictures giving Italian news editors the justification for running a relatively unimportant story with considerable prominence.

Who had sent her the pictures? Somebody who knew her home address, which did little to narrow down the list of candidates. The name Charles Seymour Elwood kept coming into her mind. It would suit him well to have the photos splashed over the media — while having a girlfriend of Gonzales' obvious talents would go down well in the pub, it would hardly endear Warham to his already jittery City investors. But this was too crude an attempt, surely, for Elwood. On the other hand, he did have a great deal to gain by blackening Warham's reputation. Warham's job, for starters.

Outside a bar in the warm sunshine, the story for news began to take shape. Dirty tricks. Somebody out to damage Warham. She was certain it would please the Editor. She ordered salad and mineral water. No point in delaying the start of the new regime.

Her walk to the British Embassy at Porta Pia, at the northern end of via XX Septembre took longer than expected and she found herself having to hurry to get there on time. The embassy is positioned in a walled garden with just enough sections of railings here and there for the curious to peek in. The large gates, set in an acre of perfectly raked gravel, were locked with a massive chain. The building, supported on marble columns, seems almost to float above the garden. It has no ground floor. Quite a statement.

The entrance to the consular section, where people waited on benches, reminded Brown of a café she and Steve had once visited back home. But instead of waiting for freshly bar-b-que'd ribs, people here queued for visas. After showing her Press card, she was admitted through a turnstile and given a pink slip of paper. This was her passport to move about the embassy.

During the course of a half-hour interview, Brown learned that Warham was a regular and well-liked visitor at the Embassy. When he was reported missing, the honorary consul in La Spezia had tipped off the local media. It was often the only way to find a missing citizen, as the *Carabinieri* did not usually take any action; adults were free to come and go as they pleased. Broadly, the British Consular Service took a similar view. Only if there was reason to suspect foul play did their interest extend beyond merely recording the matter. It took the intervention of the British Ambassador to get the police to launch a search.

The *Carabinieri* are the top tier of a bewildering array of Italian law enforcement agencies. Dealing with serious crime, the Mafia for example, they have dark blue Alfa Romeos, the helicopters and the speedboats. And the cutest uniforms. The vice consul would not be drawn on how seriously they regarded the Warham case, nor on what he personally thought may be have happened.

"Could he have been kidnapped, do you think?"

The vice consul stood up from behind his desk and walked to the window. He turned to face Brown. "Can we go off the record?" Brown nodded. "The view of our security people is that it is possible, but not likely. Kidnapping was a regular part of the serious crime scene about thirty years ago, when I first came here. Men, women and even children were taken and held to ransom. In the mid-seventies it was reaching epidemic proportions until the Ministry of Finance brought in a policy of blocking the bank accounts of families targeted by kidnappers, preventing them from paying the ransom. The number of kidnaps dropped immediately. It was really a very clever move."

"But that law wouldn't apply to Mr Warham. He's not an Italian citizen."

"Quite. But there's another reason we think abduction unlikely. Normally it is a close relative, mother, father, wife, child, of the head of the household who is taken, not the head himself. They want the person who makes the decisions to be able to organise the ransom." The vice consul looked at his watch. "Now, I really have to get away, but if I can help with anything else, please feel free to ring me. By the way, our main consulate is in Milan, not here in Rome. I'll tell you who to speak to there if you have any further questions on policy, procedures and so forth."

She emerged back into the sunshine with no story, but a potentially useful contact and a better understanding of what would have happened when Warham went missing.

Close to *Termini,* Rome's transport hub, Brown had spotted an Internet café where she could write her story and email it across to the *Post* news-desk. She picked up a taxi outside the Embassy, which hurtled through the *ATAC* lanes reserved for buses trams and taxis. Waiting to turn the final corner before *Termini* she found herself staring up at a torn poster advertising underwear. But beneath this tattered remnant another was visible. Bia Gonzales sitting on a rock beside a blue sea, wearing nothing but a fur coat. Spray painted in red across her face was the message *"STOP IL MASSACRO."*

Brown paid her three Euros for two hours on the computer and wrote her story, emailing it over to a delighted Baird. She decided to spend the rest of her allotted time on the Internet researching the Italian animal rights movement. Until the previous couple of years, campaigners had been more concerned with writing angry letters than taking direct action. But they were learning fast, particularly from activists in Britain, where the construction of a new animal research laboratory outside Oxford had become the focus of massive protest. Italian activists were organising demonstrations against any firms connected with the Oxford facility. They had also set thousands of minks free from fur farms and were using both the courts and direct action against the farmers. There was no mention of either Warham or Gonzales on any of the Italian sites, but the implications were obvious.

In the United States and Britain, threats and protests to people and businesses involved in the Oxford project had brought construction to a halt. Financiers, company directors, lawyers and bankers were listed as legitimate targets for "visits". And amongst the phalanx of names and addresses of the so-called murderers of innocent animals, there was the name of John Warham, selected not only for his involvement in the fur coat campaign, but also for a more indirect role in advising the British government on making the case for pharmaceutical research on animals.

Surely that was reason enough for the *Carabinieri* to take his disappearance seriously? But it was so much easier for them simply to hint he'd run off for a bit of naughty with the beautiful Bia.

Her two hours at the terminal were up and Brown stepped back into the sunshine and stared up at the tattered poster while she called Baird to make sure her story had arrived. It had, but he hadn't had time to read it. Brown was not ready to mention the animal rights angle, but already, the headline "Animal rights link to missing tycoon" had formed in her head. And if she didn't write it pretty damn soon, one of her competitors would.

She snapped the mobile shut and suddenly felt alone. Her friends, most of them married, many of them mothers, would envy Brown her trip to Rome. She had money to spend; she had just called on the vice consul at the Embassy and was due to have dinner with a friend at a smart seafood restaurant. She was staying at a four star hotel at her employer's expense. And she had time to do some shopping.

Grabbing a cab from the station to the via del Corso, Brown went in search of shoes. Nothing took her eye. Perhaps she was not in the right mood. Close to the Piazza di Spagna she spotted the kids' boutique she had visited once before, *Bambina*, and immediately thought of Chloë, the four-year-old daughter of her closest friend, Kate Moses. She browsed the racks, lost to a world of pastel shades and bright pinks, tiny sparkling tee shirts and miniature fatigues for brave little soldiers. Chloë was an easy child to buy for – a girly girl who adored pretty clothes. Brown's mother would have loved a daughter like Chloë, but instead she had a tomboy who preferred her bike to her dolls' pram. Brown thought of the scar, still visible on her knee, from one of her many accidents. Now her mother's ambition seemed to rest on being given a granddaughter, but Brown was not even married, let alone pregnant with a foetus of the right gender. Was Brown really such a disappointment to her? She was at the till holding a little pink and green striped shift dress and a pair of bright green trainers, when her mobile rang. She guessed, correctly, it was Baird. "Thanks for the copy Cass, the editor loves it."

"Good. Look, can I call you back? I'm just in a shop right now."

"Shoes?"

"No, as it happens. Call you in five."

"No need. Just a quick question. Paolo Vittorio in Milan is trying to reach you. Can I give him your mobile number?"

"Who's Paolo Vittorio?"

Baird sighed with enough drama for Brown to hear. "Our stringer who covers Northern Italy. I'll tell him to call you."

The shop assistant, so charming when she had been choosing Chloë's present, showed signs of impatience. Brown pulled her credit card from her wallet, the mobile cradled between her shoulder and her ear, and handed it over.

"Sure."

"See you tomorrow. About lunchtime?"

"Yeah. I'll be a good girl and come straight in from the airport." The phone was snapped shut and returned to her bag.

The assistant, a beautifully dressed woman of at least 55 with suspiciously black hair, handed back the card and the machine for her PIN. She was smiling again. "People never leave you in peace for a moment since the portable was invented."

"My office."

"Office, husband, children. They never leave you alone."

The tinny Toccata started again to prompt Brown's rapid exit to the street. It was Vittorio. Would the *Post* pay for him to go down to the Cinque Terre to work on Warham's disappearance? The investigating magistrate was, he claimed, a friend of his. She suggested he talk to Baird. This was not a decision she could make.

She walked back towards the Ambasciatori. Rome really was the graffiti and fly-posting capital of Europe, fabulous buildings defaced by spray paints and illegal advertisements. And there, on one of them, just off the exclusive via Veneto, was a poster showing a photograph of a seal with the slogan, *"Mi ucciderano per te"* — "They are killing me for you."

She was getting ready to go to dinner with Nicole, an Australian friend with whom she was at law school in Melbourne, and from whom she was hoping to discover more about the activists, when Baird rang again.

"I've been talking to Vittorio. He's going down to the coast tomorrow and I've told him to meet you there. He says you can get a train from Rome and he'll pick you up at La Spezia station at midday."

"You've done what? Please tell me this is a joke, Curley. I'm coming back to London tomorrow. First flight. Remember?"

"The editor loves the idea, Cass. Vittorio will show you around and you can file a big colour piece for the Saturday News Review. Vittorio can help you and do pictures and wire them over."

"Curley, the story is in London. Surely it's better I come back soonest and stay in touch with Elwood and what's happening there. There's nobody down the coast, as you put it. Even the family's back in London. Can't Vittorio file a colour piece himself? Why do I have to go?"

"When was the last time you had the lead story in the Saturday Review, Cass?"

"Never. But Curley, I'm a financial hack not a feature writer."

"Then this is your big chance, isn't it?"

She could sense Baird's lip curling as he spoke. It was no use arguing any further. "OK, I'll get myself to La Spezia. I'll be in touch. Now, I've got to get some clothes on or I'll be late meeting Nicole."

"And Cass?"

"Yes?"

"Don't blow it. We've both got a lot riding on this."

She had no intention of blowing it. She rang off and smiled to herself, opening her notebook to read the words copied from an Italian website:

VIVISECTORS: TODAY WE LIBERATE –
TOMORROW WE'LL BE AFTER YOU

She already had enough to knock Baird's socks off.

SECTION   News1
TITLE   Dirty
HEADING 1   "Dirty Tricks" smear on WBC chief
HEADING 2
AUTHOR   Cassandra Brown
STATUS   Live

Evidence suggesting a 'dirty tricks' campaign is being mounted against the missing millionaire businessman John Warham has surfaced in the City.

Photographs of the advertising chief and his friend, the glamour model Bia Gonzales, have been circulated anonymously.

Mr Warham, a confidante of the Prime Minister, has not been seen by his family since he walked out of a hotel in Italy a week ago. The company says it has heard nothing from him, but points out that he is still officially on holiday.

He is known to be under pressure from City investors to step down from one of the two top jobs, chairman and chief executive, at the advertising agency he founded, Warham Blazeley Cotts.

It is thought that a fierce internal power struggle could be sparked by rumours that he may have decided to quit the firm altogether.

Shares in the advertising giant have virtually halved since news broke of Mr Warham's unexplained disappearance. A leading industry expert said the City was "very worried" about the situation at WBC.

The photographs have been circulated in plain brown envelopes with no indication as to their source.

In one picture, Mr Warham is shown chatting to the model while they were on location at an advertising shoot for an Italian fur coat manufacturer. The model appeared naked in the advertisements, which were published in Italy and France last year.

Another picture shows him

and Miss Gonzales relaxing on a beach. Other photographs show the model posing nude.

It is thought that whoever is circulating the photographs intends to damage Mr Warham's reputation with City investors, leading to yet more pressure being applied to get him give up one of his jobs. Mr Warham, who earned £1.3million last year from WBC, has been resisting such calls.

A City fund manager, who declined to be named in print, said last night, "This sort of thing is not good for John personally, nor for WBC. We have already made it clear to him that we would like him to hand over the CEO's job to somebody else".

A spokesman for WBC said he had "no comment whatsoever" on the photographs, nor on who might be responsible for their circulation.

CHAPTER FIVE

ABOUT an hour north of Rome, Brown flipped open her notebook and read again the paragraph copied from the Internet:

Justice will be done and the animals will be avenged. Do not underestimate our resolve, do not underestimate the hatred we feel for those who steal the lives of animals. There is no escape from the ALF, you filthy murdering scum.

By the time she stepped from the train in La Spezia, the opening sentences of her animal rights story were already written in longhand:

"John Warham, the missing advertising tycoon, was a target of animal rights extremists in both Britain and Italy, the Post can reveal. He had enraged the activists because he not only devised an advertising campaign for a fur manufacturer, but also supported the use of animal testing by the pharmaceutical industry."

Powerful stuff.

She stood on the concourse looking for Vittorio, feeling slightly vulnerable, and very hungry. A small figure, cream chino trousers, immaculate dark blue shirt and tie, hurried towards her, his right hand outstretched in greeting.

"Cassandra. Welcome to Liguria. I hope you had a good journey. My car is right outside. Let me help you with your bags."

Brown replied in Italian. Vittorio looked late twenties, pretty much what she had expected, perhaps a little shorter. But if she had put money on the type of car he drove, she would have lost. Instead of a red Alfa Romeo, it was a Mercedes, silver. If she had put money on its inside resembling a dustcart, she would have won. The back seat was piled high with files, old newspapers, books, a fishing rod and reel, a waxed jacket. The passenger seat was clear, except for a copy of that morning's *Post*.

"I thought you might want to see what they did to your story."
He really did have a disarming smile.

"Thanks." As Vittorio pulled out into the light traffic of La Spezia, she opened the paper and was happy to see her story leading page three, the second news page. The picture of Warham at the Fashion Week party, the beautiful Gonzales clinging to his arm, had finally made its way into the paper. Brown could hardly complain. It was, after all, relevant.

For a young Italian, Vittorio drove carefully. Never aggressive, he slowed to a halt as an old lady stepped out to cross in front of them. Beside the road, on the side of a shop, a tattered and defaced advertising poster depicted a naked girl, a fur coat draped across her lap, sitting on a rock at the foot of a cliff, seemingly surrounded by a choppy sea. The slogan said simply, "Make Waves", in English. Across the bottom of the poster was the word "Naturalia." The girl was unmistakable. Vittorio followed her gaze. "Ah, Miss Gonzales. A good friend of your Mr Warham. We should perhaps try to speak to her?"

You bet Paolo, you bet. Brown made no reply. Although she had seen this and other shots from the campaign before, it only then occurred to her that using a seaside basked in sunshine to advertise furs was a very curious idea. Perhaps it was an ironic reference to the successful anti-fur campaign, in which famous models appeared naked under the slogan "I'd rather go naked than wear fur".

The town gave way to a winding road. Vittorio knew his way around, and sooner than she had expected, they were in Manarola. She climbed from the car, stretched, felt the warm sun on her back and caught that heavy scent of pine, herbs and sea, which seems unique to the Mediterranean.

Over lunch in the shade of a big umbrella, they discussed their theories, each switching easily between Italian and English. They agreed that there were two serious possibilities. The first and the most likely was that Warham had walked out. Maybe he and Ruth had a blazing row, perhaps about his involvement with Gonzales. It was common enough among successful men of Warham's age to walk out on their wives, although it did not explain why he had not been in touch, so far as they knew, with anybody. He would have seen the newspapers and would surely have contacted his office, or the embassy, if only to reassure them that his disappearance was a domestic matter and that helicopter searches and the like were not necessary. And even if he had decided to leave her, surely he would not compound the cruelty by simply disappearing?

They briefly discussed whether his wife might have killed Warham. That the same blazing row had taken place and Ruth had somehow managed not only to murder him but also to get rid of his body so efficiently that a full-scale search by the *Carabinieri* failed to find it. Not likely.

They turned to kidnap. This was the nightmare scenario for the Italian authorities. In the last few years, Italy had managed to shed its reputation as the kidnap capital of Europe, a reputation that had been damaging to both business and tourism. The Mafia were no longer much in the news, and the few kidnaps which still took place were mostly by amateurs, dangerous to the individual but of concern only to the police rather than to the government. A professional kidnap of a high-profile foreigner such as Warham could change all that.

The vice consul had explained that in domestic kidnaps it was usual to abduct a member of a wealthy family and demand payment by the family itself.

Vittorio explained that when a businessman was taken, money was demanded from his company in return for his freedom, or his life. That was why companies took out so-called political risk insurance on their most senior people. Kidnap could be a very profitable business. She thought it odd that this was not mentioned during her conversation at the embassy.

Vittorio had also found out quite a lot about the animal rights movement, which was hotly discussed in Milan, where fur was making a determined comeback. The seal poster Brown had seen in Rome was widely distributed in Milan also, and the group behind it was organising regular protests and distributing leaflets outside stores such as UPIM, Italy's equivalent of Marks & Spencer. The protest movement is international, with an Italian chapter of the British anti-Oxford group actively campaigning in Rome, Turin, Milan and elsewhere.

The two journalists walked down the narrow street, where boats for which the tiny harbour had no space were pulled up onto the road.

It was already past Thursday lunchtime, and she had to file copy for the Saturday review by mid afternoon Friday. She had about twenty-four hours in which to research and write, organise photographs, hopefully conduct some interviews and send over the copy.

As if reading her thoughts, Vittorio began to walk more quickly. "Let us check into the hotel and then make a plan of what we are to do. I think we can work well together. I have my camera and my computer. When does London need the material?"

"Pictures tomorrow morning, copy tomorrow afternoon. Look, can you concentrate on getting shots of the locality. The hotel, the coastline. And I thought that old poster from the fur coat campaign would bring Gonzales into the story. Would you mind nipping back and taking that? What do you think?"

"The pictures will not take too much time, Cassandra, we can do them this evening. Can I suggest we go to see the *Carabinieri* and try to get an interview with the magistrate? I know him a little. We may find out what lines of inquiry he is developing."

They arrived at the hotel, which was not at all what Brown had been expecting. It was, well, ordinary, commonplace. A simple little hotel in a pretty but unremarkable village. Not the sort of place where she imagined the boss of one of the world's biggest advertising agencies choosing to spend his vacation. Not exactly like Sandy Lane in Barbados, nor Paris's George V. Maybe it was Ruth's choice, but even so, it was a curious one.

The lobby was pleasant enough. A tiled floor, a small reception desk, fronted by fluted wood. She was just signing in when the wretched Toccata sounded from her bag. Elwood. "Ah Cassandra, I hope I am not calling at an inappropriate moment?"

"Not at all, Charles, it is always good to hear from you. I was going to call you later anyway. You have saved me the trouble. But you were calling me?"

"Yes, quite so. This is a somewhat, what shall we say, difficult, call for me, Cassandra, but I felt I had to put on record our displeasure, and I would put it no stronger than that, at your story this morning. I have had Ruth Warham virtually in tears on the telephone this morning, asking what we can do to stop you writing the sort of article which appeared in the *Post* today, and I have to mention to you she is talking about seeking legal redress."

"Charles, you know as well as I do there is no legal problem with that story. What exactly is upsetting her?"

"I take it you've never been married, Cassandra?"

"I have as it happens, Charles, but what's that got to do with anything?"

"Let us just say, Cassandra, that the public airing of private domestic matters is hardly helpful to a woman who is already suffering what Ruth is enduring right now."

"All I did, Charles, is report the facts."

"With respect, Cassandra, you went beyond the facts into the realms of pure speculation. To suggest that what you describe as a dirty tricks campaign is being mounted against a highly respected businessman such as John is pure fantasy, Cassandra, pure journalistic fantasy."

"So how should I interpret somebody sticking a packet of compromising photographs through my letter box in the middle of the night, Charles?"

"Fortunately, Cassandra, that is for you to judge, not me. All I am saying is that Ruth Warham finds it distressing when the question of John's friendship with Miss Gonzales becomes a matter of conjecture and innuendo. Now, you were going to call me?"

"Yes, Charles, I was going to ask firstly if there was any news and secondly if WBC had taken out kidnap insurance on John?"

"No news, I am afraid, Cassandra. But as I have said to you previously, John is not due back into the office until next week. His disappearance, so far as WBC is concerned, is a domestic matter, not an issue for the board."

"And kidnap insurance?"

"Ah. As you are no doubt aware, it would be a condition of such insurance that its existence is never disclosed. So I am afraid I cannot help you."

"Is that a complicated way of saying yes, Charles?"

"Not at all, Cassandra, not at all. It is a simple way of saying I have nothing to say on this subject. Now, I am sure you have lots to do?"

"Just two more quick questions, Charles, and then I'll get out of your hair. What do you know about the pictures? And what was John's relationship with Gonzales?"

"I can assure you I know nothing about any pictures, Cassandra, other that what I read in the *Post* this morning. As for John's private life, shall we leave it at that, private? Now, if there's nothing more, I have a meeting to get to." He rang off. Tetchy.

Vittorio had meanwhile booked them into their rooms and handed Brown her key. Behind the reception desk the hotel manager was hovering, shuffling pieces of paper but probably listening to everything being said. His face reminded Brown of an egg. He flashed a professional welcoming smile. "Welcome to Manarola, Signora, I hope you will enjoy your stay at the San Rocco. If there is anything I can do to be of assistance?"

"Thank you." Brown motioned to Vittorio to move out of the manager's earshot. "Paolo, listen, Elwood's just as good as confirmed Warham *was* having an affair with Gonzales. Do you know where Gonzales might be?"

"I know her agent and can telephone her. She's in Milan. And Mr Riolo, the hotel manager, may have some useful background for us."

At the mention of his name, even in Vittorio's hushed tones, Riolo twitched. Not much happened in his hotel that he did not know about. Brown looked across to the reception. He met her gaze and smiled. "I'll take your bags to the room." He picked up the bags and disappeared.

"He knows why we are here?"

Vittorio looked uncomfortable. "I'm sorry if that makes it difficult, Cassandra, but I used the name of the *Post* to get us the rooms."

"No problem, Paolo. Would it be a good idea, do you think, for us to go our separate ways? I want to wander around a bit, talk to a few people, maybe talk to Riolo a bit. Any chance you could get us in to see the magistrate and the police?"

"Not the *Carabinieri* I think, but the magistrate may talk to me. I think he might agree to a coffee. Shall we meet later for the photographs? Five o'clock perhaps?"

"Great. Call me if you need me."

Vittorio disappeared in the direction of his room. Brown went out onto the street. She needed to buy clothes which not only made her less conspicuous amongst the tourists cluttering the

Cinque Terre but were also more comfortable. Her heels were great for Rome but potentially lethal in the steep streets of a fishing village. At a boutique not one hundred metres from the hotel she picked up cotton trousers, two tee shirts and a pair of trainers. With luck, she would be able to claim for them on her *Post* expenses. She had one leg in her new trousers when Baird rang.

"Curley, you really do choose the most difficult moments to telephone. If you can just hold on a moment I'll finish putting on my strides and then we can talk...."

Baird carried on without a pause. He was in what was known on the editorial floor as his hyper-hyper mood. "The dirty tricks story went down well, Cass. We ran it alongside the picture of Warham and his lady friend at the party. It looked great."

"I know Curley, I saw it. Any developments your end?"

"None. The share price is still all over the place. What have you got for me today?"

She thought for a few moments. She could, at a push, file the animal rights story. She had done enough research, short of checking it out with the *Carabinieri* and the magistrate. And there was a danger if she held it back somebody else might get there first. She would be sick if it appeared first in *The Times*.

If she didn't have the big feature to write, Brown could have spent another hour or two tidying up the loose ends, sought out either an animal rights spokesman or "an expert", and put together a story which might have put her on the front page again.

But she already had too much to do, and not enough time in which to do it. "Curley, listen. I've just arrived in Liguria and have less than twenty-four hours to put together a three thousand-word scene piece for Saturday. I've got a pretty hot story on the go but it needs a lot more work. If we can leave it over until tomorrow I can do a proper job, once the feature is done and dusted."

There was a pause and a sigh at the other end of the line. "Sure, Cass. But I'm going to hold you to this. Can you give me a clue?"

"I'd rather not say too much, but let's just say I've found a grudge."

"OK, Cass. The editor's not pushing tonight as there's a big political story on Iraq. The trouble is, the other papers will be following up the dirty tricks angle and we've got to have something. The *Standard*'s already followed up, by the way."

Baird was thinking aloud rather than talking to her. "I'll put the share price as the lead to the stock market report. That way we've still got the WBC name up in lights. Oh, Elwood was trying to get hold of you again."

"I know. I've spoken to him. I've got to go, but if anything else turns up I'll let you know. OK?"

She finished putting on her trousers, added a tee shirt and put on the trainers. She looked out of the window, down to the garden. There was one couple, possibly English, sitting at a table, glasses before them. It looked like the conclusion to a very long lunch. She remembered lunch in Dublin with Hogan and his friends. It had started at twelve and lasted until closing time. It was not only in opting for the Euro that Ireland was more Continental than Britain.

In the street, the sun was blazing hot, and the tourists thronged up and down looking for – for what? The Cinque Terre had been a relatively quiet holiday area known to wealthy Europeans and poor Ligurians until an American television crew visited in the mid-nineties. The resulting footage of tiny harbours, steep streets, blue seas, towering cliffs and pretty ferryboats was irresistible, and tour operators soon block-booked the hotels. The dollars flowed in, but the essence of the place was destroyed. What was it she had read on the Internet and copied into her notebook?

"They are just five overcrowded fishing villages, every hovel turned to commerce and you will hear more American, German and English voices than on the whole of the rest of the Riviera." Quite.

But at least the hordes and the transformation would give her plenty of colour material for her piece.

She walked down towards the harbour, regularly bumped by already large people clutching ice creams. Why on earth would a sophisticated world traveller like Warham want to come here? Why would he return with his wife to a place where he may started an affair with Bia Gonzales? Was it some form of perverted conceit? Poor old Ruth, she'll never guess.

She had seen enough to get a feel for the place. She could bring into her article the romantic stuff about Paul Klee, the painter who first put Manarola on the map. She had as much background colour as she needed for the feature spread. And she had the animal rights angle for a powerful news story for Saturday morning.

Riolo was at his desk when she returned from her stroll, if a walk down a street as crowded as Oxford Circus Underground Station at rush hour could be called a stroll. He cracked his warm smile, and welcomed her as if she had returned from a long trip abroad, rather than a ten-minute walk in the sunshine. Brown replied in Italian, commenting on the weather, the crowds, the beauty of the village. She managed to include a reference to the Warhams. It was all Riolo needed. He seemed bursting to talk.

The Warhams had arrived on foot in the early afternoon on the Tuesday, having walked the relatively short distance from Corniglia. The courier had brought their luggage from Beaten Track, their tour organiser. They had spent most of the hot afternoon in their room, and at six o'clock had asked for a bottle of *Prosecco* and two glasses to be sent up. Riolo had taken the drinks himself.

"Whenever I take a tray for room service, I always listen for a moment at the door before I knock, to be sure the guests are not busy, on the telephone, in the bathroom. I heard Signor Warham speaking loudly, so I waited for a moment before knocking."

"What was he saying?"

"I was not listening, Signora Brown. I was not paying attention, but waiting for a pause, before I knocked on the door."

Not listening? Pull the other one!

"But you must have heard something. Was he angry? Was he on the telephone?"

"No, he was not on the telephone. I think he may have been a little frustrated. He was talking to his wife. I did hear one thing he said, but I am not sure it would be right to tell you?"

Brown moved closer to Riolo, still safely on the other side of the reception desk, and smiled her broadest smile. "Your hotel is very beautiful. I would like to put a photograph of it in the article for my newspaper?" Bribery maybe, if not corruption.

Riolo looked around before answering, "Signor Warham said 'it's over Ruth, it's over'."

"What did she say?"

"I did not hear her reply. She perhaps said nothing. When it was quiet again I knocked and the Signor opened the door. Signora Warham was sitting on the balcony in her robe."

"Did she seem unhappy?"

"I cannot say. I offered to pour the *Prosecco*, but Signor Warham waved me away and I left the room."

Riolo had returned a little later to serve their dinner. He said it was the last time he saw Warham. The following morning, Warham had left the hotel early, and Ruth Warham had also gone out. Riolo explained that the reception desk is not manned early in the morning, and he had been busy laying up tables on the terrace for breakfast.

"So they could have left the hotel together?"

"It is possible, Signora, but Mrs. Warham came back alone and said she had been looking for her husband. She seemed confused and very worried. The *Carabinieri* took away the video."

"What video?"

"From my CCTV." He turned and smiled at a camera discretely tucked into the corner of the ceiling.

When Warham did not return, Ruth ate breakfast alone. She repeatedly used her mobile phone, and left a note for her husband at the reception desk when she went out again into the village. Just before lunchtime Pete Nichols, the courier from Beaten Track, arrived to collect the bags, but Ruth had insisted on remaining at the hotel.

"You know the courier well, I imagine. The company does a lot of business with your hotel?"

"Yes, I see him two or three times a week. He will be here tomorrow. Perhaps I can introduce you?"

"That would be very helpful."

Riolo said he discussed with Nichols whether one of them should take Ruth Warham to report her husband missing. Nichols was against the idea, saying if Warham wanted to walk out on his wife, that was no business of the police. Riolo, or at least so he said, shared Ruth Warham's concern that he may have had an accident. In the end, Riolo did offer to take her to the *Questura*, but she refused. He then telephoned around the village to make certain nobody had been taken to the hospital, whether Warham had hired a taxi and if anybody in the village had seen him that morning. His inquiries had produced no result.

Riolo became quite distressed as he recounted the story, and

Brown found herself warming to this curious, nosey little man. It was mid-afternoon by the time they finished talking. The day was disappearing and she needed to contact both Ruth Warham and Nichols before she could start writing. But above all she wanted to talk to Gonzales. Time was running out fast.

Back in the quiet of her room, she started with Nichols and his mobile.

"Pete speaking." A fellow Australian. That might help.

"Oh Pete, my name is Cassandra Brown of the *Post* newspaper in London. I wonder if I could talk to you a few minutes about John Warham?" She allowed the intonation to rise at the end of her question to emphasise that she, too, was from the Southern hemisphere. After two years in London, she was never certain how Australian she still sounded.

"Lovely to hear from you, Cassandra. Welcome to one of the most beautiful stretches of coastline anywhere. I heard you were here. Now, how can I help?"

"I gather you helped Ruth Warham when her husband disappeared?"

"That's my job, Cassandra. To look after our clients."

"So how did you look after Mrs. Warham?"

"I'd love to help you, Cassandra, but Beaten Track have a strict policy that we lowly couriers must not talk to the media. I have to hand it all on to London. Can I give you a name and number?"

"But they weren't here Pete, you were. Suppose we talk off the record? Background only?"

"On or off the record, Cassandra, it makes no difference. If I even look at my watch and tell you the time they'll have my arse in a sling. You're really going to have to talk to London."

"Why were you against calling in the *Carabinieri* when John Warham went missing?"

"Sorry Cassandra, I really cannot talk to you about any of our clients. You'll have to talk to London."

She had been too direct, and screwed up. Try another tack. "Not to worry, Pete. Where're you from?"

"That's something I can talk to you about. Melbourne."

"You don't say. That's my home town. I'm not sure how long I'll be here, but how about we have a beer sometime?"

"Love to, Cassandra. Give me a call if I can help in any way."

She grimaced at the irony of the remark. She would get nowhere with Nichols; meanwhile her phone indicated a call waiting. She thanked him and picked up the waiting caller. Hogan, saying he was coming to London the next day.

Why did she feel embarrassed, awkward? She stared at her reflection in the big mirror, and forgot to speak until he prompted her again, asking her where she was and what she was doing. Was he merely interested or did she sniff jealousy in the question? Either way, she was not going to start accounting for her movements.

She promised to call him later when she knew at what time she would return to London. It was several minutes before she could once again concentrate. In the meantime, she telephoned the office and asked the travel people to organise a route home. Inside half an hour she was booked on the first flight from Genoa Saturday morning. Hopefully Vittorio would give her a lift to the airport.

She lay on the bed trying to think but in reality doing little more than watching the ugly ceiling fan slowly revolve. The room phone startled her from her reverie. It was "only Paolo", to tell her he had not got very far with either the *Carabinieri* or the magistrate, but that he'd spoken with Gonzales' agent and had a couple of quotes from her they could use in the story.

"Did you talk to Gonzales herself, Paolo?"

"No. But I had a long talk with her agent."

"What did he say?"

"It's a she, and she said Bia was very upset to hear John was missing."

"Did you ask her if they were together?"

"Not exactly. I asked if she knew where Warham might be, and she said no."

"So why didn't you talk to Gonzales herself?"

"Not available."

'Oh. You can tell me about it when we go to get the pictures. I'll be down in ten minutes."

Why had Vittorio taken it upon himself to telephone Gonzales? It was a call she had wanted to make. And Vittorio had not managed to talk to either the magistrate or the *Carabinieri*. Would he be able to take photographs good enough to use in the Saturday Review?

Walking to Vittorio's car, Brown decided there was no beating about the bush. "Why wouldn't the magistrate see you, Paolo?"

"He did see me. We had a talk but he told me nothing new." He shrugged with irritation, but whether it was with the question or the magistrate she wasn't sure.

"I'm sorry. I thought you said you hadn't seen him."

"No Cassandra. I said I had no luck with him. No revelations. No new leads. The man is as exciting as cold pizza. As for the *Carabinieri*, they're still furious they had to put on a show of searching for Mr. Warham, when they think he's in Milan with his mistress."

"So why don't they go visit Gonzales to see for themselves?"

"Cassandra, the *Carabinieri* do not regard it as their job to baby-sit husbands who want to disappear with their mistresses. If they did, they would do nothing else."

"So why did they mount a full-scale search, bringing in helicopters and stuff?"

He stopped so abruptly, turning to face her, she nearly bumped into him. She couldn't read his expression. "Two reasons. One, they were told to by Rome. Your Mr. Warham is a *'tres grand fromage'.*"

"He's not my Mr. Warham. And the other reason?"

"They wanted to be sure he hadn't had an accident. It wouldn't look good if he was lying halfway down the cliff with a broken leg."

They resumed the climb and reached the car. Vittorio allowed Brown to open the passenger door herself. "Do the *Carabinieri* know how he left the village?"

Vittorio sighed. His Latin temperament was getting the better of him. "No, Cassandra, they do not. They've asked lots of questions and ruled out either a boat or the train. They think he must have left by car."

"A taxi?"

"No. They've spoken to all the local taxi companies and none of them picked him up."

"He didn't have a car."

"How do we know that? You're just making an assumption Cassandra."

"So how did it get here?"

Vittorio drove slowly and carefully. The air-conditioning was too chilly, and the silence awkward.

"I thought you said the *Carabinieri* were unhelpful. It seems you've learned a lot in a short time. What about kidnap?"

"They don't think it is likely."

"Why not?"

"Firstly, kidnap victims are usually abducted when they are going about their normal routine. They are taken on their way to the office, or to school, doing something they do every day. Warham was on holiday. He was sleeping in a different bed every night. There was no routine.

"Secondly, who would organise a kidnap in Manarola? Just one winding road out of the village. And another thing, how would they know he was there?"

Nichols knew Warham was there, he knew his detailed movements, and he knew Warham was an important and wealthy guy. And according to Riolo, Nichols hadn't wanted to bring in the police. She kept her thoughts to herself. They drove into a long tunnel, the darkness stifling the conversation, which had only just begun. As they emerged into the evening sunshine, Vittorio shot his smile across the car.

"The magistrate, though, he is not so certain."

"Of what?"

"That Warham was not abducted. He seems more concerned than the *Carabinieri*."

"Did he mention animal rights? What if he was kidnapped by activists?"

Vittorio shook his head. "No, he didn't mention animal rights at all. By the way, the magistrate is from the North, sent in by Rome to oversee the investigation. He has experience of kidnap cases. I know he's dealt with at least one before. I covered the case."

Brown watched the hard rock through which the road had been blasted flash past inches from her window. Vittorio glanced across the car. "Did you know the animal rights people have made themselves very unpopular in Milan with their disruptions?"

"I'm not surprised. They're hardly top of the pops in England. Are they violent, the Milan protests?"

Vittorio pulled a packet of mints from one of the car's cubbyholes and offered one to Brown. "Not so far. But who knows how far they might go?"

Brown sucked on the sweet, then crunched it into pieces. Her best friend could always make her sweets last twice as long because she resisted the temptation to crunch and chew. 'Cassie' was always too impatient.

"Paolo, based on what you have heard from the magistrate, could we write that he is working on the theory that Warham has been kidnapped? And then bring in the stuff about animal rights?"

Vittorio began to brake as the car approached a bend. "I'm not sure there's enough to go on."

"I think there's plenty we could say."

Vittorio accelerated hard out of the bend.

"Cassandra. Why do you ask my opinion and then want to disagree? I am trying to work with you but you don't seem to trust me."

"Sorry Vittorio. I do trust you. I'm just worried about finding a strong enough storyline. We've got to put together three thousand words in less than twenty-four hours. In fact, it really doesn't take two of us to get a few photographs. When we've taken the shots of the poster I suggest you take us back to Manarola and finish them yourself. I'll make a start on the words."

Vittorio concentrated on his driving. They reached the edge of La Spezia where the road follows the coastline.

"Vittorio, is that alright?"

"Cassandra, what do you imagine I've been doing all afternoon?"

"Talking to the *Carabinieri*, to the magistrate, to Gonzales' agent. I know you've been busy. I'm not trying to criticise…."

"You may be pleased to hear this amateur reporter has already taken the photographs. All I have to do is download them to my laptop and you can choose what we send to London."

"Vittorio. I'm sorry. Honestly I am. I'd be lost without you here."

"Without me you wouldn't be here. You'd be back in London looking forward to your evening."

He smiled that smile again. Peace might be possible. Brown was, she knew, entirely in the wrong and he deserved to be treated better. He was, in fact, a thorough professional. And she liked him. She would put in a good word when she spoke to London.

Vittorio pulled into the side and parked. Opposite, the tattered Gonzales pouted down at them.

"I think she knows all the answers, Cassandra."

"Yes, but she will not tell us."

"As enigmatic as Mona Lisa's smile."

Vittorio took two or three shots from different angles.

"OK, I think that's it. Just one more. Cassandra, would you go and stand on the sidewalk under the poster?"

"Would I do what?"

"Just for me, and one for you too if you want it. I'd like it for my album."

"No way, Paolo, no way. I know you just want to compare us."

Vittorio brought his hands together as if in prayer, and smiled that smile again. He'd won. Brown went and stood obediently under the poster, while a little girl stood watching, holding her ancient red bicycle. She had a plaster on her knee. When Vittorio showed Brown the picture he had taken, he had included the child. It was a beautifully composed picture. He really was a good photographer.

As they fastened their seat belts for the return drive, Brown asked what else he had learned from Gonzales' agent. Not much. She had said Gonzales was distressed that the media had linked her to his disappearance. She admitted Gonzales was a close friend of Warham and said she was sure he would soon turn up safe and well.

"So Paolo, is Warham in some romantic Tuscan hideaway with the beautiful Bia? Is this a fantastic publicity stunt set up by her agent to get her on the front page of every newspaper in Europe? Has he been kidnapped? Killed by extremists? Tell me what you really think."

"Cassandra, have you met Ruth Warham ever?"

"Yes, I have, just once. And you?"

"No. But I suspect she knows the truth. Have you spoken to her at all since Warham disappeared?"

Now Brown was the one being questioned. She hadn't spoken to Ruth Warham and, she would admit only to herself, she had not tried very hard. Financial hacks are simply not used to touchy-feely interviews. And in any case, she hadn't much enjoyed her one encounter with Ruth Warham, the previous year, and suspected the feeling was mutual. She shook her head.

"Why have you not spoken to her?"

"Christ Paolo, you sound like my editor."

"Sorry. I was not meaning to nag."

"Well the reason, signor Vittorio, is that when I rang there was no answer so I left a message and Charles Elwood called me back and told me to leave her alone."

"Ah, Mister Elwood. Not a man to upset, I have heard. But while I drive along this difficult road, why don't you tell me about Ruth Warham?"

"She is, well, she is a classic 1960's feminist, I would say. In her time she was probably radical. She and Warham went to the same art school and I suspect she never quite forgave him for selling out to advertising."

"But she enjoyed being the wife of a millionaire who moved in the best circles?"

"Well, yes, and no. I am sure she enjoyed the wealth. But she did not like the social side of his business. She made it perfectly clear, when we met, that she did not regard herself as a corporate wife and that she would attend only those functions which interested her."

Vittorio pulled out to see if it was safe to overtake a curious little three-wheeled truck, a sort of motor scooter with a platform on the back, loaded with vegetables. No doubt they would end up being dispatched from the Italian sunshine to be squashed underfoot in a rainy side street off the Kentish Town Road. To Brown's right was a sheer rock face, to Vittorio's left, a metal crash barrier perched on the edge of a precipitous drop into the Ligurian Sea. Vittorio pulled back in again and resumed the stately 20 miles per hour journey.

"Did she not see it as part of her duty that she should support Warham at business functions?"

"No, she didn't. She told me that WBC employed Warham but not her."

"What did Warham think of this arrangement? It seems quite unreasonable to me. She enjoyed the money. She should contribute. Don't you think so Cassandra?"

She was about to take up the cudgels on Ruth's behalf when she saw the grin on Vittorio's tanned face. She swivelled slightly in the big leather seat and faced him across the car. "Paolo Vittorio, if you want me to give a good report of you to London, you had better watch what you say."

They were back in the village, Vittorio carefully parking the large car.

"Do you have a number for Ruth Warham, Cassandra?"

"Of course."

"Would you like me to call her? Might it be easier, with me a total stranger? I will be very charming and tell her I am working with you."

"You can try, if you like. I had better get back to my room and start writing."

"Before you go, Cassandra, I learned today that the magistrate also would like to speak with Mrs. Warham."

"Paolo, you are such a teasing bastard. That's really important. Why didn't you tell me before?"

"I did not know it was important." She was not sure whether brown eyes could be said to twinkle, as the term was usually reserved for blue. But if they could, then Vittorio's did. Despite the work still ahead of her, she was starting to enjoy this assignment.

On her way upstairs to her room, Bach interrupted again. She chose to ignore it and left the mobile in the bottom of her bag. She really couldn't cope with another conversation with Elwood, or with Baird. Or even with Hogan.

She was about to start writing on Vittorio's laptop when the phone announced the arrival of a text message. "Call me now – Kate." Her fingers trembled as she tried to retrieve Kate Moses' number. Kate Moses was the lawyer who had handled Brown's divorce, and after that she had also become, over the years, Brown's best friend. She had not spoken to Moses since she returned from Dublin. By the time the familiar British ringing tone was in her ear she had convinced herself that Moses' daughter Chloë had had an accident. Kate's answering voice told her otherwise.

"You devious harlot, Cassandra."

"What do you mean?"

"Conor. That's what I mean. Dublin, that's what I mean. Not telling me he was nuts about you, that's what I mean. I thought I was supposed to be your friend."

"What do you mean, nuts about me?"

Kate was laughing at the other end of the phone. Brown could hear Chloë pleading to speak with auntie Cass. "Can't you say anything but 'what do you mean?'? I've told you what I mean. I mean I've just had Conor on the phone pouring out his heart. Apparently, he said he was coming to London at the weekend?"

"Yes."

"He thought you were offhand about it and now he doesn't know whether to come or not."

"Why's he coming?"

"Cassandra, you're having me on, aren't you? He's coming to see you, or was."

Chloë's pleas to talk with auntie Cass had turned into demands. It was getting near her bedtime and tears could flow at any moment. Brown asked to speak to her.

"Have you got a boyfriend, auntie Cass?"

"I don't know, Chloë. Have you?"

"No. I want a tortoise."

"What will you call him?"

"I want a girl tortoise and I want to call her Cass, like your name. When are you coming to see us?"

"Soon. Really soon. And I'll bring you something from Italy. But not a tortoise."

"What is it?"

"A surprise. Now can I talk to mummy again?"

Brown could sense a tussle as Kate wrestled the phone from her daughter. "So, were you offhand?"

"No. I quite want to see him."

"So why didn't you invite him to stay?"

"I didn't know he was coming to see me. I assumed he was coming anyway and just thought he wanted to see me for a drink or something. But I'm not sure I'm ready to have him stay with me. Could you be an angel?"

"My wings are already in place. I said he should stay with us and we should all have Sunday lunch together. Is that OK?"

"OK? That's fantastic. I'm flying home Saturday morning. I'll call you to send him round when I've showered and dressed."

"Showered, yes. Not sure you need to worry about the dressing bit."

"Kate."

"Yes?"

"Get off the line. I've got work to do. And thanks, you're a real star."

Brown was still smiling when Vittorio knocked on the door to say he'd got through to the Warham's house only to be told that all media inquiries had to go through the WBC press office. She turned the mobile phone to silent so she would not hear Elwood ringing to complain, and they sat down together to start the article. It was more than half completed by the time they went down to the harbour for a late supper.

A surprisingly accomplished pianist played popular classics on an electric piano. Coloured lights hung from the white parasols as waiters rushed from table to table. Towards the end of Beethoven's Moonlight Sonata Brown found herself hoping that Vittorio might gently take her hand. She didn't quite know why.

SECTION   Review
TITLE   Genius
HEADING 1 Whatever happened to Mr Genius?
HEADING 2 Two weeks on there's no trace of missing ad tycoon: Cassandra Brown and Paolo Vittorio report from the Cinque Terre
AUTHOR   Cassandra Brown
STATUS   Live

TEN DAYS ago, John Warham, chairman and chief executive of WBC, Europe's biggest advertising agency, left his holiday hotel on the Italian Riviera before breakfast. He never returned.

Warham has contacted neither his family nor his colleagues at WBC, nor has he responded to appeals from the British consulate in Rome to get in touch.

So far as WBC is concerned, publicly at least, this is a domestic affair that does not involve the company. In a statement issued hurriedly after the share price was hit by a spate of rumours, it pointed out that Warham is still on holiday and so was not expected at his desk in any case.

He is due back at the company's plush Charlotte Street headquarters on Monday morning, but few expect to see the tall patrician figure step from his pale blue chauffeur-driven Jaguar at his usual time of eight thirty.

Instead, it is expected that WBC will convene an emergency board meeting to decide what to do next.

Warham is not only one of the most influential media figures of his generation; he is also a close personal friend of a number of senior government figures, and a regular visitor to Ten Downing Street.

After Warham was reported missing and WBC had put out its statement, a Downing Street spokesman said the Prime Minister was "very concerned" and promised all the help necessary.

It appears that it was

governmental concern that persuaded the Italian authorities, through the British Embassy in Rome, to take his disappearance seriously. Local police would have undoubtedly dismissed Warham's departure as a routine domestic issue of a husband walking out on his wife.

However, pushed by the British government, the *Carabinieri,* the most senior of Italy's police forces, undertook a search involving helicopters and boats.

No trace of Warham has, however, been found.

Sometime in the early morning of Wednesday, May 24, John Warham left the San Rocco Hotel in the picturesque fishing village of Manarola, one of the five villages on the Italian Riviera, which make up the "Cinque Terre", or five lands. In the quiet hours before the village became thronged with tourists, Warham walked out of the hotel at which he had spent the night. He took neither his credit cards nor his passport. He left behind nearly all the belongings he had taken with him to Italy, and a sum of cash.

He also left behind, sleeping, his wife of thirty years, Ruth, and slipped out unnoticed by hotel staff. He stepped into the near deserted street and has not been seen since. His disappearance has been marked by gyrations in the share price of WBC and accusations of "dirty tricks" following the *Post*'s disclosure that photographs of his friend, the Italian glamour model Bia Gonzales, had been circulated anonymously.

Whereas they are normally to be found holidaying with captains of industry at the de luxe resort of Sandy Lane, Barbados, the Warhams had this year opted for an organised walking holiday from Beaten Track, a specialist travel company. On the day he disappeared, they had been due to move on to a hotel in another of the Cinque Terre villages.

Warham had become familiar with the area, popular with American and German tourists, when he supervised a photo shoot for the Italian fashion house, Naturalia, last year. It was on this assignment that he is believed to have met Ms. Gonzales for the first time. The two are said to have become good friends at that time.

When Warham failed to return from what Ruth Warham had assumed was an early morning stroll, she herself went in search of her missing husband. Fearful that he may have met with an accident, she asked the manager of their hotel in Manarola to check he had not been admitted to the nearest hospital, in the Italian naval port of la Spezia.

The Warham's had been in Manarola less than twenty four hours. Shortly after lunch on the Tuesday, they had arrived on foot at the three star family run hotel a short distance from the tiny harbour. They checked into a medium-sized room overlooking the hotel garden.

Their route to Manarola from the previous overnight stop, Corniglia, had taken them along a treacherous mountain path which hugs the face of steep cliffs fringing the sea. Beaten Track, the tour operator that organized the holiday, transported their luggage.

The couple had remained in their room during the afternoon and had ordered drinks and dinner to be taken up. That was the last time anybody saw them together.

The following morning, Mrs Warham woke to find her husband gone. She became increasingly anxious about his whereabouts as the day wore on, but nevertheless refused an offer from the hotel manager to drive her to the office of the *Carabinieri* in La Spezia to report him missing.

It is understood that this was on the advice of the local courier for Beaten Track. The courier himself would neither confirm nor deny giving Mrs Warham such advice. He said it was his job to help clients, but that any media enquiries would need to be made to head office in London. A spokesperson there said it was not company policy to comment on client matters to the media.

The *Post* has established that the *Carabinieri*, Italy's most senior police force dealing with serious and organised crime, including the Mafia, were not notified until the Thursday, more than twenty-four hours after Warham first disappeared. An officer said, "By then the trail had gone cold."

Even then, it was not Mrs Warham but the British Embassy in Rome who asked for help from the Italian authorities. It is understood that the embassy was instructed by the Foreign Office, which in turn had been called in by the Prime Minister's Office on the evening Warham disappeared. Sources close to the situation say Downing Street had been alerted by the couple's son Tom.

In an exclusive interview with the *Post*, Duncan MacDonald, the vice consul at the British Embassy in Rome, said "our action in asking the Italian authorities for help stemmed from a conversation between the Prime Minister's office and our duty officer in Whitehall".

It is thought Downing Street took action because of fears that Warham may have been kidnapped. Warham is well known in Italy, largely as a result of the controversial advertising campaign he devised last year for fur coats. This brought him to the unwelcome attention of the animal rights movement.

Although the number of abductions in Italy has declined sharply in recent years, kidnapping for ransom is still a cause for concern in government and business circles.

Kidnappers' targets are sometimes businessmen, although it is unusual for foreign nationals to be taken. Ransom demands can run to hundreds of thousands of Euros. Once the police are involved, bank accounts of victims' families are frozen in an attempt to stop ransom demands being met.

For this reason, families usually want to keep the police out of the affair for fear that if the ransom is not paid, the victim may be killed. Major companies use offshore insurance arrangements to cover their senior executives.

Known as "political risk insurance", usually written at Lloyd's of London, the insurance covers both the provision of expert negotiators and the payment of ransom if necessary.

Charles Elwood, finance director of WBC, would neither confirm nor deny that the company carried such insurance for Warham. "It would be a condition of such insurance that its existence was not disclosed", he said. This is to avoid the existence of insurance cover being an encouragement to kidnappers.

Despite British fears, the *Carabinieri* are not putting kidnap high on their list of theories to explain the disappearance. They think it unlikely that kidnappers would chose to abduct a victim in a village with only one winding road out. Another factor is that victims are usually abducted while going about their usual business, not while moving from place to place on vacation.

However, the possibility that Warham may have fallen victim to abduction by animal rights activists has not been ruled out, although the authorities admit that this line of enquiry is not being actively considered.

Warham became a potential target not only because of his involvement in promoting the fur trade but also because of his behind-the-scenes role in supporting medical research using live animals.

Two days after Warham went missing, the *Carabinieri* launched a full-scale search of the area around Manarola, concentrating on the network of ancient paths criss-crossing the cliffs. The paths are regularly used both by hikers and by workers in the centuries-old vineyards, which are terraced up the steep terrain.

Using both a helicopter and a powerful launch, they repeatedly swept up and down the coast, but found nothing. Officers drafted in from La Spezia interviewed trades-people and hotel staff.

In addition to the recently

constructed road into Manarola, the village is also connected to the railway and served by regular ferries, which ply the coast.

Mr MacDonald said, "The Italian authorities were extremely helpful and acted with commendable speed".

However, an officer close to the investigation admitted they only brought in the helicopter and boat because of pressure from Rome. He said they were "leaned on heavily" to make the search look convincing, even though their own theory was that Warham had chosen to walk out.

Officers called at the hotel where the Warham's were staying and took detailed statements from Mrs Warham herself, and also from hotel staff.

Some officers think privately that the key to the mystery may lie with the fashion model Bia Gonzales, who aroused the fury of the animal rights movement with her poses for the fur coat campaign. Gonzales lives in Milan, Italy's fashion capital, and has progressed from teenage glamour model to moderate success on the catwalk.

The Italian media has printed numerous articles in the past week linking the disappearance with Gonzales. Her agent has used the publicity surrounding the mystery to generate coverage for Gonzales, and has provided magazines and newspapers with glamorous photographs with which to illustrate their articles.

However, Gonzales herself has not been interviewed, either by the media, or by the *Carabinieri* who do not regard it as their job to "search out husbands who want to go missing". The media has been kept at arm's length by Gonzales' agent.

Reporters and photographers who besieged her Milan home came away empty-handed. Her agent, who said Gonzales and Warham were "very close" and that she was extremely upset by the news, is handling all calls.

The Italian media have been

openly speculating that the two are now together, possibly staying at a Tuscan villa of a business executive. This villa has been used as a holiday home by the British prime minister, and is thought to be impregnable to photographers. Having spoken to the owner of the villa, Scotland Yard, who have been instructed by Downing Street to maintain a "watching brief" on the Italian investigation, do not share the views of their Italian counterparts.

Gonzales was Warham's guest at a recent Fashion Week party in London. She was photographed on Warham's arm arriving at the party, although a spokesman for WBC insists that it was a chance meeting that brought them together at the party. However, despite being invited, Mrs Warham did not attend the party.

Throughout the investigation, Mrs. Warham has not made herself available to the media for comment, and WBC, the company he founded in the 1970s, is handling all enquiries. In turn, WBC will answer only those questions that concern the company, not the family. When Warham disappeared,

Mrs. Warham contacted their son, the London University professor of history Tom Warham, who immediately flew out to join her and help in the search. However, Mrs Warham and her son returned to London last Sunday. Sources close to the Italian investigation say the police are keen to interview Mrs Warham again, and may send officers to London.

However, because of the involvement of the Italian and British governments in the affair, they have to approach the matter with caution. "We do not have a free hand", one officer complained.

In London, theories and rumours are rife both in the advertising world and the City, including some suggesting that WBC has financial problems. However, when WBC made its announcement, it sought to reassure investors that "results for the year are currently expected to meet market forecasts". Such a statement could only have been made with the concurrence of the auditors.

While this statement may

have calmed market jitters, it did nothing to assuage the irritation felt by leading investors at what Warham's deputy Charles Elwood described as his "inexplicable" disappearance, which has had severe implications for the share price.

They are angry that while Warham hangs on to both the top jobs at WBC, those of chairman and chief executive, he has spent much of the past few years working with government on projects such as the Millennium Dome and successful bid for the 2012 Olympic Games. At the same time, WBC has suffered some serious client losses and the share price has been under persistent pressure.

They have demanded a meeting with Warham and other board members when he returns. They are particularly upset that they learned about the situation only after rumours began to flood the stock market.

In fact, the *Post* has established that the other directors of the company were not told about his disappearance until after Mrs Warham and her son had returned from Italy.

Investors feel Warham's family kept the company in the dark. WBC directors only learned of the crisis when an Italian client telephoned Mr Elwood at home on Sunday afternoon to ask for an explanation of rumours circulating in Italy.

Italian media were told he was missing last weekend, but his name was given as "Henry Warham". It was not immediately realised that the holidaymaker reported missing was in fact the tycoon known as John Warham. His full name is Henry John Warham, but he chooses to be known by his second forename.

Whatever the facts of this mystery turn out to be, it is clear that Warham's standing in the City and in politics is irretrievably damaged.

CHAPTER SIX

BROWN bought the *Post* at Stansted. But it was not until she was secure in the back seat of the Toyota that she plucked up enough courage to look at the Saturday review section. On the cover was Vittorio's shot of the tattered poster, with the caption, "Does this woman have the answer to the question everyone in the City is asking: what's happened to Mr. Genius? Cassandra Brown and Paolo Vittorio report from Italy's Cinque Terre." Wow.

She was reading the piece for the third time, trying to work out what had been left out, when Bach broke in. Elwood. She didn't expect to enjoy the conversation.

"Ah, Cassandra, you have been busy." Friendly, a touch sarcastic maybe, but not the pompous complainer she had expected.

"That's what they pay me for, Charles."

"Quite, Cassandra, quite. I was, however, a disappointed reader of the *Post* this morning."

"Why was that, Charles?"

"Isn't it obvious, Cassandra? I thought you were going to tell me what had happened to John. But I got to the end of the piece and was none the wiser. None the wiser. Did I miss the point?"

"If I had discovered where John was, I'd have certainly shared it with my readers. But the mystery remains a mystery, Charles. That was the point of the piece."

"Who is your cohort Paolo Vittorio? He tried to call Ruth, you know. But of course you know. You would have instructed him to do so, am I right?"

"Where is all this leading Charles? Am I in the doggy do-do again, or not?"

"I do love your Antipodean turns of phrase, Cassandra. No, you are not in the, the, dogs' whatever you called it, not at all. Quite the contrary. I thought it was a well-balanced piece."

"Thanks Charles. That's kind of you."

There was a silence on the line before Elwood answered. "Well Cassandra, I expect we'll talk again over the weekend. Call me if you need me."

"Thanks. Bye."

The Toyota hammered down the M11. So what was that call all about? It was not his habit to offer praise, or even comfort. The man was such a snake – just when she thought she'd got him sussed he does some other smart-arsed thing that leaves her as confused as ever.

She tried to put him and indeed John Warham out of her mind, noticing for the first time Alex was not listening to Classic FM, nor even Radio 3, but to Radio 2. The DJ was playing, *I'll never find another you*, an ancient Tom Springfield number that had been one of her mother's ironing tunes. Brown and Steve had danced to it at their wedding reception. Brown dabbed her eyes, hoping Alex hadn't noticed, and stared out of the window at the green countryside flashing past.

If she had listened to her mother, Brown would not have the dubious status of divorcee. Standing at her ironing board in the front room of their neat bungalow outside Melbourne, on a Saturday morning two weeks before the wedding, she told Brown marriages couldn't survive on love alone. She pleaded with Brown to resolve with Steve the conflict over their respective futures – Steve was a marine biologist working on a project studying the Great Barrier Reef. Unless he was prepared to give up the project, he could not agree to move away from Australia. Brown needed to work in either London or New York if she was to fulfil her journalistic ambitions.

Since there was no solution to the dilemma, they chose to ignore it. She remembered that Saturday morning so clearly, and the row which developed. She had watched her mother carefully ironing, putting the folded clothes in neat piles, and convinced herself it was merely her mother's craving for order which lay behind her advice.

Brown felt her mother sided with Steve. She believed a wife

should tailor her own ambitions to suit her husband's. Her mother hadn't wanted Brown to take up journalism anyway – her decision to switch from law to journalism had upset her parents, who felt her expensive years in law school had been wasted. They thought Brown found law too difficult.

Brown's mother had always been too ready to compromise, too willing for her father to follow his whims and fancies. Ultimately, she had paid the price when her dad walked out on them. Brown was not going to do the same. No way. When she told her mother this, she had simply shrugged her shoulders and said, "you'll see", her favourite way of ending or avoiding an argument.

Less than a year after the wedding, Brown moved to London. Steve wasn't in Melbourne in any case, but working in Queensland. They tried to keep their marriage alive with emails, telephone calls and the occasional visit. But the ten thousand miles between them was too far to bridge. If love alone could have kept them afloat, they would still be married. But her mother was right. Steve found a new life with somebody else, while all she had was a little silver crucifix and a cupboard full of regrets.

Now she found herself looking at every man and assessing him as a potential partner. The current line-up: Conor Hogan, probably already at Kate's. Vittorio, who she had grown to like during their short time working together. And even Alex, about whom she knew nothing much more than he was scrupulously clean, polite, reliable and a good driver. She caught his eye in the mirror. "Not in the mood for Classic FM this morning, Alex?"

"I like a change at weekends, Miss Brown. You don't mind?"

What was it about being addressed by Alex as "Miss Brown"? "Not at all. I do love some of these old numbers. They remind me of home. Any plans for the weekend, Alex?"

"I'll be working, Miss Brown. Are we going to Primrose Hill, by the way?"

Brown smiled. "Please, Alex…you really should not work all the time, you know. All work and no play makes Jack a dull boy, you know."

"I'll have to risk that, Miss Brown. When you have responsibilities, you need to work when the opportunities present themselves."

Responsibilities? It never crossed her mind Alex might have

76

responsibilities. There were no telltale school photographs of toothy grinning six year olds stuck to his dashboard. He was not wearing a ring. Oh, well!

She concentrated her thoughts on her own weekend prospects. Hogan might be good fun, but he didn't seem an obvious life partner. Alex swung from the M11 onto the North Circular Road, the speedometer needle obediently hovering at 50. Brown stared out the window as IKEA, Curry's and B & Q flashed past in succession. As they turned left towards Muswell Hill the phone rang again. This time it was the City Editor, Henry Marshall. "Cassandra, well done. A wonderful piece. Congratulations. We are far ahead of the competition this morning. Excellent work."

"Henry, it's real nice of you to call. I enjoyed the assignment. I appreciate being given the chance. I'm just relieved you are pleased."

"Pleased, Cassandra. I am delighted. I'll see you on Monday." Short but very sweet.

Brown picked up the main part of the *Post*, suddenly remembering she had filed a news story as well as the *Review* feature. Her animal rights piece was not on the front page. She turned to page three, the usual overflow from page one. Nothing. She scanned the rest of the paper. The story had not been used.

So what had happened to it? Baird had certainly received it and said the news editor was planning to run the story on the front with a cross reference to the Review. Damn. Could this be why Henry Marshall had called with his soft soap? Because her story had been spiked? No wonder he was so anxious to get off the line.

Her first instinct was to call Marshall right back and demand an explanation. But picking a fight with the City editor on a Saturday morning was hardly a career-enhancing move, even if, according to rumour, his days in the job were numbered. Instead, she would call Baird. As she looked up his home number, the Toyota rattled past the end of Kate Moses' street in Kentish Town. Sod it, why foul up the weekend by getting into a row about a story? Hogan had taken the trouble to come to London to see her — the least she could do was to try to forget her bloody job for a day. If they wanted to risk being scooped by one of the Sundays, it was their decision. Instead of Baird, she dialled the Moses' number.

CHAPTER SEVEN

MONDAY morning started badly and got worse. After a nightmare in which she had to walk blindfold along a cliff path holding Elwood's hand, Brown had been awake for several hours. Too angry to sleep, mostly because of the *Post*'s failure to run her animal rights story, she repeatedly turned over the possibilities. And the words from the website kept coming back to her. *There is no escape from the ALF, you filthy murdering scum.* Poor John Warham.

So far as she could tell, this angle was not seriously considered by the *Carabinieri*. Was *anyone* actually looking for Warham, or were they all simply making assumptions? Other than the launching of a helicopter to assuage the British Embassy, there had been no signs of serious searching when she was in Italy.

But why hadn't the *Post* run the animal rights story? She tried her usual back-to-sleep strategies: camomile tea, word games, trying to remember the opening notes of all Chopin's *Nocturnes* – but none worked. When she finally went into a deep sleep it seemed only a few minutes before she was woken by the alarm. She was still cross. She should not have rushed back from Italy. If it had not been for the pressure from Hogan, she could have stayed a couple more days, continued digging, working alongside Vittorio.

In any case, the weekend with Hogan had been inconclusive – the two of them playing some sort of game, acting out roles assigned to them by others. Well, by Kate Moses, in fact. She was not sure how much she liked him, nor whether he liked her. And she didn't desperately care either way. But at least she had learnt that Hogan had been at college with Tom Warham, and had offered to fix an introduction.

She passed on breakfast and dressed without enthusiasm. Her hair felt such a mess she scruffed it up into a pleat fastened with a brown plastic clip. She picked up the *Post* from the newsagents in Regents Park Road and glanced through the news pages to see whether they had run her story. Not a word. Instead there was a short piece from Vittorio, which put her in an even worse humour. He had used a reported sighting of Warham in Milan, which seemed to come from only one anonymous source in a telephone call to the *Carabinieri*, virtually to assert that Warham had simply walked out on his wife to be with Gonzales.

Brown tried to get rid of her mood by fast walking through Primrose Hill and Regents Park before catching the Underground. But she was still mad when she reached the office and without pausing at her own desk stalked up to Baird and flung down the paper, open at Vittorio's story. Baird had been leaning back in his chair sipping coffee and jerked upright with surprise.

Brown stared down at him, feeling the advantage of height. "How could you run this garbage, Curley?"

He carefully put down his coffee. "Whoa. Hang on there Cassandra. Who says it's garbage?"

"I do for one. There's not a shred of evidence to back this up."

"I think you'll find Vittorio got it from the *Carabinieri*. Wasn't it you who told me they were the top police force in Italy?"

"They have a one-track mind, Curley. They think Warham's gone off with his mistress. He may have been murdered, had an accident, been kidnapped, lost his memory. But, oh no, they work on just one theory – he's gone off with Bia bloody Gonzales. That way, they don't have to do anything."

Baird picked up the coffee, swallowed it in one gulp, crunched the cup and aimed it at the waste bin. He was a good shot. "Hang on. Didn't I read somewhere they had helicopters and boats surging up and down the coast looking for him?"

"That's only because they were leaned on by Rome. They always believed he'd run off with Gonzales."

"Well, perhaps he did, Cassandra. Perhaps they might just know more than you do. Listen, just because you didn't write the story it doesn't mean it's rubbish."

"It's got nothing to do with me not writing it. It's about trying to get some facts before spreading gossip over three columns."

He glanced down at the paper. "Two columns, actually Cass. It was our exclusive. If you've got it, flaunt it. And we've got it."

"Got what? Some half-baked report from God knows where. You want to tell Vittorio to stop dancing to the *Carabinieri*'s tune."

"I think it's for me to decide what to tell Vittorio. You may have noticed that I'm the news editor, not you."

"And talking of exclusives, what the hell happened to the ALF story I filed on Friday. It was a bloody sight better than this. Not a bloody word of it in the paper. Why not, Curley? And if you were going to spike it, wouldn't it have been a good idea to tell me why?"

Without waiting for a reply, Brown stalked back to her desk and switched on her computer. She read her emails, including one from the editor of the Saturday *Review* thanking her for her "excellent piece." She emailed Hogan: "Week off to bad start. Hope yours is better. Thanks for coming at the weekend. Take care. Love. Cassandra." She attached a little smiley face. As a reflection of her feelings, it was a lie.

After a few minutes, Baird cautiously approached Brown's desk, sat down on an adjacent chair, and did his best to smile. He explained that Brown's story had been spiked, neither by him nor by the editor, who was not in the office at the time, but by the deputy editor, Hugo Pravin. There had been quite a debate about it at the afternoon editorial conference, when Pravin said he was not going to give the terrorists the publicity they craved. Most others at the conference, including Baird, wanted to run the story, but Pravin was editing the paper.

It was not Baird's fault; there was no point in being angry with him. "Always knew Pravin was a dickhead. I feel like stashing the bastard."

Baird grinned. "I'd call that a career-limiting event, Cass. The editor's in today and I've put the story on the morning schedule. Hopefully he'll have more balls than Pravin."

"By the way Curley, Warham's due back in his office this morning. When he doesn't turn up WBC will have to put out some sort of announcement."

He tapped his clipboard with a pencil. "I've already put a photographer on WBC's doorstep. Elwood can't complain this morning, surely. Home news have sent a reporter to Warham's house to catch him if he leaves for work. So far, nothing at either."

Brown felt her temperature rising again. "Why have home news sent a reporter? I thought this was our story, Curley, not theirs. First my story's spiked, then you run a piece from Vittorio without mentioning it and now home news is sending reporters to Warham's house. Christ Curley, what's going on? Have I fouled up or something? Am I supposed to be working on this effing story or not?"

"Wow, we are touchy this morning."

"Not touchy Curley, pissed off."

Baird swung round on the chair, snatched off his glasses, and began polishing them with his tie. His face was bright red. "You knew yesterday he'd been sighted in Milan because Vittorio rang and told you. You didn't think it worthwhile ringing the desk?"

"I didn't think Vittorio was filing."

"Then that's even more reason to call in. If it'd been left to you, we could have been the only paper not running the fucking story he'd been seen in Milan."

"And we could have been the only paper running the animal rights angle if we didn't have such jerk of a deputy editor."

Brown saw Jill Lambert slip away from the news-desk in the direction of the coffee machine. Some hardened veterans leaned back in their chairs openly enjoying the rare spectacle of somebody picking a fight with Baird. Lambert returned with coffees. "All done now?" she asked, as she put one polystyrene cup in front of Baird and handed the other to Brown.

Baird took a deep breath. "Look Cass. Nobody's trying to take the story away from you. Your piece on Saturday was fantastic. I've told you in my opinion we should have gone with your animal rights story. But Vittorio is a trusted freelance who knows his way around and I have to take his word for it. As for home news sending a reporter to stand outside Warham's house, I don't think that's something you want to do, is it, if you're honest? You and I both know he'll stand there all day and not get a thing."

Brown looked down at her shoes. Why did she ever buy them? "OK Curley, you win. Put me down for something on WBC. We can have the same bog standard story as every other paper. That way we don't take any risks."

Baird touched her shoulder as he stood up. Brown sipped the

coffee and started her "to do" list. First she needed to contact Tom Warham. When she rang, he'd obviously been waiting for the call. They chatted for a few moments about Hogan and about what fun it was spending a weekend in Dublin. He readily agreed to a meeting at six o'clock that evening.

She watched as Baird strutted off to the morning conference. Hopefully, he would get her story scheduled into Tuesday's paper.

She could even try to update her piece if the activists had had a busy weekend. She logged into the website – if animal rights lay at the heart of the Warham mystery, something might have been posted on their infamous "Diary of Actions." But there was nothing – just small stuff, gluing the doors of butchers' shops and fur boutiques and so on. There was no mention of kidnap. She was not sure whether she was relieved or disappointed.

She logged out. It was time for her morning call to Elwood. He was as smooth as melted chocolate. "Ah my dear Cassandra. I see your little Italian help-mate has been getting carried away."

"Meaning?" If she had to defend Vittorio's story to Elwood it really would be the last straw.

"Meaning, Cassandra, if John was walking the via Montenapoleone or the Santo Spirito on the arm of Ms Gonzales, as your Mr Vittorio seems to suggest, we would have known about it before him."

"How?"

"My, Cassandra, you do seem a little monosyllabic this morning. We have our ways, Cassandra."

"Interesting. You have your ways, eh? Private detectives maybe? If so, you probably know the answer to the question on everyone's lips, is he with Gonzales?"

"You can assume the former but not the latter, if that helps. And before you ask, the firm we've chosen is Stratagem Security."

"Who else, Charles, nothing but the best. I do take it, by the way, that John hasn't turned up for work?"

"Would I sound so downcast if he had Cassandra? Sadly, his chauffeur was not required this morning."

"To be honest, Charles, you don't sound downcast. I take it you've been given his job?"

"The board has asked me to carry on the day to day

management, which I am happy to do. The deputy chairman will run board meetings until John returns."

"Not exactly a surprise, Charles. Anything else going on?"

"Lots Cassandra, lots. We've got a business to run here, clients to talk to, campaigns to plan. We can't put WBC on hold until John returns. So if there's nothing more I can help you with?"

She was not ready yet to share her theories with Elwood. "Not right now. Thanks."

Baird returned from the morning conference with the news that the editor thought her story excellent, but was backing Pravin's decision. The story was to remain on hold. There was no point in arguing, but that did not mean she should abandon her research.

She went back to the Internet, looking at other pages. The focus of protest activity was without doubt the proposed new facility outside Oxford, but there were also frequent sorties to fur farms, of which Italy seemed to have many. No wonder Warham was in their sights.

This was not protest of the slogan-shouting, whistle-blowing, kind, but violence. In the first few months of the year the contractors working on the Oxford research facility were repeatedly targeted. Site machinery was wrecked, tyres slashed on trucks, sand poured into engines, building supplies damaged, fires started. The homes of directors were "visited." Paint stripper was tipped over their cars and their homes daubed with slogans in red paint. In Italy, department stores in Milan and Florence selling furs were attacked, their windows smashed and paint sprayed over the shops.

Hardly any of this had been reported in the mainstream British national newspapers. It made the news only when a protester was actually caught, prosecuted and appeared in court.

Brown beckoned Baird over to her screen and pointed out the front page of one of the online magazines.

"Let this message be clear to all who victimize the innocent: We're watching. And by axe, drill, or crowbar — we're coming through your door.
Stop or be stopped."

"They're just fucking lunatics," Baird said, "I'm not pumping up their egos by running stories on them. Just forget about this, Cass and give me two hundred on Warham not showing up for work."

What was the point? Why was she was working with such a

bunch of dubbos? Why was everything doomed to misfire? What she thought would convince Baird to fight for her story had the opposite effect. If only she had stayed in the Cinque Terre instead of rushing back. Sod Hogan.

She did her best to avoid yet another confrontation. "OK, Curley, you win. But I can do better than 'Warham fails to turn up'. I have found out WBC has hired detectives to search for him."

Baird stuck his hands deep into his pockets. "OK, but it's still worth only two hundred words. It's obvious they'd have done that."

Fuck him. Brown bit her lip. Never, since she started as a junior reporter, had she felt more like resigning. Was it simply that Baird was losing interest in the Warham story? Or was it that her outburst at him earlier that day, in front of a newsroom full of reporters, had pissed him off sufficiently to cloud his judgement. Perhaps she should apologise, before the stubbornness that had wrecked her marriage did the same thing for her career.

She settled down to write the story, calling Stratagem's London office for comment. As she expected, they would not even confirm they had been appointed. They did not get to the top of their business by gossiping about clients. Shortly after lunch — a salad from the canteen eaten at her desk — Brown delivered three hundred words rather than the two hundred Baird had requested. It included a paragraph, which she expected Baird to delete, pouring cold water on the reported sighting of Warham in Milan. She sent it through to the news-desk and went to the coffee machine. On her way back she asked Baird if it was OK.

Baird had the story on his screen. "Nice story, Cass. Do you reckon it's exclusive?"

"I think so Curley. It only came out because I asked the question."

"Then can you stretch it to four hundred words?"

The axe was buried, and not in her head. She wanted to hug somebody, looked at Baird, and returned to her desk where she added three more paragraphs and sent them through. She had calmed down enough to call Vittorio. In his position, armed with information, however suspect, from a source such as the *Carabinieri*, she would have done the same. She was pleased to hear his friendly voice. He said he would try to find out if anyone from Stratagem had visited Italy.

"Oh, and Paolo, keep close to Gonzales' agent in case our little model should make herself available for interview."

"Certainly Cassandra. How was your weekend, by the way? Did you collapse into the arms of your Irish hero?"

"Piss off Paolo, I've work to do." She spent the rest of the afternoon reading up on the animal rights movement.

SECTION Business
TITLE Dicks
HEADING 1 Missing Tycoon: WBC calls in Private Detectives
HEADING 2
AUTHOR Cassandra Brown
STATUS Live

Private investigators have been called in to help in the search for John Warham, the millionaire advertising tycoon who has been missing for more than two weeks.

WBC, the advertising agency he founded, confirmed yesterday that they had appointed Stratagem Security to investigate Mr Warham's sudden disappearance.

The news follows an unconfirmed report that Mr Warham had been seen in Milan. WBC is sceptical about the accuracy of the reported sighting.

Stratagem Security is one of the world's leading investigation agencies. The firm has developed a particular expertise in dealing with cases of kidnap, often negotiating terms of release when businessmen are held hostage.

Where kidnap insurance is taken out at Lloyd's of London, the terms of the policy usually dictate that a top investigations agency such as Stratagem be retained to conduct all dealings with kidnappers.

Stratagem were officially appointed yesterday, when Mr Warham was due to return to WBC after a vacation, although it is believed they have been working behind the scenes for several days.

Nobody at Stratagem would comment on the appointment. "All our dealings with clients are entirely confidential", said a spokeswoman.

Charles Elwood, finance director and *de facto* deputy chief executive of WBC, has been appointed to run the business until the missing businessman returns. Mr Elwood said there was "lots to do" at WBC. He added: "We've got a business to run here, clients to talk to, campaigns to plan. We can't put WBC on hold until John returns."

The deputy chairman, James Moorcroft, will run board meetings. On the stock exchange, WBC shares held steady. Dealers said they were pleased with the prompt way WBC had responded to the crisis.

The *Post* understands investigators from Stratagem have visited Milan, where Mr Warham's close friend, the fashion model Bia Gonzales, has her home.

CHAPTER EIGHT

WHEN Tom Warham arrived at the *Post*'s offices he was taken first to see the editor. Brown had finished her story and sat on the edge of Baird's desk waiting to be summoned to the meeting. They were talking about the flat she had seen.

"I suppose that means you intend to stay," said Baird as he worked his way through a pile of old press releases, only a handful of which didn't end up in the waste bin.

"I suppose it does, but if I get many more days like today, I might have second thoughts."

Before he could answer, Cameron's secretary appeared at the end of the office, beckoning Brown. The summons had come. She wished she had taken a bit more trouble with her appearance that morning.

As she entered the conference room, the same smelly glass box in which the morning, afternoon, leaders writers and all the other daily meetings for senior staff were held, Tom Warham leapt up from the uncomfortable red sofa on which he had been sat. Like his father, he was tall, but whereas John Warham was powerfully built, Tom was slight. Round spectacles, and a corduroy suit, gave him a bookish air. How suitable, but probably contrived, for an academic historian.

Brown shook the large outstretched hand and sat down opposite on another tired and grubby sofa. It had once been bright blue. Only then did she see Cameron, who had been sitting on the third sofa, also blue, beside the door. The seating formed three sides of a square. In the centre was a glass-topped coffee table, ringed with splashes of coffee from innumerable plastic cups. Journalists have a unique ability to turn decent offices into slums within weeks, if not days, of arriving.

Once the introductions were over, nobody seemed to want to

speak. She filled some empty time writing the date and "Tom Warham" at the top of the first page of a new notebook. The men sipped from whisky glasses. She was not offered a drink.

Cameron spoke first. "I've told Mr Warham, Tom, how much we appreciate him taking the time to come in and see us. I have known both his father and his mother, and indeed Tom himself, for a long time and we share the family's distress. I have said the resources of the *Post* are at his disposal. We would all like this matter brought to a happy conclusion. Now, Tom, if you will excuse me, it's the time of evening when I have to read our leaders and so on. I will leave you in the capable hands of Cassandra here."

The men nodded at each other and Cameron hurried from the room, leaving what was left of his drink behind on the table. Tom twirled his glass and took another sip. His eyes remained fixed on the dark blue squares of carpet which covered the conference room floor. Finally, he shot a glance at Brown.

"Conor said you wanted to see me."

"Yes. Look. Thanks for coming in. As the Editor said, we really do appreciate it. The thing is, I'm working on your father's disappearance, and I thought we might be able to help each other. First though, can I say how sorry I am?"

"That's nice of you. Before we get started, can I ask you something?"

"Of course."

"Would it be alright for me to see any stories you plan to print, so I can check them over?"

Brown looked down at her notebook and then turned her gaze directly into Tom's face. "Sorry, Tom, but it's not our policy to do that. But if it would help, I could certainly check back with you any quotes I intend to use. And if you ask me not to use something you tell me, of course I will respect that."

Tom's eyes remained focused on the carpet. "Conor said I shouldn't tell you anything I don't want to see in the paper. Is that right?"

Thanks a bundle, Conor. Brown put on her most sympathetically serious expression. "That's generally good advice, Tom, I have to admit. But if we can agree on what I just suggested I promise I'll not let you down."

Tom finally lifted his eyes from the floor, and the ghost of a smile momentarily lit his face. "OK, he also said I could trust you. So, let's just recap. If I say not for publication, you'll not use it. Agreed?"

"Agreed."

He seemed to relax and allowed himself to rest back on the sofa. He sipped his whisky and put the glass down on the coffee table. "By the way, I am here against the very strong advice of Charles Elwood, so you'd better not let me down."

"You asked his advice?"

"Certainly not. He gave it. Unbidden."

"How did he know you were coming here?"

"I'm not sure. I assume you didn't tell him. He seems to know too much about everything. He may even have his detectives following me for all I know. But what I think is this. While my father is away, WBC have put his car, a pale blue Jaguar if you don't mind, and driver at our disposal. I assume he keeps tabs on us through the driver's log, or whatever."

"That's outrageous. Why would he do that?"

"I don't know how well you know Charles, Cassandra, but he's a man who leaves nothing to chance. Did you know WBC have hired an outfit called Stratagem Security, allegedly to search for my father? But I expect at the same time they are digging up whatever shit they can on him for Elwood to use as he pleases."

"I heard about Stratagem today. In fact, we're running a piece on them tomorrow."

Tom looked pleased, bringing his hands together in a curious movement – a sort of slow motion, silent, handclap. Then his right hand broke free to wag its index finger at Brown. "I bet Elwood didn't tell you his spooks are forbidden to tell us anything. We get plied with questions, but get nothing back. They have to report back to Elwood then he chooses what he will tell us."

Tom gripped his hands between his knees, and grunted. Is this common with historians, the need to grunt? Like girl tennis players at Wimbledon? Brown tried to focus on his face. "Do you know if Stratagem are looking at the animal rights groups?"

He shrugged his shoulders. "No idea. As I said, they don't tell us anything."

Brown looked covetously at Tom's whisky. He followed her gaze, picked up the tumbler, and sipped. She would back off the animal rights issue for a moment. "This is a bit delicate, Tom, but one thing that has been intriguing me is the relationship between your father and Bia Gonzales."

He put the glass back on the coffee table. "Intriguing *you*? I tell you Cassandra, it's driving me mad. I don't care what he's been up to, but if he'd run off with her he'd have let us know he was alright." He paused before continuing. "He met her when he was working in Italy."

"The Naturalia campaign."

"Yes. Did you know he supervised the shooting himself? Having thought up the bright idea of having some model wear nothing but a fur coat, he couldn't resist being there. After all, what old bloke wouldn't like to see some little nymphet jumping around with no clothes on?" He allowed himself a smile at last.

"I've seen the pictures."

"So you have, Cassandra. I read your story about them."

"I'm sorry if it upset your mother."

"It didn't."

"But Elwood told me she was thinking of taking legal action against us."

"Bollocks. If you'll pardon the expression. I'm not sure she even spoke to Elwood about it. My mother, who I think you've met ..."

Brown nodded.

"... is quite able to speak for herself. If you'd upset her, she would have let you know. She wouldn't need Elwood."

He rubbed his hands together and then looked at them, as if seeing them for the first time, before continuing. "What upset her was that somebody should want to damage my father. Trust Elwood to twist things."

He stared at the ceiling, and then appeared to concentrate on Brown's breasts. Had a button on her shirt popped open? It was not the time to find out.

He went on, without shifting his gaze: "As for Gonzales, I assume Stratagem Security", he spat the name, "are keeping a pretty close eye on her. If he is with her, I think even Elwood would have let us know. By the way, that doesn't mean your story this morning is wrong. My father has friends in Milan besides Gonzales."

Brown concentrated on her notes, before looking up to answer. "Elwood doesn't believe it, by the way. Or that's what he said to me. He hinted his spooks would have found out by now."

Tom suddenly stood up and went to the window overlooking the newsroom. Brown took the opportunity to check her shirt buttons, one of which was, as she feared, undone. She struggled to refasten it before he turned back to her.

He continued to stare ahead, his back to the room, but as he resumed his monologue Brown realised he was talking to her reflection in the window. Perhaps he was embarrassed about the wayward button.

"I assume you know my father was under a lot of pressure at WBC. I gather WBC is no longer the hot-shot agency it was in the early days when clients besieged the place for a bit of the Warham magic, a touch of Mr Genius." There was an undoubted edge of sarcasm. "My father carried the can."

Brown nodded sympathetically and waited for him to continue. The door to the conference room opened a fraction, closed, and opened again. Pravin's face appeared. "Sorry, I was looking for George." The face withdrew and the door clicked shut. Brown would have liked to kick it.

The interruption allowed Tom the space to come away from the window, but instead of returning to the red sofa he came and sat close beside her. She wanted to move away slightly. Perhaps he found it easier to talk without facing her, like two lovers exchanging confidences quietly in bed, their heads close on the pillow but their eyes fixed on the ceiling. He carefully positioned one oversized hand on each of his knees.

"Elwood and his ilk like to forget it, but it was John who made WBC in the first place. Who else do you think brought in international clients like Naturalia?"

"And Naturalia wanted to make a splash at London Fashion Week so they bring over the lovely Bia..."

"You've got it, Cassandra. She attaches herself to my father, not that he minded, and I suppose her agent made sure the photographers knew where to find them."

He folded his hands around an imaginary camera, brought them up to his face, and made a clicking sound with his tongue. Brown scribbled furiously in the notebook. Tom held the whisky glass, now covered in fingerprints and nearly empty, against the light. He replaced it on the table, and looked expectantly at Brown.

She obliged with the next question. "What do you think he meant when he said to your mother, 'it's over, Ruth, it's over'?"

"Did he say that?"

"According to somebody who overheard them."

Tom stretched out his long legs, and balanced the heel of his left shoe on the toe of his right. His left shoe still had a "sale" sticker on the sole. He seemed satisfied with the strange arrangement of his feet. "When is he supposed to have said that?"

"Just before he disappeared."

"In Italy, you mean?"

"Yes. According to my contacts."

"You mean according to the little gossip who runs the hotel?"

Brown closed her notebook for a moment and looked across at this curious academic, who in his quiet and nervous way seemed to have taken control of the interview. He should not be under-estimated. "I never disclose my sources, Tom."

"Well, I can assume it was him, since he told the same story to the *Carabinieri*. I thought you would be experienced enough not to pay too much attention to him."

Brown ignored the remark. "Tell me about your mother."

"You've met her."

"Yes, but only briefly. How's she coping?"

"What do you think? She goes from fear to worry to despair to anger and back to fear. The truth is, she doesn't know what to believe. At first, she thought he must have had an accident. Then, when the search found nothing, she convinced herself he had been kidnapped. John would be a very profitable target."

His hands were now behind his head, and his body was leaning alarmingly to one side. Was he going to topple? He continued, "Then with all this stuff about Gonzales, especially in the Italian papers, she began to think maybe the *Carabinieri* were right, and that he'd walked out. If John had walked back through the door at that point she'd have killed him before asking any questions."

He permitted himself a brief smile, then suddenly sat upright and clicked the bones in his knuckles. "We were all the while waiting for a phone call from him, or a ransom note, or a call from the police confirming the worst. But nothing. That's the worst part. Our minds endlessly run through all the possibilities, none of them bring any comfort. I am used to wrestling with uncertainties in my job, Cassandra. Trying to construct viable histories on the basis of what evidence is available, realising what you don't know exceeds what you do know many times over. I guess journalism can be like that too, sometimes?"

Brown nodded.

Tom crossed his legs and lay back again. He was by now almost horizontal. He put the four fingers of each hand into its respective jacket pocket, leaving the thumbs sticking out. Brown had seen pictures of Prince Charles doing the same thing.

"Sometimes she sees John lying halfway down a cliff face, clinging to a gorse bush, his throat too parched to cry for help. Then he is locked in some ghastly outbuilding on a scruffy farm while barely literate *Mafiosi* try to write a ransom note. Then the picture changes completely. He is walking hand in hand through olive groves with Gonzales, laughing and stopping to embrace her. Then worst of all, almost, he is locked in an animal cage while men and women in balaclava hoods poke sticks through the bars. It's hell for all of us, Cassandra. We just need to know the truth, however horrible, before we can move on. The uncertainty is killing us." He sat up and brought his already empty whisky glass to his lips. When no liquid flowed, he stared at it as if it was the first time he had seen it, and then thumped it down on the table.

Brown was no longer dealing with a story, no longer pumping a source of information for all she could get, but dealing with the pain of an ordinary man thrust into an extraordinary situation. She had nothing left to ask.

Tom stood up, and walked across the small room to pick up a piece of crumpled paper left behind on the floor from the afternoon editorial conference. He looked around him. Brown indicated a small plastic waste bin already half full with used polystyrene cups. He expertly tossed the paper in and stuck his hands deep into the pockets of his baggy trousers. He remained standing, again staring down at the newsroom below the conference room window, his back to Brown. "Suppose I went through the sequence of events, as I understand them, on the day he disappeared. Would that be helpful?"

"It would, yes, thanks." Brown concentrated on her notebook. She feared looking into his eyes.

Most of what Tom told her, Brown already knew.

"There's one thing that's been bothering me, Tom, and that's why Nichols was against bringing in the *Carabinieri*."

"Probably didn't want the hassle." He began pacing up and down the small room. Brown pulled her feet back out of the way.

"By the evening, my mother was getting desperate and that's when she finally called me. I was at home for once and after talking it over with Suzie we decided to alert the Foreign Office. Well, in fact, I called Number Ten and they got on to the Foreign Office. I took the first flight out to Genoa on Thursday and took a taxi to Manarola.

"By the time I got there the *Carabinieri* had already taken statements and done some sort of search of the coastline by helicopter, but they seemed to me to have already decided John had walked out."

"Can I quote you on that, Tom?"

"Absolutely not. The last thing I need is to fall out with the Italians. Sorry."

Brown nodded acquiescence and concentrated on her notebook. On the Friday, the day after he had arrived in Manarola, he and his mother had walked the path themselves, as they still feared John had had an accident. Finding nothing, they remained in Manarola until Sunday morning when they flew home.

"Why didn't you tell WBC that John was missing?"

"It was none of their business. My father was on holiday with my mother. We decided we would say nothing to Elwood until he was due to return to work."

Brown put down her pencil and pad. "But I don't understand. Surely WBC could have helped you. Put resources at your disposal?"

"Can we go absolutely off the record?"

Brown nodded, and put her notepad and pencil on the floor.

"Because I knew Elwood would try to take advantage. To put it bluntly, he's after my father's job. It would have been playing right into his hands." He raised the glass to his lips again and immediately put it back on the coffee table.

He took a deep breath, stopped pacing and sat closely beside Brown. She wished she could put an arm around his shoulders, comfort this antsy individual with his hyperactive hand movements.

Tom shot a glance at her chest before concentrating once more on the floor in front of him. "You see, this whole disappearing thing could be about Elwood. He's put my father under a lot of pressure."

He paused, as if trying to decide whether or not to go on, before continuing. "There's a bit of him that would like to walk away from WBC, retire if you like. But he's not going to be hounded out. That's where Elwood has got it so wrong. The more he piles on the pressure, the less likely it is John will get out of his way." He punched the palm of his left hand with his right fist before continuing.

"I simply don't understand Elwood. He was a simple accountant, a ruddy bean counter from deepest Essex, until he teamed up with my father. Now he's rich and powerful. I think undermining John now is a curious way of showing his gratitude."

"OK, so if you're right, where might John have gone? And wouldn't he put your mother's mind at rest?"

Tom leaned forward, balancing his elbows on his knees and completely covering his face with his hands. "OK, it's a shit theory, but I have to cling on to something. To answer your question, I haven't a clue, except it would be in Europe, either Italy or France, and somewhere he's been before. That's why the Milan story is not as nuts as all that. And before you ask, he's never gone walkabout before. I just wish he had."

Tom again picked up his empty glass, stood up and walked over to the window, looking down over the newsroom. Brown sensed the interview was over. He pointed needlessly to the window. "What's going on down there? It looks frenetic."

Brown went and stood by his side, dwarfed by his height. "That's the back bench there. The chap in the middle, the one

George Cameron is talking to, is the night editor, responsible for getting the paper out on time. The chap at the end is the chief sub. It looks like he's just brought up the proof of the front page for George to OK. The guy sitting opposite him is the deputy editor."

"What's the main story?"

"Almost bound to be Iraq."

"My father fell out with Downing Street over Iraq by the way. He was totally against the war."

"Good for him."

He put the glass on the window ledge and stared at the scurrying figures below. Cameron nodded to the chief sub, who picked up the telephone. Cassandra found herself looking at her watch, the instinctive reaction of any daily newspaper journalist when the paper is finally put to bed.

Tom continued to stare. His eyes met hers in reflection. "Listen, Cassandra, can you do something for me?"

"I'll try."

He turned to face her. "Keep the story on the front page. Keep the stories rolling, don't let anyone forget. That's why I agreed to see you. The worst thing that could happen is people stop looking. I have no idea whether the Milan thing adds up to anything or not, but we want everyone looking out for him."

"You may not like everything we print, Tom."

"I realise that. It's the risk we take. You'll dig around in John's past and you'll find stuff ..."

"What sort of stuff?"

"For heaven's sake Cassandra, I don't know." His voice had risen an octave. "But we all have secrets. I spend my life trying to get behind the generally accepted views of public figures of the seventeenth century, and I find stuff. I find stuff people hid, sometimes centuries ago. It's a hell of a lot easier for you. Especially when, like all successful men, John has enemies."

"The ALF?'

Tom's large hands went back into the jacket pockets, his shoulders were hunched. He turned away and Brown could see his pained expression reflected back in the glass. "It was bloody stupid of him to get involved with the fur trade wasn't it?"

Before Brown needed to answer, Cameron returned to the

conference room, a copy of the *Post's* front page in his hand. Brown's story about private detectives had been cut, but at least it was on the front. "I thought you might like to see this, Tom. You see we are keeping John on the front page."

"Thanks." Tom took the proof and sat down to read. He looked exhausted. Cameron's secretary came into the room with the open bottle of whiskey and refilled the two men's' glasses. Behind Cameron's back, she waved the bottle and looked straight at Brown. Reluctantly, Brown shook her head.

Cameron broke a rather awkward silence. "Well, Tom. If you'll excuse me I have to read through the first edition and make changes for the second. I'll see you before you go." He drained the glass and put it down on the scratched glass of the coffee table.

Tom turned to Brown, as if he were surprised to see her still there, and sipped his drink. "Do you always have a drink at this time?"

"No. The office is officially dry. It's the first time I've seen drink in here since the day I joined, when my immediate boss, Henry Marshall, pulled out a bottle at the end of my shift. Now, Tom, we were beginning to talk about us finding stuff. Where should I start looking?"

Tom swilled the whisky around in the glass, as if it was a goblet of fine wine. The glass was already almost empty. "Don't misunderstand me, Cassandra. I am not saying there is anything specific. All I am saying is that in the bitchy world in which my father operates you will pick up tittle-tattle. As I said, he has enemies."

He got up from the red sofa and walked back over to the window. "Where's everyone gone?"

Brown walked over to join him. The newsroom, full of hurrying, busy-looking men and women only ten minutes earlier, was almost deserted. A few jackets hung on the backs of chairs. A young man pushed around a trolley, placing copies of the newspaper on every desk. It was as if there had been a fire alarm and everybody had run outside.

"Some have gone home. The others are taking a break between editions. They'll be back in about a quarter of an hour to work on the next edition."

Tom turned his back to the window. "John isn't just a businessman you know. He's also a father and a grandfather. We have to stay positive. The alternatives are too nasty to contemplate."

"Did he have police protection?"

"Protection, no. Were the police aware that he was a potential target, yes. Did they keep an eye on the house, yes. But of course, in Italy my parents were a long way from home."

"Can I use that in the paper?"

"I'd sooner you didn't. I wouldn't want to alert a whole load more unhinged criminals. I hope you understand?"

Brown looked at the sad stooping figure. He was probably not much her senior in years, but he seemed older. Now was not the time to push it. "Of course, Tom, if you say so."

He drained his glass and looked at his watch. "I really think I ought to be getting along. Suzie will be wondering where I am. It's bad enough one member of the family going AWOL – we don't want anyone worrying about me too. It's been good to talk with you, Cassandra. Now, I think I can find my own way out ..."

"Just a minute. Tom. I'll get the editor. I'm sure he would want to say goodbye. And you'll need somebody to walk you out of the office. If you can hang on five minutes I'll just get my coat and we can leave together. Is your car still outside, or can we get you a cab?"

"I told the driver to go home, so a cab would be nice if you don't mind. I'm going to King's Cross."

"I'm heading for Primrose Hill. We can share the journey and I can drop you off on the way."

It was drizzling rain as the cab made its way through the still-busy streets. Tom seemed not to want to talk, concentrating instead on reading the first edition of the *Post* given him by Cameron. "Suzie will be impressed, seeing tomorrow's paper this evening."

"It still gives me a thrill."

"You know, Cassandra, you don't seem quite the cynical hard bitten hack I had expected."

In silence they slowly passed Liverpool Street Station and the big roundabout at Old Street, past the Angel at Islington and around the one-way system at Kings Cross. The traffic was hardly moving.

The cabbie leaned back and slid open the glass partition, asking where Tom wanted to be dropped.

"Here, please. Right here will do fine." He sounded almost frantic. The cab pulled over and almost before Brown had a chance to say goodbye, Tom was out, hurrying away with his heavy briefcase, the newspaper under his arm, his head bent forward, as if he wanted to hide. A pale blue Jaguar drove slowly past the cab and disappeared into the traffic of the Euston Road.

CHAPTER NINE

A WEEK after Tom Warham had fled from the taxi outside Kings Cross Station, the story had stalled. Nobody claimed to have seen his father and there was still nothing from the animal rights brigade. Elwood had stopped calling. The story no longer commanded top billing. Her brief moment of glory seemed to be behind her and she had failed to keep the story on the front page.

The one positive note in her life was that her flat purchase seemed on track. But as for becoming a star reporter, Brown felt she might just as well give up, go back home to the sunshine and forget the dream. And then she wouldn't need the flat.

None of the journalists on any other paper was doing any better. She had still broken every significant Warham story and it wasn't her fault that the one strong new line she did have, animal rights, had been sat upon by the fat arse of Pravin.

According to the Internet, the terrorists had been busy again, slashing truck tyres at a quarry, sinking a rowing boat, stripping paint from an accountant's Mercedes, freeing minks. But there was no news of John Warham.

None of the ALF's antics had been reported in the mainstream British media, so the stance taken by the *Post* was common across all papers. Deprive them of the "oxygen of publicity" – a tactic and a phrase coined by the former British Prime Minister Margaret Thatcher in relation to the Irish Republican Army at the height of their eighties bombing campaign.

Without enthusiasm, Brown answered her mobile, noticing the caller's number was withheld. The person on the line introduced himself as Stephen Bennett, and he wanted to know if Brown was still following the Warham story. She considered hanging up. Instead, she answered with a clipped "yes, of course."

Ignoring her obvious irritation, Bennett said he was a forensic accountant working on a project for an investment bank, the name of which she would undoubtedly know. In the course of this he had come across information that could be pertinent to the disappearance of John Warham.

Brown was trained, both as a lawyer and as a journalist, to be sceptical of calls like Bennett's. He was probably nothing more than the telephone equivalent of a "green ink" letter writer; somebody who knew nothing but wanted the thrill of trying it on. On the other hand, he didn't sound like one of the barmy brigade. He neither ranted nor whispered about a mighty conspiracy — his manner was sophisticated and knowledgeable. Which suggested he had dealt with the media before.

Brown's curiosity weighed against her suspicion. "What sort of information?"

"Banking documents."

"And why would you want me to see them?"

"Because, Cassandra, I have a great deal of respect for John Warham." There was a pause. Brown imagined him looking around to make sure he wasn't overheard. "I think he's been badly treated by some of his colleagues."

"So how much do you want for this information?"

"I have no interest in making money from this, unlike Mr Charles Elwood's friends at Stratagem Security, who, by the way, have little experience of missing persons."

"So what's your angle, Mr Bennett?"

"No angle, Cassandra, I merely want to put important and relevant facts into the public domain. And I am prepared to sacrifice a day of my time to do so."

"So why not tell the authorities?"

"Because the Italian magistrate is bent and Scotland Yard have given up and gone home. I sense, by the way, the media has also run out of places to look."

Brown could hardly argue otherwise. There was a general sense of 'giving up' all round. Despite his promise to take Brown off all other jobs, Baird was starting to push unrelated stories her way.

There had been nothing fresh to write about. And just when the Warham mystery needed a kick-start, Bennett had popped out of the woodwork. Too good to be true?

Bennett's voice cut across her train of thought. She was sitting holding the telephone to her ear, but saying nothing. "So are you interested or shall I stop wasting your time?" he asked.

"No. I mean yes. I am interested. Can you send me the documents?"

"If only it were that easy. But I am afraid I cannot trust them to the post. We need to meet."

Brown looked at her depressingly empty diary. She had put everything on hold — her usual round of lunches with contacts, most of her private life, trips out of town — to work on the Warham story, and in both the physical and metaphorical sense she had nowhere much to go.

She could meet him immediately. "When?"

"Ah", he said, "there are a few things we need to arrange first. I am working in Geneva, but there is no point in meeting in Switzerland because if I showed you any of the papers in my possession I would break the banking laws, which I am not prepared to do."

"So are you coming to London?"

"No, but the same restrictions on me passing information would apply because of the bank's London operations."

Brown began to tire of the cat and mouse game. "So what do you suggest?"

"I am prepared to travel to either Paris or Amsterdam, but I prefer the latter. I would look to the *Post* to pay my airfare, a few hundred Euros."

A few hundred Euros was nothing to the *Post*, and even if she added in her fare the grand total would be well under a thousand Euros, about seven hundred pounds. But it was not a decision she could make. "Can I check with my editor and call you back?"

"I'm moving about Geneva and in and out of meetings all day today, so I'll call you after lunch. I will require my expenses to be wired to a certain bank at Schiphol Airport."

Brown hung up and went in search of Baird. She found him chatting up Henry Marshall's secretary, and suggested they go into

Marshall's office for a "quiet word". Since their dust up over the unused animal rights story, Brown and Baird had been polite if a little distant with each other. But Baird was surprisingly receptive to her chasing the story in Amsterdam.

"Take it to the editor, Cass. I can't authorise payment of an informant's expenses but if you explain it to him as you have to me, he'll agree like a shot."

Brown left Baird to resume his chat, went back to her desk and thought about her approach to Cameron. Should she act as if she were convinced by Bennett's story, or retain an air of scepticism?

Some old hands on the paper maintained that the best time to approach Cameron was early afternoon, when he was still feeling flush and flattered from lunch at the Savoy Grill or some other fancy establishment. But that would be cutting it too fine. When Bennett rang back, she wanted to be able to give him an answer. May as well get it over with.

As she stood up to go first to the cloakroom to check her make-up and then on to Cameron's office, Kate Moses phoned. "Hi Cassandra. How're you doing?"

"Fine, Kate. Well, OK, I think. I'm just about to go and ask the editor it he's willing to spend a grand for me to fly to Amsterdam to meet somebody I'd never even heard of half an hour ago."

"There must be more to it than that. Why would you even think about it?"

"Cos he says he's got some documents relating to John Warham?"

"What sort of documents. I don't like the sound of this."

"Jeez, Kate, I don't know. Banking documents he said."

"I'm liking this less and less. What if they are stolen?"

Brown had not thought of that possibility, but was not going to admit it. "He seems very careful about staying the right side of the law. He couldn't show me the documents in Geneva because of the Swiss banking laws. That's why we are meeting in Amsterdam — if the Editor approves the expenses."

It was time to change the subject. Brown did not want to add Moses' doubts to her own, nor hear her lawyers' caveats, which she knew already. What she needed was somebody to be enthusiastic. She closed the discussion down. "Anyway Kate, it's nice to hear from you.

Did you ring about something in particular, or for a general chat?"

"I wanted to get your take on the weekend. Conor has been on and off the phone all week, worrying because you haven't called him since he got home on Sunday. He thinks he may have fouled up with you somehow. I said I'd talk to you so here I am."

Brown took a deep breath. She didn't want to think about Hogan, let alone talk about him. It was sweet of Kate to act as a go-between, trying to fix a match between two of her friends, but her call was badly timed. Brown just wanted to get on with her work. "Jeez, Kate, could you ask him just to cool it? I'll call him when I'm ready, either before or at the weekend. And, just to put your's and Conor's minds at rest, I'm not about to draw stumps on him, OK?"

There was a pause on the other end of the line. "I'll tell him that, Cass. Sure I will. Sorry, I obviously rang at a bad time. Good luck with the Editor."

Brown felt like shit. "No, I'm really sorry Kate. It's just that Conor is, well, too anxious and to be honest, it spooks me. You must be fed up with him ringing all the time. Look, can I get this Amsterdam business out of the way and call you back? Can I pop round this evening?"

"That's more like Cassandra Brown. I'll open a nice bottle of Sancerre and get a bite to eat. You can keep me and Chloë company."

Brown had known Moses long enough to read the sub-text. Her husband went away far more often than she liked. Brown promised to be there by seven, rang off and turned her thoughts back to her meeting with Cameron. She was beginning to get excited at the prospect of a day trip to Amsterdam to meet a mysterious contact.

Cameron was in his office, talking on the telephone. She hovered by the door but he signalled for her to enter. It sounded as if Cameron was on to his bookmaker. When he hung up she outlined her proposal to go to Amsterdam. He listened carefully and asked just one question: did she think the expense might put the Warham story back on the front page? If she did, she should go ahead. Brown nodded and virtually fled back to her desk. Baird was still deep in conversation with Marshall's secretary but grinned broadly when Brown gave him the thumbs up. The day was improving.

Bennett called just before three o'clock and barely reacted when Brown said she had squared the meeting with the editor. He could, he said, meet her at Schiphol the following day at, say, one o'clock. That would give him time to collect his expenses first. He gave her the name and address. It sounded like hassle, so Brown offered to take the cash with her and hand it over when they met, but he said that since it was likely he would be under surveillance, passing a bundle of notes might be viewed with suspicion.

"And how do I know you will turn up, Cassandra? I would be out of pocket to the tune of an air fare."

Brown was feeling bouncy for the first time for days. "For that matter, Mr Bennett, how do you know the money will be waiting for you at Amsterdam?"

"Give me some credit, Cassandra. If it's not there before I leave, then I will remain in Geneva."

Brown suggested a cheque.

"No way, honey. Cash, then delivery."

She didn't like the term "honey". It made her feel like a hooker. "OK, how much?"

"Let me see. The price of a ticket from Geneva to Amsterdam is usually six hundred and seventy five Euros, so a transfer of five hundred sterling would cover everything. By the way, I'm looking forward to meeting you. I like your style."

What the hell did he mean, he liked her style?

After making arrangements with the cashiers to wire the cash to Amsterdam, Brown left the office early, picked up a bottle of wine from Tesco's, and presented herself on the Moses' Kentish Town doorstep fifteen minutes ahead of schedule. Chloë did her usual leap into Brown's arms. She carried the child through the house to the garden, where she was treated to a guided tour of a new play tent and an examination of Barbie's latest outfit before sitting down in the evening sunshine at a somewhat wobbly garden bench.

"I raided Adam's cellar for this," said Moses as she emerged from the back door and handed her a glass of chilled Sancerre. By the time they had also finished Brown's more mundane bottle of New World plonk and polished off half a kilo of smoked salmon, the difficulties of each of their days had faded into insignificance.

Flying to meet a contact in an airport lounge was a new

experience for Brown, but getting on an aeroplane while nursing a hangover was troublingly familiar. She arrived at Amsterdam's Schiphol, which was much bigger than she expected, with nearly an hour to spare. After wandering somewhat aimlessly about looking at the numerous shops in the Plaza, getting to know the geography, she went and waited, as instructed, outside the Brasserie. At one o'clock precisely, a small, neat middle-aged man in a light grey suit approached her, his right hand outstretched in greeting. In his left he carried a large black briefcase, of the type favoured by lawyers and airline pilots. He introduced himself as Stephen Bennett.

He sought no confirmation as to her identity. He was, he said, pleased she had come alone, and that if she had tried to bring anyone with her, he would not have caught the flight from Geneva. He claimed it was an essential prerequisite to the trust they needed if they were to do business together.

"How did you know I came alone?"

"I knew before you left London. You are surely aware, Cassandra, that passenger manifests, and even staff lists of organisations such as newspapers, are readily available if one has the right contacts? And I know your office only booked one ticket."

Brown nodded. "Impressive."

"You've been waiting a while. My apologies for being on time." He beamed, no doubt tickled by his own joke.

As a credentials pitch, his was a good one. Bennett remained standing, despite an empty seat at Brown's table. He looked all around him and suggested they move to another part of the airport because too many people already knew they were meeting outside the Brasserie.

Brown followed his gaze, but so far as she could see, nobody was taking the least interest in them. Brown's lips suddenly felt dry. She wanted to stay in public areas, where the presence of others ensured her safety. "I'm not sure I understand you, Mr Bennett. What sort of people? Who? Why?"

Bennett looked over her shoulder, his lips barely moving. "When you are in my business, you have to assume every phone call is being tapped by somebody. And in the present circumstances, Cassandra, you ought to do the same. Charles Elwood is a very determined man, you know."

So he knew Elwood too. Brown's scepticism receded a little. "So where do you suggest?"

Bennett handed her a small brown envelope and without another word walked off in the direction of the check-in area. She watched him disappear among the throng of people that is Schiphol at lunchtime. Only then did she open the envelope. Inside was an airport information leaflet containing a map on which was drawn, in bright orange, a route from where she currently sat to one of the cocktail bars. It finished with a cross and the message "wait here". He was certainly thorough.

Brown finished her coffee and looked at the map long enough to orient herself and memorise the route. She glanced around and, as casually as she could, walked to the area indicated, where the tables resembled huge pink ice-cream cones. Suppressing a fit of the giggles, she sat down. She was beginning to enjoy the cloak-and-dagger world into which she was being drawn. Bennett did not seem particularly frightening or threatening. He was the type of person one could pass every day and never notice.

After a few moments he came to join her, presumably satisfied that any "tails" he may have picked up had been shaken off. He neither offered her a drink nor sought one himself, but perched opposite her.

Bennett began by thanking her for the money transfer, saying that he had managed to get a slightly cheaper fare and passing her a fifty Euro note that he said was in excess of his expenses.

"This shouldn't take long, Cassandra. Do you mind if I call you Cassandra. I take it you're not wired, by the way?"

She didn't know whether to nod in answer to the first question or shake her head to the second, so did nothing. He was not, in any case looking for an answer.

Bennett looked at his watch, and swivelled his head around, glancing first over one shoulder and then over the other, to take in the full 360 degrees before continuing. He appeared to be addressing her shoes rather than her. His grey hair was thin on top, and his spotlessly white shirt was frayed at the collar. His voice was soft. "How much do you know about Warham's financial situation?"

Brown could barely hear him. She mumbled "not much" and waited for him to continue. She touched her necklace, her fingertips tracing the familiar shape of the silver.

Bennett ran his finger around the inside of his shirt collar, as if it were too tight. Maybe this rubbing had caused the fraying. "Tell me", he whispered, "how much?"

"How much what?"

"How much do you know? I don't want to waste time telling you what you know already."

Brown leaned in towards him, meeting a heavy scent of violets, an aroma she had last encountered when she went to see her grandmother in her coffin. The memory made her shudder. "Well, he lives in a smart house in Little Venice, which I guess must be his own. He's got a bundle of WBC shares, I'm not sure how many millions but it's in the annual report. He takes home a million a year or more. He's loaded."

Bennett suddenly sat bolt upright. "Aha" he exclaimed, in such a surprisingly loud voice Brown looked all around to see if he was greeting a new arrival. She again felt the urge to giggle.

"That's what everyone assumes", he continued, "but they, and I am afraid you, Cassandra, are wrong. You should never assume that the external trappings of wealth accurately reflect the reality. What about Robert Maxwell?"

Brown had heard of Maxwell but confessed she could not see the connection. Bennett explained that when "The bouncing Czech", as he was unaffectionately known, fell into the Atlantic from the deck of his £20 million yacht, the "billionaire" left debts of £4.2 billion, despite having plundered the pension fund of the *Daily Mirror*, of which he was the owner. "So you see Cassandra, you should never jump to conclusions where money is concerned."

Where was all this was going? Bennett was clearly warming to his subject and there was little choice but to give him his head.

Again he surveyed the empty tables before continuing, his voice dropping to little more than a whisper. "Did you ever hear, Cassandra, of a British cabinet minister named John Stonehouse?" He didn't wait for an answer. "Stonehouse was involved in a number of get-rich-quick schemes which failed, as a result of which he got into a mountain of debt."

Bennett stopped in mid flow as an elderly Dutch couple came to sit at a nearby table. He waited until they were settled and talking between themselves before continuing. "Anyway, Stonehouse tried to fake his own drowning by leaving a pile of clothes on a beach. About two months later he was picked up in Australia. Not far from where you were born, in fact, at St Kilda just outside Melbourne. Probably at about the same time, Christmas Eve, 1974."

Brown bristled and clenched her fist under the table. She made her voice as cold as she was able. "How did you know when and where I was born?"

"I make it a rule to know as much as I can before I meet people for the first time Cassandra, don't you?"

Of course she bloody didn't. That's why she was sitting in the corner of Schiphol Airport feeling vulnerable and stupid.

Again, he didn't wait for a response. "Anyway, why do I bring up John Stonehouse? Because people sometimes think they can disappear, but very rarely achieve it. Unless, of course, they are dead. Imagine, Stonehouse had changed his name, travelled half way across the world, and was living in a quiet suburb of a major City. He had every right to think he could remain with his secretary in blissful seclusion while his life insurance took care of his debts."

Brown nodded. She was not required to comment.

He stared at the elderly couple perched uncomfortably nearby. Brown found herself mimicking his movements, and looked down. The heels of Bennett's highly polished shoes were very worn.

"And then the police came knocking on his door. He was half the planet away from where he disappeared, but his freedom lasted only weeks. And do you know what was really sad for him? They weren't even looking for him but for Lord Lucan, the aristocrat wanted for murder." He began to rock with mirth. "Stonehouse ended up doing three years for fraud."

Bennett brought his hand up to his face and allowed the palm to slide down from his forehead to his chin. When he withdrew the hand, the grin had gone and his expression was deadly serious. After sneaking one more glance at the elderly Dutch, he again lowered his voice. "Now, I expect you're wondering why you've come here, whether this is some sort of wild goose chase. It's not, Cassandra. What I am about to give you relates to the financial situation of Mr Henry John Warham. I am going to hand you an envelope and then leave you and go to check in for my return flight to Geneva. I have a meeting there at six."

He lifted his huge briefcase onto the tiny ice-cream cone of a table and pulled out a plain manila envelope. The movement attracted the attention of the Dutch pensioners. Bennett pushed the envelope back into the briefcase. He waited, his hand still inside the case, until the Dutch resumed their conversation. Only then did he hand her the envelope. "Please put this into your bag immediately and read it only when you return to London. Wait a few minutes before you leave this table – I don't want us to be seen leaving together."

Brown did as she was told. After five minutes on her watch, which seemed more like half an hour, she walked through to departures to check the next flight to London. The meeting had taken far less time than she had allowed. Out of curiosity, she checked departures for Geneva. A flight had closed and was about to take off. It was unlikely that Bennett could have caught it. She scanned the departure board – the next flight would not get Bennett back to Geneva for a six o'clock meeting. Oh well, that was his problem, not hers. But as she headed towards a self-service cafe to grab a sandwich before checking in, she saw a small neat man carrying a large black briefcase. He was about to go through the exit signed for the railway station.

Brown quickened her step, weaving through the passengers to keep Bennett in view. She had no idea where she was going, or what she planned to do, only that Bennett's story was beginning to fall apart, and she wanted to know why.

Bennett headed for the escalators down to the train station beneath the airport – it was only a few minutes from the airport to the centre of Amsterdam. So why had he asked for a return airfare? She had no idea where he had come from that morning – but he was not going to be back in Geneva at six. But why the elaborate façade? Why hadn't he simply asked for money in exchange for the information, rather than make up a story about an airfare?

Bennett disappeared down the escalator and Brown hurried in pursuit. He paused at the ticket machine and then headed for the platform. The next train for Amsterdam Central was due to leave in seven minutes. She had time to buy a ticket.

As she stood before the machine, her finger poised above the touch screen, she began to feel apprehensive, as if she was being drawn into a trap. Supposing Bennett had deliberately put himself in her line of vision, upstairs in the departures hall, expecting her to follow him?

He seemed unlikely to have made such a fundamental error as to walk through departures at the very time he knew Brown would be there. But even if it were a trap, she would play the game. She touched the "confirm" button on the screen, and as her credit card was sucked into the machine's innards, she heard a familiar soft voice beside her.

"You can't check in here, Cassandra." It was little more than a whisper. She felt a cold feeling in the pit of her stomach, the same as she had felt when Steve told her he was seeing somebody else. There was no need to turn to see who had spoken. That smell of violets.

She could scream – there was a policeman standing not twenty metres away. She was younger, taller and probably stronger than Bennett. Her father had insisted she take self-defence classes when she was a teenager in Melbourne. She could look after herself. In any case, the station was busy with travellers; there was plenty of help near at hand. How could she be in physical danger?

The machine whirred quietly. Brown retrieved her credit card and turned to face Bennett. His arm blocked her path. She reminded herself she was fitter and faster than him. "Excuse me" came out squeakier and less authoritative than she would have liked. She pushed against his arm. As he immediately unblocked her path she saw that in his hand Bennett held a ticket. Brown looked for the first time full into his face, and was met with a smile.

His voice was soft and gentle. "You left this in the machine." He placed the ticket into her sweaty, open hand, but kept a gentle hold on her fingers. She pulled her hand free, but Bennett was still in her path. He looked around, fingered his collar and spoke quietly. "What are you doing down here, Cassandra? Were you following me?"

Brown tried for the high ground. "You told me you were flying back to Geneva, Mr Bennett, or whatever your real name is."

"Yes, that's right."

"So why were you taking the train?"

Somebody came to use the ticket machine, and Brown allowed herself to be guided by Bennett's hand gently pushing on her elbow. He was still smiling, still talking in little more than a whisper. "Cassandra, I really cannot see that is any of your business, but since it doesn't matter I am quite prepared to tell you. First, though, I want to know why you were following me."

Bennett continued to hold her elbow, and guided her towards the train platform. She could hear the sound of an approaching train. There was nothing between her and the platform edge. She wanted to resist, to break free of the gentle grip on her elbow and run. But instead she allowed him to guide her. The noise of the train increased as it entered the station.

Bennett tightened his grip. Was this what it felt like to be a shoplifter caught by the store detective, being marched to the manager's office? With a roar the train sped into the platform. Bennett's grip relaxed and then he let go. Brown turned to face him: he was still smiling. He indicated a bench. As they sat down, he turned to face her. "So?" he said, eyebrows lifting.

She took a deep breath. Her confidence began to return; her legs were no longer trembling. "I was curious. I have all afternoon to return to London. I wanted to see where you were going, because I think you were lying to me when you said you were going back to Geneva."

Bennett sniffed and looked at his watch. "If you really want to know, I missed the two o'clock flight. They wouldn't let me check in — said the gate was already closed. A bit bureaucratic really, but there was no point in arguing. The next flight doesn't get me back to Geneva in time for my meeting."

Brown had recovered her poise. She was the one asking the questions. Bennett was doing the explaining. "That doesn't explain why you were heading into Amsterdam."

Bennett laughed. A noisy belly laugh with more decibels that she believed he was capable of delivering. "But it does Cassandra, it does." He swung his head around, probably looking to see if anyone had noticed his sudden noise, then dropped his eyes and his voice. "I already told you I am working for an investment bank. Because I cannot make the Geneva meeting in person I am going to the bank's offices in Amsterdam to join by videoconference. I will catch the last flight back to Geneva this evening."

He touched her forearm gently, as if she was an old lady. "Now, my train is about to depart, and I know you are booked on the four o'clock flight into London City. I take it you've no further interest in following me into town?"

As she shook her head, he stood up without another word and

boarded the train. When it pulled out of the station, Brown could see him peering into his vast briefcase. She sat rooted to the bench for several minutes, fighting back her tears. She crumpled up the ticket, damp from her hand and then screwed up the receipt – this was one fare she was not going to claim on expenses. Hopefully, nobody at the *Post* would ever know about her humiliation.

When she returned to the departures area, there was not even time for the sandwich she had promised herself. But the trip had not been a total disaster – at least she had the envelope. Fearful the watchful Bennett would suddenly appear at her elbow, Brown abandoned her original intention to open it on the plane. When the stewardess pushed her heavy trolley uphill in the still climbing aircraft, Brown ordered a vodka and tonic, drank it in three or four gulps, leaned back and closed her eyes.

In a taxi picked up at City Airport, she opened the envelope. The first document of the small collection was a statement from a Swiss bank, showing an account with a deficit running to over twenty million Euros. The account was numbered rather than named. She could see nothing to link the statement to John Warham, and she knew enough about the arcane banking laws of Switzerland to know she was not likely to be able to associate a name with the number. She looked at the other document. It was a faxed copy of a Land Registry entry for an address, which she recognised as Warham's house, held not in his own name but in the name of a company. The copy showed there were several mortgage charges registered on the house, but it did not disclose the extent of any debts that might be outstanding. One of the mortgages was in favour of the same Swiss bank that issued the statement. So what? She could have picked this up online from the Land Registry, or had one faxed to her by one of the Registration Agents for a modest fee – which is probably exactly what Bennett had done. Such documents are freely and legally available.

There were some press cuttings relating to company failures. A building company in Birmingham, a publishing venture in London, a property business set up to convert derelict Tuscan villas into habitable homes for wealthy Northern Europeans, a proposed horseracing track in East London. Not one of the reports mentioned Warham. Finally, there was a photocopy of a letter on

WBC notepaper from Charles Elwood to John Warham, marked private and confidential, in which Warham is informed that the relevant committee of the board had considered his request for a loan from WBC, but with regret it had not been agreed. It was dated May 14, shortly before Warham disappeared. It looked as if her trip to Amsterdam had been worthwhile after all.

That evening, she lay in bed trying to put all the pieces together to see if a picture emerged. Who was Stephen Bennett? She had looked up the name on Google, but while there were many people of that name, none of them matched her 'forensic accountant'. She tried to remember every part of the conversation with him.

It was no accident he had talked about Robert Maxwell and John Stonehouse. One had stolen people's pensions, the other had tried to disappear but was caught. Could Warham be in such a financial mess that he staged his own disappearance? He could now be in hiding. With Gonzales? She was still unaccounted for.

Brown got up and went to the open window, looking down on the square. It was past midnight but the light from the moon was strong. The slightest of breezes moved the muslin curtain. She wanted to make her home in London, in Primrose Hill Village, make her stay permanent. Her thoughts of giving up, returning to Melbourne, had been banished by her encounter with Bennett, whom, she was convinced, knew more than he was telling.

Somewhere a dog was barking. Brown was beginning to be relieved she had not publicly nailed herself to the animal rights theory. If Bennett's documents were genuine, and it was still a big "if", then it was at least as likely that Warham had run away from a financial catastrophe which was about to ruin his reputation, as it was he had been abducted.

She watched a cab drop off one of her neighbours and then turned away from the window, going to the kitchen to make some camomile tea. She did not need to turn on the light, as there was sufficient coming in from outside. When she returned to bed, she switched on the radio, leaving the volume at a whisper. When The World Service gave way to a weak soap set in a doctors' surgery, she fell soundly asleep.

CHAPTER TEN

THE TELEPHONE woke Brown at seven seventeen, the BBC's *Today Programme* niggling away in her ear and sunshine flooding into her room. She reached for the phone. Was she aware, the voice asked, that WBC had put out a statement at 7am announcing the death of John Warham?

She sat up straight, swung round to sit on the edge of her bed, knocking over half a cup of cold camomile tea. The floor was wet beneath her bare feet. She pulled a crumpled sheet protectively over her chest. She was wide awake. "Dead? How? When? Who did you say was calling?"

"My name's Kathy Hill and I'm calling from the NBN News business unit. I'm sorry, Cassandra, we don't currently have any further information as to how Mr. Warham died."

"Oh. When was it announced did you say?"

"Twenty minutes ago. Cassandra, the producer wanted to know if you would be free to come into our City studio to talk about the implications for WBC immediately after the 8.30 bulletin? We could send a car to pick you up. Where are you?"

She looked at the clock. Seven twenty. Maybe half an hour to make herself presentable enough to appear on television. She nodded, but the voice from NBN News failed to respond. "Would you be able to do that, Cassandra?"

"What, Oh. Primrose Hill."

"Not far away. So could you come into the studios for a short interview? Shall we send a car at eight?"

"Oh, yes, sure." As she gave her address she was glad she was at least not nursing a hangover.

She pulled on a wrap and went to the kitchen to fix a cup of teabag tea and grab a digestive biscuit. She took several sheets of kitchen roll and mopped up the spilled tea. On the *Today Programme*, somebody was discussing the family life of the prime minister.

It was not until she emerged from the shower that the impact of the news about Warham properly hit her. Until that moment, she had focused as much on the logistics of getting to the television studio on time, and what to wear when her supply of freshly pressed suits was looking distinctly short following her visits to Dublin and Rome, as on the news she had just been given.

John Warham dead! She didn't know how, or when, or where, he had died. Surely his financial problems were not sufficient to drive him to suicide? She needed to find out more if she was going to put on a convincing performance. The programme would be seen in all the dealing rooms of the City, and would eventually syndicate around the world. The last time she had been interviewed, on NBN News, a friend had seen it from his bed in a hotel room in Morocco. Senior people on the *Post* would doubtless see the programme. If she came across well, it was a career-enhancing opportunity. She couldn't afford to fluff it, but she was hopelessly ill-informed.

She looked at the mess in the flat, still strewn with estate agents' details, half-unpacked bags, nude photographs of Gonzales, the papers she had acquired from Bennett and washing up. She had had a busy week, working on other stories. Thank God it's Friday, she muttered, before remembering that she was due to meet friends for tapas and mojitos at eight that evening. They were supposed to be planning a visit to Madrid. It had seemed a good idea when it was first discussed. Now she was not so sure.

She listened to the *Today Programme*'s business update where an analyst was predicting a sharp fall in WBC shares when the market opened. Warham's death was discussed, but the focus was on his involvement with the government rather than WBC. It was another chance for the BBC to query London's ability to stage the Olympics. Brown sighed. Years away, yet the media was already predicting failure. She flicked on the television, where the only reference to Warham's death was a brief mention in the item transmitted from the Stock Exchange. She never really understood why television was so poor at judging the importance of business news. The Australian broadcasters, with far fewer resources, seemed to cope better.

The car arrived just before eight. She put the finishing touches to her make-up, even though she knew she would be made up again for the cameras. The journey gave her the opportunity to concentrate on what she was going to say. Warham had created WBC. The agency had won all the big mandates in the late seventies and eighties, but by the nineties had become a bit institutional. The cutting edge had dulled; its campaigns had become professional rather than memorable. The client list was still as blue-chip as they come, but the multi-nationals driving the new consumer industries – mobile telephones, computer games, computers, cameras, on-line gambling – were not flocking to WBC.

She would almost certainly be asked about Warham's successor, Elwood. Would she be brave enough, she wondered, to say that he was not the future? The girl from NBN had read her the press release, but Brown could remember nothing about Elwood's elevation being temporary. It might have been better, she would say, if Elwood had been appointed chairman and that somebody new had been brought in as chief executive.

She needed to set the agenda for the interview, say something meaningful, and not simply answer obvious questions with equally obvious answers. So she would say WBC needed an injection of new talent and new thinking, which they would be unlikely to find within their own ranks. They needed to find today's equivalent of John Warham when he was in his thirties. Elwood wouldn't like it, but tough. It was not her business to please him, any more than it was his to please her.

Brown was taken straight to make-up and then to the studio, where she was offered a seat out of the way of the cameras but with a clear view of the ubiquitous sofa. A shadow minister who she recognised but couldn't name sat at the other end of the short row of chairs. Neither of them spoke – how could they, given the huge "Quiet Please" sign facing them as they entered the studio? Nobody had mentioned what they wanted her to say, what questions she would be asked. She and the politician were just two ingredients amongst many being processed into a programme. The big studio clock ticked towards eight thirty. The lights were hot on her head – how did the presenters manage to stay so cool?

She had been on television once before, but it was recorded. A live interview was something else. As the news was being read, she was led across to the sofa, had a microphone attached to her suit jacket lapel and the lead tucked round behind her bottom. As she discussed her proposed approach with the producer and the presenter, they all watched the clock. Thirty seconds before eight thirty five, the producer patted her arm and slipped away from the sofa. The presenter pulled down her jacket, straightened her back and put on her smile. Beside the camera, the studio manager counted down the last ten seconds on his fingers. As the second hand hit twelve, a light on the top of the camera flicked on.

Warham's death had been the final item of the news bulletin, providing a ready link to the interview. The presenter read from the Autocue. "With us this morning to discuss the implications of the death of John Warham is Cassandra Brown of the *Post* newspaper here in London. Cassandra, welcome. How do you think the business world will react to today's sad news?"

"It is indeed sad news. John Warham was one of the great figures of the advertising industry, one of the doyens if you like, and his death will come as a shock."

"Is this the beginning of the end for WBC?"

This was the cue for Brown to voice her opinion. "It need not be. It all depends on how the board react, how they take the business forward."

"What should they do, in your opinion?"

"Well, what WBC needs more than anything right now is an injection of new creative talent. Somebody with drive and vision to get hold of the business and grab the many opportunities available. If you like, they need to find the new John Warham."

"Do you have anyone in mind?"

Brown was not prepared for the question, and had no idea who they should appoint. In truth, she was not particularly knowledgeable about the advertising business. She uncrossed and re-crossed her legs. The camera moved back a metre or so.

"Before deciding who, the board should identify the qualities they require. They need somebody with a proven track record, somebody who has already shown they can grow a media business."

"A job for the head-hunters then?"

"Not necessarily. WBC could use its financial strength to take over one of the smaller more thrusting agencies with proven management. That way they would get an injection of new talent across the business, not just a new chief executive. WBC needs to find a new creative urge."

"So are you saying Charles Elwood, who has been named John Warham's successor, is not up to the job?"

Brown smiled in a way that she hoped would come across as knowing, conspiratorial. "I wouldn't dream of saying such a thing."

"Cassandra Brown, thank you for being with us this morning."

The camera moved forward to focus back on the presenter. As the politician was ushered into the vacant seat on the other end of the sofa, Brown was relieved of the tiny microphone, and led gently from the studio. The producer followed her out.

"Fantastic, Cassandra. Just what we needed. We must find an excuse to have you on the programme again."

She was offered breakfast, which she refused, and scarcely twenty minutes after entering the studio she was climbing back into the minicab to return to Primrose Hill. Her nerve had held. She felt she had done well. She wished she had thought to set her video recorder.

As she closed the car door, her mobile rang. Elwood, smooth as silk, considering she had just said, in as many words, that he was not up to the job he had just been given.

"Cassandra, I would just like to say how much I appreciated all that you said about John in the interview. John was indeed one of the greatest admen of his time, and it was generous of you to say so."

Brown did not actually remember saying those words, but let that pass.

"Thank you Charles. Congratulations, by the way, on your promotion."

"My, my, Cassandra, you are in a generous mood. I got the impression, however, that you did not feel I was, I was, how shall I put this, up to the job."

Brown smiled to herself. Elwood was as rattled as he would allow himself to be.

"I just think you took the wrong half of John's job, Charles. I feel you would make an excellent chairman."

"A kind thought Cassandra. By the way, I hope you didn't eat breakfast at NBN."

"I didn't. Why?"

"I was hoping to persuade you to come across to Charlotte Street for some orange juice and a croissant."

"When?"

"How soon can you get here?"

"Fifteen minutes, maybe."

She redirected the minicab from Primrose Hill to Charlotte Street, which elicited a grunt from the driver. She assumed he was a regular driver for the studio, and wondered if he treated his celebrity passengers in the same way.

Elwood's secretary was waiting for her in reception when she arrived. Brown was led past the huge mirrors and even bigger posters from some of WBC's campaigns to the lift. In the spacious fifth floor executive reception area, she was parked on a black leather sofa facing the receptionist. Above the reception desk there was a print of Andy Warhol's Campbell's Soup. More stills from some of the agency's television campaigns decorated the other walls. An office door with "John Warham" on the nameplate was closed. The lights were on and through the translucent blinds she could see movement. The eyes of the receptionist were rimmed red.

After a few minutes' wait, which she judged was deliberately imposed upon her to emphasise just how busy and important Elwood now was, she was taken along to his office. As she entered the room, he moved from his over-sized glass desk to an informal meeting area. She tentatively offered her cheek but he took her hand in a cool handshake. No air kisses for Brown today. Two sofas faced each other across a low table carefully arranged with glossy magazines. A trolley carried a large glass jug of orange juice, a basket of pastries and croissants, tea and coffee in chromium-plated vacuum jugs, two small plates, two cups and two saucers and two starched white napkins. Elwood beckoned to her to sit down. He made for the trolley. "Now, what can I get you? Orange juice? Coffee? A croissant?"

Opting for an orange juice, an apricot Danish and a cup of tea, Brown sat down and waited. For himself, Elwood took only a coffee, and she immediately felt at a disadvantage. If she were not careful, she would end up with jam round her face and crumbs on her skirt. She cut a small corner from the Danish and popped it into her mouth. It never even touched her lips. Elwood watched her every move. "So, Cassandra, a very sad day for WBC and indeed for me personally. John was such an inspiration, such a lovely man. Not an enemy in the world."

"Are you sure about that?

"Cassandra, look, I read your piece the other day about, what was it, so-called dirty tricks. You already know the family's feeling about that story, so I don't need to labour the point."

"Indeed, Charles, I do know the family's feeling. I was talking to Tom about it only this week."

If Elwood realised he had been found out misrepresenting "the family" as he put it, he hid it well. "Your story may be right, of course, but for the life of me I cannot see who might have an interest in blackening the character of such a generous and talented man. What made you think of such a notion?"

"Perhaps an anonymous envelope stuffed with compromising photographs? Can I take it they didn't come from you?" Brown smiled above the rim of the glass of orange juice.

Elwood did his best to look sincere. "Absolutely. Let me be quite clear about this, Cassandra. Quite why you should even think we might stoop to such activities is quite beyond me. Now, having got that out of the way, I thought it might be useful to, yes, useful to take stock of where we are, and where we want to go."

Elwood's fixed stare made Brown uncomfortable. Perhaps he was hypnotising himself, trying to penetrate her defences and look inside her skull. She dropped her gaze and cut another small corner from the Danish. The pastry was stunningly good.

"Have you any idea what happened to John? How he died?"

"I expect you know as much as we do, Cassandra, possibly more. Apparently he was found in the sea below some pretty treacherous cliffs. We have no details. No details at all. Doubtless we will learn more as time goes by. It really is a quite dreadful business, quite awful."

"The question is, Charles, did he jump, or was he pushed?"

He appeared to emerge from his near-trance. "Or did he fall?

They are questions for the Italian authorities, Cassandra, but as I said to you earlier, I was not aware he had enemies."

"What about personal worries?"

"Not that I am aware, Cassandra, although he was upset by the rumours about himself and that model, what was her name, Bia something? Quite unfounded rumours, quite unfair, but you of all people, Cassandra, know how the newspapers thrive on gossip."

He raised his eyes to the ceiling and took a sip of coffee. She added "hypocrite" to lexicon of unflattering words with which to describe him.

He continued. "But the world moves on Cassandra, and we at WBC owe it to our shareholders, and indeed to the memory of John himself, to drive the business forward. That's the message I am anxious to get across to you this morning, and why I thought it might be useful to have a quick breakfast together. As you know, I have been minding the shop quite a bit while John was working with the Government and while he was away on holiday. WBC is in good shape, Cassandra, good shape. I'd like to get that across to the market."

Brown nodded, her mouth being occupied with another piece of the Danish. His monologue bored her. She swallowed hard. "Before we get on to that, is there really nothing more you can tell me about how John died?"

Elwood carefully removed the smile from his face. "Not really, Cassandra. All we know is that he was found yesterday morning, in the sea, not far from where he and Ruth had been staying. He hasn't even been formally identified yet, but there's obviously little doubt. I gather there were some injuries. Such a tragedy. John was so looking forward to taking life a bit easier and seeing a bit more of Ruth and his grand-daughter."

"What do you mean Charles, he was looking forward to taking life a bit easier? Are you telling me John had decided to quit WBC?"

"Clearly, if he had made such a decision and if that had been communicated to the board, and accepted by the board, we would have announced it in the proper way. We are always mindful, as you know Cassandra, of our obligations to the London Stock Exchange."

Why couldn't the man ever answer a simple question with a simple reply? "What are you trying to say, Charles? Had he decided to give up one of his jobs, or perhaps even both of them, or not?"

Elwood retained his *sang-froid*. "What he may or may not have decided, what he may or may not have discussed privately with me, they are irrelevant now, Cassandra. Sadly, we have to face a world without John, and do the best we can for our shareholders. As I was saying earlier, WBC is in good shape." He paused, lowering his voice. "John has not been without his critics, as you know, but he has kept WBC on a remarkably steady course. Despite what you may think about our competence, Cassandra, the ship is well found. Yes, in safe hands."

He rose to signal that the meeting was over. Brown remained seated. Elwood sat down again. Brown tilted her head to one side, a mannerism which she knew was seen as cute when she was a child. "I'm sure it is Charles. I have a rather delicate question about John. Do you know if he was in any financial difficulties at all, whether he'd backed any ventures which have gone belly-up, that sort of thing?"

Elwood walked across to his desk. Brown noticed that despite the air conditioning, there were damp patches forming under his arms. "Really, Cassandra, what are you suggesting?"

Brown had with her the envelope of documents from Bennett, and she briefly considered pulling them out with a flourish, and saying something like 'don't try to bullshit me Elwood'. Instead, she asked if he knew a man named Stephen Bennett. Watching his body language while listening to his denial almost convinced her Elwood was telling the truth. Time to change the subject. "Charles, can I ask you something quite personal?"

"Of course, Cassandra, of course. Though I reserve the right not to answer."

"How long have you been manoeuvring to get the chief executive's job?"

Elwood looked into space, or perhaps at the painting above his desk. Was it really an Edward Hopper? Or was it just a print, like the Warhol in reception?

"How can I answer you Cassandra, without maligning a great advertising man. As you know, the investing institutions, our most powerful shareholders, have been uncomfortable with the roles of chairman and chief executive being in one pair of hands. There had been discussions, shall we say."

"Were you setting up a boardroom coup?"

Elwood laughed. It seemed genuine.

"No. Boardroom coups are for the headline writers, not for WBC. But, as you might imagine, the board did sound out some of our bigger shareholders last night before offering me the job. We can only assume they are happy with my appointment."

"What's your new salary, Charles?"

"Cassandra, such financial matters have not been at the front of my mind, quite the reverse. In due time, my remuneration package will be worked out by the non-executive directors and of course open to scrutiny in the annual report and accounts. Well, if that's all ..."

He stood again and this time Brown also rose, noting with satisfaction that not a single pastry crumb was stuck to her clothes. They walked out of his office into his secretary's anteroom. "Can you organise a car to take Miss Brown on, Shelly. Well, thank you for popping in this morning Cassandra. I did enjoy our little *tête-á-tête*. If you will excuse me?"

He returned to his office and firmly closed the door behind him. Brown declined the offer of a car. She wanted some air, and time to think. And another cup of tea. Back on Charlotte Street, the weather had clouded up and it felt stormy. She stood at the top of the steps in front of WBC's revolving doors and breathed deeply. The scene was entirely normal. One of the biggest names in advertising had died in mysterious circumstances, yet adland carried on as if nothing had happened. A slight breeze moved the heavy air as she walked to a little café favoured by the messengers and drivers. Her tea was steamy and large. With the *Independent* open in front of her, she listened to the chatter around her. She felt an overwhelming sadness at the death of Warham, and distaste for the world about which she had to write. Her thoughts drifted back to Tom and his words about Warham being not just a businessman but also a father and grandfather. She did not finish her tea, but went out into the street to hail a cab. The first spots of rain dropped in big circles on the dusty windscreen as they crossed Tottenham Court Road. Habitat was starting its summer sale.

Baird was walking in circles around his desk as Brown arrived. He did not attempt to disguise his excitement. "So Cass, who did it? Did he jump or was he pushed? Who's in the frame?"

Jill Lambert winked at Brown. " Can I get you both a coffee?"

"Please Jill, strong black no sugar."

"I know how you like your coffee, Curley. Cassandra?"

"Tea, please Jill." The secretary fished the required coins from the pewter tankard, a freebie from a firm of estate agents on their centenary, which served as the news-desk's coffee fund. Brown turned back to Baird.

"Christ, Curley, can't you keep still? You're making me giddy-sick, walking round and round like that."

Baird sat down on the edge of his desk. "I hear you've been on the box this morning?"

"Yes, NBN at 8.30."

"She was very good," said Lambert, returning with the plastic cups of drink in the stained plastic carrier that normally resided on top of Baird's screen.

"That suit really looked good, Cassandra. Armani?"

"No, M & S. What about the shoes?"

Lambert glanced down. "The camera never got to them."

Baird looked from one woman to the other with an expression that said he knew he was being teased. "Now the important business is done, would you mind terribly if Cassandra and I talked about tomorrow's newspaper," he barked, his eyes giving away his pleasure at being the focus of the two girls' attention, "we'll pop into Henry's office."

Neither the City editor nor his secretary had arrived. Baird unlocked the door and switched on the lights, positioning himself behind the desk and laying his clipboard down on Marshall's leather-framed blotter. Brown thought about perching on the corner of the desk but thought better of it and took the chair reserved for visitors. She crossed her legs and leaned back a little.

Baird pulled a heavily chewed pencil from his shirt pocket. "So what have we got, Cass?"

"We have Warham dead in the water at the foot of a cliff. We have Elwood installed as chief executive officer with indecent haste. No doubt we'll have tributes from everybody who thinks it may get their name in the paper. We have no idea whether he fell, jumped or was pushed. The Italians will appoint a magistrate to inquire into his death, which I suppose is likely to be the same one looking into his disappearance. Under Italian law they work in secret."

"What's your theory, Cass?"

"I've really no idea. But he was on the hit list of the animal rights mob. Also, he was involved with that model, Bia Gonzales. He may have had money worries."

Baird sniffed. "Money worries? What, about how to spend it all?"

"Don't be crude, Curley. Look, it could be an accident, suicide, or even murder. I'll get Vittorio to do some checking in Italy."

"Is Scotland Yard involved?"

Brown was becoming bored with his questioning. "Bound to be, Curley. And the private dicks will also be sniffing around."

"What did Elwood say?"

Brown stood up. She wanted to get on with her telephone calls. "He said Warham didn't have an enemy in the world" she started towards the door, "but the way he behaved was hardly the way one would normally treat a friend."

Baird stood up to follow her out. "Fuck. Are you serious? Are you suggesting Elwood had him done in?"

Brown stopped in the doorway. "Not physically, Curley, he didn't have to. He could get exactly what he wanted without resorting to violence. Character assassination. Leaves even fewer marks than a rubber cosh."

Baird continued to follow her all the way back to her desk. "Will you be talking to the son, the one who came in here the other night?"

"I don't think so, not today."

Baird put the chewed pencil in his mouth and spoke through his teeth. "I think you should. He might have something for us."

"Honestly, Curley, I really don't get you sometimes. Don't you think Tom Warham might be just a bit upset, he might be comforting his mother, who's just become a widow, or his daughter, who's just lost her granddad. No Curley, it's not on."

"OK. OK. I hear you. But I want you to play up the mystery angle. So what do we put on the news-list?"

"How about 'unexplained death of top adman'?"

"Unexplained? How very *FT.* What about 'Top adman plunges to death?'

"As you will, Curley. Whatever we say the news subs will rewrite it anyway."

Baird scribbled on his clipboard, looked at his watch, grinned, tucked the clipboard under his arm like a regimental sergeant major and strode off. He was clearly looking forward to being the star of the editor's morning conference.

Brown read through the numerous items on the newswires, and each edition of the *Standard* as it was brought in. For illustration, the *Standard* was using an official studio shot of Warham, sitting shirt-sleeved on the edge of a desk smiling for the photographer. It had dropped any references to Gonzales. No mention was made either of dirty tricks. Or, for that matter, foul play.

She had expected to hear from Vittorio, whom she felt would be best placed to dig around. She left a message on his mobile and when he rang back it was to say he was stuck in Sicily working on a different story, but he would do his best. He said he had heard a rumour that Warham's body showed signs of injury.

When Baird returned from the afternoon conference, it was with the news that, barring any late breaks elsewhere, the Warham story was to be the splash. At the end of a dismal week, Brown was back on the front page.

She was reading through the second of her two stories at about six o'clock when the estate agent rang. Although she had offered the full asking price on the flat nearly a week ago, he could still not confirm it had been accepted. The owner, he said, was abroad. Meanwhile, others had seen the flat and were also very interested. They might offer above the asking price. Isn't that called gazumping, she asked, annoyed by both the interruption and the contents of his message. He sidestepped the question, mumbling that he "quite understood her reaction" and then said he had just "taken instructions" on another very nice flat nearby. Was there no end to the pomposity of estate agents? Lawyers "took instructions" from clients, but not before they had undertaken half a decade of study. Anyone, by contrast, could call themselves an estate agent.

If she was interested, she could meet him at the property at about seven thirty? It too, sounded perfect, but then any property described by an estate agent usually does. An immaculate one-bedroom apartment, huge reception room with solid wood flooring, state-of-the-art kitchen and bathroom in a well-maintained stucco fronted house. Slightly cheaper than the other one. She agreed the appointment, had a final read through her second story and hit the send button. She began to return unanswered telephone calls.

In the taxi en route to Primrose Hill, as the evening sun won ground over the clouds, Elwood finally returned a call she had made to him at lunchtime. He was distinctly cool, but Brown nevertheless asked him about Stratagem's role, and whether there had been any further developments. He was totally unhelpful, but cautioned her against "printing any wild rumours".

"What sort of wild rumours, Charles?"

"None, I should hope, Cassandra."

She had heard more than enough from Elwood for one day. Here was a man who had been plotting to take his colleague's job trying moral blackmail. She gave him no comfort. "Listen, Charles. I'll just do my job the best I can. You can't expect me to give you heads up on what might or might not be in tomorrow's newspaper. Look, I'm about to get out of a taxi. I'll call you tomorrow."

As she looked around the flat, with its little balcony overlooking the garden, she tried to guess what Elwood had been driving at. In the end, she gave up and concentrated on the task in hand. She loved the flat. In fact, she loved it so much she told the agent she was withdrawing her offer on the other property and would pay the full asking price for this one, provided it was taken off the market. She walked the short distance to her home savouring the fresh evening air.

When she got home and had poured herself a vodka and tonic, she called Hogan. He had just heard about Warham on the evening news, and was clearly upset for Tom. She told him about her television appearance and about the flat she had just been to view. Several times during the conversation a bleeping on the line told her somebody was trying to get through. Then her mobile rang. She ignored them both and continued to chat. By the time they finally ended their call after more than an hour, she was looking forward to seeing him again.

A message on her mobile's voicemail told her she had forgotten about her evening of tapas and mojitos. She was not in a mood to give explanations or excuses – with luck her friends would assume she was still working. She changed into jeans and a tee shirt and walked up Primrose Hill, enjoying the fresh smell of wet earth. She could ring and apologise some other time.

SECTION	News1
TITLE	Admandead
HEADING 1	Missing ad man found drowned on Italian Riviera—shares plunge
HEADING 2	Elwood appointed CEO—headhunters to search for new chairman
AUTHOR	Cassandra Brown
STATUS	Live

A body believed to be that of missing millionaire businessman John Warham has been recovered from the sea. The body, which has not been formally identified, was discovered on Thursday by a fisherman on the picturesque coastline of the Cinque Terre.

A magistrate from the nearby town of La Spezia has been appointed to investigate all the circumstances surrounding the death.

The news, announced before the start of trading in London yesterday, prompted heavy falls in the share price. A record number of shares were traded.

A statement from the company, which Mr Warham founded and led for more than two decades, Warham Blazeley Cotts, said the thoughts of the whole company were with the family. He was described as "an irreplaceable leader whom we will miss immensely".

Charles Elwood, the deputy chief executive, has been promoted to the post of chief executive officer. However, the post of chairman, which Mr Warham also controversially held, will remain vacant until a successor can be found.

Mr Warham's body was discovered two weeks after he had been reported missing while on holiday with his wife Ruth. The circumstances surrounding his death last night remained a mystery. WBC would make no additional comment.

The area where the Warhams had been staying, close to the millionaire's playground of Portofino, made famous in numerous films, has treacherous paths above near-vertical cliff faces.

The death of Mr Warham deals a blow to the Government. He was one of its staunchest business supporters, and a leading figure behind the both the successful bid for the 2012 Olympic Games and, a few years ago, the controversial Millennium Dome.

A spokesman for the Prime Minister said he was "very, very sad" to hear of Mr Warham's death. "He will be sadly missed in both business and political circles."

As tributes flowed in, there was a sombre mood at WBC's London headquarters. The blinds in Mr Warham's personal office were lowered as staff worked inside.

Mr Elwood said that WBC was in good shape, and that he "owed it to John to continue to drive the business forward".

It is not yet known how long the Italian authorities will require to complete their inquiries before they release the body for return to England.

Meanwhile, there are unconfirmed rumours circulating that Mr Warham may have had financial difficulties, caused by the falling share price of WBC over the last two years.

CHAPTER ELEVEN

BROWN was daydreaming about how she might furnish her new flat when the stack of Sunday newspapers winked at her again. She sighed and picked up the first of the broadsheets. They had thousands of words but spectacularly lacked any new material; with relief she returned to sorting out the muddle left by too many trips abroad, as she planned her day. It would include a walk across Regents Park to the Conran Shop and possibly a visit to Habitat to see what was in the sale. She wanted to surround herself with sleek sofas, cool tables, and clear glass vases for bright spring flowers. Outside, the square was bright with sunlight, a sharp shadow cutting diagonally across the garden. She was still on the dark side, her turn would come around five o'clock.

Today was hers, her own time. The ironing was still piled in the corner, the fridge needed refilling, and there was a long letter from her lawyer in Melbourne to read. But for once she had time enough to see to it all, to sort everything out.

She had completed her chores and her trainers were half on when Baird rang. "Hi Cass, seen the *Sunday News*?"

"No. Should I?"

"Think you might want to. They're saying Warham was murdered."

Brown remained seated on the edge of the bed. A shiver ran through her. The floor still felt sticky from the spilled camomile tea.

"Christ, you serious? What are they saying?"

"Apparently, everyone at WBC believes he was pushed off the cliff."

"That doesn't make it true, Curley. What else are they saying?"

"That he had enemies."

"Who? Do they mention the ALF?"

"Do they mention who?"

"The animal liberation front. You know, the people I've been trying to write about for the past week, but can't get into the paper."

Baird said nothing for a moment or two. Down the line, Brown could hear his lunch being chewed as he read. "What are you eating?"

"Just a sandwich."

"Bacon and egg?"

"Mmm. Here we are. There's a quote from someone described as a close colleague, who says 'inevitably in business one makes enemies from time to time'. There's also a quote from Met Police saying they can rule nothing out at this stage."

"That all? That hardly justifies a murder claim. Anything sourced from Italy?"

"Not that it says. When can we expect you?"

"Curley, do I have to come in?"

"It'll look bad if you don't. The news editor definitely wants a story on this."

"OK, see you in an hour or so."

Brown put on the other shoe and looked at the pile of ironing. Another day put on hold. In Regents Park Road she bought the *Sunday News* and picked up a cab as it dropped a couple off for lunch at Colette's. How she envied the rest of the world, ambling along looking in the shops, choosing where to lunch, enjoying a glorious summer Sunday. And she was hungry.

"Where to, love?" She gave the cabby the newspaper's address. "Off to work, eh? Some of us have to keep the world on the move, don't we, love?"

Baird's lunch was still only half eaten, lying forlornly on his desk. She looked at the congealed fats and her hunger disappeared. A couple of subs were already at work on the pages, fitting the pre-written features around a few ads. Baird was at his most bouncy as he returned from the afternoon news conference. "You've got the splash again, Cass. The editor wants to lead the paper on Warham's murder."

If he was expecting Brown to jump for joy he was sadly

disappointed. "Except we don't know it was murder, Curley. Christ, what have you promised him? I can't stand up a murder story, any more than the *Sunday News* could. There's absolutely nothing here to back this story up. You've bloody oversold a half-baked story again. Honestly, Curley, now I'm going to be seen as incompetent 'cos I can't substantiate a story that probably isn't true anyway. Look, I'd better go and see the editor and put him straight."

Baird rammed the half-eaten sandwich into his mouth. His eyes bulged behind the large dirty spectacles. He thumped the clipboard down on his desk.

"You'll do no such fucking thing, Cassandra. Not until you've at least checked this out."

For the subs, this was rare entertainment for a Sunday, when the only arguments usually heard at the City desk were about whose turn it was for an early cut and who would collect the coffee. They made no attempt to hide their amusement.

"Let's go into Marshall's office, Cassandra, and see what we've actually got before we go running along to the editor to tell him we can't deliver."

He snatched up his clipboard and stormed across to Marshall's office. The door was locked. He stomped back to his desk, rummaged in his top drawer and produced a key. He unlocked the door and Brown followed him into the inner sanctum they both hoped, one day, to inherit.

The delay in getting into the office had softened his tone, if not his determination. "The way I see it, Cassandra, we've already got plenty to go on. For starters we have the injuries angle which still nobody has covered."

"Possibly because it's wrong. All we have is Vittorio saying he's heard a rumour."

Baird inhaled deeply and ploughed on. "Didn't you say Elwood also mentioned injuries?" He didn't wait for a reply. "And we have the comment to the *News* from somebody at WBC that people there think he was murdered."

"Alleged comment."

"OK. But we also have the Met refusing to rule out anything. You can stand that up as a pretty convincing package, Cass."

Brown picked out the *Sunday News* from the stack of Saturday and Sunday newspapers on Marshall's coffee table. Quite why it was necessary for Marshall to have complete sets of weekend newspapers delivered to his office when he never came to work on either Saturdays or Sundays was a mystery, but at least everybody knew where to find a copy if they needed it.

Brown read the story again. "Look, Curley, sure I can dress up something for the front page. I can play around with the quotes and mix up facts with speculation to make a convincing package. But we are talking about murder, here, Curley, and I don't think we should be speculating on such flimsy evidence. We don't even have the injuries story hardened up."

"Well, it's time it was bloody hardened up. You've been sitting on it for two days. Look Cass, I've got a news-list to print and pages to get out. You know what I want so just get on with it." He turned and marched out of Marshall's office.

Brown sat for a couple of minutes, alone in Marshall's office. She liked it there. Baird was right. She would either have to nail down the injuries story or be in a position to dismiss it. And she was never going to get to occupy that inner sanctum if she told the editor she didn't have the stomach to deliver the story he wanted. On Marshall's computer she called up her emails. Vittorio had called the switchboard at 9.34 that morning. It was time to return the call.

"Pronto."

"Paolo?"

"Si. Chi parla?"

"It's Cassandra, Cassandra Brown. You called me. Why didn't you try my mobile?"

"I assumed you were not working today. I didn't want to disturb you. I was about to call Mr. Baird."

Brown thought back to the previous week. While she had been taking a weekend off he had filed the bullshit story about Warham being seen in Milan with Gonzales. So was this his tactic, to try to sneak stories into the paper under his own by-line when her back was turned?

"Mr. Baird is in afternoon conference. Anything I can do? By the way, I take it there's been no more sightings of Warham?"

Vittorio laughed. It sounded genuine. "You tease me Cassandra. Now I know my story last week was proved wrong, but it was on the wires here and I thought I should at least offer it to your news-desk. Am I forgiven?"

Was she becoming paranoid? Perhaps. "You probably did the right thing, Paolo. Just a pity the story didn't turn out to be true. Anyway, that's so much water under the bridge. What do you have for us today?"

"Well Cassandra, I decided to drive down to Manarola yesterday to see what the gossip might be, and I have learned that Mr. Warham appears to have been beaten before he was thrown into the ocean."

Manna from Heaven. If Vittorio had been there, she would have hugged him, at the very least. "Are you sure? Have you been talking to the magistrate?"

"Better, Cassandra, I have spoken to the fisherman who found the body and alerted the *Vigile*."

According to the fisherman, the body was bloated and in a poor state, but there was no doubt about the head injuries. She had enough to write a decent enough piece for the front page; murder was now looking distinctly possible. And this was a chance to work in something about Warham being a target of the ALF.

Brown asked Vittorio to file all he could, and he in return asked if he could have a joint by-line. "You remember Cassandra, when you were down here in Manarola I told you it was my ambition to come and work in London, or maybe New York. A by-line would help me a lot."

Brown understood. She had had the same ambition. Now she was about to write a story, which would not only lead the paper but also set the news agenda for the following day. But she didn't want to share. She offered a line in black type saying "Additional reporting by Paolo Vittorio." Vittorio agreed – he really was rather sweet.

Brown called across to Baird. "We're OK to run with it Curley."

"For fuck's sake Cassandra, can we now get some copy moving? We could have had this angle two days ago." Baird swung irritably back to his screen and Brown returned to the sanctuary of Marshall's office. She did not shut the door. Within ten minutes, Vittorio's copy arrived, most of which Brown incorporated into her own piece. She called the Metropolitan Police press office, where the duty officer confirmed Scotland Yard was involved with the Warham case and confirmed that nothing was being ruled out.

She tried to call Tom Warham, but his mobile was turned off. When she rang the Warham's London home, somebody told her she must call the WBC press office. She didn't bother. She would try to talk directly to Elwood later.

She had virtually finished the story when Baird appeared with two coffees, slopping the brown murky liquid over the rims of the cream plastic cups. He put them carefully onto Marshall's blotter, spilling more in the process. "Sorry. So, how's it going, Cass?"

"Take a look." Brown swung off the chair. Baird slid behind the desk. The blue of the screen lit his face in an eerie way that made him look like a corpse himself. Brown shuddered at the thought of the battered bloated body being hauled aboard the *Vigile*'s patrol boat. She banished the image and watched Baird's intent face as he scrolled through the piece. He was grunting approval.

Brown sipped the coffee and looked over Baird's shoulder. To her surprise, he appeared to be wearing aftershave. "Vittorio's stuff came almost straight away. He must have already had it written. Good English, too." She was doing her best for him. "By the way, he wants to work here or in New York."

"He can have my job. I'll go and bugger around on the Italian Riviera for a few years until I retire. Only one problem."

"What's that?"

"I'd have to learn Italian."

"When you've finished learning English."

Baird tapped a cheap blue biro against his clipboard, a sign of evident satisfaction, and left Brown alone in Marshall's office once again. Her story finished, she leaned back in the big leather chair, daring to put her feet on Marshall's blotter. She really didn't like those trainers, even if they did have a Prada flash on them. She punched a number into Marshall's squawk box telephone and in an instant Elwood's unmistakable voice filled the room. "Cassandra. How delightful to hear from you. And on a Sunday, too. How unexpected."

"I hadn't really expected to find you at your desk either, Charles."

"But some of us have to keep the wheels turning, don't we? I would have thought you would have been sitting outside somewhere with a glass of chilled Chablis in your hand, rather than calling up business contacts at this time on a Sunday evening."

Was she going to get an opportunity to speak? Not yet.

"By the way, Cassandra, since you are calling, I wanted to say how much we appreciate your measured coverage of recent, what shall we say, events, yes, events. Sadly, quite the reverse is true of your Sunday brethren, quite the reverse."

She picked up the receiver. The loudspeaker clicked off. "I thought the broadsheets would have been to your liking, Charles."

"Indeed. Too kind, probably. I cannot help thinking they may be trying to gain a bigger slice of our media budgets."

"And the *Sunday News*?"

"Ah Cassandra, just when we were having such a pleasant conversation. How two such diverse titles can co-exist within the same organisation, I find quite inexplicable, quite inexplicable."

"That's easy, Charles, they both make money for their owner. Now Charles, I don't want to spoil your evening, but I thought I would let you know that we are running a story tomorrow that John's body showed signs of injury, and that neither the Met nor the Carabinieri are ruling out foul play. I don't suppose you would like to comment?"

"What can I say Cassandra? I would sooner you didn't run stuff like that based on pure speculation, especially when there's family involved, but that's your choice. Your choice. Did you ring simply to alert me, or were you seeking some kind of reaction?"

"A bit of each, I suppose, Charles."

"Cassandra, you know I respect the fact that you have your job to do, and I would be the first to, what shall we say, acknowledge that you are indeed good at it. Yes, a first rate reporter."

Brown nodded absentmindedly.

"But all of us have to be careful that we do not get carried away in our desire to advance our careers, don't you agree?"

"Oh I do Charles. But what were you thinking of particularly?" Irony, or what? It was hard not to laugh.

"What I am concerned about is that if these rumours of foul play are allowed to run around unchecked, it could be quite damaging. Yes, quite damaging. As could, of course, equally unsubstantiated stories about John's finances."

"In what way damaging, Charles? I'm not accusing anyone. And if there has been foul play, as you describe it, then surely it is in the family's interests to uncover the facts?"

"We have no problem with your reporting the facts Cassandra. Quite the reverse, quite the reverse. But supposition? Perhaps you do not always appreciate the power of your pen. All we are asking is that you are mindful of the emotional and even financial consequences for the family of starting unfounded rumours."

Was he trying to give her a bollocking? Well, he'd better think again.

"How do you know the rumours are unfounded, Charles?"

"To be honest, Cassandra, we don't know."

"And who is 'we' in this particular instance, Charles?"

"I'm sorry, I don't seem to follow you." He sounded genuinely puzzled.

"It's quite simple. You said 'we' don't know. Who did you mean?"

"I meant all of us. None of us. The board, the family, the authorities and even possibly the fourth estate, although you and your colleagues seem to have few doubts."

Oh, the sneer. Time to move on. "Charles, what did you mean when you said financial consequences?"

She imagined Elwood picking piece of fluff from an immaculate yellow Cashmere jumper. "Let us consider just two scenarios, Cassandra. The first is the possibility, no I would put it stronger than that, probability, that talk of foul play will damage the WBC share price. As you know, the market can get quite nervous about anything, anything at all, untoward.

"Secondly, we have to look at the question of insurance. We can assume John would have made more than adequate provision for his family. Indeed, his contract of employment with WBC includes a not insubstantial death in service life insurance policy. As you may appreciate, Cassandra, insurance companies need little enough excuse to delay or even repudiate payment of claims."

"I see. And does WBC have a key man insurance policy for John?"

"I wouldn't want to be quoted, Cassandra, but I think you would find it quite normal, quite normal, for companies to take out such insurance on key people. Companies can suffer serious financial consequences if they lose one of their top people."

Baird was making faces through the window of Marshall's office and pointing at his watch.

"Four times salary?"

"I think you would find that normal, quite normal. But all that is background, not for attribution. If you really want a quote, you can say WBC will do everything they can to assist the authorities and bring matters to a speedy conclusion."

Without another word he rang off.

Brown wrote in Elwood's meaningless quote and hit the send button. She cleared away the evidence of her occupation from Marshall's office and went to buy two cups of coffee from the machine. By the time she was back, Baird was making a few minor changes to her piece. He grinned from ear to ear. "The editor loves it Cass, loves it."

"What about the animal rights bit?"

"Not sure he'll go for that, but otherwise, it's spot on."

"Curley. Has he even seen it yet?"

"No, but I read over the intro. He loved it. Thanks for the coffee." He punched the key to dispatch the electronic story to the backbench, that all-powerful trio commanding the heights of the nightly production process.

Brown was determined not to get cross again about the ALF. It was not even worth arguing about any longer. OK, so the *Post*'s decision was flawed. She was not going to be allowed to run it, and that was that. She got her things together to leave. It was only when she passed the editor's office on her way out of the building she saw Cameron's chair was occupied by Pravin, the deputy editor. Pravin the Prawn. Fuck him.

Elwood's mention of a glass of chilled Chablis had taken root, and she decided to walk home, stopping at a bar she liked in Long Acre. The doors of the bar were folded right back on themselves, allowing the air to enter and the noise of the street to flood in. She had no wish whatsoever to rush home to see what, if anything, was in the fridge. She would eat where she was. After ordering her wine and moules and frites, she tried to concentrate on her new flat. She had been denied her trip to the Conran Shop and now she could not think about anything but the Warham story. Was it murder, or had she got carried away, over anxious to please the editor? Was Elwood really concerned about the family, or was he worried about becoming implicated in a plot? The wine arrived at the small round table. Through the open front of the restaurant, she watched people parading up and down Long Acre. A passing girl reminded her of Gonzales – what had been her relationship with Warham? And what might she be feeling in the wake of his death?

The waiter brought her meal. After much re-arranging of the crockery and glassware as flowers, olives, bread, butter and a finger bowl competed for space on the tiny table, a stiff white linen napkin was shaken ceremoniously and placed across her lap with the same reverence as if her jeans had been a Versace dress.

Brown ate slowly, watching the panorama before her, turning the unanswered questions over and over. What about Stephen Bennett? In the excitement of Warham's death and the possibility it might be murder, she had virtually forgotten her visit to Amsterdam. But at least she could discount one of his apparent theories — Warham wasn't faking his disappearance. But it didn't mean his finances were intact — in fact, Elwood's worries about the insurance being paid promptly gave some credence to the documents given her by Bennett.

She removed a mussel from its shell with her fork, gave it a good coating of cream sauce, and popped it into her mouth. Then, putting the fork down, used the first empty shell as the implement to pick up the remaining mussels. The frites she ate with her fingers.

It was nine thirty when Brown paid the bill and wandered into Long Acre. As she sat on the tube on the way back to Chalk farm she realised she still wanted to talk about the story. Discuss where she should concentrate her efforts. Find an impartial view from somebody she respected. Curley? But he'd never been a reporter and would simply drive her towards the next news break, almost regardless of the truth. The real experts at "spin" were not the public relations people, but the nameless journalists, the senior editors and sub-editors, who would take a collection of facts and spin them into a story, then write a headline, which ramped up the story even more. Britain's news media is the most competitive in the world. Headlines sell papers. Equivocation does not. Compare the circulations of the thoughtful *Guardian* with the rabid *Daily Mail*.

As she put the key into her front door she thought of John Douglas. Could she call him at ten o'clock on a Sunday evening? Douglas had had a successful career in journalism before he surprised everybody by moving into public relations.

He was a good enough friend to ask her to call another time if he didn't want to talk. He answered straight away. After the polite preliminaries, Brown asked if he was involved with WBC at all. He was not.

"John, I would love the chance to talk over this John Warham business with you. Any chance I could buy you lunch tomorrow."

"Sorry Cassandra, but I am out of the country all next week. Can it wait? I'm happy to chat now if it's any help."

Brown sat back in her armchair. "That'd be great. If you're sure?"

"Now, what's on your mind? By the way, it's a hell of a story. What are you running tomorrow?"

Brown suddenly felt embarrassed. "It could be murder."

"And could it?"

"Possibly. Apparently the body was quite badly injured."

"Why? By whom?"

"Don't know. But was on the animal rights hit list."

"Then isn't that what you should be concentrating on?"

"Not easy, John. Do you know Pravin, the deputy editor?"

"Pravin the Prawn? Yes, of course."

"Well, he's dead set against us running the animal rights angle and Cameron is backing him up."

"I can see his point, but it must be frustrating. OK, so where else can you look?"

"Well, I spoke with Elwood this afternoon. He was batting on about not upsetting the family and about the insurance implications."

"Do you have contact with the detectives he's using?"

"Are you kidding? They can't even tell the family anything."

There was a pause.

"Would the *Post* send you to Italy?"

"They already did. They would again."

"Then get on a plane and go. Go where the action is. Make use of your local man's contacts."

"But I don't want to miss out on what's going on here, John. I'm up against the *FT* who had three people working on it before he was found dead. God knows how many they've put on it now."

"The trouble with *FT* reporters is they always think they know best. You can beat them by plugging into the networks that have already done the legwork. The Italian police, Elwood's spooks, the family. Anyone else you can think of."

"I can't get near the detectives. Elwood's put them under strict orders...."

"Do you know their names?"

"No."

"Who does?"

"Tom Warham must. He's been interviewed."

"Then call him up and get a name. Then call Stratagem and ask to speak to them by name. Tell the switchboard it's a personal call. Once you get through, if they think you know something they'll talk to you alright, no matter what Elwood says."

"Douglas, you're great. Why did you give up journalism? I'd love to have been able to work with you."

"I needed a pension. By the way, I bet WBC's got a thumping great key man policy on Warham."

"Elwood as good as admitted it."

"There you are, then."

"There you are what? I don't understand."

"That's an easy one for tomorrow. Find out who the insurers are. There's only a handful of syndicates write key man on the sort of scale we're talking about here."

"Will they try to repudiate the claim?"

"You bet. Key man could be three or four times salary. Warham was probably on around a million, maybe a bit more. That's possibly five million they've got at stake. You bet, if they can get out of it they will."

"Can they?"

"If there's a suggestion of murder, payment simply won't happen at least until after the inquest. The same's true of suicide. Work it out. And the joy of going in on the insurance angle is that while the rest of the Street is chasing around playing catch up, you can be on a plane to Italy."

"John. That's fantastic. I'll get that going first thing. Now, there was something else I wanted to talk to you about. I had this call from a man calling himself Stephen Bennett who said he had some documents I might like to see."

"And?"

"He persuaded me to go to Amsterdam to meet him. So I went over on Thursday and picked up this envelope with bank statements and so on, but I've no idea if they are genuine. And even if they are, they were probably stolen."

There was another pause, long than the previous one, before Douglas answered. "How much did you pay him?"

"Nothing. All he wanted was his expenses."

Luckily, Douglas didn't ask how much they were. "Bank statements? What else?"

"Some press cuttings, and a Land Registry entry showing a string of mortgages secured on Warham's house. And best of all a letter from Elwood turning down a request for a loan. John, if they are genuine, Warham was in deep financial shit. I've checked the Land Registry online. It's genuine."

"It doesn't mean it's all genuine, though, Cassandra."

Brown and Douglas enjoyed a couple of minutes of newspaper gossip before ringing off. He had clarified where to concentrate her efforts: Warham's finances.

She was too excited to go straight to bed, so took a bath, put on her pyjamas and once again read the details of the flat she was already thinking of as 'hers'. On the television, BBC News 24 showed the *Post*'s front page led by her story. 'Ad chief may have been murdered'. She could just make out her by-line. She hoped the editor was watching.

But while it looked increasingly as if his financial problems may have driven Warham to suicide, he could hardly have beaten himself up.

SECTION	News1
TITLE	Murder
HEADING 1	Ad chief may have been murdered
HEADING 2	Eye witnesses say body was badly beaten
AUTHOR	Cassandra Brown
STATUS	Live

Millionaire businessman John Warham was beaten before he was drowned, sources close to the investigation believe.

The body of Warham, 58, was recovered from the Mediterranean on the Italian Riviera last week, two weeks after he disappeared from a holiday hotel.

A post mortem examination of the body is believed to have shown a number of injuries, which are thought to have been inflicted before his death.

An eyewitness who saw the body being hauled from the water said there were clear signs of Warham having been beaten up.

Neither the investigating magistrate in Italy nor Scotland Yard will rule out the possibility that the advertising guru was murdered. Police are thought to be working on the theory that his death was made to look like an accident.

Warham, one of the key figures behind the controversial Millennium Dome project and more recently London's successful bid for the 2012 Olympic Games, was close to the government. The Prime Minister has instructed officials at the British Embassy in Rome to provide every assistance to the Italian authorities.

Warham had been enjoying a holiday walking in the picturesque "Cinque Terre" ("Five Lands") in Italy when he disappeared. The alarm was raised when he failed to return to his hotel after an early morning walk. It is understood that Italian police were alerted by the British consulate in Rome after a tip off from the Foreign Office.

There has been speculation that Warham may have been

kidnapped for ransom. The discovery of his body last week in the sea suggests that if it was a kidnap operation it was bungled.

Friends in London say that they knew of no reason why Warham should have become a target. Charles Elwood, who has taken over as chief executive of the advertising giant WBC, which Warham founded, promised the firm's "full co-operation" with investigators.

In Italy, details of the investigation are, by law, secret. However, sources close to the investigation say they are working with Scotland Yard to try to establish a motive for murder. His name was listed on an Internet web site connected with animal rights activists.

A case of mistaken identity has not been ruled out. A formal identification has yet to take place.

Local people and tourists in the Cinque Terre, which covers a dramatic section of the Ligurian coastline, are shocked at the death of such a high profile visitor. The local economy depends heavily on tourism from the United States and any suggestion that it is not a safe destination could have a serious effect on hotels and tour operators.

The fisherman who found the body has been extensively interviewed by the Caribinieri, **writes Paolo Vittorio from La Spezia.**

He is understood to have told fellow fishermen that the corpse was showing serious head injuries and that his right arm appeared to have been broken. His clothing was torn.

A spokesman for the investigating magistrate would only confirm that a body believed to be that of John Warham had been recovered from the water and that a full examination would be carried out by the pathologist from the regional hospital in La Spezia.

CHAPTER TWELVE

MONDAY morning. It was nearly three weeks since Warham had gone missing. Baird was parading around the office with his chest stuck out. On Brown's desk was a white envelope.

She opened it and a grin spread across her face:

Congratulations on an excellent splash this morning. We lead the field with this story. Keep it up. The chairman has authorised the payment of a bonus of £500 in recognition of your contribution. This will be included in your June salary.

Baird stopped in front of Brown's desk. "Herogram?"

"Better than that, Curley. Herogram and a five hundred quid bonus. That'll almost pay for my trip to Dublin last month."

"For a story you didn't want to write? I think you can buy me lunch."

"Fair cop mate. The beer's on me. Now, what are you looking for today?"

"What've you got?"

"I think I can stand up a good insurance story."

"Doesn't sound very exciting. Got anything else? I almost forgot. How did you get on in Amsterdam?"

"Christ, Curley. Will you just listen for a moment? There could be eight to ten millions of insurance on Warham's head, and if the underwriters can wriggle out of paying, they will."

"Can they get out of it?"

"They can try."

"How. Isn't he dead enough for them?"

"I don't know. But the bastards'll think of something."

"I'll put it down as multi-million insurance claims in doubt."

Baird continued his rounds of the office, collecting stories to list on his clipboard for the morning conference. Amsterdam seemed forgotten again.

Brown was staring into space, wondering how to start firming up her story when Greg Jones eased himself down into the empty chair opposite her. He congratulated her on the story and asked what she was hoping to write for Tuesday's paper.

Passed over many times for elevation into the top job, Jones was in his late fifties and too generous to be resentful of the progress made by his younger colleagues. He was a sartorial and physical disaster, but could turn his hand to any story and his contacts book was the envy of the office. Brown told him what she knew about the insurance angle, which didn't amount to much at all.

Jones was so deep in thought for about a minute before speaking that Brown feared he might have nodded off, which he was certainly apt to do after a particularly good lunch, but not at eleven in the morning.

"Mmm, Lord Aldington" he said at last.

Brown smiled, her incomprehension complete. "Say again." As she looked at Jones, she imagined she could see his intricate brain whirring just under the thin skin of his bald, domed, head.

"Lord Aldington. He was chairman of Sun Alliance Insurance when it refused to pay out on the death of a man called Watts. Watts' brother dedicated his life to a wonderful campaign of vilification of Lord Aldington and in the end was arrested for libel. Sun Alliance's defence of its refusal to shell out was that all material facts had not been disclosed."

"Would they be able to claim that in this case?"

Jones lifted his arms and clasped his hands behind his head. "I've no idea, Cassandra. But let me hypothesise for a moment, which might help you. If it was murder, they will delay payment for as long as possible, preferably until somebody is charged and convicted."

Jones pulled out the bottom drawer of the desk and rested both feet on it before continuing. He was clearly enjoying himself. "Because in law, as you know, the perpetrator of a crime must not gain financial benefit from it. Now, until somebody is charged and convicted, the insurers do not know for sure who did it. But they do know that a juicy insurance policy can be a powerful motive for murder. Mrs Warham, as I understand it, was the last to see the deceased alive. She would also be a beneficiary of the insurance. The insurer would take no chances."

"Cunning bastards. You mean they suspect her?"

"Cassandra, you are not listening. Whether they suspect her or not is immaterial. What they need is an excuse to hang onto the dosh for as long as possible. That's how they make their money, hanging on to what rightly belongs to somebody else."

"Are you having me on?"

"I'm deadly serious," replied Jones, a suspicion of a smile playing around his lips.

"What about suicide?"

"Depends on the policy. Normally excluded if it is within a year of the policy being taken out. But let's look at another possibility. We don't know whether our friend jumped, fell or, according to the papers, was murdered. Suppose he fell. Suppose he fell because he suffered from vertigo. And suppose he hadn't told the insurance company."

"Oh, I get it. Failure to disclose a material fact?"

"You've got it." He didn't add the words "at last", for which Brown was grateful.

"So it looks like there's no way they are going to pay out quickly."

"That's my reading. Who are the insurers?"

"No idea, Greg. Any chance you might be able to help me find out?"

"I'll ask around." Jones kicked the drawer shut, pulled himself out of the chair and ambled back to his own desk.

Five minutes later he was back. "It's at Lloyd's." He gave her the syndicate number. The public relations office of Lloyd's appeared to be helpful, confirming all the principles Jones had told her, but they would not discuss the individual case. She then rang the syndicate direct. Somebody took her name and number and promised somebody else would call her back.

She had, however, all she needed to build a credible story. It was clear there would be no quick payouts and she could speculate around the figures and come up with an eye-catching number, which she would not feel any misgivings in inflating to "up to ten million pounds."

She was testing a couple of trial introductions when she took a call from Andrew Clarke, senior director of one of the City's top public relations agencies. "Great story this morning, Cass."

"Thanks Andy. By the way, it's Cassandra."

"Sorry. Know what you mean. I prefer Andrew."

"What's your interest Andrew?"

"No direct interest Cassandra, but one of my chums runs a certain syndicate at Lloyd's, specialising in group life and key man insurance. High-end stuff. He said you'd called and he asked if I could have a word with you."

"What's he trying to hide?"

"Nothing so far as I know, Cassandra. He's just not used to dealing with the press. You know how private these Lloyd's boys are."

"Do they insure WBC?"

"Can we establish terms of trade, Cassandra? We can say nothing on the record, and our answer when asked to comment will always be no comment. But as I explained to my friend, it is in nobody's interest that incorrect stories appear for want of a little co-operation, so I offer myself as a humble middle-man."

"Humble, Andrew, not you."

Clarke ignored the comment. In the course of the next ten minutes, he confirmed "off the record" that the syndicate did insure WBC, both for key man and for "death in service", the beneficiary of the latter being Ruth Warham. He also said his client would not be upset if she speculated that each policy could be around four times salary. When asked whether the syndicate would withhold payment, he became rather vague, but did confess that with the death having taken place in, as Cassandra herself had pointed out, rather mysterious circumstances, "it could take some time to sort things out".

Pressed, Clarke admitted, "a quick payout should not be expected." Bingo!

As she put down the phone, it rang again. The estate agent said her offer on the flat had been accepted. It was only just after midday, the flat was as good as her's, she had the bones of a cracking story and the editor had given her a £500 bonus. Quite a start to the week.

She needed to call Vittorio.

"Pronto."

"Ciaio, Paolo. It's Cassandra in London."

"Ah Cassandra. We did well this morning, I think. You sound happy."

"I sure am Paolo. Anything new?"

"I shared a glass with the magistrate last night. He is intrigued about Mr Warham's injuries. And he's hoping to appoint a pathologist today. A doctor from Milan or Rome."

"Has there been a formal identification of the body yet?"

"The magistrate has asked the consulate to organise Mrs Warham or maybe her son to come to La Spezia for identification. I am not certain when that will happen."

"Paolo, that's great. Can I call you back later? Curley will want a story about the pathologist. I'll let you know how many words."

Brown sensed, or perhaps heard, somebody behind her. Baird was back from morning conference and was standing behind her desk. He nodded in the direction of Marshall's office. As walked the length of the floor to the glass-walled office, she imagined she could feel Baird's eyes on her backside. Try as she might, she could not walk normally.

Marshall's secretary was ensconced in lonely splendour. She had opened Marshall's post, checked his supplies of mineral water and had nothing else to do except answer the telephone until the boss arrived.

"May we?" Baird asked her, gesturing towards the inner sanctum.

"Sure, coffee?"

"That'd be great."

Baird was still as chirpy, or perhaps even more so, than he had been before morning conference.

"Hope you've got something good, Cass, the editor's given us an extra page. Sport are livid. Anyway, we've still got the piece from Will Wyatt sitting on the overmatter and the piece about kidnap..."

"We can't use the kidnap piece, Curley."

"Why?"

"Cos he wasn't kidnapped, Curley. Cos he fell off a cliff for Christ's sake, remember?"

Baird reddened, but his good humour was undiminished. "He could have been kidnapped first, and then been thrown off the cliff ..."

"OK, Curley, you win. I'm sure you can tart it all up a bit."

The coffee arrived and with it the news that Marshall was just parking his car and would be arriving in a few minutes. "We'd better get out then, I 'spose", said Baird, looking ruefully at the steaming china cup on the little black tray.

"Not at all. He wants to see you both as soon as he arrives so you may as well stay here."

Baird turned his attention back to Brown. "I thought we'd get a bleached-out portrait shot of Warham, in profile if we can find one, and run a package under the strap-line 'The Warham Mystery'. The Editor loves the idea. I've asked the art room to get up a map of where in Italy he was found. Nobody there has heard of the chinky whatnot ..."

"Cinque Terre."

"Whatever. We can use that picture of him and the model at that party with the personality piece with a juicy caption. I'll get the subs to get up a chronology from the day he disappeared right up to today, and lead the page with your insurance angle."

"Ah, Curley, I gather you got the extra space for your Warham Mystery page." Henry Marshall had arrived quietly at his own office. He took his own chair behind the desk and his secretary poured a coffee and placed it before him. "I spoke to the Editor first thing this morning. He is very happy with the way we are handling this story and responded very positively to my suggestion of a whole page. The question is, my young friends, have we enough good stuff to put in it?"

Baird began to run through his ideas again as Marshall turned his Mont Blanc fountain pen over and over between his fingers, nodding in an apparent show of wisdom.

Marshall sipped his coffee, put the pen carefully alongside the blotter and laced his fingers, tapping his thumbs together. "Nice package, Curley, nice package. Now, what do we put at the top of this wonderful page? By the way, we are running an obituary on the obits page. I will write that myself. Now, tell me about the insurance angle."

Baird sighed with evident relief when Marshall looked to Brown for the answer.

"Well, Henry, I have a pretty strong line. Warham was heavily insured, both on the key man front and death in service. There may well be other, private, insurances but even without there's around ten million on his head. And you will not be surprised to hear that the Lloyd's syndicate is not at all keen to pay out, so there could be some heavy delaying tactics."

"Tell me something, Cassandra, why do you think Charles Elwood is so keen to get that story out?"

"Is he?"

"Well, I had breakfast with him this morning. He mentioned you had shown interest in the insurance arrangements. Now then, what was it he asked me to tell you? I remember, it was, 'tell Cassandra she is pushing on an open door'."

"I don't know, Henry. What do you think?"

"Perhaps he hopes the publicity will put pressure on Lloyd's for a quicker pay-out. But be that as it may, it is a strong story and certainly the page lead. The editor will, I am sure, take a cross-ref on the front. Anything else?"

"Yes. I was talking with Paolo Vittorio a few minutes ago. The magistrate is calling in a top pathologist because he's not happy about the injuries to the body. It seems Vittorio's got quite a good angle there. Oh, and the body hasn't been formally identified yet."

"We'll need to be careful with that one, Curley. Charles, Charles Elwood that is, seems particularly sensitive about the possible causes of death. But don't let that worry you. Just be especially sure that we get the facts right ..."

"I always do. Henry, really, what are you suggesting?"

"Perhaps I was addressing the rather enthusiastic tendencies of Mr Baird, here. Not too much spin, eh, Curley?" Marshall smiled, emptied his cup and rose, suggesting the discussion was over.

Baird turned and stalked out of the office, returning to his desk without a further word. Brown followed, putting her cup back on the tray as she passed and picking up a chocolate digestive biscuit. At the door she stopped, half turned, and addressed Marshall.

"If the message from the editor was anything to do with you, Henry, many thanks."

Marshall smiled. He seemed happy to take the credit, whether it was due or not.

She followed Baird to his desk. He was clearly irritated. "The Editor is very happy with the way we are handling the story, is he? Well, I don't remember Mr. Henry Marshall having anything whatsoever to do with the way we are handling the story. Bloody cheek. Not a peep out of him all weekend when we are slogging our guts out, then he takes the fucking credit."

"Curley, I think the editor knows who was responsible. Just calm down. If you give me ten minutes to paint my face I'll buy you that steak and chips at the Port Wine Club."

Baird's face cracked into its familiar smile as she slipped him the chocolate digestive taken from Marshall's coffee tray. "Thanks. I'll just call Vittorio to give us four hundred on the pathologist angle, and I'm ready to rhumba."

Brown looked at herself in the harsh cloakroom mirror, and could not help smiling. Five hundred quid bonus, a great story already in the bag, her offer on the new flat accepted. And it was still only Monday lunchtime. But she had not faced her daily call from Elwood yet. Presumably, he felt he had achieved whatever it was he wanted to achieve by smooching her boss over breakfast.

SECTION	News1
TITLE	Warhaminsurance
HEADING 1	Insurers set to delay payment on Warham claims
HEADING 2	
AUTHOR	Cassandra Brown
STATUS	Live

Payment of millions of pounds of insurance claims on the life of John Warham are set to be delayed by the insurers.

The *Post* understands that there are at least two multi-million insurance packages which are likely to be disputed. Each is for a multiple of four times the late Mr Warham's salary.

Until his recent death, Mr Warham was chairman and chief executive of Warham Blazeley Cotts, the advertising agency he founded thirty years ago. His body was discovered last week in the sea near La Spezia, on the Italian Riviera.

According to the latest annual report and accounts, Mr Warham was paid £1.3million in the last financial year, of which over £700,000 was in the form of a bonus.

The beneficiaries of the disputed insurance claims are WBC itself under a so-called "key man" policy and his widow, Ruth Warham.

"Key man" policies are frequently taken out by companies to cover the costs of disruption and finding a replacement for key personnel should they die suddenly while in office. Typically, they are for about four times the executive's annual salary. A source close to the company confirmed that Mr Warham's policy was of that order.

A personal life insurance policy, a so-called "death in service" policy was part of Mr Warham's remuneration package, it is understood. The proceeds of such policies usually go to dependents.

The policies were written at Lloyd's of London, which boasts it has never failed to meet a valid claim. A source close to Lloyd's confirmed yesterday that the same syndicate wrote both policies.

The insurers will want a much clearer idea of the circumstances surrounding Mr Warham's death before agreeing to meet the claims. Under the terms of the policies, there are various clauses to which the underwriters could point to delay or even refuse payment.

These include the possibility that not all material facts were disclosed to the underwriters at the time the policy was taken out. For instance, if it is thought that Mr Warham fell from a cliff path into the sea where he was found and if he suffered from dizzy spells or vertigo the insurers could be within their rights to refuse to pay. Mr Warham was known to be on certain medication unavailable in Britain.

More controversially, if it was believed that Mr Warham was murdered, the insurers would want to see any beneficiaries eliminated from the investigation before paying out. Under English law, a criminal may not receive financial benefit from his or her crime.

The syndicate will also want to see suicide ruled out before agreeing to make payment. Although suicide does not in itself invalidate a claim, most policies include a designated period, usually one or two years from the start of the policy during which they will not pay. This is to stop people contemplating suicide from taking out large policies in order to provide for their dependents. This would amount to fraud.

A source said yesterday that there were so many unexplained circumstances surrounding Mr Warham's death that a quick payout should not be expected.

In the event that payment is refused, or even substantially delayed, all sides are likely to resort to the courts.

CHAPTER THIRTEEN

BROWN returned home depressed. Perhaps it was just a sense of anti-climax, or possibly the glass of champagne that Baird had insisted they drink at lunchtime. He had even paid for it, though she had bought lunch. But something else nagged at the back of her mind, which she could not quite bring forward. She looked around the flat, which, considering how busy she had been, was pleasingly tidy.

Showered and once again in jeans, tee shirt and trainers, she poured a glass of Evian and carefully sliced a lemon. The sense of unease was less, but still with her.

She picked up the envelope containing the photographs of Gonzales, and spread the pictures out on the floor. The glamour shots were simply that, glamour shots of the kind that virtually every young model does to kick start her career. Some were perhaps a bit more graphic than they needed to be, but photographers could be very persuasive. She began to put them away, but then stopped, and left them on the floor.

Careful examination of the 6x4 snaps revealed more than the first impression conveyed. In one, what at first sight looked like a simple conversation taking place, albeit with one of the participants stark naked, could have been a row between them. Warham's face had a reddish tinge, not present in the other photograph, and his chin was stuck out. His mouth is open to speak. His arms are by his sides, but one hand is visible. His fist is clenched. Gonzales looks downcast, her head bent, staring at the ground. The fur coat is clutched to her chest defensively. In the background is the paraphernalia of a photo-shoot – lights, tripods and the boxes in which the gear arrived. A girl holding a clipboard is pointedly looking away from the couple.

Brown poured herself another glass of water. So what was it, a professional disagreement or a lovers' tiff? No matter how long she stared, she couldn't decide. The other snap was also interesting. Both Gonzales and Warham are looking towards the camera. Gonzales' expression is bland, but Warham looks less than happy. Had they been taken by surprise, or were they were being photographed against their will? The quality of both photographs was good, although not of the standard of either the glamour shots or the stills from the ad campaign. The pictures had a flatness about them, a lack of depth. Brown thought they might have been taken using a cheap camera – maybe a throwaway bought on the spur of the moment? She wanted to test her theories on an expert, but if she called any of the photographers at the *Post* they would need to see the pictures. She was not ready to share these with her newsroom colleagues. Kate Moses! Hadn't she studied photography at art school before switching to law?

Moses' interpretation of the relationship between Warham and Gonzales could also be useful. As a family law practitioner, Moses had seen more than her fair share of relationships between mature men and young women. Normally, but not in every case, she would act for the wronged wife and had, in the process, acquired a cynicism about the male species which made her a formidable opponent. Her clients usually emerged from the divorce process with comfortable financial arrangements.

Brown was relieved to hear Moses' voice at the end of the phone. Moses teased her a little about Hogan and, rather oddly, about Alex. She asked how the trip to Amsterdam had gone. Finally, Brown broached the subject of the photographs.

"Did I tell you about the photographs I received?"

"Yes. Have you discovered anything about them yet?"

"No. But I would love somebody other than me to take a look at them, and for all sorts of reasons I don't want to take them to the office."

"OK. Where do I come in?"

"You know a bit about photography, don't you?"

"A bit. Not much. I also, by the way, know a bit about the Warhams."

"You're not acting for anyone involved?"

"No, more's the pity. I gather the Warham's were having some sort of problem. We were actually looking forward to acting for one or other of the parties if they'd finally blown apart."

"Is that what you guys do? You're just ambulance chasers."

"Let me tell you. Every Monday morning we have a partnership meeting, and one of the standing items on the agenda is possible new business. Our press cuttings agency sends us all the gossip column pieces about marriages in trouble. The Warham's were already on our watch list."

"You bloody vultures."

"That's enough insults from you, Cassandra. Now, tell me about the pictures. First of all though, how again did you get them? They're not stolen, I hope."

"No idea, to be honest. As I said, they arrived in an anonymous package the morning I went to Rome."

"Has anyone owned up to sending them?"

"No. But I've not advertised the fact that I have them."

"Cassandra, what planet are you on? You wrote about them, remember?"

"Yes, but I didn't actually say I had them. I said they had been circulated anonymously."

"The subtlety of the distinction passed me by, darling. Anyway, who knows you've got them, other than me, you and your two million readers?"

"Curley, my news editor. And, oh, Charles Elwood."

"Why did you tell him?"

"I asked him if he'd sent them. He denied it, of course."

"Of course. Hey, listen, I've just got to put Chloë to bed and then I was thinking of opening a bottle of something. Do you fancy dropping round to help me drink it? Adam's away."

"I was hoping you might say something like that. I'll bring the photos with me."

"You'd better. And you can tell me all about Amsterdam."

"I'll bring you the package I picked up there, shall I?"

"Great. See you in what, half an hour or so?"

Kentish Town is one of those inner London areas always ready to "come up" but never quite making it. But the Moses had a beautiful, spacious house in a tree-lined road and Brown loved to visit. It had so many times provided a soft landing from the hard worlds of business and newspapers. The house smelled of good food, alongside the unmistakeable scents of childhood. The furniture was big and comfortable. The Moses were the closest Brown came to having a family in London, and she could never quite decide whether she felt more, or less, homesick after a visit. The walk there took precisely thirty minutes. Brown's finger was about to push the bell when Moses opened the front door. "Would you mind popping up to see Chloë, I promised her you'd go and say goodnight when you arrived. I'll get the corkscrew."

Brown hugged her friend and thrust an envelope into her hand before bounding up the stairs to see the four year old. She wanted to give Chloë a hug as much as Chloë wanted to see her. The new dress and trainers Brown had bought for her in Rome were beside her bed.

By the time Brown came down, the wine was poured and the photographs spread across the polished wooden floor. Moses handed Brown a glass and sat back on her heels. "It's not so many years since pictures like these were used as evidence in divorce cases, you know. Grubby little men would arrange meetings in miserable hotels, often with women the husbands had never met, to take pictures to show a judge. Thank God it is a little bit more civilised now."

"Only a little more civilised. They still have the money to argue about."

Moses picked up one of the carefully posed nude shots. "I see what you mean about the pictures, Cass, quite an interesting portfolio. She's quite a girl, but then, they usually are."

"Models?"

"No, well yes, but I was thinking more of mistresses." As the two chatted about Dublin, and Rome, men and their infidelities, children, holidays, work, Moses stared at the two snaps in turn. She went to an old wooden sea chest in the bay window of the dining room and brought out boxes of photographs. Finally she seemed to find the ones she was looking for and set them beside the two 6x4's.

"Look at these Cass, and then at yours. Can you see the similarity? They have the same sort of compressed perspective, as if everything is very close together. There's a slight blurring to the background."

At last, Brown could see what had been troubling her. She nodded for Moses to continue.

"Those pictures of mine were taken using a long lens from about 100 metres. I think that's what your snapper used."

In unison the two women came to the same word. "Paparazzi".

Once they had recovered from a fit of the giggles, Brown stared again at the pictures. "Only one problem, Kate. In the beach shot they seem to be responding to the photographer. They wouldn't do that if he was 100 metres away."

"But suppose there was somebody else much closer. I once had a case where that technique had been used – the long lens caught the couple full face when they answered a seemingly innocent request for directions."

"What was the case about?"

"I was afraid you would ask me that. It was blackmail."

Brown took a gulp from her glass and sat back on the floor, tipping her head right back until it rested on the soft seat of Moses' sofa. "Phew, blackmail. That could explain it all."

"Cass, don't be daft. All I'm saying is that a long lens may have been used. That's all. You can't jump from that to blackmail. How much have you drunk?"

"But don't you see Kate, Warham wouldn't have wanted these pictures shown around."

"So why did he agree to be seen with her at the party?" Moses stood up and fetched the bottle. Brown held out her glass.

"Kate, you're still not getting it. If he was being blackmailed, what better way of reducing the street value of this lot than by going public with Gonzales. It's like saying, 'look, I've got nothing to hide. The whole world can see me with Bia for all I care'.

Brown picked up the glamour shot taken on an elegant staircase. She knew that staircase from somewhere, but couldn't place it. She put it down again. "The guy was a mess. But the question is, have I got enough to run a blackmail story?"

"No way. It's nothing more than a theory dreamed up after half a bottle of wine."

"Legal experts believe he may have been blackmailed?"

"Nope. Look, you've got to do a lot more work here before it makes sense. And why should a blackmailer send you the pictures?"

Brown kicked off her shoes and wriggled her toes. Her toes were way too scruffy for a glamour shot. "Perhaps the pictures were worthless once Warham had gone public with Gonzales."

"So why send them to you? What shall I do with these worthless pictures? I know, I'll send them to Cassandra Brown on the *Post*. No, Cass, it makes no sense. Shall we open another bottle?"

"Do you think it'll help?"

"No, but I'm quite content to get a little pissed this evening. It's so nice to see you — it seems ages."

"It was only last week that you sent me off to Amsterdam with the Queen of a hangover."

They refilled their glasses and Moses sat on the sofa above Brown, still on the floor, and gently ruffled her hair. Brown allowed her head to rest against Moses' thigh, the warmth of it seeping through the soft cotton trousers.

Brown put suddenly put down her glass and sat up straight. "Revenge."

Moses tipped her head to one side. "What?"

Brown pulled out Bennett's envelope from her bag, spreading the documents around the floor. "Look, a bank statement showing him zillions in the red, a string of mortgages on his house and a letter from Elwood turning down a request for a loan. The poor guy was bust."

"Why would it be up to Elwood whether Warham could borrow some money?"

"Elwood was finance director, remember. He signs the cheques."

Moses seemed lost in thought for a moment. "Cass, be careful with this stuff. Is it genuine?"

"No idea, but the Land Register is. I've checked it out on-line."

Moses picked up the WBC letter. "If this is genuine, Elwood kicked away Warham's last hope. What a bastard."

At one o'clock, Brown phoned Central Executive Cars, gave them the *Post*'s account number, and gathered up the photographs and documents while she waited for the minicab to arrive. She was disappointed it was not Alex driving. A detour via Kings Cross allowed her to pick up the morning papers. The subs had done a great job on the "Warham Mystery" page. She tried in vain to focus on it in detail when she got home, but failed.

Brown awoke thinking of the photographs, or more particularly, where they may have come from, and why they had been sent to her. She knew Elwood's denial was not worth the air he had breathed to utter it, but she still couldn't see why he would have sent them. Warham was associating with a beautiful young woman who took her clothes off for a living. So what. Did he imagine the *Post* would simply publish them? In that case, given how long Brown had been sitting on them, they would probably have turned up elsewhere. The *Sunday News* would have run them like a shot. So would other papers.

Brown made some tea and began to get ready for work. The shower gave her a temporary respite from the effects of too much wine. But who other than Elwood would want her to think that Warham had run off with Gonzales?

Her musings were interrupted by the estate agent ringing to ask if she'd arranged her mortgage. Sod it. She had completely forgotten. By the time the agent rang off, she felt overwhelmed. Surely it didn't all have to be so complicated? The beneficial effects of the shower had worn off, she was still sitting, wrapped in her towel, and she didn't feel like going to the office.

The priority had to be arranging a mortgage so why not accept the estate agent's offer to help? Then she called the news-desk to say she'd be in after lunch.

The estate agents were as good as their word. She signed a few forms and the deal was done. The flat would be hers in six weeks.

Baird was remarkably relaxed when Brown arrived at the *Post's* offices. She had expected to find him pacing up and down, demanding to know where she had been all morning, but he was sitting with his feet on the desk, exposing the sorry state of his shoes.

"You need a cobbler, cobber," she said by way of hello. Baird blushed slightly and took his feet off his desk. "What are you looking for today?"

"What have you got?"

"I feel we've had this conversation before, Curley. Well, to be honest, I've not got much at all. I'm wondering if we might give the story a rest today?"

"What about your trip to Amsterdam? When is that going to yield some copy?"

"There's still stuff I've got to check out."

Baird tapped a chewed pencil against his teeth. "OK, keep me posted. The editor is bound to ask when he remembers. As for today, Vittorio's been talking to the magistrate again. He's very excited about some big cheese pathologist who's doing the *post mortem*. He also said the body's been identified by somebody from the British Embassy. None of it amounts to much but I've asked him for a five hundred word wrap we can run down-page somewhere if we need it to fill the space."

"Sounds like I'm off the hook."

Baird nodded. "Don't get complacent. You look terrible, by the way."

"Well thanks, Curley. You really know how to make a girl feel good about herself. And I have to say, you don't look too hot shit yourself. At least you can't see my socks through the soles of my shoes."

Around three o'clock, Elwood phoned "as a matter of courtesy", to let her know that Warham's body had been identified, so the boardroom changes, including his promotion to chief executive officer had taken effect. It gave her great pleasure to tell Elwood she already knew. But Elwood had more to say.

"It's the end of an era for WBC, Cassandra, and not the end any of us could have predicted or wanted. We owe it to John to move on ahead, to drive the business forward to try to recapture some of the spirit which, under John, propelled us in the past to the top of the world rankings."

Brown had the distinct impression he was reading from a prepared script.

"It is time for us to take stock, to look at the business from top to bottom, to see where we could do better. As a matter of urgency, I have been asked by the board to prepare a full review of our current position ..."

She was now convinced. He was reading, alright. There was none of his hesitation and repetition.

"And to make recommendations for the future."

She could feel her easy day evaporating. "What, exactly, Charles, are you trying to say to me? What do you mean when you say you have been asked by the board to prepare a full review of the current position?"

"Exactly what I said, Cassandra. I am preparing a full review of WBC's current position. Our market position, our financial position, our competitive, position, our USP."

There was a distinct lisp in Elwood's voice when he said "USP". She wanted to hear him say it again. "Our what, Charles?"

"USP, Cassandra. Unique selling point. I would have thought you would be familiar with the term." Brown found his irritation satisfying.

"Does the full review include your personal financial position, Charles?"

"I'm sorry, Cassandra. What do you mean?"

The temperature was rising nicely. "What I was asking is, has the board settled your pay deal yet?"

There was a pause on the other end of the line. Elwood was rattled. She had listened to his daily platitudes for long enough. She thought of the letter turning down Warham's loan request, and wanted to turn up the heat.

"I really cannot understand your interest in my compensation, Cassandra. I told you the other day, only the other day, it is not a matter of urgency so far as I am concerned. In fact, Cassandra, I would even venture to say that you are more interested in my compensation arrangements than I am."

It was a sad attempt at a joke, and she was not going to give him any satisfaction by laughing.

Undeterred, he ploughed on. "My priority is to ensure that WBC goes from strength to strength, but we have first to assess where exactly we are. Only then can we start to formulate policy going forward."

He was back under control – the carefully controlled Elwood was back on the line. Brown tried again to destabilise him.

"What about share options? Have you agreed how many you are going to get? Presumably you want to have them granted while the price is low, so as to maximise your profit when you come to sell them in three years' time?"

"Nice try, Cassandra. As I said a moment ago, nothing has been decided yet. But I think I will find common cause, yes common cause, with all the shareholders if our strategies increase the value of WBC, don't you?"

Game set and bloody match – it was time to quit. She said her goodbyes and hung up on Elwood, who had by then regained his composure so completely she wondered whether even his show of irritation had been carefully composed. She felt outclassed, and didn't like it.

The ample form of Greg Jones ambled across her field of vision, a cup of coffee slopping over his hand. He pulled up a chair opposite Brown's desk and gently lowered himself down. His round smiling face, just visible to the side of her workstation, gave Brown a sense of security.

Where some of her colleagues would, she suspected, allow her to make mistakes in order to advance their own relative positions in the race for promotion, Jones had long ago ceased to care about the internal politics of the *Post*. He just wanted to write his own column and enjoy a quiet life.

"The insurance angle worked OK, then, Cassandra", referring to that morning's paper open on her desk.

"The *Standard*'s followed it up, and I suspect others will. Thanks for your help, Greg, by the way." She shot what she hoped was a dazzling smile, which evoked a similar response. Beneath the ramshackle surface, Brown could see the little boy, clearly looking for mischief.

"Rather a lot of WBC shares traded this morning Cassandra, have you noticed?"

"No. I should have done, but I've been a bit busy signing mortgage forms so I can get my foot on the London property ladder. Do you know, I'll be paying less in mortgage than I do in rent, and getting a better flat? Anyway, what's going on in WBC shares?"

"Nearly fifty million traded, which is a lot for them. Around half past eleven the price suddenly weakened but seems to be steadier now. Something's going on."

"I've just had an earful of Elwood talking about doing a fundamental review of WBC's activities."

Jones took a gulp of coffee. "Spring cleaning time is here, Cassandra, by the look of it."

"Say again."

"Spring cleaning. Kitchen sink job, don't you think?"

"Sorry Greg, I'm not with you."

Jones explained. When a new man takes over, he often writes off large sums of money against profits made when the previous incumbent was responsible. The past chief executive's performance therefore looks less good in retrospect than it did at the time. And then the new man's performance appears even better.

"But why's that a kitchen sink job?"

"Because, Cassandra, the new man writes down the value, as the saying goes, of everything but the kitchen sink."

"But surely that'll bring the share price down."

"You bet it will."

"But that's hardly a great start to Elwood's stint as CEO?"

Jones winked. "Imagine, there was WBC going to Hell in a handcart, but in the nick of time Mr Charles Elwood stepped in to save the day. When Elwood's history is written, it will show the share price rising Phoenix-like from the depths from the time he took over. Meanwhile, he will make off with share options granted at a nice low price."

Not for the first time, nor she suspected would it be the last, Jones had put a jumbled collection of facts into perspective. Suddenly, it all made sense. Elwood was out to make big money and make himself look good. The devious bastard.

She was on her fifth attempt at writing the first paragraph when Baird returned from afternoon conference in a far from happy mood. "We've just lost a page. Bloody advertising have just sold a full page and the managing editor refuses to increase the size of the paper. That means we lose a page of editorial. You'll have to keep your piece really tight Cass."

"You didn't think much of it anyway."

"Sulking won't help Cassandra. Go and talk to the managing editor if you have a problem. It's his fucking decision, not mine."

Brown lay back in her chair, looking up to the shaft of sunlight coming through a roof light. Behind the smart new glass frontage, the *Post*'s editorial department was more like a factory than an office. A huge word factory where battery journos clucked away at their workstations, churning out stories to be packed by the subs into electronic boxes. She wished there was a window she could look out of that didn't overlook a busy dual carriageway. She wanted to see what the normal world looked like. She wanted to see children coming home from school, people doing their shopping, parks and gardens. She felt sealed inside a glass chamber.

The walls were decorated with framed front pages of the *Post*. Above her desk she had the Coronation of Queen Elizabeth II. Above the news-desk, the Invasion of Pearl Harbour. The sub editors could stare at the Sinking of the Titanic, which seemed somehow appropriate. Henry Marshall had the Abdication of Edward VIII. She could still remember the opening sentence of the story, which she had read over Marshall's shoulder when she was being interviewed for her job. "Edward VIII, thirty-eighth King of England, abdicated today for love of an American woman." How she would love to have the opportunity to write such a simple, stunning, story.

Tired of staring at the screen of her workstation, waiting for inspiration, she wandered down to the vending machine. Watching brown liquid dribble from one spout and white from another, both into a yellow plastic beaker, what had been troubling her began to come into focus: Elwood was still fighting a battle he had already won. Warham was dead and Elwood had his job. Elwood had nothing more to gain. Elwood wins. He gets the job. So what was this all about? Where was the motivation for the posthumous damage? Had he spent the years at Warham's side nursing resentment, fanning it into hatred, so that even as Warham's body lay stretched out on a slab, he needed to poison the legacy? Or was it all about money?

The vending machine had finished dispensing the hot liquid and a sub-editor was waiting behind her, filthy plastic tray in one hand and a stack of coins in the other. "You OK, Cassandra?"

"Oh, yes, I was lost in thought." She removed the cup from its station on the little drain inside the machine and made her way back to her desk. She was now pleased she was writing only a very short story which hopefully led neither the readers nor her competitors to any particular conclusion.

In Elwood she was dealing not only with a devious man, but possibly also someone dangerous.

SECTION	Business
TITLE	WBCReview
HEADING 1	WBC CEO to undertake full review
HEADING 2	
AUTHOR	Cassandra Brown
STATUS	Live

The new chief executive of Warham Blazeley Cotts, Charles Elwood, is to undertake a full review of the company's business, including its financial performance.

Speaking yesterday after he had been formally appointed to the post, Mr Elwood said the board was "taking stock" of WBC's position, following the death of the company's founder, John Warham.

It was confirmed in Italy yesterday that the body recovered last week from the Ligurian Sea was that of Mr Warham, 58. No cause of death has yet been established.

In London, WBC shares had a turbulent session as a leading sector analyst, Bruce Fentiman of the investment bank SBA, reduced his forecast of current year profits from £138million to £115m.

Mr Elwood said he had been asked by the board "as a matter of urgency" to "take stock, to look at the business from top to bottom, to see where we could do better."

CHAPTER FOURTEEN

BROWN dressed with care. She put on more than her usual amount of make-up, especially around the eyes, partly in an attempt to hide the damage done by an almost sleepless and very unhappy night. She was more generous than usual, too, with the perfume. She leaned forward into the mirror. It was just possible to look down her shirt. Brown was going hunting, and if she was taken for a high-class hooker in the process, so be it.

Her quarry, at eleven thirty that Wednesday morning, was Elwood. Shortly after eight o'clock, she had called to ask him for an urgent meeting on neutral ground. To her surprise, he had readily agreed, and they were meeting at a rather old fashioned Knightsbridge hotel, the Berkshire, where the booths in the foyer were so private that even the waiters frequently failed to find you.

Somewhere around two am, she had woken from a dream about Steve. They were still married, on holiday at Coffs Harbour. It was evening. Steve had gone sailing, crewing in a race on a delightfully calm Pacific. She was in the garden of their rented holiday home, preparing supper for when he returned. The tinnies were in the cooler. The wine was on the table, lemon-scented candles lit the scene and kept the insects at bay. She waited and waited, but he didn't return. Around midnight, she ran to the harbour. The boats were all long back from the race, tied up at their pontoons. Nobody had seen Steve, but somebody gave her a jigsaw puzzle. All she had to do was fit the pieces together and Steve would arrive back. She tipped all the pieces out onto the pontoon and one slipped between the planks, as it lay in the water she could see it was part of Steve's face, but she just couldn't reach down to pick it up because the gap between the planks was too small for her hand.

Then she woke. In an attempt to put the dream out of her head, she had made camomile tea and put Beth Orton on her iPod. If Steve had been there with her, in her bedroom in Primrose Hill, he would have woken and made love to her. But he wasn't. He was the other side of the world, and she didn't even dare ring him. He would, she knew, be kind and gentle and supportive, but it was not fair on him, or on his new partner. What was over, was over, and had been for more than two years. She had made her decision then and Steve had made his.

It was while she was sleeplessly contemplating the consequences of ambition, she had thought again about Elwood and his plotting to overthrow Warham, long before he went missing. That he coveted Warham's job was an open secret in the advertising world. He never passed up an opportunity to knock Warham and was probably behind the move to force him to give up one of his jobs. It was Elwood who talked with investors, he was WBC's face in the City, a face he kept scrupulously clean. And why else would Elwood have been so keen to imply that Warham's disappearance was a result of some "extraordinary behaviour" of his own volition? And the photos. Yes, the photos. What was she supposed to make of them? And why had she been singled out to receive them? Who sent them? Elwood or somebody else? Why had he turned down Warham's request for a loan? And was Elwood's ambition was sufficient to drive him to murder?

Eventually she drifted into sleep, only to wake with the sunrise and the questions still on her mind. So at eight fifteen she had called Elwood, before she lost her nerve.

It was ten thirty and Alex was already waiting by the Toyota. Brown could have taken a taxi to the Berkshire, but she needed her own transport, even Alex's cronky minicab, waiting outside. She didn't want her session with Elwood extended into a lift in his car.

The small tape recorder was in her bag, a new tape and fresh batteries installed. There was also the packet of photographs, together with the envelope in which they had arrived. And there was the copy of the letter to John Warham.

Baird seemed in a remarkably good mood when she called to say she would be in by lunchtime. From the somewhat muffled way he was talking she judged he was engrossed in his mid-morning snack.

There were a few minutes to spare before she needed to leave so she read again the letter from the estate agent. All was going ahead. Her mortgage was confirmed. Her sitting room window was open and the white muslin curtains billowed in the warm breeze. She looked out the window at the Toyota, Alex standing beside it as if it were a top-of-the-range Mercedes. He glanced up and she smiled down; he was probably too far away to notice a slight blush shading her cheeks. At a quarter to eleven, she put on her jacket, had a last look at herself in the bathroom mirror, removed a white thread that had settled itself on her trousers and went down to the car.

"Beautiful day, Miss Brown." Alex was as fresh and sweet smelling as ever, but the scent was not his usual.

"New after-shave, Alex?"

"Givency, Miss Brown. I hope you like it?"

"A present from an admirer. Alex?"

"Perhaps I shouldn't say, Miss Brown." The use of her surname by Alex always had a charge to it, and she wondered if it showed. A glance in the mirror suggested it did.

"Where to, Miss Brown?"

"The Berkshire, Knightsbridge, please Alex."

They sat in silence for a moment. The radio was, as usual, tuned to Classic FM, and the Ride of the Valkyries issued softly from the speakers. He started the engine and the Toyota clattered away from the curb. Alex took a route around the Outer Circle in the middle of Regents Park and down Baker Street where there was already a knot of tourists taking each other's photographs outside the Sherlock Holmes Museum. Within a few minutes they had reached Park Lane and were sitting in a queue of traffic waiting for the lights to change, when Brown had an idea. The photographs had been waiting for her on the morning she went to Rome. "Alex, do you remember you picked me up very early last week to drive me to Stansted?"

"Of course. Miss Brown."

"I had a letter waiting for me on the mat. It had been hand delivered. You didn't see who delivered it, I suppose?"

Alex looked up into his mirror. "I did, Miss Brown, certainly. Somebody arrived in a white Jaguar E Type, a real beauty, parked up and walked into the square. He was looking at the house numbers and then posted something though your door. I didn't think to mention it as I saw you had the envelope in your hands when you came out."

"Thanks, Alex. You didn't notice who was driving it, I suppose."

"No, not really. He was well dressed, looked like a businessman I suppose. I was more interested in the car. Sorry."

"Alex, you're a genius."

Alex nodded as he swung into the giant roundabout at Hyde Park Corner. It was still only five minutes past eleven. Brown asked Alex to drive around the block and park opposite the hotel. She didn't want to hang about the hotel lobby for too long as her willingness to be mistaken for a hooker had evaporated. Also, she wanted to see Elwood arrive. Her wait outside was brief. Elwood's car swept into the service road in front of the Berkshire. A uniformed commissionaire stepped forward and opened the door. Elwood was on the telephone, and the commissionaire stood holding the car door open until he emerged. Elwood looked around but took no notice of the ancient Toyota parked opposite.

"OK, Alex."

The Toyota pulled out from the kerb, swung across the road and stopped right behind Elwood's Mercedes. Even though the Toyota was not the sort of vehicle that usually graced the paved semi-circle, the commissionaire was instantly at the door. Brown put on her Ray-Bans and leaned forward to get out of the car. She noticed the commissionaire's eyes were not on her face.

"Half an hour at the most, Alex."

She found Elwood waiting in the foyer. He took her hands and air kissed her on both cheeks. "Cassandra, how lovely to see you. A pleasure I had not been anticipating until you rang."

He led the way to one of the booths. Was this a good idea? The bright idea of the early hours was starting to tarnish. He had already seized the initiative. She was no longer even sure what she intended to ask. A waiter addressed Elwood by name. He was four points in the lead and she had not even opened her mouth. He ordered coffee for two. She smiled and ordered tea. She had clawed back one point.

"I'm sorry. Never assume, eh, Cassandra?"

Brown took a deep breath. It was now or never.

"Thank you for agreeing to see me at such short notice Charles, and for dragging all the way over here. I hope it was not too inconvenient for you."

"Not at all. Cassandra. It is good to get out of the office for an hour. As you can imagine, it is rather busy at the moment. Now, what is it you wanted to talk to me about?" A smile was glued to his face, his silver hair immaculate, highlighting a hint of a tan. His suit had Savile Row written all over it. But the white shirt and blue tie of Elwood, finance director, had given way to a strong pink tie against a pale pink shirt. A silk handkerchief of the same strong colour spilled from the top pocket of his suit. Elwood, advertising chief, was dressing for his new job. While the waiter fussily arranged pots and jugs, cups and saucers and a plate of biscuits, Brown took the opportunity to think about her opening gambit. Christ, why had she come? Good ideas in the early hours are sometimes that, good ideas. But not always, and this one was beginning to drop firmly into the "bad ideas" box. The waiter retreated and Elwood looked expectantly.

"I wanted to talk to you, Charles, about the pressure John was under. As I understand it, he either remained chairman and gave up being chief executive, or vice versa."

"With respect, Cassandra, isn't that a little academic now, given that you've already written about this."

"Well, I thought it might throw some light on things. Of course, if it is a problem to talk about it."

"No problem, Cassandra. You have your job to do and I have mine. Now, how can I best put this? John was, shall we say, aware, yes painfully aware, even, that he had to relinquish one or other of his two roles."

"And he was resisting?"

"Correct. However, some of the more active of our investors were making life, how best to put it, difficult for him. Yes, quite difficult."

Brown pulled her earlobe. She had forgotten to put on her earrings. "Where did the board stand in all this? In particular, what was your personal position, given that you wanted the CEO's job yourself?"

She sat back, surprised at the words which had just spilled from her own mouth. Damn, she had forgotten to turn on her tape recorder. Elwood busied himself pouring her tea, enquiring whether she wanted milk or sugar, and then seeing to his own coffee. Eventually he leaned back in the green velvet banquette, carefully arranged his fingertips so they touched each other and rested his chin down onto the extended fingers. He looked straight into her eyes.

"We are off the record, Cassandra?"

She nodded.

"Well, the last year or so has been a very difficult time for me, very difficult. On the one hand, John is, was, one of my oldest and closest friends. He brought me into WBC at an early stage and we took on the advertising establishment and we won. Nobody else could have done that, Cassandra, and I certainly could not have done anything without John. I owed him an enormous debt of loyalty."

Brown nodded leaned forward. Elwood's eyes finally left her face for an instant, flicking down and back again. Brown looked down in what she hoped was a modest way, picking up her cup to take a sip. Elwood was getting into his stride.

"But on the other hand, I have to listen to our investors. I was, I am, the, what shall I say, the conduit between the City and WBC. As you know, we have had a challenging couple of years, yes, challenging, and this has encouraged our shareholders to focus on our management issues. They do own the business, after all, so when they say jump we must, to some extent, ask, how high?"

It was Elwood's turn to concentrate on his coffee. He did not take a biscuit.

"You've not quite answered my question, Charles. Where, exactly, did you stand?"

"I've tried to answer you as best I can, Cassandra, but let me try again. The board, even John himself, recognised we had to change the way we did things. Not only were the two jobs too much for one man, but also John was quite involved with helping the prime minister on certain delicate relationship issues with business."

"Such as pharmaceutical research using animals?"

Elwood ignored her interjection.

"The board insisted that these political activities should be quite separate from WBC. Quite separate."

He picked up his coffee, extending the back of his free hand under the path of the cup *en route* to his mouth. He changed his mind and replaced the cup in its saucer. "You may ask why would John get involved in politics? Well, I guess when somebody judges they have climbed to the top of their particular tree they might start to look for other, shall we say, recognitions."

"Such as a title?"

"You said it Cassandra, not me."

Brown allowed a silence to hang between them for a few moments before speaking again. She wished she could find some way of turning on her tape recorder.

"Was there a campaign to get John out of the CEO's job and you into it?"

"A campaign, Cassandra? Mounted by whom?"

"Why, you, of course." Brown smiled as sweetly as she was able, and leaned forward in what she hoped would be interpreted as a conspiratorial, if not seductive, manner. Elwood responded by leaning back. He smiled so broadly it was even possible his humour was genuine.

"What do you expect me to say, Cassandra?"

"I expect you to deny it, Charles."

"Consider it denied."

"And now you've been given the half of his job you were plotting to get."

Elwood's fingers again met below his chin. Brown remembered a childhood action rhyme, "Here's the Church and here's the steeple, look inside and here's the people." Elwood didn't get beyond the church.

"As ever Cassandra, it does not do to under-estimate your powers of invention. Can I tell you something that must not, and I mean not, ever be traced back to me?"

Brown nodded, once again leaning forward.

"I have your word?"

"Yes."

"Since you are so interested, I think it safer, yes, safer, to let you have the facts. Yes, John *had* been given his ultimatum. The Thursday before he started his holiday was our regular board meeting and it was made clear, very clear, in fact, that we needed to listen to our shareholders and bring our management structure into line with best practice."

"What was his reaction?"

"He promised to give the matter some thought while he was away. John may have been stubborn, Cassandra, but he was also a pragmatist. Other than that, I cannot say."

"Was he upset?"

"What do you think, Cassandra?"

"Enough to ..." She did not want to say the words 'commit suicide' so raised her eyebrows and slid her finger across her throat. She knew immediately it was a stupid gesture.

Elwood shook his head, "As I said Cassandra, John was a pragmatist."

Time for another sip of tea. If only the tape recorder was on. She dabbed her lips with the starched white linen napkin thoughtfully provided to catch any biscuit crumbs, and ploughed on.

"Tell me about the photographs, Charles."

"There is nothing I can tell you about them. I haven't seen them and have no wish to do so."

"So you didn't send them?"

Elwood's composure was beginning to crack. "No, of course I didn't send them. It is not the way we do things."

Brown was nearly through. One more question. "Why did you refuse his application for a loan?"

Elwood drummed his fingers on the table, and then his hand went up to signal to the waiter for the bill. "Cassandra, I'm always willing to help you, as you know. But you seem intent on straying into the realms of pure fantasy, wild speculation. I would urge you to be very sure of your facts before you write. Now, as I was saying earlier, we are pretty busy working on the review right now, so if you'll excuse me, I'd better get back to the shop. I'm relying on you to treat our discussion with sensitivity and discretion. In return I will forget you ever asked me that final question." He scribbled a signature on the bill and stood up. The interview was over, and they walked out together into the bright sunshine.

To the casual observer they would have looked like two old friends, or maybe father and daughter.

As Elwood leaned forward to air-kiss her cheek she whispered in his ear, "Who drives a white E Type, eh, Charles?" She put on her most innocent expression and walked to the Toyota, where Alex was already standing, the back door open. He had enough style to be behind the wheel of a Bentley.

Elwood put his head down and hurried to his own car. It was as close to a declaration of war as she dared to go. She was going to nail him, one way or the other.

"Office, Miss Brown?"

"Please, Alex." Her hands were trembling and she felt sick. She took a deep breath, slipped her feet out of her mules and wriggled her toes.

The minicab slid out into the Knightsbridge traffic. "Oh Miss Brown, I was talking to Mr Elwood's driver. I've known him for years from when we both worked in the directors' car pool at Imperial. I mentioned the E Type I'd seen outside your flat in Primrose Hill. He knows the car. He's seen it outside WBC and at Mr Elwood's home. Said he wasn't quite sure who owned it, but thinks it might be a Mr Clarke. I don't know if that's helpful?"

"Helpful, Alex, that's brilliant. I owe you a good dinner."

Alex appeared to concentrate on the traffic and made no answer. Brown was embarrassed. Not only did she look like a hooker, she was beginning to behave like one. She did up two buttons on her shirt and tried to focus on the extraordinary encounter she had just had with Elwood. But at least she knew who had delivered the photographs, if not why, or on whose behalf.

CHAPTER FIFTEEN

BROWN wanted to write about the implications of the ultimatum delivered at the board meeting. There was a man under probably the heaviest pressure of his working life. Directors he had brought onto the WBC board, including his lifelong business partner Elwood, had turned against him, backing the City shareholders. It might have been enough to drive him to the edge of the cliff, and then to jump. The story would have the rest of Fleet Street trailing in her wake.

But she had promised Elwood their conversation was "off the record". The term was itself virtually meaningless. To some people, "off the record" meant the story could not be published at all. To others, it meant the story could be told, but the source could not be revealed. To others, it was a way of helping the journalist to understand a situation, for background only.

The simplest way of finding out what Elwood had meant was to call him. She regretted, now, the whispered question in his ear, especially since she now knew who drove the white E Type. It was an impetuous thing to have done, and she was embarrassed to face Elwood, even on the telephone. She thought about writing the story anyway. There are times when a journalist will deliberately break her word. Even in her own department, attitudes would be divided. Baird would argue, she knew, that people should not tell secrets to journalists if they don't want to see them in the paper. Marshall would say that "off the record" meant it could not be published.

Against that, the ultimatum could hardly have been a secret. It had been delivered at a board meeting where there were probably a dozen people present, if not more. No doubt a few of the largest shareholders would also have known of it. She needed to find somebody other than Elwood from whom she could authenticate the story. That way, she could convince herself she was not being unethical.

The WBC annual report was on her desk and she turned to the page listing the directors. The same band of great and good non-executives that appeared around the boardroom tables of virtually any of the largest companies. Merchant bankers, senior industrialists, a lawyer – all picking up their £50K a year for attending a dozen board meetings. She knew none of them well enough to expect them to tell her anything, let alone something confidential.

There was one other possibility. Bruce Fentiman, the investment analyst she knew was close to Elwood. He would probably know about it – and even if he didn't, he could find out.

She picked up the phone, just as Baird strode up to her desk. "So Cassandra, how was Elwood this morning. Tell you anything interesting? The editor wants a strong story on WBC today. He believes the others are catching up and we are in danger of losing our lead."

Brown replaced the receiver, Fentiman's number undialled. She did her best to curl her lip. The lack of sleep was catching up with her. "Christ Curley, I've broken every story first so far, ahead of the *Financial Times*, The *Times* and even his beloved *Independent*. I have every intention of continuing to do so. I've been awake half the night thinking about it. So what the hell's he on about?"

"Whoa, calm down. Don't shoot the messenger. So what have you got for us today? Knowing you it'll be something good. I still haven't heard what you got in Amsterdam."

"Don't try to patronise me, Curley, especially not today. I'm pissed off up to here with this story. Do you know the *FT* has a team of three working on it? I'm on my own and I'm still breaking all the exclusives. It would be nice if the other end of the paper could recognise that, instead of just piling on the pressure. As for today, I have discovered Warham was given an ultimatum at a board meeting two days before he went on holiday. He was told he had to choose one job or the other – he couldn't keep both. Then the poor sod goes on holiday to try to patch up his marriage after the Gonzales business ..."

Baird cut in "And throws himself off a cliff? Hell's teeth, Cassandra, that's sensational. That'll lead the paper. There's bugger all else about."

"Too simple Curley, too neat. He was a pragmatist, remember." She was surprised to hear Elwood's words coming out of her mouth. "I don't think he was the sort to throw himself over."

"Anyway, it's a great story Cass."

Brown leaned back in her chair, and put her hands behind her head.

"Only I can't write it." It was like poking her tongue out at a policeman.

Baird looked more puzzled than angry, although his temper would, she knew, flare soon enough. He removed his spectacles and attempted to clean them with the bottom of his tie. "Why?"

"Elwood told me off the record."

"Fuck that. If he didn't want to see it in the paper, he shouldn't have told you. He's a big boy, Cass."

"I'd like to run it, Curley, but unless I can firm it up from an alternative source, I can't."

"Shall we let the editor decide what should and should not go into his newspaper? This story's going on the afternoon list and you can wrestle with your precious conscience tomorrow." Baird did not wait for a response, but stalked back to his desk, knocking a precariously balanced pile of *The Economist* from Greg Jones' desk as passed. He didn't even look round to see what had fallen.

Brown was close to tears. She was tired, she was upset and she was compromised. But the worst thing, the very worst thing, was that she felt stupid. Reluctantly, she picked up the telephone to call Fentiman. She would have to sound bright and cheerful as usual.

"I thought I might hear from you this afternoon", Fentiman said, after the usual polite introductions. He sounded less than pleased.

"Why?"

"Well, I don't know what you said to Charles Elwood this morning, but I was talking to him a little while ago and he was less than flattering about your methods."

"Really?" she answered as casually as she could, while adding "frightened" to the list of her current emotions. "Why, what am I supposed to have done?"

"Something about accusing him of sending out those anonymous photographs. Did you?"

"Bruce, I did no such thing. Any more than I would accuse *you* of sending out anonymous photographs. You didn't, by the way, did you?"

"Cassandra, I did no such thing." His repetition of her words suggested he was lightening up. Perhaps he figured there was little point in falling out with one of his best media contacts. "Anyway, what can I do for you?"

But could she trust him? If she asked him about the ultimatum, would he simply get straight back on to Elwood, who would then know she was on a fishing expedition? She could not risk asking him outright, but she would try to steer the conversation in that direction.

"So, what's going on then, Bruce, anything I should know?" She felt her stomach begin to relax. Fentiman would surely respond to her friendliness.

She hurried on. "I've got the editor on my back for a story and frankly, Bruce, I don't know what the hell to give him."

"I could make a few suggestions, but I don't think you'd like them much." Harmless or offensive? She wasn't quite sure. She never was with Fentiman. But she sensed a smirk, best ignored.

"Seriously, though, Bruce, I'm really interested in how much pressure Warham was under. To be honest, I'm surprised he got away with it so long."

Would he take the bait?

"Well, he wasn't going to get away with it, as you put it, much longer."

Yes! Yes, hook, line and sinker!

"What do you mean, Bruce?"

"As I said to you the other day, everyone was getting fed up with John clinging on to both jobs. They wanted action; sooner, rather than later. They had made it very clear to certain non-executive directors that they expected them to give Warham an ultimatum."

"And had they?"

"Yes"

"Do you happen to know when?"

"Before he went on holiday. But look, Cassandra, you know all this, don't you? Charles has told you all about it, I gather. I cannot see what I can possibly add when you already know what happened."

An edge was in his voice. "As you know, Cass, I'm always ready to help you, but only if you are straight with me. As it happens, I can't see what objections Charles has to you telling the world the board had finally got its act together, but it's his call, not mine. So if I were you, I'd pick up the phone and ask him if you can use it, and stop pissing me about."

"Bruce, I'm sorry. I didn't mean to, well, it's a great story and I need a second source, otherwise...."

"Wouldn't it just be easier to get back on to Charles rather than running all around the houses with people who've got their own work to get on with?"

"Thanks for the advice, Bruce. I'll get out of your hair."

There was no choice but to ring Elwood, or go sick. Fentiman would probably tell Elwood she'd called, and she would be even deeper in the mire. Elwood might then speak to Henry Marshall, her boss, if he hadn't already. Ringing Fentiman had been a mistake, a big mistake. Her second in two hours. She couldn't afford any more.

Reluctantly, she dialled Elwood's direct line, and was relieved to hear his voicemail rather than his voice. She left a message. Would he mind calling her when he had a moment.

After her calamitous morning, Brown was hungry, and in need of some ordinary conversation, to talk to somebody who had no agenda, no games to play. Jill Lambert was at her desk, so the two of them walked across to the canteen, following their usual route through the newsroom. It was a quiet time of day; the couple of hours when only a few sub-editors are on shift and most of the reporters and specialists are out. As usual, the heads swivelled to follow their progress.

As she passed the editor's office she could see Baird inside, speaking excitedly to Cameron.

Elwood was, of course, charm itself when he returned her call. Clearly he had already spoken to Fentiman, and was willing to do a deal. Provided she did not identify him as her source, he had no problem with her running the story.

"Had I realised, Cassandra, that you were so, ehm, enthralled, by a detail which is, after all, already known to a wide circle of people, I would have been happy to talk about it this morning. But I would ask you to be discreet and I would prefer it if you didn't mention my name at all. If you need something from us, can you say a spokesman for WBC refused to comment, or some such words?"

"I'll call your press office to cover myself, shall I?"

"Do that, Cassandra. I am confident they will refuse to comment, since they don't know anything anyway."

"Thanks, Charles, you can rely on me to be discreet. Journalists never, as you know ..."

"Reveal their sources. Quite so, quite so, Cassandra. Now, I wonder if I could ask something from you in return?"

"Depends what it is, Charles."

"Of course it does Cassandra, of course. But don't worry, I am not about to ask you to the opera."

"Oh," was the best she could manage.

"But to ask that you please accept that I have absolutely no knowledge of any photographs. One more thing, Cassandra, you asked me a question as we were leaving the Berkshire this morning. As your driver has probably told you by now, Andrew Clarke drives such a vehicle and, before you ask, no, he is not retained by WBC."

Brown was quite without words. Elwood had gone head to head and had, of course, won. Rarely had her self-esteem taken quite such a bashing in just a few hours.

At least, though, she had her story. Doing her best to impersonate somebody confident and assured, she caught Baird just as he was about to leave for the afternoon news conference. He grinned from ear to ear when she said she was now able to run the story, having been released from her "off the record" pledge.

"That's a relief. The editor was none too pleased when I told him we couldn't run it unless we found a second source."

"Did you do that Curley? Thanks."

"We have to stick together up here, Cass. By the way, how did you swing it?"

"Charm, Curley, charm." She wished it were true.

SECTION	News1
TITLE	WBCUltimatum
HEADING 1	WBC gave chief ultimatum over jobs split
HEADING 2	
AUTHOR	Cassandra Brown
STATUS	Live

The board of WBC, the global advertising conglomerate, gave chief executive John Warham an ultimatum to split the roles of chairman and chief executive just a day before he departed on holiday, the *Post* has learned.

He had been told at a crucial board meeting that he must chose either to remain chairman, or chief executive. He could no longer remain in both positions, the board had resolved.

The board's decision followed a period of intense pressure from City shareholders. It is regarded as unacceptable under current corporate governance conventions for a single person to do both jobs.

It is understood that Mr Warham, who died shortly afterwards in mysterious circumstances while on holiday in Italy, was reluctant to give in to the board, but had accepted that the split had to take place. To refuse would have been to run the risk of being sacked from both jobs at the company, which he founded.

Mr Warham was reported missing shortly afterwards when he left his hotel room on the Italian Riviera early one morning and failed to return. An extensive search, which included a helicopter, failed to find any trace of him.

Some two weeks later his body was recovered from the sea below treacherous cliffs. An Italian magistrate is investigating Mr Warham's death. He has called in a top pathologist to establish the cause of death after wounds were discovered on Mr Warham's body.

There has been speculation that his death could have been murder or suicide, and Scotland Yard have said they are "ruling nothing out" at this stage.

It is understood that Mr Warham felt the board was siding with the City in trying to loosen his hold on the company. His claim to retain both titles had been weakened by the recent financial performance of WBC, and compounded by the loss of a number of key advertising accounts.

It is understood he was told by the board that his preference as to which job to retain had to be given to the board at the July board meeting. Even then, the board said it was under no compulsion to accept his proposal.

Certain City figures had indicated they would like to see Mr Warham retain the role of chairman, with a new chief executive. It is thought likely, however, that Mr Warham would have opted for the more powerful role of chief executive.

When his death was announced, WBC moved to fill the vacuum by appointing Charles Elwood, who was previously finance director, as chief executive officer. The board has instructed headhunters to find suitable candidates to become non-executive chairman.

After Mr Warham disappeared, there was evidence that a "dirty tricks" campaign was being mounted to discredit his reputation. A portfolio of photographs showing him with the Italian fashion model Bia Gonzales were circulated anonymously. Ms Gonzales, who appeared nude in a series of advertisements for an Italian fur company, was Mr Warham's companion at the opening party for the London Fashion Week.

CHAPTER SIXTEEN

ANDREW Clarke called just after Brown arrived home.

"Hello, Cassandra?"

"Yes?"

"Oh, Cassandra, it's Andrew here, Andrew Clarke, I hope you don't mind me ringing you at home."

All the same if I do. "Not at all, Andrew. What can I do for you?"

"I know this is really cheeky, Cassandra, but I'm just around the corner from you and I wondered if you were free for a drink?"

However casual he wanted to sound, it was clear Clarke's call was neither social nor coincidental. Either he wanted to bend her ear on behalf of his insurance friends at Lloyd's or, much more likely, Elwood had warned him he'd been identified as the deliverer of the photographs, and he was eager to put his spin on things. Either way, she was ready to listen. There was a story here somewhere. But first he could dangle a bit.

"Well, ehm, I do have a couple of things to do right now. This is not a social call, I presume?"

"Not exactly, Cassandra, although it does seem ages since I last saw you."

In fact, Clarke had never met Brown on a one-to-one basis. He liked to spend his time with City Editors rather than humble hacks, and would sooner buy Henry Marshall a glass of Champagne in the Savoy than share a pint in a pub with a reporter. Clarke was one of those people whom she doubted knew the meaning of friendship. In its place were networking opportunities. He even went on holiday to places where he expected to rub shoulders with the great and the good. But he was one of the most successful financial public relations operators around, and as such wielded considerable power and a great deal of influence.

"What do you want to talk about, Andrew? I'm really feeling a little tired."

Brown was not going to flatter his already oversized ego by jumping at the chance of a drink with the master storyteller. She wanted to establish that she held the cards, and for once it was him in the weaker position.

"I'd like to talk about philosophy, or music, or the film I saw at the weekend, but in fact I need to talk to you about a much more prosaic matter. I'd sooner do it over a glass of bubbles than over the telephone. Could you possibly spare me half an hour of your evening? I'd really appreciate it."

He had pleaded sufficiently. "When you say you are just around the corner, where exactly are you?"

"I've just come out of a meeting in Harley Street, so I'm just across the park. I could be in Primrose Hill in five. Do you know Colette's Wine Bar? Shall we meet there?"

Brown nodded, lost in thought. The last time she had been to Colette's was with Hogan. It had been a happy lunchtime in a good weekend. Clarke waited for an answer for nearly a minute.

"Cassandra, are you still there? Is Colette's OK?"

"Oh, yes, sorry. Yes I'll see you there shortly."

Brown was desperately tired, but the prospect of a glass of champagne with a rather witty, urbane and well connected public relations man, even one as seemingly shallow as Clarke, didn't feel like a chore. And a story loomed. She could feel it.

She took her time getting ready. Clarke could wait while she took a shower and dressed in something more relaxed than the suit she had put on many hours earlier.

Clarke was as immaculate as ever when she saw him sitting outside the wine bar, a bottle of decent champagne already in the ice bucket, smoked almonds and olives on the table. He was dressed in a dark suit that showed no signs of having coped with a sweltering London day. She guessed it was silk. White shirt, a quiet silk tie, shining shoes. Not a hint of a seven o'clock shadow. Brown was glad she had taken the time to put on something fresh. As she approached, he snapped shut his phone and slipped it into his top pocket. He stood and offered both hands in front of him for her to take before the ritual double air-kiss. The man was such a bullshit artist, but he was good at it, she had to admit. A class act.

"Cassandra, how good of you to spare me some of your evening. You really are so fortunate to live in Primrose Hill."

She smiled at the thought that Clarke, with houses in Kensington and Dorset, might envy her a rented flat in a north London suburb. The thought remained in her head as she picked up her glass, above which she hoped her eyes might be twinkling.

"Well, I like it here. In fact, I'm about to buy a flat. What do you think, about my timing that is?" Two could play the flattering game.

"You should know better than me, Cassandra. You're the financial expert. But people tell me it is never wrong to buy good quality central London property." She noticed the chunky gold ring on the third finger of his left hand as it silently drummed the table. She saw for the first time there were a few tiny beads of sweat on his top lip.

Brown took a second sip. She was beginning to enjoy herself, drinking good champagne at somebody else's expense, watching the buzzing street. And in contrast to her miserable encounter with Elwood, she, and not Clarke, had the ace. Sooner or later, he would have to broach the subject on his mind. She was not planning to help him. He looked around and nodded as a well-known young actor sauntered past their table.

"Did you recognise him, Cassandra?"

"Are you kidding?" Her gentle sarcasm sent him up nicely. "A friend of yours?"

"Well, not exactly a friend. A friend of a friend I suppose you could say. He's a decent regular guy, you know."

"Yeah. I've seen him in the greengrocers here. Buying carrots, as it happened."

Clarke looked up and down Regent's Park Road, no doubt seeing if there were any other celebrities to whom he could nod. He returned to his guest. "This is nice, Cassandra. Having a chance to talk to you in person, instead of the usual hurried conversation over the telephone. And it is such a beautiful evening. I hope I didn't interrupt anything important? You look terrific, by the way."

"Thanks. No, you didn't interrupt anything important at all. I was just trying to decide whether to take a walk in the park or do my chores when you called. I'm afraid the offer of a glass of champagne won hands down. You made up my mind for me." He did not appear to be listening, and she followed his gaze to a white Jaguar E-Type parked across the road.

Clarke topped up the glasses. "I gather you saw my friend Charles Elwood today, and that my name came up in conversation."

So, he was getting to the point. No doubt he had a business dinner to go to and wanted to spend no longer than necessary with a relatively junior reporter.

"Your name didn't come up in conversation, exactly, Andrew, but in the parking area outside the Berkshire Hotel." She smiled, took an almond from the dish and popped it into her mouth without it touching her lips. Clarke's fingers drummed more urgently on the white linen tablecloth. He waited for her to continue as she munched the little nut, and washed it down with another sip of champagne. "Let me just say, I solved a mystery today, with the help of a minicab driver." There was a danger that her smile would become a smirk.

Clarke took a quick sip from his almost untouched glass and raised one eyebrow.

"Did you learn that from Roger Moore, Andrew?"

The brows were dark and, she noticed, as well groomed as his hair. He pushed a lock of stray hair from his forehead. "No, he learned it from me."

Brown almost choked on her drink. Clarke really was witty, even when under pressure. He leaned back in his chair, uncrossing and then re-crossing his legs, which were projecting untidily into the space between their table and the next, causing the waitress to divert around them as she hurried about her business. Did he have to be noticed by everybody?

"Now, tell me about your little mystery. Would I be right in thinking you believe me to be somehow involved?"

"You've got it in one, Andrew. I found out today that a package of photographs, which were posted through my door two weeks ago, came from you. Apparently you delivered them yourself. I'm afraid your rather distinctive car gave the game away."

As she finished talking, she picked up her glass a little too quickly and a few drops spilled over her hand. Clarke offered his napkin and smiled.

"What did you think of them?"

"I thought they were very pretty, but that's hardly the point, Andrew, is it? What I want to know is why you gave them to me, and in particular why you delivered them to me anonymously in the early hours."

"I thought they might be useful to you."

"What made you think that?"

"I assumed you would be trying to find out all you could about John and why he might have disappeared. I thought the package might shed some light on him for you. If I am wrong, then I apologise. Just put them in the nearest shredder."

"But why send them anonymously? Who are you working for Andrew? Is it Charles?"

The question hung there, unanswered. Clarke looked across the road to where his car was parked, and for the first time Brown noticed the driving seat was occupied. In response to a wave from his employer, Clarke's driver got out of the car and picked his way across the road to their table. Clarke was scribbling something on a small oblong of cream paper taken from his pocket memo pad. As he folded the note and handed it to the driver, she could see even his memo paper was embossed with his initials. He asked the driver to deliver the note to the Reform Club and to take the car back to Kensington. Clarke would get a taxi home.

Brown grinned. She was on the front foot, and was enjoying the sensation. "Have you just blown out your dinner date, Andrew? I hope it was nobody important."

"I had a sort of informal arrangement to meet a chum this evening but, to be honest, it is so nice sitting here in the open air with a bottle of champagne between us that I don't feel like moving. Now, where were we? Oh, yes, you had some questions about the photographs. What were they again? By the way, I don't suppose you've eaten?"

Brown shook her head as Clarke nodded in the waitress's direction. She was at their table instantly and handed out two menus. "What's good to eat tonight?"

The waitress ran through the "specials" of the day, by which time Brown had decided not to refuse supper as she was, in fact, rather hungry. She had also decided, once they had ordered, that Clarke had had long enough to come up with answers to her questions.

"So, Andrew, first question. Why did you send me the photographs? And why anonymously?"

The eyebrows lifted again. "Didn't I even put in a compliments slip?" He smiled so warmly and innocently that Brown could not resist smiling back.

"Andrew. You know you didn't. Now, would you mind answering the question?" She tried her best to sound stern, but it came out more like flirting.

"When you have been in public relations as long as I have, Cassandra, you learn that journalists can be a cynical bunch. I have lost count of how many times I have tried to help somebody, only for them to look for an ulterior motive. So I thought I would try to avoid that by being discrete. Can I just say I am full of admiration for your persistence in discovering I was the source of the package. One under-estimates your investigative skills at their peril."

"But why send me the photographs anyway, if you've no ulterior motive."

"I see you will not be fobbed off. No wonder Henry was singing your praises to me only the other day. You should ask him for a raise. So, I confess I did have a motive. One of the reasons I enjoy working in the tawdry business we call public relations is that I like to make things occur. I like to drop a word into this ear or that, pull a little string here or there, and try to shape a particular outcome. I like to be a cause to an effect, regardless of whether or not I have a commercial or vested interest in the situation."

He took another sip. "I was in possession of that little portfolio and decided to put them into the public domain to see what happened. To see how John would react. At that time, of course, I did not know he was dead, and I am just so relieved that you chose not to publish them. Poor Ruth Warham has enough on her plate right now."

"But what have you got, or rather had, against John Warham? Photographs like that in the public domain could only do him harm, and from what I have found out in the past two weeks the poor guy had enough troubles piled up on his plate. Wasn't it rather cruel? Or was it simply business? You still haven't told me who you are working for."

Clarke tapped his ring against the stem of his glass. "With the benefit of hindsight, Cassandra, I cannot deny it was thoughtless. I am afraid I let my enthusiasm for mischief get the better of me. But I can assure you I had no ulterior motive other than to create a bit of a stir. And I am not working for anybody involved with WBC."

"What about your chums, as you like to call them, at Lloyds. Could these have something to do with the insurance money?"

He shook his head. "My call the other day was simply to help out an old pal on a one-off basis, and I hope you would agree it also helped you. But no fee was involved, I can assure you. The photographs are nothing to do with anyone but me and you."

"I'm not sure I believe you, Andrew, but let's assume for a moment I do. Why did you drop them off at such a strange time of night, or rather, early in the morning?"

"That's easier to answer. It's quite straightforward. I was on my way home."

"What? At a quarter to six in the morning?"

"As I am sure you know, given the intrusive nature of the media's diary columns, I need to unwind after a hard day's work, and usually a business dinner. So I occasionally like to visit the tables. Other times I might drop into a night shelter, near Kings Cross, you know the one?"

Brown burst out laughing. "What, to sleep?"

"To wash up. Help get a meal. Take in some supplies. A box of fruit. That sort of thing." He flushed. It was the first time she had ever seen him less than totally composed. "As it happens, that morning I had left the shelter after a really interesting chat with an old boy who, believe it or not, used to be a hack on some paper down on the South Coast."

"So what about the pictures?"

"They were in the car addressed to you and I simply dropped them off on my way home."

He paused. "Now, shall we have another bottle to go with our supper or would you prefer something different?"

"I'll just have mineral water from now on, thanks. I think I've had enough for one evening. Now, where did you get them? And I don't want any bullshit about them being dropped off anonymously in the middle of the night. Time for a bit of honesty, Andrew."

"How unkind. Surely you are not suggesting I would tell you anything but the truth, the whole truth."

"Yeah, and nothing but the truth. OK, so where did they come from?"

"On that matter, I am afraid my lips are sealed. Oh, what exquisite timing, here's our supper. Now, can we talk about something else while we eat? I wouldn't want either of us to suffer indigestion. By the way, have you ever been to John Warham's house. As you might expect, it is very beautiful. Very elegant. In fact, you may remember a feature spread your Saturday pages ran on it a couple of years ago. John was really very chuffed."

Brown had her mouth full of roasted cod, and simply shook her head.

Once it had gone, Brown put down her fork and stared into Clarke's eyes. "You don't happen to know a man called Stephen Bennett, I suppose Andrew?"

It was his turn to shake his head, but not because his mouth was full of roasted cod.

Clarke poured the last of the champagne into their glasses. Brown looked again at the gold ring and wondered what it could possibly be like being married to an outrageous flirt who didn't roll home until the early hours, night after night, because he was either at a swanky club or a night shelter for the homeless.

They spent the rest of the evening talking about the media, business, the cinema. He really was great company, full of anecdotes, names dropping from his lips like confetti. Around ten thirty, they went their separate ways. She doubted his evening was yet over.

As she walked the short distance to the square, she reflected on the way Clarke never wasted a word. He really was a very smart operator. But the reference to Warham's house had left her mystified.

CHAPTER SEVENTEEN

PERHAPS it was eating late, or maybe it was the champagne, but for the second night running Brown was wide-awake at three in the morning. It was stiflingly hot and she had been dreaming again. The dream had been about Chloë. Brown had left her in a car while she went across to a seafood shack somewhere on Australia's Gold Coast. When she came back, Chloë was gone. Vanished. Brown ran to the beach, her feet sinking deep into the sand. She could move only slowly, but in the distance was a giant beach umbrella with the WBC logo on it. When she eventually got there, Brown was naked except for a silver crucifix at her throat. But Chloë was sitting safely under the umbrella with her mother.

Pulling on her wrap, Brown walked through to the kitchen and made herself some camomile tea. She thought about her extraordinary evening. Clarke certainly could turn it on, and she had enjoyed herself. But she was no nearer knowing why he had sent the photographs, nor where he had got them. Was it really because he wanted to "see something happen. Be the cause of an effect"? Maybe. But she had learned this much about Clarke: he does not relax, however smooth the exterior. His conversation is as controlled as a well-edited story – not a word is wasted, nothing said that doesn't mean to be said. So why had he suddenly asked, when she was pushing him about the photographs, if she had ever been to Warham's house? Why should she? Some of the more senior people on the paper had probably been invited, George Cameron maybe and possibly Henry Marshall, but lowly hacks do not get welcomed to top people's dinner tables. So, what was Clarke telling her? She could hardly invite herself to Warham's house, but she could look at the feature he'd mentioned.

Back in bed, she tried to turn her thoughts towards Hogan, in the hope she could conjure something dreamy. But it just wouldn't happen. Hogan seemed so keen, she didn't have to make any of the running. But it was only fair for her to make the next move. She could pay another visit to Dublin or invite him to London, or to a weekend in the country somewhere. Eventually she fell asleep.

Brown arrived late in the office. Her telephone was ringing. She ignored it, flung her bag down on her desk and made off in the direction of the cuttings library. It was in the basement of the old part of the building, with eighteenth century vaulted brick ceilings dating from its days as a storage warehouse. The bricks had been meticulously cleaned and carefully lit, so the effect was one of warmth, quiet and order. On the telephone, the librarians could be brusque, but if a journalist took the trouble to visit them in person, their response was usually as warm as the ambiance of their room. The head librarian was, as usual, sitting behind a large antique desk. His name, Innis, seemed appropriate, although she could never quite think why.

"Cassandra. How nice to see you. You've been keeping us pretty busy. Now, let me guess, you'd like the personality file for John Warham?"

"Nearly right. What I am really looking for is a piece we ran in the Saturday Review about John Warham's house, about two years ago?"

Innis tapped on his keyboard. "Here we are: 'A Little Venetian Treasure – the Home of John and Ruth Warham.' Did you want just the text? Or did you want the pictures?"

"The pictures, if you don't mind."

He disappeared behind one of the long sets of filing shelves. The cabinets holding the shelves were mounted on rails running along the floor, and as each one was moved it revealed another line of shelves behind. He came back with a folder. "This is what you are looking for I think. Can you just sign for them?"

As Brown headed back towards her desk, she could not resist looking inside, even though there was a danger that loose cuttings would fall out. There they were. The sweeping curved staircase. The marbled entrance hall. The modern art. All it lacked was the naked young woman standing at the foot of the stairs. No wonder the location had looked vaguely familiar. She wandered slowly back to her desk.

The message on the unanswered telephone was from Hogan. Brown mentally kicked herself for not calling him first, having decided that she could not expect Hogan to accompany her for another celibate weekend. To her own surprise she found herself offering him a weekend in Paris, with her footing the bill. But despite the offer, which he immediately grabbed, she felt he was nursing resentment because she'd not called him sooner.

As she came off the phone she sensed somebody behind her. Baird was back from morning conference and had perched himself on the next desk, waiting for her to finish her conversation. How much he had overheard?

"So which lucky man has won the trip to Paris?"

"Curley, do you mind. I was having a personal conversation. So, what do you want?"

Baird shifted his weight from one foot to the other. His stomach strained his shirt buttons to bursting point. "Actually Cassandra, I wasn't really listening. I'd only just arrived and heard the bit about somebody meeting you off the Eurostar. Sorry, anyway. Do you have anything for the news-list? It's looking a bit thin."

"Since you heard me making an arrangement for next weekend, any chance I can have the Friday off? I'm owed a day because I worked last Sunday."

"No problem. Now, anything for the news-list?"

"I'm not sure at the moment. There are a couple of angles I'm looking at. Just put down "WBC developments" for now and I'll try to come up with something. At the very least we can probably follow up on the ultimatum story."

Baird grimaced. "Haven't you got anything fresh? How about a piece saying how useless the Italian Police are?"

"Why should I write that? We've got no grounds."

"Well, they've not come up with a thing. Not a blinding thing."

"We don't know that, Curley."

"Then what. What have they come up with?"

"We don't know because they work in secret. It's the law out there."

Blair sniffed and walked away.

Brown stared at the article, trying to make sense of what she saw. The Warham's home had been used as a location for photo session with Gonzales. So, did he take them, and if so, how did Clarke get hold of them? She was getting no nearer to solving the mystery. "A mystery wrapped in an enigma" is how Churchill once described Russia. She now knew what he meant.

Defeated, she decided to book her trip to Paris instead of beating her brains on an insoluble problem. Eurostar booked online, the hotel by telephone. Two nights at Hotel de l'Église, where she had stayed once before, would set her back the best part of her bonus. But it is a fantastic little hotel, tucked away off the Boulevard St Germain. Only as she put the telephone down did she remember that the double room in which she had stayed before actually had two beds pushed together rather than one large *matrimonielle*. She smiled to herself. She would enjoy teasing Hogan.

She emailed him details of the proposed trip and returned to the question of the photos. Fascinating though they were they did not, in themselves, make a story. Part of a larger story, certainly, but she had no idea what that was. She called the photographer who shot the pictures for the *Review* to ask if he had booked the house for a modelling session? Not only was the answer "no", but also he did not think the house was available for photographic work. So Warham must have taken the pictures himself, or at least commissioned them. But why would a married man take such a risk? It was making less and less sense.

After two cups of tea, discussions with Jill Lambert about clothes, and a Kit Kat, she telephoned Tom Warham, who seemed almost pleased to hear from her. When she said she wanted to meet him, he said he could meet her at about five o'clock somewhere near King's College. He needed to be back, he explained, for a reception at six. They agreed to meet in the bar of a smart new "boutique hotel" on the edge of theatreland.

"By the way, Tom, am I right in thinking your father was a keen photographer?"

"Yes. It was his first love really. After money, possibly."

"Thanks. I'll see you at five."

Brown cleared her timetable with Baird, who seemed remarkably relaxed that she didn't have a story for him. At four o'clock Alex was waiting outside to take Brown first to Primrose

Hill to pick up the photographs, and on to the chic and no doubt expensive bar.

Tom strode in, his height and ramshackle appearance contrasting sharply with a party of business-suited Japanese. She ordered the drinks.

He looked around the unfamiliar room. "Is this the sort of place journalists hang out these days? I thought they went to the Cheshire Cheese."

"I'm afraid only tourists go to the Cheese these days. Sadly, Tom, journalists don't really gather anywhere any more. Not like it was in the old days, so I'm told, when they were all located around Fleet Street."

"Anyway. What can I do for you? As I said, I have to be back for a reception soon after six. You're welcome to come by the way."

Brown ignored the invitation but could not help thinking that possibly physical appearance was not the only characteristic Tom had inherited from his father. She pulled out just one of the photographs from the envelope, first making sure they were not overlooked. Tom stared at it for a few moments and then laid it face down on the table. "Why are you showing me this, Cassandra?"

"You recognise the location?"

"Of course I bloody do. Where did these come from?"

"I'm sorry, I can't tell you."

He picked up the photograph and handed it back to her. "You'd better put this back in the envelope before anybody else sees it. Why didn't you tell me before that the pictures were taken at the house?'

"I didn't know, Tom. I've never been to your parents' house."

He looked at his watch. "I suppose if you had known, you'd have felt you had to mention that too in your wonderful Dirty Tricks scoop. If you'd shown them to me when I first asked to see them I could have helped you do a proper demolition job. Read all about it. Only son spills the beans on Mr Fucking Genius."

His voice was rising and his arms seemed out of control. The Japanese stopped talking.

"I'm sorry, Tom. I didn't want to ..."

"What? You didn't want to what?"

Brown shifted uneasily in her seat. "Well, I didn't want to upset you. Sorry."

To her astonishment he suddenly smiled. What was it with this guy? His mood swings? His pent-up anger itching to get out?

He stood up, and she thought he was leaving. But he just did a circumnavigation of their table and sat down again. The anger seemed to have evaporated. "Do you remember, when we met, I said to you that if you dug around you'd find stuff?"

"Yes."

"Well, I am not sure what else you have found in the last couple of weeks, but we have discovered my father had a lot of secrets and these," he pointed to the envelope between them, "are yet another. The man was a fake."

"How's your mother holding up?"

"Well, they want her to go back to La Spezia. The magistrate wants to ask her a barrow-load of questions, but I can't see the point. For that matter, I can't see the point of talking to a newspaper. My father is dead and the sooner we bury him the better."

"Don't you want to know what happened?"

"I'm not sure I care – let the Italians come up with their equivalent of death by misadventure or whatever."

"But what if he was murdered?"

"Even if he was, what help would it be for us to know? The sooner he's buried the sooner you guys can stop digging around for dirt." Angry man was back.

"I'm sorry, Tom. I'm not looking for dirt, but there is considerable public interest in this story."

"Correction, Cassandra, the public might be interested. But there is no public interest issue whatsoever."

Tom picked up his whisky glass, then put it down again the contents untouched. He rubbed his hands down his trouser legs. "Look, I'm sorry I got a bit ratty, but if I am honest I am not sure what I want, other than to wake up and find I have been having a long bad dream. And that's not going to happen."

He picked up his glass again and this time took a mouthful, wiping his lips with the back of his hand. "OK, you may as well hear it from the horse's mouth, 'cos you'll probably find out anyway. In his luggage we found some pills my mother didn't recognise. One was for high blood pressure. The other was a form of tranquilliser. But they are both sometimes prescribed for stress."

"Hardly surprising he was stressed, with Elwood piling on the pressure."

"Right" He paused, seemingly undecided as to whether or not to go on. "But the thing is, neither of them were made up in London. They were both dispensed in New York. In fact, I'm not sure you can even get them over here."

"So what are you saying, Tom?"

"I suppose what I am saying is that John had a secret life. Mother was really angry. She'd always thought John, despite his faults, was basically honest with her. And now you present me with these photographs. What am I supposed to make of them? What the hell was she doing there? I really don't want my mother to hear of these. Are you planning to write anything?"

Brown looked down into her bloody Mary. "No ... well, not immediately. To tell you the truth, Tom, they don't on their own make a story. Well, not for the *Post* anyway. And by the way, nobody at the office has seen these. I've deliberately kept them out of sight."

The Japanese were getting noisy and the evening crowd were beginning to fill up the bar. The bill paid, they walked out onto the Aldwych pavement, a blast of warm air liberally laced with diesel fumes hitting their nostrils. They headed towards the bottom of Kingsway, opposite Bush House, and stopped at the kerb.

"Well, as I said Cassandra, I've got to get back for a reception. Thanks for the drink. Would you just let me know if you are going to do anything about the pictures? I'd like to try to prepare my mother somehow ..."

"Thanks for meeting me ... I promise I'll let you know."

Tom Warham's earlier invitation to Brown to attend the reception was not renewed.

It was really too early in the evening for Brown to have a large Bloody Mary inside her, and she needed a walk. Surprisingly, she had not heard from Baird, not even a call to ask whether she was going back to the office. The traffic was virtually stationary in Fleet Street as she walked down past the Royal Courts of Justice where a television reporter was speaking to camera. The *Standard*'s billboards were full of President's Bill Clinton's memoirs. Monica had been a "dreadful mistake". With no particular destination in mind, Brown crossed Fleet Street to the south side and walked under an ancient archway down a cobbled street she had never noticed before. All around were old buildings, Georgian probably, with cream-painted plaques carrying the names of barristers. The Inns of Court were a quiet sanctuary from the scramble of Fleet Street which, despite having long ago lost its status as the home of British newspapers, retained a somewhat frantic air. Under a large plane tree, Brown sat down to write up her notes. She was every bit as confused as Tom, but unlike him, she wanted to find out what had really happened to John Warham, and why.

The first green ink letter was waiting for Brown when she arrived at the office next morning. Rarely does anything interesting come through the post, and she opened the typed, correctly addressed envelope expecting to find a boring week-old press release about the latest innovation in one-way valves or some other such material destined for the rubbish bin. But it was a neatly typed, or word-processed, letter.

Dear Cassandra Brown,

You might like to know WBC is mounting an investigation into Warham's expenses.

That was it. No details, no signature, no date. She turned it over but the back was blank. She retrieved the envelope from the bin and looked at it. There was no indication it had been through the post at all, so it may have been hand-delivered. So where had it come from? Surely not Clarke again? What about Stephen Bennett? Perhaps he was impatient that she had not written a word so far on the stuff he had given her?

She walked across to Greg Jones' desk, which was precariously piled with back issues of the *Spectator* and the *Economist*. Jones had left just enough room, at one corner, for his feet. The keyboard of his workstation was balanced on top of the computer screen. Jones looked up from the magazine he was reading. "Ah Cassandra, would you like to hear my money-saving tip of the week? Don't buy the *Economist*." He chuckled at his own wit, and waited for Brown to speak. She handed over the letter without a word.

Jones read it and put it down on his desk. He nodded towards an empty chair pushed against the wall. "Mind how you sit down. The back's given way." Brown sat gingerly on the grubby swivel chair, glanced at Jones and didn't need to ask how it got broken.

Jones lifted his feet from the desk and allowed his chair to sit back on all its four feet. "Where did it come from?"

"It was on my desk when I arrived this morning. Not sure whether it came in the mail or by hand."

Jones leaned back again, tucked his hands behind his head, and surveyed the office. "The mail's not come yet. You know the Post Room like to leave it to mature for a while before bringing it round, just in case it's urgent."

"Greg, I'd really value your advice on this one."

Jones put down his magazine and picked up a ballpoint pen, which he twiddled between his fingers. "I'll tell you what you shouldn't do, you shouldn't tell Baird. Not until you've found out a lot more. You daren't go off half-cock."

At the mention of his name, even above the noise of the newsroom and at a distance of twenty metres, Baird glanced in their direction. He didn't miss a thing but was obviously not curious enough to walk over, being engrossed in typing the first news-list. Greg nodded towards Baird and raised his eyebrows.

"So Greg, do you think this is a green ink job from a nutter or should I take it seriously?"

Jones was still holding the letter. He held it up to the light. "It's not green and it's not ink. It's on decent paper and doesn't have any spelling mistakes. I think this is a case of smoke and fire, if you catch my drift. In other words, I would take it seriously until you are in a position to rule it out."

"But how? How do I take it seriously? What do you think I should do? I can hardly ring up WBC and ask them, can I?"

The two journalists were silent for a moment. Baird glanced uneasily over in their direction but continued with his typing, in between slurps of coffee from a pale yellow plastic cup. Jones spoke first. "In a normal company, that is a company with normal boardroom structures and the required checks and balances, this sort of thing would be handled by the chairman. Now, we have a complication, don't we, because Warham was himself the chairman? He'd hardly be investigating himself, would he? So who would?"

Brown had the distinct impression that Jones already knew the answers to all the questions he was posing, and was carefully tutoring her on the intellectual processes that needed to be completed before any conclusions could be drawn. She was ready with her answer. "Elwood."

"But in what capacity, Cassandra? How would he acquire the right to investigate his boss's expenses?"

"He was finance director. It was his hands on the purse strings."

Brown had not mentioned the documents she had been given in Amsterdam, because she seriously doubted they were genuine. Neither Baird nor the Editor had pressed her on the success or otherwise of the visit, and she didn't want to raise the matter, and thus appear naïve, unless she had to.

But the latest letter did fit with the thrust of what the documents suggested: that Warham was in deep financial trouble. She could trust Jones to help without patronising her. "Wait a minute Greg, I've some other things to show you."

Jones looked carefully through the papers she placed on his desk, unfolding each one and then neatly refolding it and replacing it in the envelope Brown had been given by Bennett. He stared for a long time at the letter turning down Warham's request for a loan.

"It all fits, Cassandra, doesn't it? In fact, it fits so neatly it makes me doubtful. Shall we get a coffee?"

They made an incongruous couple as they headed towards the vending machine. Baird rose from his desk and followed them down the stairs. "What are you two hatching? Anything I can put on the news-list? Mind you, it'll have to be good. We are tight as a tick today and I've already got enough to fill the pages twice over." Without waiting for an answer he strode off, clipboard under his arm, in the direction of the editor's conference room.

Back at Jones' desk, the two sipped their drinks, Brown waiting for the next pearl of undoubted wisdom to fall from his lips. She did not have to wait long. Jones' face lit up. "Cassandra, did you ever hear of a man named Rocky Ryan?"

"No, I don't think so. Is he a boxer?"

"Not a boxer Cassandra, a hoaxer. A man who dedicated his life to pulling wool over journalists' eyes."

"And they fell for it?"

Jones picked up his coffee, sipped a little, continued. "You bet they did, time after time. The lure of an exclusive, however far-fetched, was too strong. And do you know his golden rule, 'always tell then what they want to hear'. I think, Cassandra, we may have another Rocky Ryan on the loose."

"Why should it be another one, Greg?"

"Because, like your Mr Warham, Rocky Ryan is dead."

So was this what her trip to Amsterdam had boiled down to, a hoax? For once, she was not going simply to accept that Jones was right. If the documents were genuine, money worries on top of health problems could have been a motive for Warham to take his own life.

She thanked Jones for his help and went back to her desk. With Baird not hassling her for a story, she had space to think. In fact, the plot seemed to be falling neatly, piece by piece, into place. Warham's life had been unravelling. And sooner than face humiliation, he had taken action one morning on a cliff-top. And Elwood had not denied the story of the rejected loan request, merely ridiculed it.

"The auditors."

Brown looked up with surprise at Jones, blocking the light. "Sorry Greg, I'm not with you."

Jones grabbed a chair, sat down and leaned towards her. She noticed for the first time, and with some surprise, his eyes were the deepest blue, like a baby's.

"The auditors. The auditors, Cassandra. If they had expressed a doubt about Warham's expenses, they would have told Elwood."

Got it. "And he would have confronted Warham."

"Not immediately Cass. First he would have asked them to dig deeper."

"Surely the whole board would have had to know?"

Jones looked in the wastepaper bin, and finding it empty, turned it upside down. He then propped up his feet on the bottom of the bin. "I don't see why. Picture this. The head of the audit firm rings up Elwood and says, 'Oh Charles, we may have a little problem. I wonder if we could have a spot of lunch to talk about it?' So Elwood says, 'What sort of problem?' and he replies 'It's very delicate so I'd rather not discuss it over the 'phone. Could you possibly pop round tomorrow?'

Jones' chair was in danger of toppling. The upturned waste bin moved an inch or two away from him. He continued, "Elwood would be busting to know what it was all about so goes round the next day, where the audit partner says the "little problem" is with Warham's expenses. Should he dig a bit deeper? Music to Elwood's ears, methinks. 'Oh yes, he would say, but you are to report solely back to me'."

"Greg, you're brilliant, that's it, the auditors. I'd have never thought that in a million years."

"Hang on Cassandra. It's only a theory. But I have to admit it myself, it does stack up."

"Would they confirm it, do you think, if I called them?"

"Not a chance. They take their secrets to the grave. You'll have to confront Elwood if you want to run any of this."

"Suppose he refuses to comment?"

"Then you're probably stuffed. But I don't see why he would refuse. Especially if you say something like 'I have it on good authority'. It's a chance for him to drive in another nail."

"Pardon?"

"Another nail, Cassandra, it's a chance for him to drive another nail into poor John Warham's coffin."

"I'll call him now?"

Jones looked thoughtful. "What's the hurry? Why not wait until Monday?"

"Why wait?"

A mischievous smile spread across his rosy cheeks. He looked more than ever like a schoolboy. "Well, firstly Baird has already said there's no space in tomorrow's paper, so your story will be cut to shreds. Secondly, even if there was space, you don't want to waste this story on the Saturday readers. They only buy the paper to check they've still got the best mortgage deal. Thirdly, if I were Elwood I would listen to you politely and say nothing. Promise to get back to you while trying to cast enough doubts to stop you running the story. Then I would tell my version to the *Sunday Times* or the *Sunday Telegraph*, and bang goes your exclusive.

"Hold your horses and hit him with it on Monday afternoon. That way you can even pre-write most of it first, get it lawyered in good time and just top it up with any comment he might make. And I assume you know you can't libel the dead."

She wanted to kiss him. Instead, she asked if he fancied a glass of wine at lunchtime.

When Baird returned from the editor's conference. He was grinning like the proverbial Cheshire cat. She had no idea why.

CHAPTER EIGHTEEN

WHEN Brown woke on Monday morning, she was looking forward to going to work. Over Saturday and Sunday, she had convinced herself that the expenses story must be correct, that her anonymous informer had to be a well-placed WBC mole, in a position to know about an investigation that had not been disclosed even to all the board.

The good feeling evaporated the minute she arrived at the office. Baird was in a black mood, even for him. She could feel the tension as she came through the swing doors. He snatched at the phone whenever it rang, snarled at any reporter foolish enough to try to talk to him and repeatedly stood up to try to tuck his shirt into his trousers.

This was a time to adopt a low profile, rather than seek to discuss a possible story still based on nothing more than an anonymous letter and a few bits of circumstantial evidence.

Jones was, surprisingly, already at his desk, but head down in whatever it was he was doing, probably his column for Tuesday, and did not look as if he would want to be disturbed. Brown was keen to talk to him, to seek his advice on how best to approach Elwood without coming off worst. She had suffered too many defeats at Elwood's hands recently and did not relish another humiliation. She looked again at the letter, which she now knew by heart.

Dear Cassandra Brown,

You might like to know WBC is mounting an investigation into Warham's expenses.

There was something in the choice of words, the choice of "You might like to know", that stank of Elwood. It was certainly pompous enough. And: "mounting an investigation". Why not simply "investigating"? Why use three words when one would be enough? But she couldn't face another standoff with the man, which she feared would end up with her again being made to feel foolish. She folded the letter back in to the envelope and resolved to keep her suspicions to herself.

She would tackle Elwood later, once she had talked to Jones. But should she let Tom Warham know? He had, after all, told her about his father's secret medication – didn't she owe it in return to warn him that tomorrow's *Post* might contain an article that effectively claimed his father was a thief? She had no choice, and in any case she would like to include a comment from him. Perhaps he could be encouraged to say it was nothing more than a witch-hunt.

But she wasn't pleased about having to dish the father of somebody she had grown to like. How right John Douglas had been when he warned Brown, just after she arrived from Australia, not to get too close to the people she would write about. "It's not money that corrupts journalists, Cassandra, it's friendship." Too right, John.

But first, she had to stand the story up and talk to Baird. By the time he strutted off to morning conference, his humour appeared to have improved — Brown had not overheard an expletive yelled down the phone for several minutes, but that could have been down to the fact that Baird had not talked to the advertising department during that time.

While waiting for Jones to finish his column, Brown wrote part of the story and a number of different introductory paragraphs. Satisfied with none of them she went to the coffee machine. When she returned, Baird was not only back from conference, he was seated at her desk, reading from her screen. His face told her all she needed to know.

"I was coming to see you Cassandra, to tell you the editor insists we run something on Warham tomorrow. I see you are already ahead of him. This is sensational stuff. Where did you get it?"

"I have to harden it up yet, Curley. I'm even sure if it's right."

"The editor will want this on the front, Cassandra. It'll make a change from Iraq all the time. I'll try to get him to make it the splash."

"Curley, you're not listening. I just said I'm not sure it stands up. I haven't even checked it out with Elwood yet."

Baird continued to stare at the screen, scrolling the text up and down in front of him. "Great story. How much did he nick?"

"Curley, will you please pay attention. I'm not sure he nicked anything. Elwood may deny the whole thing."

"So what?"

Brown noticed Jones stop typing. Was he about to come to her aid? "Well, if he does deny it, we can't run it. It's based on an anonymous tip."

"Fuck that, Cassandra. Of course we can run it. The dead can't sue us anyway. I don't see what you're worrying about. It's sensational."

She was such a nong to leave the story on her screen. She couldn't even complain about Baird reading it, as it was the *Post's* policy that all screens should be hibernated whenever a journalist left her desk.

There was no retreat, no matter how much damage it might do. Sometimes hers really was a shitty job. "Curley, can I just ask that, please, you don't tell the editor about this until I have run it past Elwood."

"OK Cass, but you'd better get on with it because its going top of the afternoon news-list, right or wrong. Either we run with the story you've got here" he tapped the screen, "or we run with Elwood's denial, or even with a refusal to comment, if that's the way it turns out."

Brown scowled and made no reply. Denials printed in newspapers wreak as much damage as confirmations, usually because editors sanction them only when they believe they are being lied to. "MP denies affair with rent boy" is as damning a story as "MP admits affair with rent boy".

But if the story was wrong, then she couldn't simply accept Baird's position, even if the dead couldn't sue. This was one occasion when she might have to go above Baird's head and ask Henry Marshall to over-rule him. It would dent her relationship with Baird for a while, but if it stopped the story it would be worth it. She cursed herself again for leaving her screen live.

She telephoned Elwood on the dot of two thirty. He was in his office, and as sarcastic as ever.

"Oh Cassandra. How delightful to hear from you. I had

assumed you had moved on to a more interesting topic than WBC. I was beginning to miss our daily chats. I gather you had a nice supper with Andrew Clarke, by the way. I assume I'm now in the clear as far as John's holiday snaps are concerned?"

She might have guessed that Clarke's admission only came because he was being leaned upon by Elwood. The man was everywhere. Brown was in no mood to banter and came straight to the point. "Charles, I am ringing to find out more about the investigation into John's expenses."

Elwood paused just long enough before answering for her to know she had scored a direct hit. "Which investigation would that be, Cassandra?"

Two could play at answering the question with a question. "I only know about one, Charles, are you telling me there's more than one?"

"Are you looking for a comment from WBC, Cassandra, in which case I will offer my usual 'No comment'. Yes, no comment."

"I was hoping to broaden my understanding, Charles. I wouldn't want to damage anyone's reputation here, especially when such words as 'witch hunt' are flying around. I thought it would be in everyone's interest to get the story right."

"Well, Cassandra, you have our comment. But, as ever, you have assessed matters with some perspicacity. Let us talk background only. As you have managed to uncover, a matter had arisen concerning the use of WBC's," he paused while he appeared to search for the right word, "resources. Yes, resources. Let me emphasise here, and I cannot over-emphasise, that we are not talking about the sort of sordid penny piece cheating some of your fellow journalists are rumoured to get up to ..." He waited for the slur to sink in"... but the extent to which it might be thought reasonable for a director to use company assets, yes, facilities, for non-company business. This is a matter which the auditors, yes, the auditors, have asked us to address. In fact, I think I am right in saying they have asked all their audit clients to address the issue, so it's not something related specifically to WBC. Not at all."

"But there was, is, a specific issue relating to John?"

"There is, Cassandra, something quite specific. This was one of the issues on which John was, sadly, out of step with the board."

"So what was it?"

"You may not know, Cassandra, because I am not sure when you came to our shores, that John was closely involved with the Government, in fact with the previous government too, with the Millennium Dome project. I have to say he believed in it, yes, wholeheartedly, and undertook to try to persuade some of his clients to put their weight, yes, and their financial backing, behind it. He argued that the time he spent working with the government on the project was an investment for WBC. It would, he believed, lead to better relations with government and thus to a possibly greater volume of business from that source."

"So what has this to do with the auditors, Charles? It sounds a plausible argument to me."

"A plausible argument maybe, but sadly not one borne out by subsequent events. To be frank, Cassandra, not only have we not received one bit of government business but also we have lost clients who resented being strong-armed by their advertising agency."

"But why the auditors, Charles? It's none of their business."

"I am getting to the point Cassandra, if only you will be patient. The auditors are concerned that John used private charter aircraft paid for by WBC to engage in what could be seen as his private work for the government. He also hosted a couple of receptions here at head office, but that was a minor matter of no consequence here or there. It was the use of the airplane that has worried them."

"Why wasn't it questioned at the time?"

"As you yourself said, John had a plausible argument. Although I have to say, some members of the board were never really happy about the arrangement."

"So, why didn't they complain? And why has it only surfaced now? Is it part of your campaign?"

"Cassandra, if you were not a very dear friend, I would hang up now. There was no campaign, only issues that needed to be addressed. And it has come up now because we changed auditors last year and they have been looking back at past audits to satisfy themselves they were properly conducted."

"Was John being asked to pay the money back?"

"It was under discussion."

Just beyond her desk, Baird was hovering. She looked down at her notebook. "How much was involved?"

"Cassandra, I think I may have already told you more than I should. I am relying on you to treat our conversation with the utmost discretion. On the record, we are saying, 'No comment'. Is that clear?"

"Perfectly, Charles. I have no problem with that."

"And Cassandra, before you get too carried away, remember that this was an issue raised by the auditors."

"And they were appointed by you?"

"By the board, Cassandra. By the board. And by the book." He chuckled at his own joke. "Now, if you've no more questions, I have a visitor waiting."

Brown jumped up from her chair and punched the air. "Yes, yes, Elwood confirmed it. It's even better that I thought. Warham was using private planes to jet around and charging them to WBC."

All trace of Baird's earlier black mood had disappeared. He was grinning so broadly his face was in danger of splitting in two. "What sort of planes?"

"For Christ's sake Curley, I don't know. Executive jets I suppose. Trust you to ask a question like that."

Baird sat down at Brown's desk and began drawing on his clipboard. "We'll do a piece for the front and then clear a whole inside page." He drew a line across the top of the page. "We'll do a top hamper on the cost of hiring a private jet. Our Transport Correspondent can do that. By the way, what was he using the planes for?"

"That's the best bit, Curley. He was jetting around trying to drum up support for the Dome."

"You are having me on, aren't you?"

"Straight up. He was charging WBC for doing the government's business."

Baird continued to scribble. "I'll get up pictures of the Dome and some executive jets. He didn't take his girlfriend with him, I 'spose?"

"Not so far as I know. It was probably before he met her."

"Pity. Look, can you give me 800 words for the page. We need something as a sidebar." He pointed to a vertical line he had drawn down the right hand side of the page.

Greg Jones looked up from behind his pile of papers. "How about a history of the Dome? It's a few years ago now and some readers may have forgotten about it. I've finished my column and can pull it together for you."

Baird looked doubtful. "Ehm. Not sure. Ill-fated Dome claims another reputation, something like that?"

Jones leaned right back in his chair and stroked his chin. He spoke slowly and deliberately, as if addressing a child or somebody who didn't understand the language. "OK, Curley, but just for the record, the Dome wasn't a disaster. What happened, if you remember, was that there was a projection that the Dome would attract 12 million visitors a year. That was always totally unrealistic and it was made to get the thing built. When the numbers fell short, it was deemed a disaster. Not true. But I can write anything you want. Any spin you like. I have been around long enough to know not to let the facts get in the way of a good story."

Baird removed his spectacles and rubbed them vigorously with the end of his tie. When he replaced them over his scowl, they looked no cleaner. "According to the editor, the Dome was a disaster. That's all I need to know, and all you need to know. We don't need a debate about it."

"Anything you say, Curley. But can I just remind you that the reason he, and virtually every other editor, was so negative, was because a whole load of them were left standing on Stratford Station for a couple of hours and missed half the Millennium Party."

"OK, OK. I said I didn't want a debate about it. If you can give me something on the people involved and the reputations lost that'd be great."

Jones put his chair back to the vertical. "Fancy a coffee, Cassandra?" He pointedly did not offer to get one for Baird, who continued sitting in Brown's seat, planning his page. He'd already drawn a childish sketch of an executive jet.

Brown felt she should warn Tom Warham, who answered his mobile immediately. He remained silent while Brown outlined the story.

"So, now we know. My father a thief as well as a liar, a philanderer and a megalomaniac. Oh, and a hypochondriac. The world needs to be told. It's in the public interest. What are you waiting for? Get writing."

Why had she bothered to call? She took a sip of coffee and spoke as gently as she was able. "Tom, there is no question of your father being a thief. I didn't suggest that for a moment. But ..."

"But what?" Tom shouted.

"But there is an investigation going on about WBC's money being used to drum up backing for the Dome. I can't ignore it."

Tom's voiced moderated. "But he did that for WB effing C. It was hardly a secret. He was trying to save a project he desperately wanted to succeed. How can you make something out of that?"

"It's not me making something out of it, Tom. According to Charles Elwood it was raised by the auditors."

"Oh, sure. And pigs can fly."

"Tom, I want to make this as positive as I can for John. Can I quote you?"

"Quote what?"

"Quote the bit about John working on the Dome on behalf of WBC. And that it was hardly a secret?"

"Oh, sure. Quote what you bloody well like."

"It's out of my hands, Tom. I can't take a decision about whether or not to run a particular story."

"You are just obeying orders. Now where have I heard that before?"

Brown ended the brief conversation as cordially as she could. The story would probably end her association with Tom Warham. She was going for broke with this one.

Baird returned from afternoon conference in a strop. The editor had decided not to take Brown's story for the front and had made it second lead in an inside page, which meant about 350 words only and no picture.

"Cameron's still looking after his mate, even if he's dead. You come up with the most sensational fucking story and he's as good as spiked it."

"Hardly spiked, Curley. It's still a page lead."

Baird grunted and clumped back to his desk, his plans in tatters. Brown suspected that immediately she hung up on Tom Warham, he had called the editor.

While using a company-financed plane on political business was a good story, it was not as if Warham had been pocketing the money himself, or had been using the plane to visit his girlfriend in Milan. In fact she now knew, from the picture library, that he had even been photographed by the *Manchester Evening News* at Manchester's Ringway Airport arriving in the company of a government minister. The two of them are standing in front of a business jet, which Curley immediately identified as a Falcon, one of the plushest on the market. A great picture to substantiate the story, but proof that the trip was no secret.

Jones abandoned his piece on the Dome and brought Brown a coffee. "How's it going?"

"To be honest, Greg, I'm struggling. Although there's an investigation going on, it was all pretty open and above board. I'm really having trouble dressing this up as a scandal."

"But it is a scandal, Cassandra. You don't need to dress it up. How can it possibly have been justified for Warham, who was no doubt looking for a knighthood, to spend shareholders' money on his own pet project? When the shareholders hear of this, they'll really kick up a fuss, believe me. Have faith in your story Cassandra. If you don't, nobody else will. By the way, have you spoken to any shareholders to get their reaction?"

It had not occurred to Brown to do so. She shook her head. "Who do you think I should talk to?"

"Go to one of the big pension fund managers. I'll give you a couple of names if you like. I can tell you, Cassandra, they'll be outraged when they hear about it."

"Thanks Greg. You're a star. A real star."

One of Jones' contacts refused to comment, but the other two were every bit as upset as he had predicted. One added he would be taking the matter up with WBC "at the highest level". Finally she had her story. She was putting the finishing touches to "WBC faces City outrage over private use of executive jet", when Elwood telephoned.

"I gather you've been speaking to some of our shareholders, Cassandra. In view of that I thought I had better let you know that WBC has been advised to issue a clarifying statement, in order to make sure the facts are properly disclosed to the market."

"Don't you trust me to do that, Charles?"

"With respect, Cassandra, that is not your job. We need to

assure our shareholders that matters are being properly dealt with by the board. It is a matter of observing the correct procedures. Yes, the correct procedures."

Brown could see her exclusive story, which had already caused her considerable anguish and which was likely to cause her even more, slipping away. If WBC issued a statement, then all the newspapers would have the story, not just the *Post*. It was worth trying to stall Elwood.

"When are you putting out the statement, Charles?"

Jones was within earshot and hurriedly scribbled a note, "ring off—call back", which he held up for Brown to see. Before Elwood answered, she made an excuse about another call coming in from overseas and rang off, promising to call back in a few minutes.

"We've got to try and stop him putting out a statement, Cassandra, or at least delaying it until tomorrow."

"Otherwise my exclusive is fucked. But how can we do that. Any ideas?"

He grinned broadly. "Not a clue Cassandra, not a blinding clue, but time is on our side. He's only got forty five minutes to get something to the Stock Exchange, otherwise it will have to go out tomorrow anyway."

"But he can just put something out on the newswires. He doesn't have to stick within the Stock Exchange's timetable."

"No, but I think he will on something as serious as this. There's just one trick I can try. One of the people I put you in touch with, the man at S & G, is a very good mate of mine."

"I gathered that."

"And I am not sure he will share Elwood's enthusiasm for WBC issuing a statement. He's the sort of person who would sooner things be managed behind closed doors. I could suggest he gives Elwood a ring. What do you think?"

"Greg, as ever, you're brilliant. Could you try?"

Attracted by the discussion and the worried faces, Baird hurried across the office to join the discussion. "Why did you have to ring Elwood, Cass? He's going to screw us now."

"Because, Curley, if I hadn't rung Elwood I wouldn't have had a story."

Baird stalked off muttering. Jones was already deep in a

telephone conversation with his friend at S & G. He grinned and gave a thumbs up to Brown. As he put down the telephone, the grin broke into an open smile. "He's going to call Elwood now. He'll say he's had a call from you about the matter in hand and that he'd like the opportunity to discuss the matter in person with Elwood before any public statement is made."

"But will Elwood listen?"

"If he wants to hang onto his job he will. He's not going to mess with S & G when he's only just got his feet under Warham's desk. By the way, he didn't take any persuading. He was horrified that WBC was rushing out a statement about something that happened five years ago. He doesn't want his name mentioned, by the way."

Brown waited half an hour before telephoning Elwood. "I've been watching my screen, Charles, but I haven't seen anything yet. Are you hoping to put something out tonight?"

"I have remarked before, Cassandra, that you journalists are so impatient. Why on earth would we be rushing to put out a statement about a matter which is, after all, several years in the past? In fact, I am not sure we will say anything at all. I do hope, by the way, you are keeping this, this matter in perspective."

"Absolutely, Charles."

She was increasingly sure that Elwood himself had sent the anonymous letter, but she was not going to risk another humiliation by accusing him to his face. Not yet, anyway. A favourite saying of her Dad's came into her mind. *There's always free cheese in a mousetrap.* But who was supplying her cheese?

SECTION	News3
TITLE	Warhamexpenses
HEADING 1	WBC faces outrage over use of private jet by former chairman—probe launched
HEADING 2	
AUTHOR	Cassandra Brown
STATUS	Live

WBC, the multinational advertising group, has launched an investigation into expenses incurred by its late chairman, John Warham, in connection with his political activities.

The *Post* has learned that the probe was triggered during a routine evaluation of past audits by the new auditors appointed last year.

The auditors have queried the use by Mr Warham of chartered aircraft, paid for by the company, during his campaign to raise funds for the controversial Millennium Dome several years ago.

Mr Warham and government ministers embarked on a "whistle stop" tour of Britain to drum up support for the project, which at the time looked as if it might founder because of inadequate funding.

The investigation has come to light in the wake of Mr Warham's still unexplained death while on holiday in Italy.

Although there appears to be no question of Mr Warham gaining personal financial benefit from the use of the aircraft, questions have been raised as to whether WBC should have financed the trip.

At the time, it is understood the board reluctantly agreed to the plan when Mr Warham assured them that WBC would benefit from additional government work as a result. In the event, no such work has materialized.

Shareholders contacted by the *Post* yesterday expressed anger that company funds had been used for political purposes.

One, who refuses to be identified publicly, said he

would be taking it up with the company "at the highest level".

"This is an abuse of power at the centre", he said. "While we recognise companies need to have good relationships with the government, this is seeking to carry favour at our expense."

Charles Elwood, who was appointed chief executive following the death of Mr Warham, would not comment on the matter.

WBC chartered a Falcon, one of the plushest executive jets on the market, for the trip, which is likely to have cost upwards of £25,000.

Meanwhile, the ongoing investigation into Mr Warham's death continues. His body was found in the sea two weeks after he disappeared while on holiday with his wife.

CHAPTER NINETEEN

"HE'S STILL working on the two theories, Cassandra. Theory one is that Mr Warham was under so much pressure he took his own life. Theory two is that Mrs Warham pushed him off the cliff in a fit of jealous rage." So, after weeks of investigation the magistrate in La Spezia had managed to come up with the two most obvious theories. What do they pay these drongos for?

Brown loaded her cereal bowl into the dishwasher, picked up her coffee and walked through to the bedroom. Outside was bright sunshine. The white muslin curtains twitched in a slight breeze from the open window.

Brown looked at the clock next to her bed. It was already after nine and she was running late. She really didn't have time to listen to a lot of waffle. "I guess you must have heard something or you wouldn't be ringing me. Can you share it with me?"

"It sounds as if you may be in a rush, Cassandra. Shall I call you later."

He was more intuitive than she gave him credit for. "Paolo, that would be great. We'll talk when I get to the office."

She was choosing what to wear when the mobile rang again. She had finally managed to get rid of the irritating Bach and instead had a nice old-fashioned ring. On the screen was the name Tom Warham. She took a deep breath. She would have to answer it. To her surprise, Tom's opening gambit was totally friendly. "Hello, Cassandra, it's Tom. How are you?"

"Not bad, Tom, and you?"

"I'm fine. Well, I would be if it wasn't for this business. I've just been speaking to the British consulate in Milan. We want to get my father home, but the Italians are refusing to release his body. It really is pissing me off. You can imagine how my mother feels. To be fair to the consulate, I think they are doing all they can but the magistrate is being bloody-minded and obstructive. I wondered if a heart-rending article in the *Post* might shame them into action ... "

Brown spread out her clothes on the bed. "I'm not sure it would help Tom, but I'm willing to give it a go. Look, can we meet up sometime today to talk about it. I think I'm free all day, so if you have a spare half hour?"

"I'm over at Kensington this morning at a conference. In fact, I'm there now. It finishes about twelve. Could we meet up then?"

Brown needed to get to him before he changed his mind. "Shall we meet for lunch?"

Tom sighed. "I really only have time for a quick sandwich and then I'm back to the Strand. I could see you at the Strand at about half twelve."

"It's a fantastic day. Shall I pick up a couple of sandwiches and we'll find somewhere to eat them?"

"Do you know Temple Gardens, Cassandra, just on the embankment more or less in front of the college?"

"I'll find them. Shall I meet you there? What would you like in a sandwich?"

"Anything. Oh, cheese and pickle. I'll see you later. And oh, by the way, in case you were worried about the article you wrote in yesterday's paper, I thought you were very balanced. I've no complaints."

"Thanks. That's a relief. I'll see you about twelve thirty."

Brown completely forgot about her promise to call Vittorio. She spent her time at the office outlining Tom Warham's proposition to Baird, who seemed distinctly unenthusiastic. This story was firmly in tabloid territory; it had left the arcane world of business. She was used to writing about companies rather than individuals, take-over bids rather than personal anguish, captains of industry, not grieving widows. She wrote a few alternative opening paragraphs and showed them to Baird, but received little encouragement.

At midday Alex was outside the *Post*'s offices. Instead of his usual immaculate grey suit, he had on a crisp white shirt, silk tie which Brown guessed was an Hermes, and dark trousers. The Toyota's interior smelled of something expensive. Verdi's Requiem was playing gently on the radio. She could shut her eyes and imagine herself in the back of a big bouncy limo, if it wasn't for the rattles.

"Was it Temple Gardens, Miss Brown?"

"Yes, but I need to pick up some sandwiches on the way please Alex. By the way, I love your tie."

"Thank you Miss Brown. It was a gift."

"From an admirer?"

"I couldn't say, Miss Brown. Now which number Temple Gardens would you like? I can drive in from Tudor Street."

"It wasn't a particular number, Alex. It was the gardens themselves I meant, near King's College. I'm meeting somebody there."

Alex smiled into the mirror. "I know where you mean, I think. Inner Temple Gardens, would it have been? Temple Gardens is a row of barristers' chambers."

Brown nodded. "I have a poster of Temple Gardens on my bedroom wall, Alex, but not the one we are going to."

Alex grinned through the mirror. "You mean the Paul Klee, Miss Brown? Do you happen to know where the original is?"

Brown admitted she didn't and a slightly awkward silence descended in the car. She shouldn't have mentioned her bedroom. They passed St Paul's Cathedral, the west front thronged with tourists, coaches lined nose to tail along Cannon Street and Ludgate Hill. Half way down the hill, Alex stopped outside a sandwich shop. He turned round in his seat. "What would you like me to get, Miss Brown?"

"No. It's OK, Alex. I'll get them."

While she waited in the sandwich shop, Alex stood by the car, ignoring the hostile looks from the drivers who had to manoeuvre their buses and coaches past the parked minicab. A traffic warden walking down the hill waved an acknowledgement to Alex, but made no attempt either to issue a ticket or move him on. Networking operates at all levels.

A few minutes later Brown was walking around the Inner Temple Gardens pondering on the incongruity of Alex, and of the coincidence of the reference to Paul Klee, who had done much to celebrate, through his paintings, the Cinque Terre, when she came face to face with Tom. It should not have been a surprise, but it was nevertheless. They found a bench and sat down. He looked hot, flustered and unhappy, in a heavy grey suit, carrying his enormous briefcase. He immediately drank most of the bottle of water Brown handed him from the paper carrier bag.

"So, you've got problems with the Italian bureaucracy?"

He looked down at the gravel path, suddenly bending and pulling up one sock. "They are refusing to release the body. They won't tell us why, nor how much longer they plan to hang on to it. I do think the consulate are doing all they can, but nothing seems to make any difference."

Brown turned slightly sideways on the bench so she could face him. "Is it because they haven't finished all the tests they want to do?"

"That's the official line and the one they are giving to the consulate, but I think there are other issues."

Brown opened the bag and handed him a neatly wrapped package. "I think that's yours, mature cheddar cheese and pickle. I got you wholemeal bread; I hope that's alright. What other issues had you in mind?"

Tom put the package in his lap and began slowly to unwrap the greaseproof paper. It reminded her of her Dad when they used to play pass the parcel, when she was just a happy little Vegemite before her dad left home. He always unwrapped really slowly, to make sure the little gifts went to the children. Tom looked up and down the path. "I think they are holding on to the body in the hope my mother will get so frustrated she will go out there again." He took a huge angry bite from the sandwich.

Brown began to unwrap her own package. She picked up one quarter of a smoked salmon sandwich. "Why do they want her to go to Italy again, and why wouldn't she want to?" The pigeons waited hopefully around their feet.

"They want to interview her."

"Have they said so?"

"Yes. The request was made quite properly through the vice-consul, who passed it on to us. Our lawyer advises her not to agree, nor to travel to Italy until this matter is cleared up."

"Tom, you've been very straight with me and I want to be straight with you. I heard from a source in Italy that the magistrate, how can I put this?"

He supplied the words for her. "Suspects my mother of murder?"

Brown nodded. "Police the world over look for the easy answer, because it's often the right one. They understand jealousy. They probably understand about insurance. And I don't suppose they want to look too far."

Tom gulped some water, crushed the bottle and tossed it into the wire bin beside the bench. He took off his jacket and laid it carefully over the back of the back. His underarms were soaked with sweat. "The trouble is, there are no easy answers. Even to us, my father becomes more of a mystery every day. It's as if I didn't know him. By the way, his stupid doctor thinks he may have had a breakdown."

"And what do you think?"

"Cassandra, John Warham was as tough as old boots. He liked to appear the sensitive creative soul, the talented photographer who fell into business almost by accident. Bullshit, all bloody bullshit. Breakdown my arse. My father caused breakdowns. He didn't have them."

His face had turned puce, his hands shaking. Brown was afraid he was about to cry or have a heart attack and touched his arm. He pulled away and concentrated on carefully refolding the greaseproof paper in which his sandwich had arrived. He shook the crumbs onto the ground and their feet were immediately surrounded by pigeons. He turned to Brown and to her surprise placed his hand above her's, squeezing it so gently the action could have been accidental. "Do you fancy a drink, by the way?"

"OK. A juice or something would be nice." She wanted to finish her sandwich, but he was in a hurry. She wrapped the sandwich back into the paper and slipped it into her bag. The pigeons weren't getting her smoked salmon. As he withdrew his hand and bent forward to pick up the briefcase, Brown wondered, not for the first time, about Tom's sudden mood switches. She had just seen a transformation in an instant from angry, mourning son to may-be philanderer. Like father like son? He picked up his jacket and hung it over one shoulder, its loop securely through a finger, his briefcase in the other hand. They walked up through the gardens and out into Fleet Street where he turned without hesitation to the left and into Ye Olde Court Tavern. He was obviously known there. After the bright sunshine outside, the pub seemed impossibly gloomy. Fizzy orange juice from a bottle was not exactly Brown's favourite tipple, and she glanced covetously at Tom's pint. They sat in silence for a short while. One trick Brown had learned from in Melbourne was the tactical value of silence. If one sits silently, eventually your interviewee will feel obliged to say something. And as likely as not it will be something they did not intend to say. But when Tom did speak it was not about the matter which had brought them together.

"So how's it going with Conor?"

The question took her by surprise. Clearly the discussion about Warham's death was concluded – hadn't he signalled that with the abrupt change of mood in the gardens? Now they were into a social situation, two acquaintances finding some mutual ground to inhabit while they had a drink together. "Fine. He's fun isn't he?"

"He's really fond of you. I don't blame him, by the way. In his shoes ... well, maybe we shouldn't go there."

This was not a conversation Brown wanted to have and she sought to change the subject, back to Warham.

"You said his doctor thinks your father may have been on the edge of a breakdown. On what grounds?"

"I went to see him yesterday about the pills we found in John's luggage. He said they were a fairly typical prescription for stress, but maintained it was irrational to have sought medical help in New York when he had a regular doctor in London. But then he would say that, wouldn't he? Professional jealousy and all that. I expect there's a lot of that in your business?"

"Well, not so much jealousy as competition." She looked at her watch ostentatiously. Tom's pint was nearly gone. She could escape. "Well, I guess I'd better find my way back to the office. It was good to talk to you again Tom. I'll certainly write something about the Italian authorities being difficult. Can I just check again, though, what reasons they are giving?"

Tom picked up his glass and drained the rest of his beer. "Well, there's this cock and bull story about needing to do further toxicology tests. He wasn't poisoned for God's sake, he was drowned. And maybe bashed on the head first. That's another thing. Do you know how tall my mother is?"

Brown shook her head.

"Five feet two. My father was over six foot. How is she supposed to have bashed him over the head with a rock and pushed him off a cliff? She's not exactly Superwoman."

Even in the gloom, she could see Tom's colour rising again. He really was a very angry young man. He looked towards the door and watched as a girl walked to the bar to join a friend already perched on a stool. When he turned back to Brown his colour had already begun to subside. "Do you want the other half or do you really have to rush off?"

She was in no hurry to get back to the office. Ignoring his protests about paying she went to the bar and bought the drinks, returning to the dark table where he had chosen to sit. "Did they say what they were looking for in the tests?"

"No. But I would have thought all the usual tests would have been carried out as part of the regular *post mortem*, wouldn't you?"

"Tom, forget for a moment your mother could be a suspect. Surely you agree it's possible he was murdered. When I mentioned animal rights to you the other day, you implied he had received threats. Could there be a link, do you think?"

Tom look a long swig at his beer and looked around the pub. There were few other drinkers to overhear him. Nevertheless, he lowered his voice almost to a whisper. "I've been talking to Scotland Yard about that. You know he was quietly working for the government trying to persuade companies to back the Oxford Project. Anyone involved with that is routinely harassed by activists as you no doubt know. I just don't know how far they would go. Nobody does. But if you look at some of the websites you'll see that moderation and argument are not what they are about."

He bent again to pull up his socks, shooting a glance at the legs of the girl on the bar stool, before continuing. "Talk of murder's all a bit far fetched, though, isn't it, even for a newspaper reporter?"

Brown again looked at her watch. "Well, Tom, I think I'd better get back. As I said, it was good to see you and I'll certainly get something in the paper in the next couple of days about the problems you are having in Italy."

As she left the pub, Tom was heading back to the bar, glass in hand. Whether it was to get his third pint, to chat up the girls or simply to return the glass, she was not sure.

Vittorio had filed copy by the time she returned to the office. It was on her desk with the message "Curley wants your opinion on this." Most of it was unusable.

Reluctantly, she picked up the telephone and dialled Vittorio's number. "Hi Paolo, Cassandra. Thanks for your copy. Sadly we can't use it as it is because of libel laws in this country. You should have spoken to me before filing. I would have saved you a lot of work."

"But I spoke to you this morning Cassandra, don't you remember?"

"And we arranged to speak again later. I didn't tell you to file. We are running something about the investigation tomorrow, and I'll see if I can work any of your stuff in."

"Can we have a joint by-line?"

"I doubt it. Depends how much of your stuff I am able to use. Where are you by the way, in Milan or at the coast?"

"I had a spare day Cassandra, so I came down to the coast. Is there anything I can do for you while I am here?"

"It depends. Can you talk to the magistrate again? Or the police?"

"The Police, no. The magistrate, maybe. What do you want to know?"

"I want to know why they refuse to release Mr Warham's body for burial. And why they want to interview Mrs Warham. I thought your authorities were supposed to be sympathetic to widows, not harass them?"

"I suppose they will want to talk to Mrs Warham because she is a suspect. I don't know why they are refusing to hand over the body."

"Well, can you try to find out and call me back as soon as you can."

Brown was amazed at her own arrogance. But Vittorio had asked for it. He hadn't covered himself in glory by again filing copy behind her back. He needed putting back in his box. It didn't make her feel good, but it did work. Within half an hour Vittorio came through with answers to both her questions, confirming exactly what Tom had told her. The magistrate had instructed the *Carabinieri* to interview Ruth Warham again and he had indeed ordered more toxicological tests on the cadaver, because he wanted to establish whether or not Warham might have been drugged before he entered the sea. Vittorio had however, found out one additional piece of important information: the wound on Warham's head had been inflicted while he was still alive.

She finished the story and sent it to the news-desk. She again visited the web to check up on the animal rights angle. It was the usual – animals "liberated" from farms, the words "murderers" and "scum" daubed on the walls and material damage to property.

Lists of "legitimate targets" were growing daily. In top place were buyers of animals for vivisection – animal experimentation is described as torture and the researchers as torturers or worse.

Brown clicked on the "politics" section of one of the more extreme sites, and accepted the invitation to "search the site." She typed in the name John Warham and moments later a "biography" was across her screen.

John Warham: Paid millions from animal torturers to lobby on their behalf. Chairman of WBC, the advertising agency which works for pharmaceutical companies, cosmetics companies, food manufacturers and fur coat makers. Warham takes blood money from anyone who pays him enough. Government toady.

Below the entry were Warham's office and home addresses, telephone numbers and details of his company car. She made a mental note to warn Tom he should not use the blue Jaguar.

What more did the magistrate want? Warham was lying dead in a *camera mortuaria*. Why wasn't he looking at the animal rights issues? Maybe Bennett was right: the magistrate was bent and Scotland Yard had lost interest.

She went to see Baird, who was putting the last few stories into the afternoon news-list. As he continued to type, she explained about the website and the so-called "biography" she had found.

"So, Curley, do you think we'd be able to get this into the paper? I could angle it on the Italians' refusal to follow up the most obvious lead?"

"I thought you were writing about the Italians' refusal to release the body?" he questioned, distractedly.

"Well, yes, I am, but I thought."

"So this story still stands?" He tapped the screen with his pen at the line "Widow's anguish as Italy refuses burial".

"Yes, but."

Baird swung his chair so his back was towards Brown and nodded to Jill Lambert. "Gone, Jill." Lambert stood by the printer waiting for the news-list to appear, and hurried off to the copier to make the fourteen copies needed for the afternoon conference.

Baird unnecessarily reminded Brown that the Editor did not favour stories about the animal rights movement, on the grounds that they gave them the very thing they most craved, publicity. The "human interest" angle of a grieving widow not only being deprived of the opportunity to bury her dead husband, but also being harassed by the Italian Police, had more potential.

When Baird returned from the editor's office, it was with the news that her story of the grieving widow would lead the paper. Brown was back on the front page. But it was not the story she wanted to write.

SECTION	News1
TITLE	Bodystuck
HEADING 1	Widow's anguish as Italians refuse to release adman's body
HEADING 2	
AUTHOR	Cassandra Brown
STATUS	Live

Italian authorities were last night accused of "gross insensitivity" for their continued refusal to release a businessman's body for burial in England.

The body of advertising guru John Warham is effectively impounded in the Italian Navy port of La Spezia, weeks after it was pulled from the Ligurian Sea.

Despite protests from the British Embassy in Rome, the magistrate in charge of the investigation into Mr Warham's death wants yet more tests before allowing the family to take their loved one home.

Mr Warham, 58, disappeared while on holiday with his wife of thirty years, Ruth. Two weeks later, his body was found in the sea at the foot of treacherous cliffs.

It is understood the magistrate has ordered further toxicological tests to try to establish if Mr Warham was drugged before he fell from the cliffs.

A family friend said "Ruth just wants to be able to return John's body to Britain so that his loving family can say their farewells. She was his lifelong sweetheart and is devastated by his death.

"One would think the bureaucrats would be a bit more understanding."

Mr Warham was a close friend of the British Prime Minister, and the family are considering asking him to intervene personally in the matter.

A spokesman for the Prime Minister's office said that if the Warham family ask for help the request would get sympathetic treatment.

The Italian authorities have asked Mrs Warham to travel to Italy for questioning, but she has so far refused to do so on the grounds that she told them everything she knew when she reported him missing. It is suspected that the magistrate is retaining Mr Warham's body as a bizarre bargaining chip, refusing to release it unless Mrs Warham meets his demands to return to Italy.

Meanwhile, the future of tens of million of insurance claims remains in doubt.

CHAPTER TWENTY

BROWN called Moses from the Eurostar and took a cab from Waterloo to Kentish Town. She dropped her bag in the hall and fell into Moses' warm embrace. In the sitting room, on the coffee table, were a bottle of white, two glasses and a box of tissues. Chloë was in bed. Adam was away.

"So, what happened?"

"Kate, how long have I known him?" She didn't wait for an answer. "Known me five minutes and he thinks he owns me. He is just the most jealous, possessive, ignorant son of a bitch. It was an absolute nightmare."

Moses poured the wine. Brown took a gulp and went on. "The crowning glory was this morning. Paolo called me on the mobile about ten o'clock. Do you know what Conor did?"

"Tell me."

"First of all he snatched up his book and started to read. Then he slammed it down again, threw off the duvet and stomped into the bathroom, locked the door and started crashing around in there. So I've got Paolo in one ear rabbiting on about the state of the Warhams' marriage and I've got my own so-called relationship falling apart in front of my eyes. I hadn't even got out of bed."

Moses started to laugh.

"What's so funny?"

"It's just the way you tell it, Cass."

"Oh. Anyway. I got rid of Paolo and knocked on the bathroom door. Conor does one of his famous grunts. I'd had enough so I banged on the door and told him to hurry up 'cos I wanted to use the loo. Which was true, by the way."

Moses topped up Brown's glass, stifling another giggle. The humour was infectious.

"Eventually he comes out. I didn't speak to him, but just went in and shut the door. It was a scene straight out of George Feydeau. I took my time, and when I emerge he's sitting slumped in the only chair, his bag packed and by the door."

Brown was feeling more composed by the minute. Moses' Sancerre was hitting all the right parts.

"So I said to him, what was all that about? And do you know what he had the front to say?"

"No, tell me."

"He didn't appreciate me talking to other men while I was in bed with him. So, quick as a flash, I said, 'don't worry, it won't happen again'. He thought for a minute I was apologising, and then he clocked my expression. Anyway, enough of that. How are you, how's Chloë?"

"She's asleep, thank God. So, then what happened?"

"Well, I picked up my clothes, took them into the bathroom and got dressed. I wasn't giving him a free peep show."

This was clearly too much for Moses and she burst out laughing. "Sorry Cass, but it's just the way you tell it. I know it's not funny. Was it all awful?"

Brown searched her mind for any positives during the weekend, but came up with very few. Right from the moment she stepped off the Eurostar, it had been tense. Hogan was waiting at the barrier and seemed irritated, even though Brown could hardly be blamed for a ten-minute delay in the train's arrival. Anyway, he had almost snatched her bag and, without a word, headed off towards the taxi rank.

Like virtually every railway terminal in any major city, Gare Du Nord sits in the midst of a perpetual traffic jam. Instead of spending the next half hour watching a taxi meter rack up the Euros as they tried to get clear of the station, Brown had suggested they take the Metro. Hogan argued it would be full of beggars and pickpockets.

He gave in grudgingly, and they went down the escalator, each carrying their own luggage. Brown slipped Hogan a Metro ticket from a *carnet* she had bought in London. They stood side by side on the platform, she enjoying the smell of the hot rubber of the train tyres, the proximity of the drains and the fumes from the electric motors. It could only be Paris. Opposite, a huge poster advertising Lejaby underwear seemed to have claimed Hogan's attention. When the train came, it was stifling, but scarcely ten minutes later they had negotiated their luggage through a set of automatic doors and climbed the stairs into the evening light of the Boulevard Saint Germain des Pres. The air was good enough to breath. The threatened thunderstorm had headed off in another direction. An old man in a beret squeezed traditional music from a piano accordion. The traffic honked and weaved. A one legged man knelt on the pavement, overdressed in rags, a paper cup in front of his knees. Hogan had put his hand into his pocket, but added nothing to the beggar's cup.

Brown had had misgivings about staying at L'Eglise. On their only visit to Europe together, soon after they were married, she and Steve had taken the train from London to Paris. The hotel had been recommended by a friend and was just the perfect blend of comfort and Parisian chic. They spent two nights there. She loved it. He was miserable. Steve was uncompromisingly Australian. He liked the open air, the ocean, a big steak and a cool beer. He found the smell of Paris offensive, the noise torture, the food too fussy and the hotel room too small. He had no grasp of the language and no wish to shop. Throughout the weekend, they had tried to make a joke of their differences, because neither wanted to spoil it for the other. But Paris revealed a faultline in their relationship.

Brown explained to Moses, over her second glass of wine, that she had taken Steve to the Jardin du Luxembourg in the hope that the sight of trees and grass would help, but it didn't. So they spent the weekend being polite, rather than honest. The trip marked the beginning of the end of Cassandra and Steve, the weekend when Brown realised she was never going to persuade her husband to live in Europe, but that she couldn't live anywhere else.

Despite all that, like an old lag, she had returned with Hogan, not only to the same city but also to the same hotel, perhaps even to the same room. How could she have been such a lamb-brain?

Brown downed her glass. "Enough of all that. Thanks to the crass behaviour of Conor Hogan I've got a present for Chloë. I picked up a nice old book from a second hand stall by the river. I had been planning to give it to him."

"Sure you don't want it as a souvenir?"

It was Brown's turn to laugh. The two women spent the rest of the evening discussing the inadequacies of the male species. Brown did not go home, and woke feeling slightly confused in the Moses' spare room, with Chloë climbing into the bed beside her. Brown reached into her bag and handed the child a parcel, watching as she carefully unwrapped a 1948 edition of *L'Histoire de Babar,* bought from a beautiful woman on the banks of the Seine.

"Read me, Auntie Cass, read me," whispered the little voice beside her. Brown read the story, Chloë seemingly unconcerned that it was in French. Brown then told her the story of the elephant who travels to Paris, where he is befriended by a rich woman who buys him clothes. He returns to the jungle and weds the beautiful Celeste. As she told the child the story for the second time, Brown could not help feeling Hogan would find his Celeste somewhere in his native Dublin. And she realised she didn't give a stuff.

Brown eventually arrived at the office around eleven. Marshall's room was dark. His secretary was not in. His calls were put through to the news-desk and messages taken by Jill Lambert. By lunchtime, *Post* reporters were receiving calls from mates on other newspapers asking if it were true that Marshall had been fired. A hack on the *Mail,* an inveterate gambler by the name of Brian Murphy, had opened a book on the runners and riders to replace Marshall. Baird was three to one. Brown was a twenty-five to one outsider. But within the *Post* itself, there was no news. Marshall's mobile telephone rang through to voicemail. Baird was tight lipped and irritable; when one of the reporters suggested he should go and ask the editor to put business staff in the picture he didn't even answer.

Brown's immediate concern, however, was not Marshall's whereabouts but Greg Jones'. He seldom arrived early, and Brown watched anxiously for his lumbering, smiling, presence to amble through the newsroom. He finally arrived after lunch. She waited while draped his jacket across the back of his chair, and sauntered across to his desk, perched on the edge and told him about her suicide theory. Could he find out if there were other insurance policies on his life, besides those taken out by WBC?

Jones shook his head, "I suppose, Cassandra, you would think me dull and defeatist if I were to mention needles or haystacks?"

"I would never think you dull, Greg" she replied as she pushed down behind her with both hands and slid back to sit more firmly on his desk. At the far side, a pile of old newspapers cascaded to the floor. "Oops, sorry, let me pick them up."

Jones told her not to bother and promised to try to get some information. Before she went back to her own seat, she picked up all the papers. Some of them were four years old.

Whether it was the distraction of the speculation about Marshall, or the impossibility of the task, Jones failed to discover the low-down on Warham's private insurance. His contacts at Lloyd's of London had heard that there could be a big policy with a specialist Swiss life company, but he had been unable to find out which.

This left Brown in a dilemma. She was sure Andrew Clarke would be able to find out the details from his "pals" at Lloyd's, but journalists do not like being beholden to public relations consultants, particularly those as powerful as Clarke.

But this was a story that would stand or fall on the details, and she had none. Ergo, no story. She was on the point of resorting to Clarke when a smiling Jones approached her desk. He emptied the contents of her waste bin into her neighbour's bin, well, most of it, the rest going onto the floor, turned it upside down and sat on it, his knees almost level with his chin. He looked more gnomic than ever. "Guess what, Cassandra, I'm apparently three to one to take over from Henry. Same as Curley. What do you think, should we put a bet on?"

Brown put the telephone back into its cradle. "I wouldn't put a penny on your chances when you can't come up with even the most basic information in a sector in which you are supposed to specialise, Jones. Not a cent."

"Suppose I told you I have just taken a call from an old mate giving me the low-down on the Warham's insurance arrangements?"

"I still wouldn't bet a penny until I'd heard the story." Not for the first time in her life, Brown wanted to hug Jones. Without doubt, he was the most well-connected reporter on the paper. He was also one of the most generous, and the funniest.

"OK. This is how it works. Last December, your late friend took out a whole life policy with Geneva Life for three million Euros. It was on standard terms, the beneficiary being his wife."

"Greg, that's fantastic. What does standard terms mean?"

"It means there were no special clauses in the policy. But here's the bad news. It also probably means that suicide was excluded for the first year. Now, are you going to put a tenner on me at three to one?"

Brown could feel her story beginning to fray at the edges. "Do you think he would have known suicide was excluded?"

Jones took a chewed pencil from his top pocket and twirled it between his fingers. "Well, if he was contemplating suicide when he took out the policy, then he probably would have checked the policy wording first."

"Which sort of blows my story out of the water, doesn't it?"

"Not entirely. You could still write that just six months before his mysterious death, John Warham took out a massive new insurance policy. No need to mention suicide. Let our readers jump to their own ill-informed opinions."

Brown looked down at the dishevelled figure crouched on the waste bin. "Do you want the job?"

"Pardon, Cassandra?"

"Do you want Henry's job, assuming it's vacant?"

"You must be joking. I'd have to learn to drive that obscene car of his."

Brown stared down at the thin freckled skin covering his scalp and gave him a playful prod with her toe. "So why do you want me to waste a tenner on you?"

"I want shorter odds than Curley. Can I get you a coffee while you pick up the phone to Geneva Life? They will tell you absolutely sod all, of course, but you shouldn't miss out on the fun of a chat with the lady they laughingly call their director of information."

"Do you want a joint by-line if I write the story, Greg?"

"What, and blow my cover? Certainly not."

Jones pulled himself painfully up from his diminutive perch and wandered off in the direction of the coffee machine, stopping to talk to various other reporters on the way. Brown looked up the telephone number of Geneva Life's London office and dialled. She was re-routed to Switzerland with commendable speed, but there the efficiency of the operation collapsed. The "director of information" said she could not disclose details of clients. Asked whether Warham had been a client simply generated one "no comment" after another, no matter how many different ways Brown tried to frame the same question. Eventually, she rang off. She at least had an on-the-record "we do not comment on our business with clients" to put into the story. It would show she had done her homework.

At six twenty, much to everybody's surprise, Henry Marshall strode in to the office. All work effectively stopped, and reporters and subs gathered in small knots to discuss what this could mean. Baird glowered. After a couple of minutes, when the gossip showed no sign of reverting back to productive writing, Baird approached the nearest group and sent them back to their desks. They continued their discussions on the office email.

Brown sent her copy through to the desk at six thirty precisely. It was to be the splash in the business section with a short story on the front page. Baird was in a taciturn mood, and merely grunted when she asked if the story was what he wanted, and whether it was alright for her to go home. She took it as a "yes" on both counts.

The air had cleared after the rain, and the evening was warm but not stuffy. Brown decided to walk home, even though it would probably take nearly two hours. She wanted time to think, time away from the telephone and the pressure of deadlines and demanding men. She turned off her mobile and glanced at her reflection in the tinted glass front of the London headquarters of Geneva Life, which was no more than one hundred metres from the *Post*'s office. Her suit looked crumpled and she never did like herself in flat shoes, even if they were the only sensible footwear for a four-mile walk. Crossing the footbridge high above the traffic speeding along the dual carriageway below, Brown turned up past the Monument commemorating the Great Fire of London. This was the insurance district, and she was amused to think that the people passing her on their way home would probably be talking about her story the following morning.

In the distance, the dome of St Paul's still dominated the skyline, despite ferocious competition from the newest office towers. She thought of the news photograph hanging in one of the *Post* conference rooms. St Paul's Dome is highlighted by fires blazing all around, as smoke swirls across the foreground. So much of the City burned during the War.

She did not need a jealous lover. Her life was too unpredictable.

She needed to be able to go away at short notice, stay as late in the evening as was necessary to do the job, go to dinners, meet contacts. She needed to be able to accept evening engagements, go drinking with other hacks and public relations people. Get drunk and roll home at three thirty in the morning. That was her life, and she loved it. She could not, would not, accept the restrictions that a jealous man would impose. She could not deal with endless cross-examination and suspicion. It was ironic that Steve, who she missed more than ever, did not seek to restrict her life. He accepted that her job was not like a so-called "normal" job. She could come home, sometimes the worse for wear, in the early hours and he would be asleep. He would turn to her and draw her close. He accepted that she loved him, and never demanded explanations. Having sacrificed Steve on the altar of journalism, she was buggered if she was going to compromise her career for Hogan. How dare he get in a huff because she had a conversation with another reporter? His jealousy was his own problem. She had no intention of making it hers.

As she walked up the gentle rise of Fleet Street, she tried to imagine the scene twenty years earlier, before the 1986 revolution started by Rupert Murdoch took the power away from the printing unions. By shifting *The Times* and *The Sunday Times* over the course of one weekend to Wapping, Murdoch made the production of newspapers the preserve of electricians and information technologists rather than ink-stained artisans.

The *Daily Telegraph* building still stood, but the paper had followed Murdoch to Docklands, leaving an investment bank to take up residence. The black fronted former home of the *Daily Express*, one of a trio of identical buildings put up in London, Manchester and Glasgow, no longer reverberated to the thrum of the presses churning out two million copies a night.

She never tired of hearing stories about the glory days of Fleet Street. Perhaps she would take Greg Jones out to dinner at one of the old journalists' haunts, get him to reminisce. Dinner with Jones would be welcome light relief from ardent would-be lovers and devious business contacts. He kept his private life to himself. He was rumoured to have a long-term partner somewhere in East Anglia. Jones lived in the Docklands. A sartorial disaster, he was not the archetypal Gay Man in London. Brown imagined he spent his weekends in second-hand bookshops rather than designer clothing boutiques or furniture stores. He was a good friend always ready to help, and Brown felt the very least she could do was to buy him a decent dinner.

She imagined Fleet Street jammed with vans, the names of the newspapers painted on their sides, as they shuttled back and forwards to the main railway stations. The journalists and printers would be packed into the pubs, talking about the day's events. She had never seen where the *Post* was printed. The paper had no presses of its own, and was printed by a series of specialist companies, close to the centres where it was sold. The nearest one was less than a mile from the *Post*'s offices, just across the river. But no longer did millions of newspapers board night trains from London – instead, electronic signals flashed over dedicated telephone lines to printing control centres which looked like operating theatres.

Walking across Regent's Park, Brown decided that, as soon as she reached home, she would telephone Hogan to tell him that she had thought hard about things, and that she really didn't think it was fair to either of them to try to continue their relationship. As she left the park to cross the Regents Canal bridge and enter Primrose Hill, her steps began to falter. She did not want to make the call. Instead, she began to compose in her head a letter, which she would write by hand on the notepaper her mother had given her one Christmas. How long did mail take to reach Dublin? Could she keep Hogan at bay, avoid talking to him, until he received it? Probably not. She would have to make the telephone call after all. It would be fairer, too. Having come to the decision, it was only right she let him know as soon as possible.

She could smell the flowers as she came up the front path. They were tucked into the porch, and the sight of them made her heart sink. The card left no room for optimism. "Sorry" was all it said. She had no choice, she would have to phone Hogan. She looked at her watch. Nine fifteen. She would call Moses first to seek moral support. Meanwhile the flowers needed water, and she needed a drink. She was just pouring vodka straight from the freezer when the distant sound of her mobile filtered through from the sitting room. She snatched up the phone, saw it was the office, and answered briskly. Baird told her Henry Marshall had resigned.

It seemed the perfect moment to write that letter.

SECTION	Business
TITLE	Warhamnewpolicy
HEADING 1	Warham took out massive life policy before he died
HEADING 2	
AUTHOR	Cassandra Brown
STATUS	Live

John Warham, the advertising tycoon, took out a multi-million insurance policy on his own life just six months before he died. The policy, for three million Euros (£1.8million) is understood to name his widow, Ruth, as the beneficiary.

The *Post* has established that the policy was taken out last December with Geneva Life, a specialist insurance company.

The insurance was in addition to other policies, totalling some £10m, taken out at Lloyd's of London by WBC, the advertising group of which he was both chairman and chief executive.

Mr Warham, 58, disappeared from his hotel while on holiday with his wife. Two weeks after he was reported missing by his wife, his body was recovered from the sea, at the foot of cliffs close to where he was last seen.

Geneva Life refused last night to comment. "We never comment on matters involving our clients," said a spokeswoman, speaking from Switzerland.

The revelation that Mr Warham had taken out the policy comes only a week after the *Post* disclosed that the millionaire businessman's use of a company financed plane in connection with his political activities were being investigated.

Documents seen by this newspaper show that the house used by Mr Warham and his wife in London's fashionable Little Venice was held in the name of a company, and had a number of financial charges, or mortgages, against it.

Mr Warham was a substantial shareholder in WBC, but over the past two years had seen the value of his shares tumble as the previously high flying share price came down to earth.

Mr Warham's body is being retained in Italy while the authorities there look into the circumstances surrounding his death. It is understood the investigating magistrate is awaiting the results of certain toxicological tests before deciding when to release the body for burial.

Witnesses who saw the body brought ashore say the businessman appeared to have been beaten before Mr Warham entered the water.

CHAPTER TWENTY-ONE

"DID he jump or was he pushed?" John Douglas whispered in Brown's ear as he greeted her arrival at his usual breakfast table in the River Restaurant of the Savoy Hotel.

Brown put on her most innocent expression. "Who? John Warham?"

With exquisite timing, the waiter slid the chair towards the table as she sat down. He flicked the pink table napkin open and laid it across her lap. Douglas had already ordered tea for her, which he poured from a silver pot. A breakfast menu was placed beside her plate.

"I was talking about Henry. There doesn't seem much doubt about Warham, if what you have been writing is even half-correct."

"Did you know John, that actually they are both Henrys? John Warham was christened Henry Warham. John is his middle name. That's why there was a foul-up when he was first reported missing."

Brown had not seen Douglas for several weeks, but it had been he who had encouraged her to pursue the insurance angle. She was looking forward to chatting about newspapers, stories, angles, personalities and politics.

There was, though, little doubt that Marshall had been fired, and the description of his departure as "a resignation" was at best euphemistic and at worst a blatant untruth. Douglas was sure that George Cameron had already decided who would take over. He thought it unlikely that he would have fired Marshall until a successor was already signed up.

Brown loved breakfast at the Savoy, especially on a morning when the Thames was in flood tide and the sun shining. From the window she could see the magnificent curve of the river, the tourist boats already being washed down for the day's work, the London Eye reflecting the morning sun. She ordered scrambled eggs and smoked salmon.

Their food arrived with fresh coffee and tea.

"So, John, who's going to get the job?" Brown took a tentative forkful of the fluffy concoction and guided it carefully into her mouth. Douglas carved off a tiny piece of kipper and loaded it onto his fork. He held it a few inches above his plate and grinned across the table. "Have you looked at the changes George Cameron has made since he was appointed editor, Cassandra? They all have one thing in common. He has poached top journos from other papers. Names he can boast about on his front page." He slipped the piece of kipper between his teeth.

Brown put down her fork and stared at the river sparkling below her. "So where does that leave me?"

"Sitting pretty, Cassandra. You are one of Cameron's rising stars. You're breaking story after story, and Cameron is giving you your head. Whoever is appointed City Editor he will make sure you are looked after."

He forked another piece of kipper. "You've got plenty of time to climb into the management tree, which believe me is a lot less fun than it looks from the ground, so for the time being I would concentrate on reporting."

Brown was about to reply when the immaculate figure of Charles Seymour Elwood appeared, it seemed from nowhere, at their table. Douglas stood to shake hands and Brown felt a hand on the shoulder. She fingered the collar of her shirt. Although she had spoken to him, she had not seen Elwood since she had whispered in his ear just before they parted outside the Berkshire nearly two weeks earlier.

Elwood was as charming as if the incident had never happened. "What a delightful way to start the day. Beautiful weather, an agreeable breakfast and then to see two of my dearest friends enjoying a little, shall we say, *tête-à-tête,* together."

She felt his hand pushing down, very gently, against her shoulder and felt his finger trace the outline of her bra strap.

"I would love to talk to you later, Cassandra, if I may be so bold. There is something I would like to discuss." He lifted his hand away and put it into his jacket pocket. He had done with Brown, clearly, and turned to Douglas. "Such a shame about Henry, isn't it?" He paused for a moment, but before Douglas could respond, Elwood brought his heels together, and executed a mock bow. "John, as ever, a pleasure to see you." And then he was gone.

They watched Elwood depart. "I'm still trying to come to terms with being one of Elwood's dearest friends, Cassandra. That man is such a bullshit artist, isn't he?"

"With friends like, him, John, who needs enemies? Which brings me back to Warham. What next, do you think?"

Douglas traced a pattern in the tablecloth with his knife. "Well, I think you've probably done the insurance angle. You've had some great stories, but there's a danger of diminishing returns. If I were you, I would try to plug into the investigation. Your man in Italy seems to be doing a good enough job, but with Scotland Yard and Stratagem on the case there must be a lot of angles to chase. Did you phone Stratagem, by the way?"

Brown admitted that she hadn't. Douglas looked out of the window. He turned back to her with a grin.

"Now, Cassandra, what about Beaten Track Holidays? You know, I suppose, they've retained our mutual friend Andrew Clarke?"

Brown choked on her tea, a few drops splattering her white cotton shirt. The waiter rushed forward to remove the half-empty cup and brimming saucer. She declined the offer of a fresh cup. Douglas continued while Brown recovered her composure. "Yes, apparently they are planning to float the company on the Stock Market next year and have employed Andrew to make sure there's no bad publicity ahead of the flotation".

"Bad publicity such as?"

"Oh, I don't know. About anyone meeting a nasty end on one of their holidays, perhaps?"

"You are joking, I take it, John?"

"Never more serious, Cassandra. And I suppose you know why John was on a Beaten Track holiday, and not in Barbados with the other captains of British industry?"

"I had wondered. I just assumed it was because Ruth talked him into it."

Douglas nodded to someone passing the table, stirred the tiny amount of coffee remaining in his cup and began to fiddle with the spoon. "Mmm. You may well be right. But it may also be because WBC won the Beaten Track advertising account for the coming season and Warham thought it would look good if he spent some time on a fact finding mission."

"Now you are having me on, John Douglas." Brown laughed out loud. "You cannot be serious."

"Never more so, Cassandra." He looked at his watch and signalled to the waiter. "Well, it was so nice to see you. Mary sends her love, by the way." Douglas signed the bill and as they were getting up to leave a bellboy in his brown uniform came hurrying across to the table. "Miss Brown?" She nodded and he handed her a slip of folded pink paper. The message read "Staff meeting, editor's conference room, 10.30. Car sent to River entrance". She handed the note to Douglas, who had diplomatically looked the other way. "Looks like your career dilemma is solved, Cassandra."

Douglas headed off towards the front hall, Brown went the other way, down the chromium staircase.

Alex was already waiting beside the Toyota. His back was towards her and he appeared to be deep in conversation with Elwood. Over Alex's shoulder, Elwood saw her approaching, gave her a wave, and almost dived for his own car. Alex spun round. "Beautiful morning, Miss Brown. The office?" Neither of them mentioned Elwood during the short journey to the *Post*.

Staff were already making their way to the conference room when Brown arrived. The atmosphere was jovial rather than tense. Baird still had his jacket on and was in a clean shirt. He clung to his clipboard and seemed to be avoiding eye contact with anybody. By ten forty-five the entire business desk was crammed into the small room. Cameron, jacket off, came in and the chatter only slowly subsided. Deference is a not a quality found in many journalists, even to an editor as tough as Cameron.

"Now," he said, "you will all know by now that Henry has decided to leave us to take up various consultancy roles in the City and elsewhere. He has asked me to thank you all for your support during his time as City Editor, and to say he will be organising a leaving drinks party, to which you will all be invited, in due course.

Meanwhile, he has asked to leave the *Post* with immediate effect, and I have agreed to his request. Until we announce his successor, Curley here will be in day-to-day charge of the section, while Greg will be responsible for analysis, opinion and comment. They will both report directly to me. I know you will give them both your full support."

Cameron was turning to leave the room when Tony Ward, the stock market reporter, put his hand up. "Have you appointed Henry's successor yet?"

"As I said Tony, we'll be announcing his successor in due course."

"Yes, but have you appointed him?"

"Can I just say, Tony, that we expect to make an announcement soon."

"So you have somebody in mind?"

"In mind, yes."

Jill Lambert suddenly spoke up. "Is it an internal promotion, Mr Cameron?"

Cameron looked longingly at the door. "I really can't tell you anything more at the moment." His patience, never abundant, was wearing dangerously thin. "As soon as we have something definite to say, you will be the first to know. Now, we all have a paper to get out." He turned and left the room. Brown glanced across at Baird, who was bright red and furiously polishing his glasses. He jammed them back on his nose and hurried out. As Brown left to make her own way back to her desk, she could see Baird standing in Cameron's outer office, talking to his secretary.

Jones was a step behind Brown. "It would have been nice if Cameron had told me beforehand that I was suddenly doing half of Henry's job," he muttered. "Fancy a coffee?"

"Good idea. I'll fetch it."

"Shall we go out for one, Cassandra? I need a change of air."

"And I need a clean shirt. Let's nip into the City for half an hour."

They walked in the sunshine through to Leadenhall Market where they stopped for coffee. Jones was in fact quite pleased to have been put in charge of the comment section, which was really just a recognition of the role he had been fulfilling for months, given that Marshall's visits to the office had become steadily more unpredictable. They agreed that Baird would be bitterly disappointed not to have been given the job, and was likely to be difficult to work with over the next few weeks. They strolled along to Marks and Spencer where Brown bought a plain white tee shirt, not quite as stylish as the designer number which was now splattered with brown tea stains, but perfectly good enough for work. As she was paying the bill, her mobile rung. It was Cameron's secretary. "Cassandra, where are you? George wants to see you in his office soonest. How quickly can you get back?"

"Ten minutes."

"I'll tell him fifteen. See you. You're not in trouble, by the way."

Brown breathed a sigh of relief and looked round to see Jones examining a rack of ties. "The editor wants to see me Greg, I'm going to have to rush back."

"Right. I'll see you later. I'm going to hang around here and go straight to lunch. Thanks for the coffee. And good luck with George."

Brown looked up and down Gracechurch Street for a taxi. There was none in sight, so she began to walk, looking over her shoulder every few seconds to see if one approached from behind. By the time she reached Monument Underground Station, it was scarcely worth looking any longer, as it was quicker to walk. Even so, she made it back to the office in just over ten minutes. Breathless, but at least no longer tea-stained, Brown hurried into Cameron's secretary's office. His door was open and she could see him leaning back in his chair, feet on the desk, reading the *Financial Times*. A tray with coffee pot and two cups and saucers was before him. He waved her in. She sat down in front of his desk, acutely aware of the shortness of her skirt. He nodded towards the tray. "I would offer you coffee but I expect it's half cold by now."

"I'm sorry, George, but I was just down in the City. I came as soon as I heard you were looking for me."

Cameron raised both eyebrows, removed his feet from the desk and leaned forward. "Quite so Cassandra. You'll never find stories sitting at your desk, eh?"

Brown did not know whether he was being sarcastic or not, and simply mumbled "no".

"Now, Cassandra, have you experience of news editing."

"Back in Oz I ran the desk for a while, yes, but…"

"But you didn't enjoy it?"

"Well, yes, I mean no. I prefer reporting."

Cameron got up from his chair and went to the window overlooking the newsroom. He had his back to her. "I wonder if you'd like to stand in as City news editor for a little while. You see, Curley was disappointed that he would not get the City Editor's job this time, so I've told him to take a few days off." Cameron turned to face her. His eyes were a soft brown. "I need your help for a few days. What do you think?"

"Of course. Thanks. It might mean the Warham story taking a bit of a back seat, though."

"I'm quite sure you won't miss anything important Cassandra. Oh, and of course there will be financial recognition."

Brown stood up from her chair, feeling slightly wobbly. She had just been promoted, albeit to a job she didn't want. But it showed she had made her mark with Cameron, and confirmed what Douglas had said earlier about her being one of his rising stars. And with a new flat to finance and furnish, some more money was very welcome. By the time she was back at her desk, an email setting out the new arrangements for the City desk had been sent to the entire paper. She went and sat in Baird's chair. For the first time in anyone's memory, his desk was clear except for the clipboard which already had the morning's news-list attached.

"Morning conference is about to start", said Jill Lambert. "I've made fourteen copies of the news-list." As she hurried off back to the editor's conference room, where she would probably be the only woman present, Brown wished she were wearing trousers.

CHAPTER TWENTY-TWO

BROWN'S stint as City News Editor lasted just over a week. Late on the second Friday evening, as she worked on the page proofs of the first edition and was giving instructions to the chief sub-editor on the changes she wanted in the next edition, Cameron called her to his office. Brown had so far avoided the wrath and sarcasm she had seen inflicted on others, especially the arts editor who regularly received public tongue-lashings, but as she hurried along towards Cameron's office her palms became sticky. She had failed to recognise the importance of some economic news — a statement by the Treasury regarding the Euro – released the previous day, and prepared herself for the worst. At least her humiliation would take place in the relative privacy of Cameron's office.

But Cameron made no mention of the missed story. He wanted to tell her Baird would be back after the weekend, to thank her for her support and to promise there would be a little something extra in her July pay. "How much, George, how much?" The words remained unsaid. But it might be enough to buy a rug for the sitting room or a new television set. Not bad for a week's experience on the news-desk, which had convinced her beyond doubt that she never wanted to become News Editor.

After a weekend finally catching up with domestic chores, she was enjoying the opportunity to pace her preparations for work on Monday morning when Baird telephoned. "Hi Cass. Just thought I'd let you know I'm back in harness and that you're off the hook." He sounded remarkably cheerful.

She tucked the telephone under her chin and went to her ironing basket to find clean underwear. "Glad to have you back,

Curley. I don't think I could have taken the strain for much longer."

"From what I hear you did a great job. I thought I'd better get back before they gave it to you permanently."

"No chance, Curley, I'm not going to fight you for that number. Are you OK with things now?"

"Well, it's not what I wanted, as you well know. I still think I could have led the team and beaten the shit out of the opposition. But, well, Cameron crossed my palm with silver and gave me a title. And there's always next time."

"A title, eh? What do we call you?"

"Associate Editor, Business. Not bad, eh? Now, do you have anything for the news-list this morning? We've not carried anything on the Warham story for more than a week."

That's what made Baird such a good news editor — he never missed a beat, even when he was away from the office, never let his team off the hook. His appetite for news was insatiable. The Warham story was just one of a number of running stories — he always managed to stay on top of them all. "I think there may be enough bits and pieces to cobble something together, Curley. Just put it down as 'WBC developments' for now."

"Will do. No need to hurry in. Everything's under control."

Brown took Baird at his word. She had been in the office for a minimum of twelve hours a day every day for the past week, and she felt a late start was more than justified. She looked again at the handwritten envelope bearing the Irish stamp, but drew back from reading the letter again. She had not expected Hogan to agree with her.

Strolling across Regents Park, she remembered the unexplained incident outside the Savoy after her breakfast with John Douglas, when she spotted Charles Elwood apparently in deep conversation with Alex. Her first call, when she arrived at the office, would be to Elwood to ask him what had been going on. Tom Warham was convinced Elwood was keeping tabs on him through the loan of Warham's car and driver. Was he also keeping a check on her? Could Alex be in the pay of Elwood? Unlikely, but Elwood wanted to know everything. That was why he had hired the private detectives as soon as Warham disappeared. Brown remembered with embarrassment she had not yet telephoned either the detectives or

Scotland Yard. She had a lot of follow-up calls to make, most of them suggested by Douglas. Was there any significance that Beaten Track had retained Andrew Clarke, who also happened to be "helping an old mate" at Lloyd's with the insurance issues, as their public relations consultants? Or that Clarke was also a pal of Elwood's? There was still so much she didn't know.

Baird was still in a bouncy mood when she arrived at the office. A rumour was doing the rounds that he'd been "bunged an extra five grand" in salary, and the demeanour of the new Associate Editor did nothing to make anyone doubt it was true. A box of business cards bearing his new title was on his desk. Cameron certainly knew how to get what he wanted.

Amongst Brown's messages was one that Tom Warham had telephoned. She had not spoken to him for well over a week, certainly not since she had written the last insurance story and not since she had told Hogan their romance was not to be. She was not sure what sort of reception she would get, but then with Tom Warham she never was.

He answered immediately, as if he had been sitting there at his desk waiting for the phone to ring. There was no preamble. "Why doesn't anyone believe it could have been a simple accident, Cassandra, that's what I'd like to know? I'm not singling you out; I know you try to write reasonable stuff. As you said, that's your job." He was almost hysterical. "But what about people who should know better? The bloody Italians are making such a meal out of it. They still won't give us any indication of when they will release the body. How long do a few bloody tests take, for God's sake? And we've just been told, only just been told, that the coroner will want another post-mortem here when the body does come back. What's a post-mortem in Britain going to tell anybody that ones in Italy haven't already, I ask you? And why can't the pathologist get on a bloody plane and go and do it now?"

He paused only long enough for Brown to mutter "see what you mean, Tom, it must be frustrating," before he was off on another tirade. "And what about Elwood? What's his game? He lends us a car so he can keep himself informed of everywhere we go. It's probably fitted with a tracker device and wired up with a tape recorder so he can listen to everything we say. He's appointed private detectives, did you know that, but they don't tell us a thing. And then there's Scotland bloody Yard. A couple of detectives want a few weeks' holiday in the sun so they make out there's some great mystery to be solved. My old man was a mess but he's gone. He fell off a cliff. That's all we need to know. Stop. End of story."

"Well, surely they do need to get at the truth."

"I know, but it's so frustrating Cassandra, I really have had it up to here. I've got a family to think about. And a career. I was supposed to deliver a paper in New York this week but with all this going on I had to back out."

His voice was suddenly sad, rather than angry. "I'm sorry I sounded off at you, Cassandra, but I don't know who to talk to. My mother can only talk about my father and Bia bloody Gonzales. Suzie's fed up with the sound of my voice and suggests I need counselling. It's not counselling I need, it's co-operation."

"I'm surprised you feel you can talk to me, given that all I do is write stories you'd sooner not read."

Tom laughed. "At least you tell us in advance when you are going to stitch us up. Not like Charles bloody Elwood who spends his life stitching people up behind their backs. I don't blame you for chucking Hogan, by the way."

The abrupt change of subject took her by surprise. "Oh?"

"What a drip he's turned out. Seems obsessed about your Italian friend. He believes the Italian phoned you in Paris because he was jealous you'd gone away with him. How an intelligent man can get so up his own backside is beyond me. He even suggested I had ulterior motives towards you. The man's unhinged, Cassandra. Talking of ulterior motives, do you fancy a sandwich lunchtime? My turn to buy."

"Why not? What time?"

"One o'clock in the usual place."

Brown did not need to leave the office for at least an hour. She called Vittorio who admitted that, like her, he had been distracted by other stories but agreed it was time they tried to warm up the Warham mystery again. He promised to talk to the magistrate and call her back if there was anything to report. Jones arrived at his customary eleven thirty, his additional duties seemingly making no difference to his lifestyle. In fact, it was now clear that Henry

Marshall's contribution to both the running of the department and the paper's editorial position on business matters had been virtually zero. The office was, to all intents and purposes, functioning in exactly the same way as it had done for months. The only change was Baird's mood, and his new suit.

An excited Vittorio rang back after a few minutes. "I have learned from my friend that Mr. Warham was hit on the head by a heavy rock before he drowned. And they now know exactly from where he plunged into the water. And Cassandra, listen, they have found his camera."

Brown glanced across at Baird and switched to Italian. "Are they sure it's his?"

"No doubt."

"It sounds as if you have enough for a decent story about the injuries. Don't write anything about the camera yet, and don't mention it to Baird. I'll call you back and let you know how much we can take."

Baird was scrolling through a week's newswire stories. "Did I miss anything while you were away then Curley?"

He had had a haircut and bought new shoes. Even his glasses looked new. He spoke without taking his eyes off the screen. "Not that I know of. But we've got a miserable list today and I was just trolling through to see if there was anything we could warm up." He looked away from the screen and took a gulp from his coffee mug. "So what's happening on the Warham front?"

Brown explained that a head wound had been inflicted by a rock, and that the *Carabinieri* had identified the spot from which Warham fell.

Baird continued to stare at the screen. "Good story, Cassandra. It'll keep Cameron happy, especially if Paolo can wire a picture over. But it's all for the front of the paper – is there anything for our pages? What about the insurance angle? Something we can hang a pound sign on."

"I'll see what I can do, but I think I've just about squeezed the lemon dry."

When Brown left the office to keep her appointment with Tom Warham, it was not Alex and the old Toyota but a different driver waiting beside a silver Audi. In a few minutes she was at

Temple Gardens, where she found Tom Warham sitting on a bench reading the *Standard,* a small paper carrier bag beside him. He patted the seat beside him and Brown obediently sat.

"I've decided, Cassandra, we are both on the same side. It's you and me against the world. Or at any rate you and me against devious business sharks, second rate policemen, creepy PR men and Italian bureaucrats."

"Not to mention beautiful fashion models?"

"Ah, let's not go too far Cassandra. I'm sure Miss Gonzales could be tempted to join our ranks."

"I'm not sure we need her, Tom."

"What a pity. I was looking forward to trying to find out what my old man saw in her."

"I would have thought that was obvious. You saw the pictures."

"Yes, but you didn't let me keep them."

"Simmer down sport. Now, can we be serious for a moment. What's going on in Italy?"

Tom Warham picked up the carrier and pulled out two paper napkins. Next came two packages, both containing cheese and pickle sandwiches on malted grain bread. Between mouthfuls, Tom Warham said there was no movement at all, so far as he was aware. It appeared to be a standoff between the family and the police – until Ruth Warham agreed to an interrogation, they would refuse to release the body. He had not heard the latest developments about which Vittorio had told Brown that morning.

"But I can't see that would change anything, except possibly make my mother rather less of a suspect. I can't see her following my father up to a cliff top and whacking him on the head with a rock, can you? Mind you, I wouldn't blame her."

As she finished her sandwich the wind snatched the napkin from Brown's lap. Tom Warham ran off after it, a lanky comic figure with oversized feet trying to stamp on a paper napkin as it danced down the path towards the forbidden grass. He returned and dropped the screwed up paper in the bin. "You don't fancy a drink, I suppose?"

They walked up the gentle hill towards Fleet Street. "Has your mother heard anything more from the insurers, Tom?"

"No, not really. They are hanging on to their money and are clearly not going to pay up this side of an inquest."

"Is that a problem?"

"No, I don't think so. My father wasn't as wealthy as everyone thinks he was, and certainly not as wealthy as he should have been given how much he was paying himself, but I don't think my mother is short of ready cash."

They entered the musty pub, dark after the sunshine outside. Brown bought the drinks and they sat at a table near the door. Tom Warham downed nearly half a pint in the first draught. No wonder he carried a potbelly on an otherwise skinny frame. "Did I tell you Elwood has offered to send someone to Italy to try to speed things up? So I suppose he's not all bad. I won't use the car any more, by the way. We told him to take it back."

Brown sipped her pineapple juice, sweet and sticky, and looked longingly at the pint glass on the other side of the table. "God, that's a horrible drink. I think I'll get myself some water. Did he say who he was thinking of sending?"

He looked anxiously around the pub, as if afraid he was being watched. "No idea. Might have been some PR guy who he says has good connections in the area." He was still not looking in her direction, and Brown searched the bar to see what might be unsettling him. He drained his glass and stood up.

"Same again?"

"No way. I'll just have some mineral water."

"You do know how to enjoy yourself, don't you? I thought you hard-bitten hacks could easily do a bottle of claret at lunchtime. No wonder the pubs round here are so dead and alive."

When he returned with the drinks, he was again focused. "You mentioned a camera. Do you happen to know what's on it?"

Brown shook her head. "Not yet. I'm hoping to hear from Paolo. Can I call you later if I do?"

Tom Warham chatted about his daughter, his wife, his work. Brown talked about her new flat and how nervous she had been at the editorial conferences. She described how Cameron had turned on the arts editor one morning because he "never produced any news stories". They left the pub together.

On her way back to the office, Brown phoned Vittorio. He did not know any more about the camera, other than that it did contain some pictures.

Brown meanwhile still had no new leads. "Insurers continue to delay payment on Warham" was certainly not going to get into the paper, let alone earn her a promotion. But as she walked into the office, she remembered the tip-off from John Douglas that Beaten Track Holidays was planning to float on the stock market.

Baird had his jacket off and his shirt hanging out. He had his old glasses back on, the ones with sticking plasters around the tips of the arms to stop them digging into his ears. He was shouting at somebody on the other end of his phone. Jill Lambert looked happy for the first time in days. Once he had completed his string of expletives to the advertising manager, he turned to Brown, took off his glasses and began polishing them with his new tie. Curley was back, grinning broadly as she outlined the Beaten Track story. She left to return to her own desk when Baird snatched up his phone and began ordering photographs of white beaches and bikini-clad girls from the picture desk.

Andrew Clarke was less pleased to hear from Brown. He was not ready for the Beaten Track flotation story to be made public. Such stories usually appear first in the Sunday papers, where reporters are given the "exclusive" in return for a favourable piece. Clarke's first tactic, doomed to failure, was to offer to give her "the full story, exclusively" in a few weeks' time if she would agree not to write the story she had.

"No way, Andrew. I've got quite enough to go on already. I would like more detail but you and I both know I don't need it."

"Ah, but the question, Cassandra, must be whether it would be ethical for you to run it, given the circumstances in which it was obtained."

"What the hell do you mean, Andrew?"

"What I mean, Cassandra, is that John Douglas is a bad loser. He and I were in competition for the Beaten Track account, as I am sure you know. Information was given to both of us in confidence, and that confidence has to be respected as much by the loser as by the winner. In other words, Cassandra, Douglas had no right to tell you. Now, I'm not going to make an issue of this, but if you are determined, despite our long and cordial relationship, to play hard ball then the consequences will rest on your shoulders. And before you deny that Douglas was the source, I thought I might just mention that Charles Elwood and I enjoyed a most pleasant breakfast together at the Savoy the other day."

"I'm really not interested in who you may or may not have had breakfast with, Andrew. Now are you going to play ball or not? Speaking of ethics, Tom Warham asked me earlier if he could have copies of those Gonzales pictures. I don't suppose you've got another set."

Clarke burst into laughter. "God, you're a tough cookie Cassandra. Let me speak to the client about our little dilemma and get back to you. I'll see what I can do."

Half an hour later, Clarke was much more helpful and Brown learned the timing and the price of the planned stock market flotation.

She sensed Clarke was about to hang up, when he lowered his voice. "Oh Cassandra, just one thing, I hope you will not find it necessary to mention that John Warham was on one of their holidays when he disappeared."

"Mention it, Andrew? I can hardly write the piece without saying John was on a fact-finding trip having just won the advertising account can I?"

"We'd sooner you didn't, if that's possible. It's hardly relevant, and might even detract from the main story, if you see what I mean."

"As you might say to me, Andrew, I'll see what I can do." The story she put across to the news-desk just before six o'clock contained no mention of John Warham.

Brown had still not telephoned either the private investigators or Scotland Yard, partly because she was unfamiliar with the conventions of crime reporting. Do crime correspondents meet their detective friends in dark bars close to Scotland Yard; is there a "lobby" system under which reporters are briefed by policemen on the understanding that they are not identified? Do detectives need to be plied with drinks? But at the very least, Brown owed it to John Douglas to follow up his suggestions.

Tom Warham answered his phone almost before it rang. He was brisk and businesslike – yet another manifestation of the Tom Warham personality. Were all the Warhams so difficult to predict? At the conclusion of a two-minute conversation, her notebook contained four names, two from Stratagem and two from Scotland Yard.

Neither of the policemen was at their desks, but the call to Stratagem was more successful, even if it was hard to take seriously a man named Rocco Suarez. Initially disinterested when Suarez learned about the camera, he became enthusiastic for them to meet. She was obviously a step ahead of him, enough to make her wonder why Elwood would pay for such expensive detectives. She suggested Suarez come to the *Post*'s offices. He in turn proposed the lobby of the Ambassador Hotel on Park Lane, a place favoured by Americans and high-class hookers. There was little point in arguing. "When? I could be free from the office in an hour or so."

"That would be perfect, Cassandra. Shall we say seven thirty?"

"How will I recognise you, Mr Suarez?"

"You will not need to, Cassandra, I will make myself known to you."

Brown felt an irrational irritation at his use of her first name, and decided she did not like Mr. Rocco Suarez, not only because of his ridiculous name. And how would he recognise her? Had Elwood asked them to watch her too? She shivered at the thought of Suarez sitting outside her flat in some nondescript car, noting down her movements.

She was about to call Central Executive Cars to order a minicab to take her to Park Lane when she remembered the incident outside the Savoy. Why had Alex been talking to Elwood? Just to be on the safe side, she would hail a cab on the street.

She arrived at the Ambassador a deliberate ten minutes late. She did not wish to be taken for a hooker loitering in the lobby, and was in any case not much looking forward to the meeting. As she emerged from the revolving door and was confronted with the vulgar brass staircase, a small man with startlingly black hair was at her side. He offered a damp handshake. Brown found it almost impossible to take Suarez seriously. He led the way to a table at the far corner of the lobby, where there was already a half-finished drink, the shape of the glass suggesting a Martini. Did he take three measures of Gordon's and one of vodka, shaken not stirred? She ordered a tonic water and listened as he told her how well connected he was and how impossible it had been to carry out his "assignment", as he insisted on calling it, because Elwood would not authorise a second trip to Italy. But he had done a lot of research into the animal rights movement in Italy, and seemed convinced that if foul play had caused Warham's plunge from the Cinque Terre cliff path, animal activists were most likely to be behind it. He did not, however, have any evidence, because, he claimed, of Elwood's refusal to sanction the expenses of a second trip.

"So, Mr. Suarez."

"Call me Rocco, please, Cassandra."

It was not worth arguing about forms of address. "So, Rocco, where do we go from here?"

"I am not sure, Cassandra. Now, if the *Post* were to retain my services, I could come up with some very good stories for you. And of course, you would get the credit, Cassandra."

So that's why he was so keen to meet. Brown took a sip of tonic water, picked up a peanut, which was far too salty, and tried to appear thoughtful. She knew, however, that there was no way the *Post* would agree to pay a private detective. "I doubt, Rocco, the editor would agree. I will see what I can do." She made as if to leave.

"Are you leaving already, Cassandra? Wouldn't you like to hear what was on the camera found at the scene?"

"I thought you didn't know about it."

"I have been working on another case, so I didn't know about the camera until you told me", he looked at his watch, "approximately two hours ago. As I said, I have good connections in Italy. Very good connections, helpful people, and they are emailing the pictures to me. When they arrive, we can look at them together. Since you tipped me off, I think that is fair don't you? One good turn leading to another. It's the way I like to work."

Brown settled back into her chair. Not half she wanted to see the pictures, even if it meant sitting side by side with Suarez, peering into the laptop he had placed on the table. He opened the lid and the machine began to run through the start-up procedure. "Another drink, Cassandra? Would you like something in your tonic this time?"

"Vodka, please." Self-denial has to have limits.

He waved to a waiter and ordered a vodka tonic and a vodka Martini. Disappointingly, he did not specify whether it was to be shaken or stirred. The waiter seemed to know him.

They watched the laptop screen for a moment. Brown broke the silence. "By the way, how did you recognise me? Have you been keeping me under surveillance?"

Suarez forced a laugh. "No. I watched you on television when Mr. Warham was found dead. By the way, I knew the previous evening his body had been found. If we had been in contact then, you would have had quite a scoop."

Brown believed him. The drinks arrived. She nodded thanks and took a sip. It was a double, if not a treble, and it tickled her tongue in all the right places.

Suarez bent over the laptop. "Now, here we are, the email has arrived. We'll just download the pictures."

The photographs, about twenty-five of them attached to four separate emails, could have been almost anybody's holiday snaps. Ruth Warham is posed against a variety of scenic backdrops. She looks relaxed and happy. In a few of the shots, Warham himself is in front of the camera. There is one of them together on a boat, with the cliffs in the background, and another of them toasting each other at a restaurant table. There were a few more artistic scenes. Boats in a harbour, a sunrise, a shot down the cliff-face to the blue water below, so clear the rocky bottom of the sea is visible in sharp relief. There were a few long-range views. Finally there was one of a cliff path winding into the distance, where the roofs and tower of a village are defined against the green hillside. The last picture Suarez left on the screen.

"Not many clues, there, eh, Rocco?"

"A few, though, Cassandra, if you know where to look. For instance, we can see by the shadows it was taken early in the morning. It is looking southeast towards Manarola from the northwest. There are very few people about. In fact, we can see several hundred metres of path, and there is only one figure. We could take a closer look at him, or her." He began to zoom in on the man, but before he was recognisable, the picture began to break down into individual pixels. "I'll have that one re-sent in a higher definition, if you've a few moments to spare."

Suarez dialled a number on his mobile, picked up his Martini and took a sip while waiting for an answer. He then spoke in excellent Italian, but let go nothing to indicate who he was speaking to.

"It is on its way, Cassandra. Now, would you like another drink?"

Brown shook her head. Suarez had downed two Martinis in the forty minutes she had been with him, and was about to order his third. The question of who would pay had not been discussed. She guessed it might be her, since it was she who had initiated the contact. She thought about the amount of cash in her purse. This was going to be a credit card venture. As if reading her thoughts, Suarez cut in, "since Mr Elwood will not allow me to go back to Italy, I think he can afford a few drinks, don't you, Cassandra?"

She nodded. Suarez was much sharper than she had given him credit for. "Why do you think Mr. Elwood doesn't want you to return to Italy, Rocco? Surely that's where the story will be found."

Suarez grinned. He even had a gold tooth. The man was straight from Central Casting Agency. "To be honest, Cassandra, I don't think he is interested any more. He brought us in when Mr. Warham was missing, you will remember, because he wanted to find out where he had gone. He thought Mr. Warham was with Bia Gonzales, and sent us first to Milan. Once we had established he wasn't there, Mr. Elwood seemed to lose interest in the matter..." Suarez broke off to answer his mobile, which must have been set to vibrate rather than ring, and thanked his caller in Italian. "Anyway, as I was saying, he was not even keen for us to visit Manarola. Now, that picture should be here."

He opened his laptop. After a few taps and clicks, he turned the screen in Brown's direction. The entire screen was filled with the image she had seen a few minutes earlier. "Now Cassandra, let us see who might have been awake as early in the morning as Mr Warham."

He began to zoom in on the cliff path. "The resolution is excellent. This was taken on an expensive digital camera, Cassandra. I would guess it was probably the Canon EOS, which would have cost Mr. Warham several thousand pounds. Over sixteen million pixels ... we can't quite see all the man's face, but we might see enough to hazard a good guess as to who Mr Warham's stalker might have been."

Brown held her breath as the picture enlarged. "Jeez, it's Pete Nichols. I'd swear it. The man from Beaten Track Holidays. Do you know him?"

Suarez closed the laptop as the waiter approached, bearing a fresh Martini on a tray. "Oh, yes, Cassandra. Well, I cannot say I know him, because he is a man who does not wish to be known. I met him when we went to the Cinque Terre. He said he would like to help, but would lose his job if Beaten Track knew he had talked to us. After a few beers he loosened up a just a bit, but still told us nothing. We ran the data on him down under and he didn't check out, he didn't check out at all. So either he's not Australian."

"He is, believe me. It takes one to know one, and he's a true blue OK."

"Or, as we suspect, he is not Pete Nichols. We are working to find out who he really is, but as Mr. Elwood."

"I know, will not allow you to go back to Italy."

"Well, it is difficult if we cannot interview him."

Brown leaned forward and opened up the laptop again. There was no doubt. It was the man who had introduced himself as Pete Nichols, courier for Beaten Track. He had been nervous, too, when Brown had tried to talk to him, referring all her questions to head office. It was probably in his interests that Suarez and his colleague were not returning to Cinque Terre. Brown thought about the form an "interview" with them might take, and felt suddenly cold. It was time to depart.

She finished her vodka tonic and stood up to leave. "I suppose there's no chance you could email me the photographs."

Suarez shook his head. "If it was known that the pictures had been circulated outside the investigation, my contact would be in very serious trouble."

There was no point in arguing or pleading. "Will you report this back to Elwood, Rocco? If so, I'd sooner you didn't blow the gaff on meeting me."

He grinned, but not enough to show his gold tooth again. "Of course. I'll report the facts back to my client, but will not mention your name."

After another damp handshake, Brown hailed a cab on Park Lane. She looked regularly out of the rear window. If Suarez was following her, he was being very discreet about it.

SECTION	Business
TITLE	Beatenfloat
HEADING 1	Beaten Track heads for £300m flotation
HEADING 2	
AUTHOR	Cassandra Brown
STATUS	Live

Beaten Track Holidays is planning to come to the stock market in a three hundred million pound flotation.

The company has appointed merchant bankers, brokers and financial public relations consultants to handle the deal, the first in the holiday sector for several years.

Beaten Track, set up less than a decade ago by a group of friends to organise walking holidays abroad, has grown into a major force in mid- and up-market holidays for active people.

Unlike others in the sector, the company has concentrated on planning and packaging both off-the-peg and tailor-made holidays. It has steered clear of the ownership and operation of either planes or hotels, preferring to use the excess capacity in the industry to drive hard deals with suppliers.

The *Post* understands that bookings for the current season are some 20 per cent ahead of last year, providing a solid underpinning to the directors' flotation plans.

The company has built up a strong reputation in the industry, and claims that half its business now comes from "repeats", customers who have taken a Beaten Track holiday previously.

Sources close to the company say that most of the proceeds of the public offer for shares will be used to develop the business.

The company plans to draw on its customer base, overwhelmingly from the ABC1 social groups, to market its shares. It is planning to offer preferential terms and discounts on holidays booked by shareholders in a bid to encourage both brand and shareholder loyalties.

The company is undergoing a financial reorganisation, as part of which its capital will be doubled. The new shares will then be offered for sale, with customers who have booked or taken two holidays or more receiving preferential treatment in the event that demand for the shares exceeds supply.

A major advertising campaign will support the September flotation.

CHAPTER TWENTY-THREE

BAIRD bounced back from morning conference, later than usual, and pointed to Marshall's office. His secretary was, as usual, reading. It had been over a week since Cameron had promised to make "an early announcement" about Marshall's successor, and although the rumour mills had been working overtime, no name had emerged. Marshall's office had already acquired the look and feel of an empty house. There were dark patches on the faded beige hessian wallpaper where some personal pictures had once hung. The bookshelves were virtually empty and the "in" and "out" trays contained nothing more than an internal telephone directory in one and the remote control for the large television set in the other. Nobody had heard from Marshall since he was fired, despite the promise that he would be organising a farewell party.

"Coffee?" asked the secretary as they entered, no doubt welcoming the interruption to yet another day of inactivity. Baird settled back into the big leather chair, and began to swivel madly from side to side.

She didn't trust the look on Baird's face.

"How do you fancy going back to Italy for a few days?" Baird swivelled so far he had his back to her and turned round only when he saw the coffee tray arriving.

"I'm not sure there's any point, Curley. Shall I pour?"

Baird took a chocolate biscuit from the plate, broke it in half, put one half on top of the other as if making a sandwich and put the whole thing into his mouth at once. Cheeks bulging, he tried to speak, emitting a fine spray of digestive crumbs.

He licked smears of dark chocolate from his finger and thumb in turn. He picked up the remote control from the "out" tray, fiddled with it a moment or two, and put it back. "Cameron wants us to give the story one more heave before we give up on it. At the very least, you could put together another double pager, 'the ongoing riddle of Britain's top Adman'."

"But I've got nothing new to write."

"OK, I know it will cover a lot of old ground, but you could pull all the strings together. And, so far as we know, the corpse is still stretched out on a slab in Italy when it should be brought home for a decent funeral. What do you think?"

Brown was about to argue when Jill Lambert put her head around the door. "Editor wants to see you, Cass. Right away."

Baird winked as she hurried from the room.

She emerged from the editor's office ten minutes later with a pay rise, and having agreed to go back to Manarola to "wrap this Warham business up", as Cameron had put it.

She needed to contact Vittorio. Initially sceptical, he agreed to meet her in Manarola two days later. Brown had not spoken to him since she had seen the contents of Warham's camera.

How carefully had the *Carabinieri* looked back into the camera's memory? Would they find some rather tasteful images of a beautiful young woman standing at the foot of an elegant curved staircase?

She had not managed to find a way of writing about the latest pictures. "Dead holidaymaker took snaps" was not a story to set any pulses rating. "Holidaymaker takes snap of company representative" was hardly front-page material either. Especially since she did not even have copies of the pictures herself. Vittorio still hadn't seen them.

"They're mostly holiday snaps, Paolo. Warham and his wife, that sort of thing. There is a strange thing about one of the photographs, though."

She paused. Should she tell him everything, or keep the Nichols angle to herself? She chose the latter. "There's this guy up there on the path. He's some way away but might have followed Warham up there. You haven't heard that the police have pulled anyone in for questioning in the last couple of days? You see, you can tell from the shadows the picture was taken early in the morning, it's the last one in the camera and was taken on the day Warham disappeared."

Vittorio promised to find out.

Greg Jones was grinning from ear to ear. He, too, had been to see the editor and over the coffee machine confessed he had been offered more money to take over writing economic leaders for the front of the paper. Much to Brown's relief, he would remain on the Business team. Cameron was making sure key people were kept sweet ahead of announcing their new boss.

Vittorio called back within fifteen minutes with the news that no one had been interviewed since the pictures had been found. And they were not looking for anyone. Incompetence or conspiracy?

"You didn't mention I'd seen the pictures, did you Paolo?"

"Certainly not Cassandra. What do you take me for, an idiot? If the deadheads in the *Carabinieri* can't be bothered to do their job properly, it is not up to us to tell them. It would give me great pleasure to embarrass them with our story. When are you coming to Manarola? Shall I book the hotel?"

"Day after tomorrow. And, yes please, can you book us in somewhere. If it's the same place can you use false names? I don't want our friend Riolo gossiping around that we are returning. I'd like to keep an element of surprise."

Vittorio was obviously amused. "So who would you like to be, Cassandra?"

"You can use my former married name. In fact, I still have a passport in that name I use occasionally."

"You were married Cassandra? You never told me. You must have married very young ..."

"I did. Now, my former surname was Tasker. So I will be Mrs. Cassandra Tasker for a few days."

"So will I be Mr. Paolo Tasker?"

"Dream on Paolo. Well, not unless you want to sleep on the floor. Otherwise you'd better book your own room in whatever name takes your fancy."

Chloë answered the telephone when Brown called to ask whether she could come over with a bottle. After a conversation about pre-school, the child allowed her mother to come on the line. Moses was facing an evening on her own, Adam again being away on business. She promised Brown a take-away curry if she could get there before Chloë had to go to bed.

She arrived at the Moses' door at same moment as the young man delivering the meal. Chloë grabbed Brown's hand and led her to the garden. A table for three had been laid with a cloth printed with elephants chasing each other around the perimeter, and paper napkins printed with balloons, suggesting that Chloë, who was being allowed to eat with them, had chosen them. Glasses picked up the evening sun.

Moses came to the table and sat down. "So, what gives?

"Well, I've been given a pay rise."

"You don't look very cheerful about it."

"It'll come in handy, with the move and everything, but I had been hoping for promotion."

"Give it time, Cass, there's no hurry."

Chloë slipped off her chair and stood beside Brown, who pulled the child on to her lap. Moses disappeared to get the food. Chloë was unusually quiet and didn't want to eat.

Brown mopped the last of the vegetable curry from her plate with a piece of naan. "Oh, there's another thing. I'm going back to Italy for a few days. And guess what, I'm going there as Mrs. Cassandra Tasker." Moses raised her eyebrows and told Chloë it was time for bed. Brown carried her upstairs and once again read the French Babar. She then told her the story in English.

When Brown came downstairs Moses had cleared the dishes and made tea with fresh mint. The evening was warm, but the insects were starting to be a nuisance. Moses lit a citronella candle and poured the tea. "Now, Cassandra, you're not telling me, are you, that you're going to Italy with Steve?"

Brown picked up her spoon and looked at her reflection in the bowl. She was upside down. Turning the spoon around, she saw herself with an exaggerated nose and a pointed head. "Sadly not, Kate. No, I'm just borrowing his name so I can get a hotel booked without the whole of Manarola knowing. It'll be weird, though, using my married name again. I haven't used it for more than two years."

She felt her throat tightening. She needed to change the

subject. "By the way, Chloë seemed very quiet this evening. Is she all right? Not sickening for something?"

"No, I don't think so. The truth is, she overheard Adam and I having words because he was going away again. I know it's not his fault, but I am tired of being a one-parent family. Anyway, it's nothing serious and he'll be back again in a couple of days. The trouble is, half Chloë's class have been through a divorce, and she's frightened."

She poured more tea. "But what about you? Is there any chance for Conor? At least he's stopped ringing me every night for comfort, so perhaps he's accepted that things are not going to work out between you."

"They never would, Kate. He's an amusing guy who deserves a nice life and even a nice wife, so long as he can get over his jealousy. But it won't be me. And guess what? The cheeky bastard only agreed with me that we weren't cut out to be together. He was supposed to be devastated. Now, can we talk about something else?"

From the corner of her eye she noticed Chloë looking out of her bedroom window. Brown smiled up, put her hands together and rested her head at an angle against them. Chloë's face disappeared.

Moses raised her eyebrows but did not look up. They sat in silence for a minute, sipping the tea.

Brown put down her cup. "I want to ask you about photographs. Not the ones I showed you before, but some that were found on Warham's camera. Imagine you are a policeman investigating the death of a businessman in mysterious circumstances. You find a camera, which was owned by the deceased, and you download the pictures. The final picture shows somebody on a cliff path taken on the day the man died. What would you do?"

Moses thought for a moment. "Find out who it was if possible, and pull them in for questioning."

"Quite. There is such a photo. I have actually seen it and know who it was on the path. So isn't it strange that he's not been questioned?"

"Enough suspense, who is it?"

"Guess."

"Ruth Warham?"

271

Brown shook her head.

"Elwood? Tom Warham? The Australian from Beaten Track?"

"You've got there at last."

"Show me."

"I don't have them. I saw them on a laptop in the lobby of the Embassy Hotel. Some extraordinary character from Stratagem Security, called Rocco Suarez if you can believe it, showed me. Anyway, so far as I've been able to find out, my young Australian friend has not been questioned by the *Carabinieri* since before Warham's body was found. I think he has some explaining to do, don't you?"

"So that's why you're going back to Italy, Mrs Tasker?"

"Kate, please, don't call me that even in fun. Now, was there anything left in that bottle?"

Around ten, Brown called a minicab to take her the short distance home. It was still light. As she was leaving, Moses put an arm around her shoulder. "Cass, take good care of yourself. When you get back, Chloë and I will come over and help you with your packing."

On the way back to the square Brown realised Moses might have liked her to stay over. Sometimes she was not very good at reading signals.

CHAPTER TWENTY-FOUR

ALEX stopped the Toyota outside Heathrow Terminal 2 departures, and handed over the chit she needed to sign.

It was now or never. "Oh, Alex, there's been something I've been meaning to ask you."

"What's that, Miss Brown?"

"Well, the other day, when you picked me up from the Savoy, as I came out you were talking to Mr. Elwood. Was he trying to get you to keep tabs on me?"

She handed the chit back to him.

He looked her in her eyes and laughed. "Yes, I was chatting to Mr. Elwood, but not about you."

"But why would you talk to him, Alex?"

Even as the words came from her mouth, the penny dropped. Why was she sometimes such a dunderhead?

Alex looked on with evident amusement. She raised both hands to hide her reddening face, and did her best to laugh. "Oh. I see. I mean, Mr. Elwood was, I mean, you are ... maybe I shouldn't have asked."

"It's no secret, Miss Brown. No secret at all."

She quickly opened the car door and fled into departures. She was glad to be leaving England.

Her plane arrived twenty minutes early at Milan, where she had to wait over an hour for the connection. Time for a coffee, always her first indulgence in Italy.

As she leafed through *la Repubblica,* something made her look up. Across the lounge, standing at an Alitalia check-in desk was a young woman. Brown could only see her profile, but she looked familiar.

Brown drained her coffee and stared. In apparent slow-motion, the woman's bags were loaded onto the moving belt by a burly man who could only be a minder, tagged, and sent on their journey. As the last one disappeared, the woman turned. Despite the sunglasses, there was no doubt. Bia Gonzales was leaving the country.

Brown snatched up her bag and hurried across the hall, her trainers squeaking on the tiled floor. What was she going to do? Confront her? Seek an interview? Take a picture? She remembered the camera in her bag, stopped and pulled it out. By the time she looked up again, Gonzales was already at the Departures Gate, her minder standing back to allow her to go through. It was too late.

But where was Gonzales heading? Brown walked back past the long check-in queues to the desk where she had first spotted her – business class passengers were checking in for Buenos Aires. Bia was going home.

Brown wanted to call Vittorio, but her call was diverted to voicemail. She left a message in English: "Hi Paolo, I've just seen Gonzales check in for Buenos Aires. See you later."

Baird. She needed to call Baird. The *Post* should have a reporter waiting for Gonzales when she arrived at Buenos Aires.

He answered his mobile on the second ring. He was at Wimbledon, as a guest of a public relations company anxious to make friends, waiting for the rain to stop so he could watch some tennis. He was in the company of other journalists and made the most of asking, in a loud voice, how the weather was in Italy. She told him it was lousy, before explaining how she had seen Gonzales about to board a plane for Buenos Aires.

"You sure, Cass?"

"Positive."

"OK, I'll make sure foreign get their stringer to meet her at the airport. I'll get them to phone you if they need any background."

The sad weather followed her as far as Genoa, but as she left the airport for the train the rain stopped. By the time she stepped down in Manarola, the sun was again shining on hoards of the tourists pouring off the ferries. Vittorio was waiting at the hotel, where a clearly confused Riolo was hovering.

Brown had dressed as a tourist, not like a journalist from

London. They were already checked in and together they wandered down to the harbour to discuss their plans in the shade of a café umbrella.

"So Paolo, what did the magistrate tell you about the photographs?" Brown asked once they had ordered.

"He said they were regular holiday snaps, and there was nothing of any significance in them."

"That's odd, Paolo, because there was somebody on the path on the day John Warham was killed."

"You still haven't told me who it is, Cassandra."

"I haven't told anyone, Paolo. But it was Nichols, the Beaten Track man."

Vittorio whistled. "I saw him in the hotel this lunchtime, before you arrived. He was collecting somebody's bags. He nodded when he saw me."

"He knows who you are?"

"Oh, he knows exactly who I am. He and Riolo seem very good friends."

Brown sipped her orange juice. "I'm going to ask Nichols if he can join us for a drink this evening. Shall I say here rather than at the hotel, do you think?"

Vittorio nodded, just as his portable began to ring. Leaving him talking, Brown walked down towards the waterfront. She found a place to sit on the wall, and pulled Nichols' number from the phone's memory. He answered immediately. "Hello Cassandra. How nice to hear from you. How you doing? What's the weather like in London?"

Brown had the distinct impression that Nichols already knew she was not in London. What's this bastard's game? "Hi Pete. I'm fine. I'm not in London, though, but in Manarola. I wondered if we could meet up for a beer later?"

"That'd be really great, Cassandra, but I'm not working in the area right now. They've sent me half way across the country. Anyway, as I said to you before, I'd get fired if London found out I had been talking to you."

Brown watched a ferry come into the harbour. "When are you back this way? Surely you can have a drink with a fellow Australian, Pete. Who's to know anyway?"

"No, it's more than my job's worth. Sorry."

"What if I promise not to fire questions at you?"

"As I said, I'd love to but I'm not in the area. Some other time maybe."

"Suppose I was to put things another way?"

There was a pause on the line. "What do you mean Cassandra, another way? In any case the answer's the same. I'm not in the area."

"What I mean, Pete, is that I've a couple of questions that you might prefer I put to you directly, rather than put to your head office."

"Why would I prefer that?" The veneer of fellow Aussies' engaging in friendly banter was coming unstuck.

"Because you value your job?" She allowed the message to sink in, before continuing. "Alternatively, Pete, if you're not going to be around I could just pop along and see the magistrate, or the *Carabinieri*. In fact, I'm surprised they haven't spoken to you already."

"I'm still not with you, Cassandra."

"Let's just say you take a lovely picture, sport."

"What do you mean?"

"I'll leave you to think about it. You know where to find me if you change your mind."

Brown hung up and walked back to the cafe. Vittorio was back at the table. "I've just put the shits up one little Aussie courier, but he's not cracking. We know one thing for sure, though, Paolo, Nichols is a lying bastard. He said he's not working in the area at the moment. He must have forgotten you saw him this morning."

"You would not mistake him for Einstein, would you? By the way, that was Gonzales' agent returning my call. She was pretty taken aback when I asked her why Gonzales was going to Buenos Aires, and demanded to know how I knew. In the end, she told me that she was going to see her mother, who is not well."

"True or false?"

"Who knows? Who cares? Let's find something to eat."

After a couple of glasses of *Prosecco* and a rare *tagliata di manzo*, Vittorio persuaded Brown that once they had filed their copy for the *Post's* double page spread, they should stay an extra day and have some fun at the newspaper's expense. He had his fishing gear in the car and had arranged to borrow a small motorboat for the weekend.

Brown had no interest in fishing, but she was already hooked. A weekend of sunshine and swimming was what she needed.

Brown groped for her phone as its ring battered through her subconscious. She stretched out her arm – Vittorio was no longer in her bed. She did not recognise the number illuminated on the screen, but even in her groggy state, she did recognise the voice on the other end.

"Cassandra?"

She managed a cautious, "yes."

"It's Pete. Can we talk, are you alone?"

She felt the depression in the mattress beside her. It was cold. Vittorio must have gone back to his own room ages ago. "Of course."

"I've been thinking about what you said. I've a proposition."

"A proposition? What the hell are you talking about Pete? It's," she looked at her watch, "half past five in the morning."

"I'm willing to meet you."

"Go on. Now you've woken me completely I may as well listen."

"No. Not now. Face to face."

"When."

"This morning."

The window was beginning to be lit by the sun. Outside, there were a few early morning noises. The sound of boats being dragged down to the harbour, possibly. The birds' dawn chorus. Brown sat up in bed and pulled the sheets across her body. "I thought you said you weren't in the area?"

"Well, I am at the moment."

"I could meet you for coffee?"

"I don't want us to be seen together." His words tumbled out in rapid succession. "Meet me now, above the village, on the path out towards Corniglia"

"Where?"

"There's a seat on the path."

"How will I find it?"

"Turn left out of the hotel and just keep walking down the hill. Before you get to the harbour there's a gap between two houses

277

on the right. There's a red and white way-mark. That's where the path starts. Follow it up the steps and then turn left after the cemetery."

"Why all this cloak-and-dagger stuff? Can't you just come to the hotel?"

"As I said, I don't want anyone to see us together."

"OK. But I'm bringing Vittorio with me."

"No. Just you."

The phone clicked as the connection was closed.

Brown piled the pillows behind her head and laid back. Her mouth was horribly dry. She stared at the mobile, willing it to ring again, for Nichols to call to say he was only joking. But this was no joke. Nichols was serious, and she was scared. She watched the slow revolutions of the ghastly ceiling fan. Was this what happened to John Warham? Did he take a call early in the morning, go out, never to return?

It would be mad for her to go, but Nichols promised the biggest scoop of her career. Her clothes lay scattered around the floor. The shower. Somewhere to think. Mechanically, she showered and towelled her hair dry, pulled on cotton trousers and a bright orange tee shirt. Easy to spot from a distance. Almost as an afterthought, she picked her silver crucifix from her bedside table and fastened it around her neck.

She was ready to go. She should at least let Vittorio know where she was going, but if she woke him, he would insist on coming with her.

If she were going, she would have to go alone, but she could already see the headline: *Warham mystery: reporter missing. By Paolo Vittorio.*

Brown picked up her telephone to compose a text to Vittorio. Her last Will and Testament? She took another drink of water and stared at the blank screen. She keyed in "Meeting Nichols now on path to Corniglia", selected Vittorio's number but did not push the send button.

Holding her breath, she slipped out of her room, and along the corridor. She stopped outside Vittorio's room and pressed her ear to the door. She could hear nothing. Her knuckles were about to tap on the wood when she regained her resolve and walked on, soundlessly save for the squeak of her trainers on the floor, to the deserted hotel lobby. The front door was not yet unlocked, so she turned the latch and walked out. The empty street was still in shadow, the sun striking the very tops of the buildings. She had seen nobody, and so far as she was aware, nobody has seen her. Only Riolo's CCTV would have stored her image on its tape. Once outside, she let go the breath she had been holding, looked up the street to the right before turning left, down the hill, towards the gap between the houses.

If Paolo had stayed the whole night, she wouldn't be doing this. Should she turn back, before it was too late? But she was committed. And she wanted that story.

CHAPTER TWENTY-FIVE

BROWN reached the gap between the houses, and looked up and down the street. Nobody in sight. She pulled her mobile from her pocket and pushed the "send" button to start the message's journey to Vittorio's in-box. Would he be awake? Did he turn off his telephone when he slept? How long would the text take to reach him? Where did it have to go? To London and back? To the US, India, the moon? Did he take his mobile with him, or was it still somewhere in the jumble of her room? Why did he sneak back to his own room? Had she snored? *You don't have to say you love me, just be close at hand.*

Ancient stone steps led up between the houses. On the wall she found the faded red and white way-mark. She climbed a few steps to where she could not be seen from the street and sat down. It was still cool in the shade and the stone was cold enough through her trousers to make her shiver. She composed a second text. "Need help. Come quickly." Again she did not push the "send" button.

The path climbed steeply past the little terraced vegetable gardens marking the outskirts of the village. Neat rows of lettuces and beans. Tomato plants, tall already, the heavy red fruit weighing down the stalks. Far down beside the harbour, a group of divers, sinister in their black wet suits, held harpoon guns. A waiter moved from table to table outside the café, wiping off the moisture. Men were preparing their boats for the day ahead. Two *Carabinieri* leaned against a dark blue Alfa Romeo parked alongside the harbour. She thought she could smell the smoke from their cigarettes.

Dry gravel crunched beneath her feet. She stopped frequently, listening hard and hearing only the sound of her own heartbeat. She could see nobody behind her, nobody ahead. In the distance she heard the sound of a train as it rushed from tunnel to tunnel. Out in the bay, an inflatable boat sped towards the harbour.

She stopped for breath and looked down, her heart jumping when a small black cat brushed against her bare calf. She bent and tickled the cat's neck. It responded with a purr. Her mobile beeped, far too loudly. The cat started, jumped onto the cemetery wall and ran along the top. Vittorio had got her first message and replied: "*Faccia attenzione. Sono sul mio modo*" — be careful, I am on my way. She slipped the mobile back into her pocket. She was no longer alone. All she needed to do was find Nichols before Vittorio found her.

The cemetery lay to her left, perched precariously on the side of the cliff. Followed by the cat, she reached the junction of the paths and turned left. The long drop to the sea was now on her right. Now what? Where was Nichols? How far along this path should she go? Was he watching her? Or the hotel? Would he see Vittorio leave? Had she delayed too long? After less than one hundred metres, the path turned once more to the left, and began to descend back towards the village.

Again the smell of tobacco smoke. Brown thought she heard a noise behind her and spun around. No one. When she looked ahead again, Nichols' head was slowly coming into view as he climbed up towards her, turning frequently to look behind him. She gripped the telephone in her left hand, the index finger poised.

Nichols was carrying something. A lump of rock maybe? The same as he used on John Warham? A gun? She stopped and screwed up her eyes against the morning sun. It was only his mobile. A wire led to his earpiece. Brown swallowed hard and tried out her best "isn't this fun" voice. She waved the mobile. "Hi Pete, we could have done this on the phone instead of getting up at sparrow's fart."

The young man again looked behind him, and then back to Brown. He put his finger to his lips. Her finger itched to send the second message. Nichols stopped and moved the mobile into his right hand while his left disappeared into his pocket. Brown fingered the crucifix. Slowly he retrieved a pack of cigarettes, pulled one out, and lit up. That was one jumpy guy.

Listening for Vittorio's footsteps, Brown heard nothing except the muffled sounds of a village waking up. It had been stupid to agree to come alone. Was Vittorio also in danger? Would he even find her, given she was no longer on the main path, but behind a cemetery with somebody whose real name she did not even know. Why did she come? She was a financial hack, for God's sake, not a private detective. This was fine for Rocco Suarez and his ilk, but not for a soft city girl from Melbourne.

They met at a viewpoint high above the village. Fishing boats had begun to put out from the harbour. Several miles offshore, the misty grey shape of a warship headed north, in the direction of La Spezia. Cigarette ends lay in the dust under an ancient seat. Far below, Brown picked out the roof of the hotel. Had Vittorio left yet? Brown instinctively moved as far back from the cliff edge as possible. Nichols gave one last look round and flopped down at the end of the bench. His head hung and he appeared to be concentrating on the dust beneath his feet. He looked as if he had not slept for days. Brown sat at the other end, her mobile still firmly in her grasp. He took a long drag on his cigarette and ground the barely smoked butt under a dusty trainer.

Brown looked out to sea. "So what's the story, Pete? Why drag me up here?"

Nichols lifted his head and turned toward her. He straightened his back. "What did you mean yesterday, about going to the *Carabinieri*?"

Words from the Mozart's *Requiem* sung inside her head. The *confutatis maledictus. When the damned are cast away.* How she had enjoyed singing that with the university choir back home. She turned to face Nichols. His assertiveness was no more than bluster. "You were up here when John Warham was killed, weren't you?"

"What makes you think that?"

"A photograph now with the Magistrate."

She watched the colour drain from Nichols' face. His reaction gave her no pleasure. *Bowed down in supplication I beg thee, my heart as though ground to ashes: help me in my last hour.*

"If it's any comfort, Pete, I'm not sure the Magistrate knows it's you. He's had the photos for more than two weeks and from what I hear he hasn't come looking for you."

"Where did it come from?"

"John Warham's camera."

"Fuck."

"So why don't we cut the crap. You were on this cliff when Warham was killed. I know it, and you know it. And by the way, just in case you were thinking of teaching me how to fly, the spooks working for WBC also know it and so does Vittorio. So, bumping me off won't help you one little bit. Quite the reverse, in fact."

"I didn't have anything to do with Warham's death."

Brown traced a pattern in the dust with her trainer. She found she had drawn a cross and quickly rubbed it out. "But you were here."

"OK. I saw what happened."

He was staring intently at Brown, sizing her up maybe, in case it came to a fight? Or was he looking over her shoulder? She could not be sure. She thought she heard a noise behind her and swivelled round. The path was deserted.

"So. Give. What did happen? You look jiggered by the way."

Nichols stood up and walked towards the cliff edge. He turned to face her. "Can we cut a deal, Cassandra?"

Please say he's not going to jump. "Can you come away from the edge, Pete?"

He came and sat on the bench. She tried to smile. "Thanks. I couldn't think when you were over there. Now, what sort of deal? Do you want money?"

He managed a momentary grin. "Are you offering?"

"No way."

"I don't want my name mentioned, OK? Not to anyone." Nichols looked at his feet, and moved a few cigarette ends around in the dust. "So, you leave me out of the paper? And if the police come knocking, you tell them to rack off?"

"Why?"

"I don't want to get involved. The last thing I need is the police crawling all over me."

"I'm not interested in whatever shonky little racket you're running Pete. But, for the record, I guess you're dealing?"

He nodded. "Nothing serious. But there's a lot of kids here in the season and they're always asking me where they can get stuff."

"So you set up shop."

He seemed almost proud of it. "Nothing heavy. A little skunk, a few sticks and fifties. Whatever's around. Look, I'm just a regular Joe Blow trying to make a crust out here. OK?"

Brown again thought she heard something, got up from the bench and walked a few paces back the way she had come. Vittorio? But he would not know where to find her. He would not know she was behind the cemetery. She went back to the bench and sat down.

He moved a little closer, turning his mobile over and over in his hands. "So Cassandra, do we have a deal?" His voice was hoarse. Beneath the bold exterior lurked a small-time drug dealer scared shitless that he was going to be banged up for years in an Italian jail.

"Why should I agree to any of your conditions, Pete? All I've got to do is tell the Magistrate you're in Warham's photo album and you're stuffed."

"Fair enough, but you still won't know what happened."

Nichols turned his face away from her, rose slowly from the seat and moved toward the cliff edge, where he stopped and turned. His cheeks were wet. He walked to the bend in the path, where he lit another cigarette before walking back and sitting down. "It's your call. I can just leg it right out of the country and you'll still know nothing."

Brown stood up and moved in front of Nichols, looking down at him. She was no longer frightened. "Why should I believe you? Nothing you say is on the level, Pete. Even your name is bogus. How do I know you're not dealing me so much horse-shit? What kind of drongo do you take me for?"

The cliff was behind her. If Nichols were to rush her, she would suffer the same fate as Warham. She turned and sat down on the other end of the bench.

His cigarette stub joined the others in the dust under the bench. "You don't have to listen, but can you at least give me time to get out of town." He stared out to sea. "I might have guessed you'd be holier than bloody thou."

"At least tell me your name. Level with me that far. Meet me half way."

"You've got to be joking." He ground out the still smouldering cigarette.

Brown strained her ears for any sound of Vittorio's approach. Nothing. "So what did happen?"

"Does that mean we have a deal?" Nichols was back at the edge, his back toward her.

"Agreed."

He turned to face her, sweat beads showing on his forehead.

"You are going to level with me, aren't you Pete, because if you make me look a dill in front of my editor I'll come after you, I promise? And if I do, you'll be wishing the *Carabinieri* had you banged up safe and sound."

His lips moved, but no noise came out. He kicked a stone. She heard it bounce down the cliff face.

Brown spoke softly. "Pete, whatever your bloody name is, for fuck's sake give, otherwise I'll be chucking myself over. And please come away from the edge. You're giving me vertigo."

He stopped pacing and stepped closer to the seat. "I was sitting here waiting for someone. I had no idea Warham was up here until I saw him, just round the path, over there. He'd stopped to take pictures. He stood there for ages, looking down the cliff. Then he seemed to stagger and went arse over tip. I watched him bounce down the cliff from rock to rock. Then he disappeared and I heard the splash. I reckon he was dead before he even hit the water."

"What did you do?"

"The funny thing was, he didn't yell, or shout for help, or anything. The only sound was him crashing against the rocks, and the rocks going down with him and them all hitting the water."

"So what did you do?"

"What do you mean?"

"For Chrissake, Pete, it's not a difficult question. What did you do?"

Nichols walked forward again and stared down the face of the cliff. When he finally spoke, it was a whisper. "I legged it."

"You didn't try to help him?"

"There was no point. He was already a goner."

"So you just nicked off? I can't bloody believe it."

"Look, if I'd gone shouting off about it I'd have ended up in deep shit."

There was no point in prolonging the exchange. Nichols was a cheap bastard who legged it instead of phoning for help. Some people are just like that.

"Where exactly did he fall?"

"From there. From right there." Fifty metres away a tattered piece of chequered police tape fluttered in the soft morning breeze. It seemed suddenly very quiet.

"Straight up, Cassandra, I know you think me as crooked as a dog's hind leg, but there was nothing I could do for him. He was already scuppered."

Slowly, Brown rose from the seat and walked towards the spot. Nichols followed her. They stood side by side on the path, Brown fingering the end of the tape, still attached to a metal spike driven into the ground.

The narrow strip of grass between the path and the cliff edge was trampled, and the undergrowth broken. She followed Nichols' gaze down the face of the cliff. Some of the rocks had circles of white paint on them. Inside the circles some dark stains were visible. The sea lapped gently against the foot of the cliff.

At the harbour, the *gommone* backed away from the wall, wet-suited figures sitting on the fat rubber gunwales. As it turned seawards, she heard the engine accelerate and watched the white wake slowly disappear.

In the village below, several of the tables outside the café where John Warham liked to take his coffee were already occupied. Soon, the ferries would begin to arrive. People would pour off them to buy ice creams and tee shirts. All so sodding normal. Walkers would be setting out from every one of the five villages, tens of thousands of photographs would be taken. Without incident. Without death.

He didn't jump. He wasn't pushed. He fell. He just bloody fell. How many newspapers is that going to sell? The *Requiem* kept singing in her head. *Culpa rubet vultus meus: guilt reddens my face.*

Beside her, Nichols stood motionless, staring at the void just beyond their feet. He took out his cigarettes and offered one to Brown. She shook her head.

Down at the harbour, the two *Carabinieri* climbed into their car. The siren screamed. From the distance came the noise of an approaching helicopter. And Vittorio was running up the steep path.

Panic rose on Nichols' face, "You didn't, did you?"

"Give me some credit, sport. Of course I didn't." She put a restraining hand on Nichols' arm, and tried to smile, first at Nichols and then at Vittorio who, apparently reassured, slowed, puffing, to walking pace. Nichols stepped back from the edge. The police siren softened into the distance as the helicopter passed rapidly, disinterestedly, high above their heads, heading straight out to sea.

Meanwhile, a handful of kilometres away, a large, talented, but devious man lay in a refrigerated stainless steel drawer, stripped of his internal organs.

In Buenos Aires a young woman visited her mother, who was not ill. In the Cinque Terre a shoddy little drugs racket ended because the courier decided to leave Italy in a hurry. The share price of WBC took a hit, and then recovered.

A finance director became a chief executive. A widow was burdened with too much knowledge. A son discovered how hard it could be to forgive a parent. A little girl wondered where her grandpa went. A wiser journalist was promoted.

Up and down the coast, the ferries come and go. People take spectacular photographs from precarious positions. Mostly, nothing happens to them.